AMERICA'S BEST PLACE TO LIVE

A NOVEL BY

CONRAD BAR

Cover design by Charlie Bar & Conrad Bar

Library of Congress Control Number is available upon request.

ISBN: 979-8-234-02346-9 (paperback)

ISBN: 979-8-218-74276-8 (ebook)

First Edition

For Julie

Prologue

Roughly 10,000 years after the Anishinaabe people settled near the shores of a great lake, later renamed Superior by some guy who was not a Native American, five highly respected climate scientists were preparing to publish their peer-reviewed paper that focused on this forgotten region in America. The objective of the five-year study was to determine the best climate havens on Earth. In the end, the study only strengthened the climate scientists theory that geographic relocation is the best, and possibly only option left for humans to defend themselves against the devastating effects of climate change.

The five climate scientists—two Americans, one French-Canadian, one Costa Rican and one Pole—went to great lengths to keep the study a secret. Even Stan Zbikowski, arguably the most successful realtor in the Upper Peninsula and one of its most connected residents, didn't know about the secret study. But he should have.

Dr. Marquette, no relation to Fr. Jaques Marquette—a French Jesuit missionary who was the first European to settle in the U.P.—was immediately taken with Stan. Most of the men she knew took themselves way too seriously and were a bore to hang out with in social situations, but not Stan. He possessed an unpredictable self-deprecating sense of humor, which conveyed a certain confidence that Dr. Marquette had never seen before in a man. Despite the fact that Stan was kicked out of Northern Michigan University, failed the Michigan real estate license exam twice, and still only read the sports section of *The Mining Journal,* the climate scientist and the realtor became fast friends. The relationship eventually grew intimate...emotionally.

Six months into the relationship, Bianca stopped hiding her feelings for Stan. It almost got physical on more than one occasion, but Stan was still in love with his wife and never let it go too far. Except for the one time he gave Bianca a ride home and was slow to stop her advancing hand.

In Stan's defense he was buzzed and completely engrossed with Bianca's passionate rant—fueled by four espresso martinis—about the need for an ecosystem of interconnected solutions to combat all the growing threats to human life caused by rapidly rising sea levels. It was when he heard her say, rapidly rising, that Stan happened to look down to find Bianca's hand where it shouldn't be. He brushed her hand away, pulled his newly leased GMC Denali to the curb, and yelled at her to get out of his massive suv. Embarrassed, Bianca whispered sorry, blamed her roaming hand on the four espresso martinis, and exited the suv.

The five-year study began shortly after the group of prominent climate scientists, led by Dr. Marquette and Dr. Parizek, agreed that climate breakdown had begun. All but guaranteeing that record-breaking heat, drought, wildfires, rising sea levels, and extreme weather events will only become more frequent and more destructive in the near and distant future. Last year was the hottest year on record and this year will probably break last year's record. Most people have become painfully aware that every place on Earth is becoming more vulnerable to extreme weather events, however, some regions will fare much better than others. But there's one place on Earth that will fare the best, according to the study. After analyzing hundreds of regions around the globe, Dr. Marquette and the other four climate scientists behind the study became fascinated, borderline obsessed, with a small but incredibly unique region in America known simply as the U.P.

Dr. Marquette had been the first one in the group to move to the Upper Peninsula. Less than forty-eight hours after arriving in Whisper Dunes, she started work on the scientific study that would prove there is no better place to live on Earth than in the Upper Peninsula of Michigan. An immeasurable force of nature is how Dr. Marquette described the U.P. to her colleagues and friends. A place where the weather and the landscape collide in a tempestuous display of beauty, nearly every day of the year. A four season paradise. But even before Dr. Marquette first stepped foot in the Upper Peninsula, she was well aware that the driving force behind all the beauty and life in the U.P. is Lake Superior. Originally named *gichi-gami* by the Ojibwe tribe, Lake Superior is the largest freshwater lake in the world by surface area, holding ten percent of Earth's surface fresh water.

The people who live in the Upper Peninsula of Michigan are called *Yoopers* by the people who live in the Lower Peninsula of Michigan. *Yoopers* are proud people, so much so that when visiting any town in the U.P. it's common to see people walking around wearing hats and shirts that read: YOOPER.

The first thing that stood out to Dr. Marquette was that *Yoopers* always seemed to be in a jolly mood. Maybe because most *Yoopers* possess a grateful attention to the beauty of life. They figured out a long time ago that the key to a happy life is knowing when you have enough. *Yoopers* pride themselves on being incredibly resilient, helpful, fiercely independent, and trustworthy. That's not to say the folks in the U.P. are without their flaws. Most *Yoopers* are heavy drinkers...six days a week. But that number increases to seven in the winter. Their view on drinking is identical to their view on gossiping, it's just a fun way to loose track of time. If *Yoopers* have one defining similarity with other Americans its that they like to gossip. They don't think twice about spreading a rumor that isn't connected to a single fact, and they're suckers when it comes to buying into a conspiracy theory. The more delusional the better.

Yoopers are very protective of each other and their environment. They leave behind an almost non-existent carbon footprint. They hate to travel outside of the U.P. Because when you're surrounded by friendly people in a four season paradise, why would anyone ever bother to travel? *Yoopers* will tell you that travel is for people struggling with extreme boredom.

Another thing about *Yoopers,* although they would never admit it, but most walk around with a chip on their shoulder. Only three percent of Michigan's population actually lives in the Upper Peninsula, and the feeling that comes with being ignored by most of the people in your own state, not to mention the entire country, has created a rather large chip on the shoulders of most *Yoopers*.

Even though the Upper Peninsula is closer to Minnesota and Wisconsin, no state in the Upper Midwest wanted to adopt the land as their own. Back then it was considered a wild and harsh land, but that's only because the territory was still heavily populated with Native Americans. Shortly after becoming the twenty-sixth state in 1837, Michigan was persuaded to adopt the Upper Peninsula. But the lower peninsula of the state didn't acknowledge the Upper Peninsula as part of the state until large copper and iron deposits were discovered throughout the U.P. The discovery created an economic boom for the state that lasted nearly a century.

       Stan never told Dr. Marquette that he got kicked out of Northern Michigan University. After moving back to his parents house, which was only seven miles from campus, Stan got his real estate license while completing his degree in history at the local community college. But Bianca did know that Stan began teaching history and civics at the only public high school in Whisper Dunes while spending his weekends trying to launch his real estate career. Bianca had little interest in real estate but liked asking Stan about his teaching days. She loved that he required his students to read Howard Zinn's, *A People's History of the United States.* And that he encouraged his students to become pen pals with Native American kids attending high school on reservations. Bianca also knew that Stan devoted an entire semester each year to *The Council of Three Fires* which consisted of the Ojibwe tribe (keepers of the medicine and faith), the Odawa tribe (keepers of the trade), and the Potawatomi tribe (keepers of the fire). Stan refused to pass his senior class until they memorized the 1833 Treaty of Chicago, which forced the Ojibwe, Odawa, and Potawatomi tribes to give up their 5,000,000 acres of land to the United States government and move west of the Mississippi River.

       Knowing that the study was coming to an end, Bianca decided to take a few days off and enjoy the Whisper Dunes night life. Stan's wife and kids happened to be out of town that weekend, and because it was the end of summer, Stan was open to hanging out with Bianca late into the night. She kept her eyes locked on Stan as he made her laugh loudly in between conversations about nature conservation, the next real estate crash, best strip clubs in Montreal, and a longwinded story about the time he bumped into Keith Richards at the local public library while studying for his real estate exam. Even though Stan reminded Bianca at least five times it was a true story, this was the only story Stan told her that she didn't believe.

On the drive back to her place, Bianca had planned on inviting Stan up to her apartment. She was finally going to tell him about the study she'd spent the last five years of her life working on, but she never got the chance. The espresso martinis kicked in, turbo charging her horniness, and leading her right hand on an expedition up Stan's leg. But even if the night had gone according to Dr. Marquette's plan, and Stan was told about the climate change study, there was no way he could have foreseen the chain of events that would transpire.

Almost a year had passed since Stan kicked Dr. Marquette out of his suv on that unseasonably warm June night. Stan hadn't thought about his drinking buddy—a.k.a. the climate scientist from Montreal—in quite some time. But had Dr. Marquette popped into his head recently, Stan might have gotten the urge to search her on the internet. Had he done this, he would have come across Dr. Marquette's recently created website, which advertised her upcoming speaking engagements ahead of the study's publication. The greatly anticipated study was slated for a late September publication, and the first stop on her speaking tour was the public library in downtown Whisper Dunes. The same public library where Stan claimed to have bumped into Keith Richards.

If you've met a *Yooper*, then you know how much they pride themselves on always being prepared for the next big storm. But for Stan Zbikowski, and every other *Yooper*, there was nothing they could have done to prepare for the storm that was about to hit the town of Whisper Dunes.

1

Stan Zbikowski stepped outside through the side door of his 110-year-old craftsman style house and onto the covered porch that wrapped around to the front of the house. Like he did most mornings, even in the middle of winter, Stan walked to the front porch to take in the sweeping views of the beautiful natural surroundings. The Zbikowski family had neighbors, but you couldn't see their homes because of all the pine and spruce trees covering the area. Stan sipped his coffee as his eyes moved from a tall birch tree in the front yard, his favorite tree, to the expansive lawn. The lawn was in desperate need of a mow he thought, but Stan decided right then and there he'd wait until it finally rained to mow the lawn. Kind of a fuck you to his lawn obsessed, climate change denier neighbor down the road.

Despite his success as arguably the best realtor in the Upper Peninsula, Stan refused to hire someone to mow his lawn. His dad taught him how to mow when he was eight years old, and he quickly found the chore to be therapeutic. Stan still liked the chore, but most days he was busy brokering real estate deals and struggled to find time to mow the grass that covered his three acre property. He had tried to convince each one of his three boys to mow the lawn, but kids from their generation successfully used their screen addiction as a way to avoid doing chores.

Sixteen days had passed since Stan mowed the lawn. He told his wife, Lisa, that he wouldn't cut it again until they finally got some rain. It had actually rained three times in the last sixteen days, but by the time Stan got home from work he was drunk from celebrating closing another real estate transaction. He had been on a hot streak the last five months, and when that happened Stan was known to close down a bar or two.

Stan had lived his entire life in Whisper Dunes and never experienced a heat wave in June. Of course, most people around the globe would not consider a stretch of low eighties warm enough to qualify for a heat wave label. But in Whisper Dunes, or any town in the Upper Peninsula of Michigan, hitting the low eighties in June for more than two consecutive days was without question a heat wave. Every town in the U.P. usually struggled to reach seventy degrees for a high in June. Most summer mornings in the U.P. require a sweatshirt or light jacket, but for the past week the temperature had hit seventy degrees by ten a.m. and gone over eighty by mid-afternoon.

A long driveway was located on the left side of the Zbikowski house that led to a detached garage. If you walked up the driveway you'd normally see a basketball hoop, but not today, because there was a large pirate ship float parked in front of the basketball hoop. Every year for the past seven years, Stan and his two best friends, Duane and Randy, had built a pirate ship float for the town's 4th of July parade. The guys had won a first place trophy every year except last year so this year they decided to go bigger. They had already dropped nearly six grand on the float, but Duane was still waiting for Stan and Randy to Zelle him their share of the cost.

Whether you won a trophy for the bike category, stroller category, or float category, all winners received the same size trophy, which Mayor Russ Tillinghast personally purchased every year from Down Wind Sports for ten bucks a trophy. But for some reason, dating back to the eighties, the group who won first place in the float category treated the trophy like it was the Stanley Cup, and they had the post celebration photos to prove it.

Stan and Lisa bought their large house ten years ago, when Lisa was pregnant with baby number three. Stan wanted something newer and closer to the beach, but Lisa fell in love with the old house. She especially loved the original woodwork, along with the five spacious bedrooms and the wrap around porch. It took some convincing but eventually Stan agreed with his wife that it was the perfect home to raise their family in. After Stan's real estate career took off and he was closing multiple deals a week, Lisa was finally able to see her decorating dreams become a reality. She spent a year carefully overseeing a renovation job that brought contemporary updates to the home while maintaining its original details. Even though the project went over budget by almost two hundred grand, Stan never complained once to Lisa. Except during Thanksgiving 2018, but Stan complained about a lot of things that day. He was drunk before the turkey was even halfway cooked, and because he had been mixing it up with his in-laws for two straight days, Lisa was not surprised when Stan let loose and went on a repetitive, foul mouthed, four minute tirade. He hasn't spoken to his mother-in-law since.

Stan took another sip from his coffee cup while admiring the rose bushes Lisa planted a few months after they moved into the house. He set the coffee cup on the railing and stretched his left hamstring, then his right. At forty-six, Stan was still blessed with an athletic body and handsome face that had barely changed in the last twenty years. His brown, wavy hair was longer than usual because it helped cover up his greying temples. Stan still drank at least four nights a week, but he worked out nearly every day and still could impress his three sons by dunking a basketball.

Stan walked down the five porch steps and strolled up his driveway. He looked at the pirate ship float and seemed pleased. Randy Daugherty, his t-shirt covered in paint, didn't notice Stan approaching because he was focused on painting the right side of the float. Like Stan, Randy had defied middle-age. He was one year older than Stan but his round baby face made him look like he was in his early thirties. Unlike Stan, Randy was African-American and had a college degree. Randy also graduated from law school with hopes of being a lawyer in a big city, but instead he'd been practicing law in Whisper Dunes for the past twelve years. Randy may have looked younger than Stan, but he struggled to keep off the belly fat. Compared to Stan, Randy was only a moderate drinker, yet he had a big beer belly. The result of working too many hours and struggling to find time to exercise, even a little.

Randy continued to paint with laser focus. Stan was standing two feet away, sipping his coffee while fidgeting with his balls, but Randy didn't notice. Stan seemed mesmerized for a moment by Randy's quick brush strokes. Having already spent most of the last three days working on the float, the close friends had run out of things to talk about.

Stan walked over to the makeshift plywood table. On the table was an architectural design drawing of the float, along with a dozen empty beer cans, an iPhone, and a JBL portable speaker. Stan picked up the iPhone and selected a song. Pearl Jam's, "Seven O'Clock," started to blare from the speaker. Stan bobbed his head as he put a construction belt around his waist.

After looking over a few different tools, Stan finally grabbed a nail gun from the table and walked over to Randy while his head continued to bob along to the PJ song. "I drove past the marina yesterday," Stan said. "That thirty-eight-foot speed boat is still for sale. Duane said he's in, we're just looking for a third partner to close the deal."

Randy stopped painting and stepped back to inspect his work. "Stan, if I wanted to know what it felt like to own a boat, I'd sit in a cold bath and burn hundred dollar bills every weekend."

Stan looked disappointed. Randy finally turned and met Stan's angry gaze. "There's more to life than saving for retirement," Stan said.

A man in his early fifties was walking his big German Shepherd past Stan's house. He stopped and analyzed the front yard. He shook his head in disgust. The disgruntled man finally looked in Stan's direction and shouted, "Hey, Zbikowski! I've seen better looking lawns in downtown Detroit! Ever heard of weed killer?"

"Yes, I have. It contaminates our drinking water and causes a variety of cancers. But don't worry, Bob, while you stay busy in your man cave listening to podcasts and jerking off to the latest superhero movie, the few adults left on Earth will keep focusing on important issues. Like trying to figure out a way to prevent our planet from burning."

Bob was unable to hide his embarrassment, but he was able to muster up the courage to flip Stan the bird. He then lowered his head as if he'd already forgotten about the confrontation and continued his walk. Stan glanced at Randy for a reaction.

"You know, I have a theory about people who obsess over their lawns," Randy said.

"I know, you've told me. It's spot on. You could host your own podcast on that theory. But your too damn classy to go and host a podcast."

Randy was about to say something but got distracted by his ringing phone. He looked at his phone to check the caller ID then answered. "Hey, Duane. Did you get the boards? Hang on." Randy looked at Stan and said, "He stopped at Lucky Dogs. Do you want a chili cheese dog or a Chicago dog?"

"Two Chicago dogs, and tell him to pick up a case of beer."

"Make that two chili cheese dogs and two Chicago dogs, and pick up a case of beer on the way back," Randy said into his phone. "Yeah, Stan already brought up the boat...again. Not interested, pal. Because I can barely afford to take my family to Wisconsin Dells every summer. Duane, I'm done discussing the fucking boat." Randy pressed the "end call" icon and put his phone back on the table.

Stan looked ready to continue the boat conversation, but his demeanor quickly changed at the sight of a maroon Chrysler mini-van pulling into the driveway. Stan looked uneasy. He turned down the music then glanced at Randy. "If Lisa asks, tell her I just got home."

"I can't lie to my own wife, how the heck am I supposed to lie to yours?"

"I got an idea, how about you practice by lying to my wife?"

Randy looked perturbed as he turned his back on Stan and started painting an area on the float that didn't need more paint. Randy avoided confrontations whenever possible. He knew Stan might try to drag him into his ensuing confrontation with Lisa, so he pretended to be deeply focused on his paint job.

Lisa Zbikowski stepped out of the mini-van and walked toward Stan. Lisa was forty-seven and a natural beauty who seemed to become more beautiful with each passing year. She was five feet six inches with long brown hair and a skinny frame. When she found a reason to flash her big smile Lisa looked like she was still in her early twenties. At least that's what Stan liked to tell her.

Stan forced an uneasy smile as Lisa approached. But before he could tell her how good she looked in her belted yellow summer dress, the sliding door of the mini-van opened and Stan and Lisa's youngest son, Brendan, exited the van. The eight-year-old headed straight for the house while staring at his phone.

"Hey, Brendan, how was camp?"

"Fine," Brendan said as he stared at his phone.

"How about a hug, big fella?"

Stan let out a frustrated sigh just as Brendan entered the house through the kitchen door. He looked over at Lisa and said, "Ever since you got him that damn phone, he stopped giving me hugs."

Lisa rolled her eyes before smiling at Randy. "Hi, Randy."

"Hey, Lisa."

"What a tragedy that my son would rather stare at that mind fucking device instead of stopping to have a quick chat with his old man. It's not his fault though. The entire human race is controlled by those machines now. If it were up to me..."

Lisa knew exactly what Stan was going to say, so much so that she mouthed the words to herself as Stan continued: "I'd ban smartphones and social media in schools and all public spaces."

Randy nodded in agreement as a discouraged look appeared on his face. "The smartphones have destroyed human relationships, and the human experience. People are no longer attached to their real feelings because they can't think for themselves anymore. Humans are controlled and violated by their smartphones, except for the few brave souls who refuse to own one."

"I only have one because I'm a realtor. I don't have a choice. But if I did, I'd go back to using a walkie-talkie."

"You can't hack a walkie-talkie or a fax machine," Randy said.

"Fuckin A."

Lisa glanced at Randy and asked, "How are your girls doing?"

Randy's face lit up with an excited smile. "Oh, they're both fantastic. Sophie just got back from the Princeton Math Camp, and Zooey's almost fluent in Italian. She's only ten and can already speak three languages."

Lisa looked impressed as she flashed a smile. "That's incredible."

Randy exhaled slowly through his nose. It was evident to Lisa that he seemed a bit emotional. "Well, having an amazing mom helps quite a bit," Randy said in a sincere tone.

Lisa's kind smile vanished as she was suddenly overwhelmed with the thought that she wasn't doing enough to encourage her three boys to reach their full potential. God knows Stan wasn't any help in this department. He taught his boys how to add and subtract by analyzing point spreads in football and basketball games.

Lisa's cold eyes regarded her husband, who was loading nails into the nail gun. "Why aren't you at work, Stan?"

Without hesitation, Stan said, "I took the afternoon off so I can help Randy and Duane with the float. It's kind of a make or break day for us."

Lisa folded her arms as she glanced at all the beer cans on the table. Randy looked just as uneasy as Stan did. Lisa acted more surprised than disappointed as her brown eyes finally met her husband's shaky gaze. "I'm surprised there were no E.R. visits today."

"Most of those are Duane's," Stan said. "He went home to sleep it off."

Lisa's eyes narrowed as she stared at Stan. She was thinking about the last time she had to rush Stan to the E.R. after he almost cut his index finger off with a Swiss Army knife the kids had gotten him for Christmas. The most recent trip was two summers ago when Stan broke his ankle after falling off the float in the middle of the 4th of July parade.

"Don't give me that look, Lisa. I can broker deals from home just as well as I can from the office. Probably better actually."

Once a very patient woman, Lisa's patience and even respect for Stan had eroded over the past twenty years of marriage. Stan was well aware that Lisa took pretty much everything he said with a grain of salt. They still loved each other though. Still found time to go on their weekly date night. Still made love—sometimes as often as five times a week—but the relationship had suffered through the years. Mainly over trust issues.

"Don't get cocky, yesterday was a fluke," Lisa said dryly.

Randy glanced at Stan with curious eyes. "What happened yesterday?"

"I sold my biggest commercial property ever, and I suddenly got multiple bids on that 200 acre lot south of M28," Stan said. He looked surprised, almost as if he still didn't believe the big deal actually happened.

Impressed, Randy nodded and asked, "Who were the buyers?"

"No idea. A trust was used to buy the mix-use building and four different trusts submitted offers to buy the 200 acres."

Randy lowered his head as an uneasy thought crossed his mind. Lisa walked over to Stan, put her hands on his waist, and flashed a slight smile. "I'll be the happiest woman in Whisper

Dunes when you find someone to buy the 5,000 acres earmarked for the spaceport site."

"Yeah, that's a little trickier, honey. All that land has been in a trust for the past forty years. I've yet to meet anyone who knows the actual owner of that land."

Terry Lutterbach walked up the driveway. At fifty-six he was still a fit looking fella, who looked like he just finished playing golf. In fact, Terry always looked like he just finished playing golf, even in the dead of winter. He gave Lisa a long look as he slowly made his way up the driveway. Lisa diverted her eyes from Stan and spotted Terry approaching. "Hey, gang," Terry said in his deep, raspy, voice. "How's everyone doing?"

"Hi, Terry," Lisa said.

Stan nodded and smiled before he said, "Afternoon, Deacon. Hitting the links before you volunteer at the soup kitchen?"

Terry cracked a smile at Stan before he turned his attention to Lisa.

"Can I borrow you for ten minutes, Lisa? I'm getting new plush carpeting in the basement and I've narrowed it down to three colors. I'd love to get your opinion."

"Sure."

"Super."

Terry faked a smile as he glanced at Stan and Randy. He then regarded the pirate ship float for a few seconds before he flashed an energetic thumbs up. "Float looks terrific, guys. Really something."

"Thanks, Deacon Terry. It's been a team effort," Stan said. Randy, however, couldn't bring himself to say a word, or even nod at the Deacon.

Lisa walked with Terry toward his house, which happened to be next door. You couldn't see the house though because it was fifty yards away and there were a few hundred pine trees between the Zbikowski house and Deacon Terry's house.

Randy closely watched Terry and Lisa as they walked down the driveway and made a left down the street. When they were out of sight, Randy turned his attention to Stan. "I don't know how you can trust Lisa around a guy like that."

Stan looked genuinely confused. "What are you talking about?"

"Your friendly new neighbor wants to do the forbidden polka dance with your beautiful wife."

Stan closed his eyes in frustration. His right hand slid down his face as he took a deep breath through his nose. He finally said, "I think you're fishing in an empty swimming pool with that theory."

"I'm a lawyer. My intuition is different than yours. Trust me. Terry would like nothing more than to put his banana in your wife's fruit salad."

"You're nuts! The man's a Deacon for Christ's sake!"

Randy's eyes widened as he regarded Stan. "Did you see the way he looked at Lisa? Trust me, he's into your wife...Big time."

Stan started to consider the possibility that Randy might be right. He was suddenly overcome with a disgusting image in his mind, which led his emotional state to be upended by a tidal wave of jealousy. In hopes of calming down, Stan was forced to take short, deep breaths.

"The only reason Fr. Carey hired Deacon Lutterbach is so that he can take more weekends off in the summer. Who knows if he's even a real Deacon...he acts more like a golf pro if you ask me," Randy said.

Stan clenched his jaw as his mind started to produce images that he didn't want to see. He struggled to take a breath as another sexually explicit image popped into his mind, based on the worst case scenario. Stan shook the gut wrenching image from his brain and started walking quickly through the pine tree forest. Stan and Randy walked across a narrow dirt trail covered in pine needles. With each step on the pine needle trail, the sharp, minty smell cooled Stan's nostrils while also comforting his fragile state of mind. The scent was fast fleeting, but it didn't matter because ever since Stan was a young boy the smell of pine needles always brought him serenity. The infuriating, vomit inducing images of Deacon Terry caressing Lisa's large breasts while bending her over the kitchen counter and taking her from behind had been replaced with images of Christmas morning from Stan's youth. Stan took his first easy breath in over two minutes as he thought back to that precious Christmas morning when he got a Lionel electric train set. His dad helped him set it up around the Christmas tree, and Stan and his two brothers spent the rest of the morning watching in awe as the train moved around the seven-foot blue spruce.

The smell of pine needles faded as they reached the end of the trail. Stan and Randy moved quickly across Deacon Terry's backyard. With the aid of cancer-causing chemicals, the lawn was incredibly well cared for and had just been cut by a reliable lawn care service.

Stan locked eyes with Randy and pointed at the window next to the chimney on the side of the house. Randy nodded and followed closely behind Stan as he jogged toward the east side of Deacon Terry's two-story brick house. The house was built in the mid-90's by the most respected home builder in Marquette County. Unlike most brick houses built in the 90's, this one stood out because it wasn't ugly.

Stan and Randy reached the side of the house and exchanged another look. Randy hunched down so he could look through the window next to the chimney. He spent about thirty seconds peeking through the window. "I don't see them," Randy said. He turned around but Stan was out of sight.

Stan, without really considering his options, walked down the steps that led to the walk-out basement. He had sold the house twice, including most recently to Deacon Terry, and knew the home's layout. Stan reached for the door knob of the steel, windowless, door. The door was unlocked to Stan's surprise, but he hesitated to enter. He finally put his hand back on the door knob just as the door opened from the inside.

"Jesus!" Deacon Terry said.

Lisa and Terry both looked startled at the sight of Stan. He acted casual as he glanced at Lisa then Terry, but his forehead was covered in beads of sweat, heightening the awkwardness of the situation. Lisa caught her breath and blurted out, "What the hell are you doing, Stan?!"

Stan refused to make eye contact with Lisa. His eyes were focused on Terry, who stood there with a not-so-bright look on his face. Stan finally glanced at Lisa before his eyes moved back to Terry. "Well, if Deacon Terry can borrow my incredibly beautiful wife for a carpet color debate, I thought I could ask the good Deacon if I can borrow a paint brush. What do you say, Terry, can I borrow a paint brush? Duane used my brush yesterday, but forgot to rinse the paint off so now it's rock hard. Can't paint with a hard brush."

Terry's eyes widened as he finally got the courage to look Stan in the eyes. In his mind, Stan thought Terry looked like a man who was hiding something. Terry finally forced a friendly smile and said, "Sure, Stan. No, problemo."

Stan grinned as he kept his suspicious eyes on Deacon Terry. "Thanks, Deacon Terry. I'll be working on the float all afternoon so bring it over when you can."

Lisa glanced at Stan with her angry eyes as she walked past him. She moved quickly up the stairs and back to their house. The uncomfortable situation grew more tense as Stan and Terry locked eyes. Neither man blinked, but as soon as Stan's nostrils started to flare, Terry blurted out, "Tell you what...wait right here and I'll get you a brush. A brand new one."

"Okey-doke."

Stan stood alone in the doorway. "Fuckin Randy," he mumbled to himself. He couldn't help but think that if it wasn't for Randy trying to convince him that Deacon Terry was a world-class womanizer, he wouldn't be in this situation right now. Stan scratched the stubble of hair on his chin. That's not to say Randy's personality profile of Deacon Terry was incorrect. Stan was thinking, ever since Deacon Terry moved next door he was always overtly nice whenever he was around Lisa. Stan hated how Lisa always laughed at Deacon Terry's well rehearsed jokes.

Stan's mind started to wander back to the time when he was convinced Lisa was cheating on him. For almost six months, Stan had this awful feeling that his wife was sleeping with not one, but two other men. The hostility between them peaked when Stan finally accused Lisa to her face of cheating on him with his brother and his former mentor, who's now deceased. The weird thing was, Lisa didn't deny the accusations at first. Instead, she kicked Stan out of the house and they didn't speak for two days. Through Stan's other brother, he learned that Lisa had been busy planning his surprise 40th birthday party for the past six months, which was why she was acting so secretively.

Although no longer a surprise, the party went on as planned. Stan felt bad and apologized more than once, but it didn't matter. The circle of trust between Lisa and Stan had been broken. Throughout Stan's 40th birthday party Lisa barely spoke to him. Stan couldn't even remember if she wished him a happy birthday. They posed for a few photos throughout the night before Lisa started drinking copious amounts of red wine. Before he had a chance to blow out his forty birthday candles, Stan found his wife passed out in the guest bedroom on the first floor.

Lisa was still wearing the sexy white summer dress she bought just for the special night.

The trust issues between Stan and Lisa have persisted ever since. In hopes of taking a step toward restoring the circle of trust in their marriage, Stan had considered telling Lisa about that night when Dr. Marquette tried to give him a handjob. He spent a lot of time thinking about it, but ultimately decided that nothing good could possibly come from telling Lisa about that night.

Terry finally appeared with the paint brush. "Here you go," Terry said as he handed Stan the paint brush. He patiently waited for his thank you.

Stan nodded and finally said, "I'll be sure to wash it and return it when I finish."

"Keep it."

Stan stared at Deacon Terry with suspicious eyes. He had no intention of returning the brush, but still managed a barely audible, "Thanks."

Lisa leaned her lower back against the kitchen island, waiting for Stan's arrival. Since before they were married she knew that Stan was a passionate man, who could get jealous on occasion. As she stood alone in her quiet kitchen, Lisa thought about how she loved that Stan still got jealous. It turned her on. Of course, that's not something she would ever tell Stan. She put her long brown hair in a high ponytail as she continued to wait for Stan's arrival. In the early years of their relationship when Lisa would put her hair in a high ponytail it was her signal to Stan that she was in the mood to give him a blowjob. Now, the high ponytail signaled to Stan that his wife was furious with him.

Lisa flashed an angry look at Stan as he finally entered through the back door. "You are such an asshole," Lisa shouted. Stan knew Lisa would be waiting for him but still struggled to find the right words to explain himself. "I can't believe you were spying on me."

Stan did not hide his embarrassment. He nervously licked his lips then finally got the courage to look Lisa in the eyes. "I'm sorry, Lisa. That was a stupid thing to do."

"We've been married almost twenty years, and I've been nothing but a loving, faithful wife, who hasn't even come close to fucking another man."

Stan furrowed his eyebrows as he tilted his head. "Wait, on a scale of one to ten, how close have you come?"

"Fuck you, Stan!"

"Okay, I deserve that."

Lisa blushed with guilt. She felt bad for saying fuck you and considered apologizing for a moment but ended up not saying anything.

Lisa and Stan stared at each other for almost a minute. The silence wasn't uncomfortable, instead it seemed to relax them both. Lisa felt her anger dissipating, replaced by a sudden desire to make love to her husband. She was about to step toward him, but instead, Lisa turned and walked slowly out of the kitchen.

Stan, also turned on by the silence, followed Lisa through the living room and up the stairs, like a helpless, insecure puppy.

"Lisa, I trust you with my life. I have no reason to doubt you."

"Then why did you creep over to Terry's and spy on us?"

Stan followed Lisa down the long hallway, the original wood floor creaking with each step, and into their master bedroom.

"I'm sorry I did that. That was a mistake, but Randy got in my head. He made me think that Terry has the hots for you and was going to make a move. I guess his insecurities finally rubbed off on me."

Lisa looked surprised to hear this. "Really? Randy made you think that Deacon Terry has the hots for me?"

Stan nodded then ran his fingers through his hair. "I swear, I think he's having marital problems. He's been acting weird the past few months."

"How so?"

"He's more guarded than usual. When I'm talking to him I can tell his mind is somewhere else."

Stan tried to mask his surprise as Lisa started undressing in front of him. "Has he talked about his marriage with you lately?"

"God, no. We both consider it bad luck to talk about our marriages."

Lisa removed her bra and tossed it on the queen-size sleigh bed with a rustic cherry finish. Stan took a slow breath through his nose as he stared at Lisa's large, teardrop shaped breasts. She could see that her husband was quickly becoming aroused. Lisa had undressed in front of Stan thousands of times, but each and every time his eyes would narrow slowly as he looked Lisa up and down. Stan stood before his wife, completely awestruck, as if he was seeing her naked for the first time. Lisa noticed and always appreciated how Stan was able to remind her how beautiful she was with his eyes. It was the gratitude and admiration Stan conveyed to Lisa with his eyes that kept her in love with him.

Stan was both aroused and confused as he watched his naked wife remove her silver watch followed by her one-carat diamond wedding ring. Stan bought Lisa the ninety-dollar watch for her thirtieth birthday. Lisa and Stan both believed that buying an expensive watch was equivalent to walking around with your bank statements taped to your forehead.

As soon as Lisa's brown eyes met Stan's gaze he pulled off his shirt and went to unbuckle his belt. Lisa put her hands on her narrow hips and said, "What are you doing?"

"What do you mean, what am I doing? Aren't we having makeup sex right now?"

Lisa was perfectly still as her eyes looked Stan up and down. She closed her left eye and tilted her head to left. She never got tired of teasing Stan. Lisa finally let out a long, "Hmmm."

"I am so hard right now, I could dent the bottom of a family-size baked bean can."

Lisa walked slowly over to the dresser and grabbed her hair brush. "Stan, we can't have makeup sex every time we have an argument."

Stan watched Lisa brush her hair for a moment before he said, "Dr. Calloway has been very clear about the importance of makeup sex in our relationship. Makeup sex is an enriching reminder of the love and passion we still have for each other. Her words, not mine."

Lisa rolled her eyes as she stopped brushing her hair. She turned toward Stan and said, "Oh, give me a break. We went through four therapists before you finally found one who strongly advocates for makeup sex."

"Dr. Calloway is the best damn therapist we've ever worked with and you know it. Please, Lisa...if I didn't have a bum knee I'd be on my knees begging."

Stan's eyes moved slowly from Lisa's sun-kissed breasts down to her ankles and back to her beautiful face. She slowly turned her back on Stan and looked at herself in the full length, arched mirror as she went back to brushing her long brown hair. Even though it wasn't even mid-summer, Lisa's skin was tan with no white lines. The result of taking advantage of the warmer than usual June and sunbathing naked on the back deck whenever Stan was at work and her kids were at camp.

"How's your summer chore list coming along?"

Stan was in a trance state of arousal while he watched Lisa brush her hair. She brushed with a delicate rhythm that looked like it might come to a stop after each brush. The tingling sensation covered Stan's skull then moved slowly down his neck.

"Stan? The summer chore list. How's it coming?"

The thought of doing a single chore broke Stan from his trance.

"I plan on knocking out at least four chores this weekend, which should get me to the halfway mark."

Lisa set the brush on the dresser and glanced at herself in the mirror before she turned around and faced Stan. She met his gaze before glancing at Stan's erection. Lisa sighed, bit her lower lip, then said, "Give me five minutes to wash my hair then you can join me."

Stan let out a sigh of relief. He smiled and nodded as he watched his gorgeous wife walk slowly into their master bathroom. He glanced at his watch and said, "See ya in five, hon. And don't worry about me, I'll keep it up."

Stan's phone started to ring. He glanced at the screen but the number was blocked. Stan's first instinct was to let it go to voicemail, but after the fourth ring he answered his phone thinking it might be a potential client interested in his latest listing. Realtor rule number one: always answer your phone when an unknown number pops up on the screen. Stan said, "Zbikowski Group, Stan speaking."

After a few seconds he heard a familiar voice. "Hello, Stan...it's Bianca."

Like a bridegroom who just farted in church as he finished the last sentence of his marriage vows, Stan blushed and his knees buckled. He was forced to sit on the edge of the bed before he could utter a word. His face was tomato red and his chest was tight. Stan took a few deep breaths before he quietly said, "Hello, Dr. Marquette."

Bianca didn't say anything for a few seconds. That was the first time Stan had ever called her Dr. Marquette. Bianca finally started talking and told Stan that she was in town and wanted to meet. Stan cut her off mid-sentence and said he had to run. But before he hung up to join Lisa in the shower, he told Bianca to try him again tomorrow.

2

Denise Lyons stood near the double-hung window in her bedroom that let in the most sunlight. Her back was to the window as she stared at her phone. The curtains were about halfway open, allowing the late afternoon sun to light up most of the spacious bedroom and warm Denise's long back, which like the rest of her body was tan from spending most of her summer afternoons at the beach. Denise had turned thirty-five a week earlier but easily could pass for a woman in her mid-twenties. She was a unique beauty who attracted long looks, from men and women, wherever she happened to be walking. But it was her piercing blue eyes that were the first thing anyone noticed when they looked at her face. Before a person became awestruck admiring her beautiful face with high cheek bones and a seemingly perfect jaw line, they stood flatfooted and mesmerized as they stared at her blue eyes that twinkled like expertly cut blue sapphires. If you saw her face or body in a photograph you would immediately suspect that the photograph had been extensively photoshopped. Denise stood at five-ten and had a perfectly sculpted body, the result of instructing two pilates classes a day, six days a week. She also instructed a clothing-optional hot yoga class three nights a week for select students.

The popular pilates and yoga classes—they were always full—took place in the ground-floor studio, directly below her apartment. Denise had rented both the studio space and the only apartment in the building for the past four years. The two-story brick building, built in 1890, was located on the corner of a quiet tree-lined street that was three blocks from the lakefront.

Denise, wearing turquoise yoga pants and a black square-neck tank top, looked tense as she walked slowly around the bedroom while searching for a particular video on her phone. Her spacious bedroom, with a ten-foot ceiling, consisted of a four poster king-sized bed with a headboard and canopy, matching light brown nightstands each with a Tiny Terri round accent lamp, and a long dresser that was purchased recently at a custom furniture shop. The white walls were bare except for a twenty-four-by-thirty painting depicting a pack of wolves in a snowy forest, which hung on the wall above the dresser.

Denise finally found the video she was looking for on her phone. She was about to email the video to *Canadianpicklelover@gmail.com* but she hesitated. What she was about to do was something she had done many times before, but suddenly she was overwhelmed with guilt. This was not a feeling she was used to experiencing. Denise glanced at the fresh cut yellow daisies in the glass vase on her nightstand for a moment. She closed her eyes tightly for a few seconds, and when she opened her eyes she tapped the "send email" icon on her phone. She tossed her phone onto the bed and quickly put her long and wavy sandy-blond hair in a pony tail. She then got herself into a difficult yoga pose—the destroyer of the universe. Denise stayed in the pose for exactly one minute before disentangling her body from the difficult pose and standing upright. Denise then slowly bent down, touched her toes, and held the pose for ten seconds. She stood back up, closed her eyes, and tilted her head right then left.

Denise walked tall with her shoulders back, from her bedroom to the open kitchen of her apartment. The old wood floors creaked with nearly every step, but because Denise lived alone in the only apartment in the building, there was no one to hear the creaky floors, or the rock music she liked to play very loud in the morning, or the moaning and screaming that echoed off the bedroom walls most nights. Denise glanced at her watch, fourteen minutes until her next pilates class started.

Randy sat behind the desk in his small, messy office. He slurped diet root beer through a paper straw as he stared at his laptop computer. Randy was not a well-paid lawyer and had the office to prove it. His shabby office was on the second floor of a two-story building on Front Street. Built during the late 19th century during the Upper Peninsula's golden era, fueled by the mining boom of iron ore and copper, the ornate building originally housed an Irish pub on the first floor and a high-end brothel on the second floor. But now the building was in desperate need of basic repairs and hadn't been updated since the early eighties. The first floor was occupied by a four person accounting firm. Before Mulcahy & Associates took over the lease, the space was occupied by a now disgraced chiropractor.

Daugherty Law Group was stenciled on the frosted glass door that led to his office, but Randy was the only one practicing law in the group. Not that long ago, he did have two associate attorneys and a secretary, but they left for better-paying gigs in Green Bay. Randy's law practice focused on workers' comp, but a few years ago, thanks to a referral by Stan, he became the sole legal advisor to Russ Tillinghast, the longtime mayor of Whisper Dunes. The advisor role only paid Randy a thousand dollars a week, and most of that money went toward paying off his student loan debt. Although last year, Randy used some of that money to finance a romantic weekend getaway with his wife to Traverse City.

Randy's parents encouraged him to go to law school in case his dream of becoming a novelist didn't work out. They reminded him constantly that some of the most successful novelists of all time had become lawyers before they wrote their first novel. By the time Randy graduated from Wayne State Law School, his artistic dreams were crushed by the pressure to find a job so he could start paying off his massive student loan debt.

Unlike his two best friends, Stan and Duane, Randy still cared what other people thought about him. He was one of those kids who hated to disappoint his parents. But now it was his wife and two daughters whom he desperately tried not to disappoint.

Randy took a big bite from his turkey sub sandwich then grabbed his phone off the desk. He took another bite while scrolling through emails on his phone. The desk was littered with manila folders and large binders, but he was able to find a spot for his forty-eight-ounce diet root beer and his twelve-inch sub. He squinted his eyes as he continued to scroll through the emails. Randy's thumb stopped moving as soon as he came across the email from Denise. Finding an email from Denise Lyons clearly caught him off guard. Randy had never received an email from Denise. Even stranger, he had never shared his email address with her. He looked uneasy as his index finger tapped opened Denise's email. Just as he tapped the video link, he slurped the rest of the diet root beer from his giant cup.

Upon hearing Denise's voice yell, "Slap my ass! Slap it, Randy! Slap it harder, you little bitch!" Randy spit out the diet root beer all over the legal documents on his desk. His wide eyes froze, along with the rest of his body, as he watched the sex video for another ten seconds. Randy looked like he might pass out as Denise screamed, "Fuck me like I'm your ex-girlfriend from college!"

"I don't have an ex-girlfriend from college!"

Denise stood in her kitchen wearing a black silk robe that was loosely tied. She had no expression on her face as she reached for the blueberry smoothie on the kitchen island. Randy stood on the other side of the kitchen island. His face twitched with a tidal wave of emotions. Denise flashed a sly grin right before taking a long sip of her blueberry smoothie.

Randy's hands clutched the edge of the butcher block countertop. Denise watched in amusement as he started to dry heave. While waiting for Randy to catch his breath, she used her right thumb to wipe the blueberry smoothie from her top lip.

"If you're going to throw up, please hurry to the bathroom," Denise said. She casually took another sip from her smoothie. Randy closed his eyes and took a long, deep breath, which allowed him to finally gather his thoughts.

"Want a sip?"

Randy's eyes narrowed as he regarded Denise. He stared into her big blue eyes for almost a minute before he finally said, "When did you make this video?"

Denise gave Randy a smart ass look. "Well, obviously when we were fucking."

"I'm mean, why...why would you secretly record us having sex?"

Denise regarded Randy, thinking she'd give him at least a minute to come up with the answer to his question. Randy started to become overwhelmed with emotions again, and Denise knew that he had figured out the answer. Randy processed the worst case scenario then said, in a barely audible tone, "Are you trying to blackmail me?"

Denise's right eye narrowed while her left eye twinkled with bewilderment. "I'm not trying to blackmail you. I am blackmailing you."

Randy lowered his head in agony. He thought for a second that maybe he should start ripping her place apart in hopes of finding the sex tape. He outweighed Denise by over a hundred pounds. *She couldn't stop me, could she?* Then Randy quickly recalled how Denise had dominated him during each of their encounters in bed. Denise was strong and limber from head to toe. Randy knew he had no chance if things got physical.

"I also got great footage of you eating kale chips off my tits."

"That was your idea!"

"I thought you'd have fun with it. You didn't want to do any lines off my tits so I thought my homemade kale chips were the next best thing."

"I've never done cocaine in my life!"

"Good for you. But if you ever want to do a few bumps off my tits, just ask."

Randy shook his head in disgust.

"Okay, lets get down to business," Denise said. "I'm pretty sure that if your wife ever saw the video of me playing with your sturdy cock, she would get the sudden urge to divorce you. Even if she happened to hire the worst divorce attorney in the world, the sex tape will guarantee that your wife gets half of all your assets, and full custody of your two kids."

Randy started to get light-headed as his knees began to shake. He pressed his hands on the countertop to prevent a hard fall to the floor. He winced in pain while trying to get his breathing under control. He was about to hyperventilate until a vivid image suddenly came into his mind. His breathing slowed down and his mind stopped racing as he envisioned walking on the beach with his wife, hand in hand. Randy looked at Denise and quietly said, "I love my wife...very much. Please..."

Denise interrupted Randy with a loud laugh. Not in a mocking way, just surprised. "Well, I really hope it works out between you two."

Randy looked embarrassed. He thought he might cry so he glanced toward the living room until he got control of his emotions. "I made a mistake, Denise. My wife and two girls are all I care about. Please don't destroy my life."

Denise suddenly had the desire to comfort Randy. She reached across the counter and gently grabbed his hand. "I'm not looking to ruin your life, Randy."

Randy looked at Denise with confused eyes. He wanted to believe her, but didn't.

"Don't feel bad. You'd be hard pressed to find any man who enjoys having sex with his wife after twenty years of marriage. That would be like bumping into someone at a bar who enjoys drinking tequila endorsed by a celebrity, who doesn't drink alcohol."

"My wife is the only woman I've ever desired to be with."

"That's sweet."

Randy finally started to have some clear thoughts that allowed him to speak with conviction. "I never had any desire to be with you. But you invited me up here after that hot yoga class and hypnotized me with your perfect breasts. The only reason I even showed up to that class was because you offered me a two week free trial that night you drove me home after we got shitfaced at Stuckos Pub."

Denise finished the rest of her blueberry smoothie. As Randy watched her slowly lick her lips, he couldn't help but think that the situation made no sense. *Why would Denise blackmail me? I don't have any money.*

Denise singed up her robe and smirked as she noticed the beads of sweat covering Randy's forehead. "Sure you don't want me to make you a blueberry smoothie?"

Randy's eyes narrowed as he looked down at the countertop in a daze. He was angry with himself and very confused as to how he ended up in this position. Randy loved his wife very much, and had never considered cheating on her. He lifted his head up and looked Denise in the eyes. He realized that he was dealing with a very cold, calculating woman. Until this encounter, Denise had been nothing but sweet and carefree around Randy. He'd always been self-conscious around women, but Denise made him feel at ease. Now that he thought about it, maybe it was Denise's cannabis infused kale chips that made him so comfortable around her.

Randy tried to compose himself in hopes he wouldn't completely lose control of his emotions again. "I thought you were this incredibly sweet-natured woman. You're so casual and carefree about everything. I honestly believed you were one of those unique women who doesn't realize how beautiful you are."

Denise looked dumbfounded. "What? No, I'm well aware that I'm the most beautiful woman in any room I enter. I've been aware of that fact since I was eighteen."

"I only know you as this kind, gentle woman, who's full of positive energy. I just can't believe that I'm now looking into the eyes of a cunning, cold-hearted monster who set out to ruin my life."

Denise felt a lump in her throat, but flashed a hard look to prevent herself from conveying any remorse or compassion. She kept her eyes on Randy as she walked around the kitchen island and sat on the bucket bar stool. Thinking he could give his shaky knees a break, Randy sat down on the other bucket bar stool. He eased into the teal blue leather-upholstered stool that swiveled, but Randy was in no mood to swivel. He sat perfectly still and upright in the stool while giving Denise a blank look.

"I didn't set out to ruin your life, Randy. Every man I've ever met would have given up just about anything to get a chance to spend the night with me. But I only start a relationship with a man if he has something I truly want."

A confused look crossed Randy's face. Thoughts started spinning around his head before he stopped the crazy thoughts with two blunt questions. *Since the beginning of time, many, many men have been blackmailed by a beautiful woman. But don't only important men get seduced and blackmailed by beautiful women? I'm an underpaid attorney, who still has student loans to pay off. I'm barely in the middle class. What the hell could I possibly have that she wants?*

Denise took a long, hard look at Randy, who still seemed to be having an internal conversation with himself. She was no longer trying to be sexy, or sweet. She had morphed into a cold, cunning woman. She looked like a judge who was about to sentence a person to life in prison, albeit a judge who was only wearing a small black robe that was barely covering her perfect breasts. "Other than the mayor, you are the only person in this town that has access to the feasibility report," she said.

The confused look still hung on Randy's face. "I'm an attorney for the city of Whisper Dunes and top advisor to the mayor, I read lots of feasibility reports. I'm afraid you'll have to be more specific."

Denise leaned her body forward. Her face was now only inches from Randy's bulbous nose. She looked him in the eyes and said, "I'm talking about that bullshit report from that non-profit science research institute."

Randy's blank stare didn't give Denise any indication that he had read the report.

"You know, the report that contradicts the Michigan Space Association's claim that the proposed rocket spaceport will create an economic boom for the town."

Randy's eyes slowly widened. He no longer looked confused or emotional. It all made sense now. Randy had never understood why Denise invited him up to her apartment after the hot yoga class and suddenly started going down on him while he was enjoying the best blueberry smoothie that he had ever tasted. After their first encounter, six months ago, Randy had considered the possibility that Denise was attracted to his winning personality, and his dry sense of humor, and even his dad bod. But now he knew exactly why Denise invited him up to her apartment and seduced him. Randy took an easy breath. He no longer felt embarrassed or dejected. He was a blackmail victim, but for some reason that fact gave him a certain confidence that he had never experienced before. Randy slowly scratched his chin, calmly looked at Denise and said, "Ahh, that feasibility report. Yes, I read the whole thing. It strongly recommends that the rocket launch spaceport not be built."

"The mayor hasn't read it yet, has he?"

"No. Mayor Tillinghast doesn't like to read reports filled with charts and graphs. He only reads the reports that I tell him to read."

Randy continued to stare at Denise as he thought about some of the hard truths in his life. Like nearing the age of fifty and still being years away from paying off his student loan debt from law school. Still driving a 2012 Ford Explorer with nearly two-hundred thousand miles on it. Still only able to afford to take his family to the Wisconsin Dells for vacation, but dammit, for the first time in a long time, Randy couldn't help but feel important...really important. Like a powerful politician, or the CEO of a publicly traded company, or a banking executive, or the dean of admissions of an Ivy League school, Randy was the target of a well-conceived honey trap.

Randy became so consumed with his thoughts that he was no longer looking at Denise. He was suddenly filled with a certain arrogant confidence that was unfamiliar to him. Randy looked to be enjoying the thoughts going through his mind. *If only Dad were still alive to know that I was important enough to be caught in a honey trap. If there wasn't video evidence, I highly doubt that any of my buddies, or my wife would believe that a beautiful woman, who should be working as a supermodel, would have the desire to seduce me in order to blackmail me.*

"Randy!"

He finally shook away his arrogant thoughts and looked into Denise's big blue eyes.

"How in God's name did you get your hands on that report? Only the mayor and I have access to that report. Wait, are you screwing Russ too?"

Denise smiled as she pat Randy on the cheek. "No."

Randy rubbed his chin as he stared at Denise with suspicious eyes. "Now why would a pilates instructor care about a feasibility report on a potential rocket launch spaceport? That just doesn't add up."

"That's a fair question." She slowly placed her right hand on Randy's right thigh. "But the only thing you need to worry about is making sure that report isn't made public before September 1st," Denise said in a sexy voice.

Randy looked uneasy as he glanced at Denise's hand, which remained gripped firmly on his inner thigh. He grabbed Denise's wrist and gently removed her hand from his thigh as he looked into her eyes. "According to the report, the annual revenue generated from a rocket launch spaceport would have the same revenue impact on our town as the addition of two fast food restaurants. A far cry from the 1,000 jobs the Michigan Space Association predicted would be created. The report strongly recommends that no investment be made in constructing and operating a rocket launch spaceport in Whisper Dunes, or any other town in the state of Michigan."

Denise put her hand back on Randy's thigh and leaned toward him until her lips were just a few inches from his lips. He could smell the blueberry smoothie on her breath as she inched closer. Randy looked intimidated, but couldn't help himself from sneaking a peek at Denise's round perky breasts as they popped out of her robe. "If you don't want your wife to ever see those tasteful videos we made together then I recommend you bury that report."

Randy's mouth became very dry. He struggled to swallow as Denise's steely blue eyes stared him down. "If the mayor reads that report, or God forbid, it becomes public before September 1st, I'll have no choice but to email your wife the videos of you putting your crooked cock into me."

Randy let out a long sigh as Denise leaned her body closer to him. Her breasts pressed against his chest, which caused Randy's entire body to start perspiring. But to his credit, he did not get an erection. He stared at Denise and calmly said, "I'll do everything in my power to bury that report for as long as I can. But we both know that the vast majority of people who live in Whisper Dunes strongly oppose a rocket launch spaceport being built here, or anywhere else in the U.P. Can you blame them? Who wants to see a heavy industrial rocket launch site on the coastline of the largest and cleanest freshwater lake on Earth?"

Denise slowly pulled away from Randy as she closed her robe. "Want to know who? The geniuses at the largest space company in the world, and they don't give a shit about a bunch of whining environmentalists," she said in a cold tone. Having never heard her speak in that tone, Randy suddenly had goose bumps on the back of his neck.

"Wait, do you secretly work for Space O?"

"Space O isn't the largest space company in the world. Space D is."

"Do you work for Space D?"

"No. It just so happens that my business partner owns the 5,000 acres along Lake Superior that Space D wants to build their rocket spaceport on."

"Wait, I thought Beige Origin wants to buy the land for their spaceport."

"They do, but Space D is going to outbid them. But they'll only go through with the deal if we can get the town to agree to rezone the land. The planning commission scheduled the rezoning request for a public hearing on August 31st. As long as the report doesn't become public before then, the zoning change will be approved the next day and Space D will pay my partner one hundred million for the land."

Randy slowly scratched the stubble on his chin as he tried to play it cool. He finally said, "What's in it for you?"

"I get ten million once the deal closes."

Randy, impressed, let out a long whistle. "That's a lot of dough."

Denise flashed her sexy smile and said, "Yes, it is."

Randy stood up from the chair and was ready to leave when Denise put her lips close to his left ear and whispered, "I hope you can find time to stop by soon for some fun on top of the feathers."

Randy's eyes started to look around the kitchen, wondering if there might be a camera on him right now. He let out a long sigh as he regarded Denise. "You blackmailed me, and have threatened to ruin my life. I will follow your orders, Denise, but I want absolutely nothing to do with you. Understand?"

Denise actually looked disappointed. She kept her eyes on Randy as she took off her robe and set it on his shoulder. "You're a sweet guy, Randy. I enjoyed fucking you," Denise said jovially. "I'll keep an open spot for you in my Wednesday-night hot yoga class, just in case you get the urge to pop in."

Randy's face remained listless as he watched Denise walk toward her bedroom.

"I'm going to take a shower. Please lock the door on your way out, sweetie," Denise said without turning around.

Randy closed his eyes for a few seconds until he heard the bathroom door slam shut. He then pulled out his phone and looked at his calendar—**July 5th: discuss spaceport feasibility study with Mayor Russ**. Randy tapped the edit button and changed the meeting to **September 7th**.

3

Stan Zbikowski was awakened by his alarm clock that dated back to his college days. He rolled out of bed, wearing boxer shorts with faded Santa Clauses on them, and started doing pushups. Stan counted out loud, but as he got closer to thirty his arms started to fail him. "Twenty-six, twenty-seven...twenty-eight," he shouted out as he ran out of breath and strength. Stan's face was flushed with blood as he attempted to complete his thirtieth pushup. He got close but his arms failed him and he collapsed to the ground. Stan yelled, "You bum!"

Stan took several deep breaths as he made his way toward his closet. He was one of those guys who always looked for a chance to get a couple micro workouts in throughout the day. He entered his closet and glanced at both biceps until he decided it was finally time to put a shirt on. Stan selected a blue golf shirt, but before he could put it on, the phone rang. He put the shirt on, walked over to the nightstand, and picked up his phone. A restricted number appeared on the screen. Stan contemplated whether to answer before he finally cleared his throat and tapped the green "accept button."

"Bryce Dunlap speaking, Mr. Zbikowski's second assistant," Stan said. As Stan listened to the caller, a curious expression came across his face. Stan quietly said, "What time?"

Stan, now dressed in grey shorts and a blue golf shirt, entered his sunlit kitchen that opened to a huge family room. The family room had vaulted ceilings and a brick, wood-burning fireplace. He grabbed a coffee mug from the cabinet that one of his kids made him for Father's Day a few years back and filled it up with the remaining coffee in the pot. He set the mug on the countertop, grabbed the carton of organic half and half from the refrigerator, and poured a little into his mug. Just as Stan took his first sip, he noticed a piece of paper taped to the outside of the sliding door. The sign read: *I stole a box of Fruit Loops from your cupboard. Consider it a down payment for the 46 grand you still owe me. Mr. M.*

Stan looked furious as he stared at the note while taking another sip from his coffee. He mumbled, "You son of a bitch, Duane." He opened the sliding door and ripped the note off the glass.

Stan's small home office was messy and poorly decorated. Faux-wood Venetian blinds hung from the only window in the room, and two different golf bags were on the stained area rug, which covered most of the wood floor. Twenty lawn signs that read: STOP THE ROCKET! were piled up in the corner. Leaning up against the wall in the opposite corner were thirty ZBIKOWSKI REAL ESTATE GROUP lawn signs. On the wall behind Stan's desk was a framed photo of him and Lisa on their wedding day. On the table behind the desk were family photos of Stan, Lisa, and their three sons as well as four framed photos of Stan on various golfing trips with friends.

There was a poster board taped to the wall—clearly written by Lisa—that read: *Stan's Summer Things To Do List.* Twenty tasks were listed but only two had been crossed out with a black marker. Like a guy who decided to play thirty-six holes of golf with his buddies when he could have spent the day with his beautiful wife on their sailboat making love, Stan's messed up priorities had a tendency to leave Lisa disappointed. Unbeknownst to Stan, his actions continued to give some hope to the eligible bachelors in town that one day they might have a chance with Lisa Zbikowski.

Stan sat behind his desk with reading glasses slumped on the tip of his nose, staring at his laptop. This small office was once the place where he did his best thinking, but that was before online gambling became legal and Stan, like tens of millions of other people, developed a terrible addiction. For Stan, he knew he had hit rock bottom when he bet twenty grand on the Puppy Bowl and another forty grand on the Super Bowl two years ago. The next day, he confessed to Lisa that he had a problem and told her that he would delete every online gambling app from his phone, which he did, and quit cold turkey...which he didn't.

Stan had not made a single sports bet online since that disastrous Super Bowl weekend. But the day before March Madness tipped off, Stan decided to place a few harmless bets with his close friend, Duane Murphy. Back in college, Duane started a book making operation and over the past thirty years he had established himself as one of the most respected bookies in the Upper Peninsula. Because of all the rolling hills and dense forests, less than half the folks who live in the U.P. have access to reliable internet, and even for those who do have reliable internet they have minimal faith in online banking, much less online gambling. There are a few other bookies in town, but Stan had never placed a bet with anyone, except Duane.

In the corner of the messy desk was a landline phone that Stan currently had on speaker mode. "I don't care how much I owe you, Duane, that doesn't give you permission to break into my home and steal a box of my kids' favorite cereal."

"Hey, there are consequences when you owe the Iceman a lot of dough."

"I'm the Iceman! That's my nickname going back to my high school basketball glory years. You can't steal my nickname," Stan said as his face turned red.

"I thought that was your nickname in college because you slept with the entire women's ice hockey team at Northern."

"Oh, come on! You know that rumor's not true."

"Pay me back in full, Zibs, then I'll give you back your nickname."

"That's bullshit, Duane..."

"Hey! You got off easy. What I should've done is shat on your favorite chair in the family room."

"You'll have your money by the end of the week, or by the end of next week at the latest. But no more breaking into my house to steal cereal and God knows what else. If my kids see you lurking around our house, how am I supposed to explain that?"

"I'll just tell them what I always do when I pass out at your house. Uncle Duane doesn't drink and drive, ever, because I'm a man of high character, and I lead by example. Uh-oh, I'm about to lose you. Walking into L&M's to get a new pirate flag and a dozen two-by-fours."

"We don't need a new pirate flag, Duane. What we need is a smoke machine so it looks cool when we shoot water balloons out of the cannon." Stan glanced at the caller ID as his cell phone started to vibrate on the desk. "Duane, I gotta take this call. I'll see you in an hour."

Stan picked up his cell phone and tapped the speaker button. "Hey, Lenny."

Lenny sounded hungover as his voice finally came over the speaker. "Hey, buddy, just returning your call. What's going on?"

Stan grabbed his lower back in pain as he got up from his chair. He walked over to his golf bag and pulled out the putter. "Remember that check for two grand I gave you last month?"

"Not really."

"I gave you a check for two grand after you said you would install the new shower heads at all of my properties within a week."

"Ok, it's ringing a bell, but I don't remember giving you a time frame on when I'd complete the job."

"You cashed the check, but for some reason you still haven't installed the shower heads."

Stan shook his head in frustration as he heard the sound of a beer can being cracked opened, followed by a loud burp. Lenny finally said, "I'm packing for Florida right now. Can I install the shower heads tomorrow?"

A look of bewilderment crossed Stan's face. "You're leaving Whisper Dunes, a summer paradise, to go to Florida?"

"Yeah. Naples."

"Ah, Naples. The swingers capital of Florida."

"No, no, no. You're thinking of Jupiter. Naples is the divorce capital of Florida."

"I thought that was Palm Beach?"

"No, Palm Beach is the Chinese massage parlor, slash whore house capital of Florida."

"What about Fisher Island?"

"Cuckold capital of Florida."

"Marco Island?"

"STD capital of Florida."

"Boy, for an unlicensed plumber from the Upper Peninsula, you sure know a lot about Florida."

"All I know is that I like F-L-A snatch and the summer green fees."

"Oh, before I forget...make sure you say hi to Mrs. Houston for me."

"It's Mrs. Wadsworth now. She went back to her maiden name. How do you know I'm seeing her?"

Stan took a long sip from his coffee cup. "There are no secrets in Whisper Dunes. You know that. Half the town knows you're banging Hubert's ex-wife."

"How'd you find that out?"

"Fr. Carey."

"I'm in love with her, Stan."

"Fantastic. I want those shower heads installed today. Understand? All my properties have tenants so make sure you knock loud and long before entering."

"I always knock before I enter."

Stan shook his head in frustration. He then closed his eyes and rubbed the bridge of his nose. "What about the time you walked in on Mrs. McDougall going down on Mr. McDougall? What about the time you walked in on Gary banging his sister-in-law on the kitchen counter? What about the time you walked in on a group of stay-at-home moms trying to negotiate a fair price for a bag of magic mushrooms from one of my oldest tenants?"

Lenny's defensive voice came over the phone speaker. "Hey, when you call the pipe-master for emergency plumbing services, I'm coming in hot. And I will not apologize! Because sex acts should be performed in bedrooms, and a drug deal should take place in an empty church parking lot, not in the middle of an open kitchen!"

"Knock. Don't knock. I really don't give a shit. But at the end of today, I expect every one of my units to have a new shower head."

Stan tapped the "end call" icon, dropped the phone on his desk, and walked over to the list of chores tacked to the wall. He glanced at the poster board with twenty chores listed, ripped it from the wall, and stuffed it in the trash bin. He looked relieved, like a nagging weight had just been lifted from his broad shoulders. Stan walked back to his desk as his phone started to vibrate. He checked the caller ID and quickly answered. "Hi, honey. Good. How's your day going? No, I'm not headed in that direction today. Because that pompous couple from Green Bay canceled on me. That road has plenty of signs already. Well, I think there's such a thing as putting up one too many protest signs."

A 2006 white Chevy cargo van was parked on the corner of Michigan Street in front of a two-story, Italianate style, red brick building. The corner building stood out because it had been beautifully preserved since it was erected in 1890, but also because it was the only apartment building on the block. The rest of the block consisted of single family homes, most of which were built during the 1950's.

Lenny Trubisky, who looked young for a man approaching fifty-four, slowly exited his van. On the driver side of the van it read: *THE PIPEMASTER: 24-Hour Emergency Plumbing Service. 906-270-6900.* On the passenger side it read: *Sometimes A Flush Is Better Than A Full House.* Lenny, wearing black jeans and a gray t-shirt, walked toward the rear of the van to retrieve his tool box. He was rail thin and maybe an inch shy of six feet, but his muscular arms and strong hands were proof that he'd been doing manual labor since he was a young man. Lenny's wavy brown hair was just starting to gray, the only noticeable indication that he had reached his fifties.

Lenny walked past a large cast stone planter filled with geraniums that was positioned a few feet left of the front door. The front door was painted dark green and had a half-moon window. Lenny pressed the apartment buzzer with his right thumb and waited all of four seconds before pressing the buzzer again. On the first floor of the building was Denise's pilates studio. The floor-to-ceiling glass windows, with no window treatment, made it easy to see inside the studio. Lenny peeked through the glass, hoping to find Denise setting up for her next class, but he was bummed to find the studio empty. He pressed the buzzer again.

"It's Lenny Trubisky, the pipe master," he said in a voice normally reserved for a radio commercial. "I'm here to replace your shower head. Hello-hello-hello! Anyone home?"

Lenny pressed the buzzer once more. No answer, so he pulled out a master key and unlocked the front door. Lenny entered the building and walked slowly toward the end of the dark hallway. He turned right and huffed and puffed his way up the wide stairs to Denise's second floor apartment.

Lenny's tool box was on the kitchen counter, next to a wooden bowl full of apples. But he wasn't clutching a wrench or a hacksaw, instead he was clutching a tooth pick as he carefully inserted it through two Pimiento stuffed olives and a thick pickle. He then dropped the olives and pickle into a tall glass filled with vodka and spicy Bloody Mary mix. He added a dash of celery salt, stirred his beverage with a spoon, and took a sip. He licked his upper lip and seemed more than satisfied with his beverage.

Lenny looked at his Casio watch, and a thought immediately popped into his head. *It's Friday, almost noon...what the hell?* He set the tall glass on the counter and added a little more Crystal Head vodka to his Bloody Mary. He mixed his drink with his celery stick, took another sip, and let out a long, "Ahhhh." Took another sip and said to himself, "Oh, good, good, good, good."

Lenny had not been back inside the apartment since Denise moved in. He couldn't remember how many years it had been since she moved in, maybe four he thought, but he did remember doing a few last minute quick fixes right before she moved into the apartment. Lenny thought it was a bit strange that he hadn't been asked to fix something since Denise moved in, especially considering that the building was very old. Most of Stan's tenants who lived in his older apartment buildings frequently submitted maintenance requests. Maybe Denise was a handy girl who liked to fix things herself, Lenny thought as he sipped on his Bloody Mary.

He looked impressed as he walked around the spacious and nicely decorated apartment. No one would know it to look at him, but Lenny had been inside so many buildings and homes in the Upper Peninsula over the past thirty years that he had developed quite an eye for interior decorating. He always looked for visual texture and was quick to criticize a room that didn't have a good flow.

Lenny looked up at the twelve-foot ceiling and noticed two different water stains. The high, white coffered ceiling made the living room feel bigger than it actually was, causing Lenny to bump his shin on the corner of the rectangular coffee table. "Fuck!"

He walked off the pain shooting through his left shin as he wondered why Stan hadn't called him to fix the water leak in the attic. Maybe Denise never reported the leak, he thought as he rubbed his throbbing shin. Lenny admired the rustic wood bookcase in the corner, but he wasn't much of a reader so he didn't bother to glance at any of the books on the shelf. Lenny took another sip from his Bloody Mary then fixed his eyes on the white wall that was crowded with framed nature photographs. The opposite wall was reserved for small canvas paintings. Lenny looked interested in the paintings, which were comprised of landscapes and a few nudes. He noticed that most of them were signed, *D. Lyons.* Lenny continued looking around, not sure why there were no photos in the living room of Denise posing with family or friends.

Lenny looked more frustrated than buzzed as he stood over the sink in Denise's master bathroom. He tried to remove the new shower head from the thick plastic packaging but couldn't seem to do it. With vengeful eyes, he whipped out the switch blade from his back pocket and popped up the blade. As he attempted to slice open the box, he instead sliced opened his thumb. Lenny dropped the switch blade and grabbed his badly cut thumb. He glanced at his bleeding thumb then looked at himself in the mirror and yelled, "Lenny, you grossly, incompetent, fuck!"

He leaned his left hand over the sink and rinsed his bloody thumb under warm water. He turned off the water and grabbed a hand towel to wrap around his thumb. Lenny then started to search around the bathroom for a first aid kit. He opened the bathroom closet and immediately froze like a boy who just walked in on his mom pleasuring herself. Lenny's eyes and mouth were wide open. On the top shelf were six boxes of condoms, four bottles of hydrating organic lube, four bottles of sweet almond body oil, and a dozen tubes of chapstick. On the shelf below, Lenny found two long black dildos, a pink dildo, a double-ended glass dildo, a magic wand vibrator, two pairs of handcuffs, a whip, and four scented candles.

Lenny looked dumbfounded. He mumbled to himself, "What the hell's going on around here?"

Lenny was mesmerized while he looked at the double-ended glass dildo, but his trance was broken when he noticed that some of his blood had dripped on the wood floorboard. He grabbed another wash cloth, knelt down, and quickly wiped up the blood. But as he wiped the floorboard he could tell that it wasn't connected to the other floor boards. He knocked hard on the floorboard with his right hand and saw the floorboard loosen up some more. He carefully removed the floor board and then another board before discovering a secret hiding place. Lenny removed two more floor boards and discovered an eighteen-by-twelve-by-seven clear plastic storage box. He lifted the box from the hiding spot, set it on the floor, and popped the top off.

Lenny's wide eyes stared at the contents in the box: a camcorder, a GoPro Hero10 action camera, a DJI Pocket 2 camera, an audio recording camera pen, four laptops, two external hard drives, and eighteen USB flash drives. Lenny scratched his chin as he considered why Denise would bother storing these devices in a secret hiding place. The only other box in the secret hiding place was an orange Nike shoebox. Lenny reached his hands into the hiding place, picked up the shoebox, and removed the lid. He looked inside the shoebox for a few seconds before a confused expression appeared on his face. Lenny lowered his right hand into the shoebox and his eyes slowly started to move from left to right. "Oh...my...God."

Lenny took a deep breath and exhaled before he removed a red leather-bound journal from the shoebox. He thumbed through the first few pages of the journal and saw names that he didn't recognize written neatly in all caps, along with home addresses, emails, and phone numbers. Multiple dates were written under each name. Some names had nearly a dozen different dates written under the name, other names just had one or two dates under the name. Lenny continued to flip through the journal until he came across some names that he recognized. He turned the page and recognized even more names. "Randy Daugherty," Lenny said quietly to himself. His state of shock heightened as his eyes landed on the only thing remaining in the orange shoebox.

Lenny's van sped down Front Street past a late-19th-century, red sandstone building on the corner of a busy intersection that was frequented this time of year by kids holding ice cream cones. On the ground floor of the building was Marge's Ice Cream Parlor, a popular establishment that opened nearly eighty years ago. Because it was a perfect summer day, eighty and sunny, the line outside the ice cream shop was larger than usual.

Lenny, the blood soaked towel still wrapped around his left thumb, glanced nervously at the orange shoebox on the passenger seat. He then glanced in his rearview mirror and saw a police siren flashing behind him. He held out hope for a few seconds that the Whisper Dunes police suv was headed toward a crime in progress, but all hope was lost when he saw the police

suv speed up until it was directly behind his van. The officer
flashed his headlights twice, which prompted Lenny to turn on
his right blinker. He hit the steering wheel with his right fist as he
yelled, "Son of a bitch!"

Lenny slowed down and steered his van toward the side
of the road. He put the van in park, rolled down his window, and
put his hands on the steering wheel at the ten and two position.
He was clearly nervous as the police officer approached with an
angry stride. Officer Freddy Soller, his gut proudly hanging over
his belt buckle, finally got to the driver side door. He slowly
removed his sunglasses as he regarded Lenny. "Are you fucking
high, Lenny?" Soller asked in a stern tone.

Lenny looked a bit confused as he finally made eye
contact. "God, no. I'm sorry I was speeding, Freddy, but I need
to get to the E.R."

Officer Soller glanced at the blood soaked towel wrapped
around Lenny's left thumb. "I don't give a flying moose about
your thumb. You were going fifty-two past Marge's. Do you have
any idea how many kids run across the street on a day like today
to go to Marge's?"

Lenny looked like he was actually trying to come up
with a number. "Gotta be seven dozen kids at least."

Officer Soller glanced at the orange Nike shoebox on the
passenger seat before he put his sunglasses back on. Lenny
looked to be in pain as he readjusted the bloody towel around his
thumb. "I need to get to the E.R. But I realize that's still no
excuse for speeding past Marge's. That was a dipshit move on my
part, Freddy. I apologize. Won't happen again."

Officer Soller nodded as he aimlessly scanned the area.
He then placed both hands on the van door as he looked at
Lenny. "My wife's been busting my balls about installing an
outside shower next to the gazebo. Finally bought one, but I have
no idea how to install it. What do you say you swing by the house
tomorrow and work your magic?"

Lenny nodded and said, "No problem."

"Great. Stop over around nine for a Blood Mary
breakfast then you can get to work."

"I'll be there at nine sharp. Now, if you'll excuse me, I
need to get my pie-eating thumb stitched up."

Officer Soller headed back to his cruiser as Lenny's van
sped away.

4

She had asked to meet Stan at Elizabeth's Chop House, a popular restaurant on Front Street that had a patio with beautiful views of Lake Superior. But Elizabeth's Chop House was a sentimental place for Stan and Lisa, so there was no way he was going to meet Bianca at that place. Instead, Stan told the renowned climate scientist that he would meet her at noon at The Wooden Nickel, a popular bar with Northern Michigan students and quite possibly the oldest bar in Marquette County. Stan used to drink at The Wooden Nickel back in his college days and well into his late twenties, but hadn't been inside in over a decade. He was fairly certain he wouldn't be recognized by any customers or employees.

It was a few minutes before noon and the only people in The Wooden Nickel was the bartender, four regulars sitting at the bar, and Stan, who was sitting at a high table for two in the back. He was wearing his typical realtor outfit: sport coat, button down shirt, and dark blue jeans.

Stan had spent about ten minutes reading emails on his phone before he started thinking about the first time he met Dr. Bianca Marquette. It was at a bar in downtown Whisper Dunes. He had no idea she was one of the most respected climate scientists in the world, and Bianca—Dr. Marquette to her colleagues and former lovers—had no idea that Stan, according to his website, was the top producing realtor in the Upper Peninsula for the past six years.

It was a Friday night, and after another week of analyzing depressing climate data, Bianca was desperately looking for a reason to laugh. Stan's drinking buddies went home early so he was more than happy to entertain the gorgeous woman with the French-Canadian accent sitting alone at the end of the bar. Stan and Bianca had exchanged glances throughout the night, but it was Bianca who walked over, smiled, and introduced herself. Twenty minutes later, Bianca was laughing hysterically and Stan was ordering another round of drinks. It was Christmas time so Stan told her a dirty joke about why Santa Claus didn't have any kids. Bianca laughed so hard she choked on her gin and tonic.

Stan smiled, thinking about that night. But his smile faded as he thought about the last night he ever saw Bianca. A week after the attempted hand job incident in Stan's Denali, he called Bianca, but her cell phone was out of service. Concerned for her well being, he contacted the dean of Northern Michigan University's science department, where Bianca had told Stan she was a visiting professor. Stan felt like he was sucker punched when the dean told him that he had never heard of Dr. Bianca Marquette. Bianca had no social media profile, but when Stan looked her up on the internet he discovered that she was in fact a climate scientist, based in Montreal.

Stan felt betrayed, and tried to keep her out of his mind. It wouldn't be accurate to say that Stan had a crush on Bianca, but he did think about her every time the topic of climate change came up. Before meeting Bianca, Stan never thought about climate change, but that's what Bianca liked to talk about. Sometimes she would ask Stan real estate questions, specifically zoning laws and whether or not it was possible to develop along Lake Superior's rugged coastline. But Bianca never once mentioned she was leading a highly anticipated climate change study that would forever change the lives of the people who call the Upper Peninsula of Michigan home.

Stan's wandering mind froze at the sound of the metal chair across from him being dragged along the concrete floor. Stan felt a nervous flutter in his stomach as he looked up to find Dr. Bianca Marquette sitting directly across from him. She smiled sweetly, but Stan couldn't muster up a return smile. She looked more youthful than Stan remembered, maybe because he had never seen her dressed so casual. She was wearing tight black jeans, a loose fitting white t-shirt, and no makeup. Her shoulder length hair was now a lighter brown, and her face and arms were tan, as if she'd just got back from a beach vacation.

They didn't attempt to hug or kiss each other on the cheek. No handshakes either. Bianca finally said, "Hello, Stan. It's nice to see you."

"I'd say hello, but I don't know who I'm talking to."

"Yes, you do. The only lie I told you was about being a visiting professor at Northern Michigan."

"So your real name is Dr. Bianca Marquette?"

"Yes, and I'm a climate scientist from Montreal. I've been engaged twice but never married. My dad works for Greenpeace and I haven't spoken to my mom in eight years because she and her husband are climate deniers."

Stan was without expression until his eyes narrowed with suspicion as he tugged at his left ear lobe. "What about that story from your cousin's bachelorette party? Did that really happen?"

Bianca, clearly embarrassed, leaned her forehead into the palm of her left hand. "Jesus, I forgot I told you that story. Yes, that happened."

"Wow."

"Everything I told you was the truth, Stan. I just couldn't tell you the real reason why I moved to Whisper Dunes."

"Why?"

"I was in the middle of working on the most important study of my life. When you're working on a scientific study that will have a major impact on peoples lives, you're not allowed to talk about it until the study concludes."

"Yeah, I get that."

The bartender shouted across the bar, "Either of you need a drink?"

"Bloody Mary. Spicy," Stan said.

"I'll take one too."

Stan relaxed his shoulders and exhaled slowly through his nose. He didn't seem uncomfortable that Bianca was looking him right in the eyes. Bianca's eyes narrowed slightly as her long back leaned against the metal chair. "Can we go for a walk after our drinks?"

"No, I have to get back to the office."

Bianca didn't hide her disappointment. "Are you still upset about that night in your gas guzzling suv?"

Stan sighed while trying to avoid Bianca's watchful green eyes. "Why did you want to meet, Bianca?"

Bianca rested her elbows on the metal table and leaned toward Stan with a sincere expression. "The study I was working on is going to be published at the end of September."

"What were you studying?"

"Climate havens. Geography, not technology, is the best way to combat against the brutal effects of climate change."

Stan looked like he had something he wanted to say, but kept his trap shut as he recognized the serious look on Bianca's face. He was very familiar with that look, which Bianca always seemed to convey when discussing climate change and the Earth's future. She looked around the bar to make sure no one was approaching then leaned her face close to him.

"When our paper is published, it will change the lives of everyone who lives in the Upper Peninsula."

Stan felt a nervous feeling in his stomach. "Mind elaborating a tad more?"

"Our study's main objective was to determine the best climate havens in the world. Three years into the study, it became clear to us that there was one place on Earth that stood out as the best climate haven...the Upper Peninsula of Michigan."

Stan's face was no longer without expression. A shot of adrenaline started to run through his body, which made it hard to sit still. "That's very interesting," Stan said. He was so stunned, he hadn't realized he just spoke out loud. They looked at each other for almost a minute before Stan said, "So, based on your scientific study, the Upper Peninsula is the best place on Earth to live?"

"Yes...because of Earth's rapidly changing climate."

Bianca regarded Stan while he tried to slow his racing mind. He looked confused as he tried to process the information.

"In November of 1856, Eunice Foote, a housewife and self-educated scientist, published the first scientific paper on global warming. She spent years conducting experiments in her kitchen that proved emitting carbon dioxide into the Earth's atmosphere warms the planet."

"I'm guessing that paper did not resonate with a broad audience," Stan said.

"Good guess. The most recent data confirms that the global carbon dioxide emissions last year was 182 times higher than the amount of carbon dioxide emitted in 1850. Human-induced global warming has caused horrible changes to the Earth's climate that can't be fixed. Over six trillion tons of ice has melted in Antarctica and Greenland since the early 1990's, and it's only getting worse. The Earth is now shedding around 1.2 trillion tons of ice each year. Large regions on Earth are already becoming uninhabitable. In less than a decade, Earth's average temperature will likely increase by 1.5 Celsius. Once that happens...Earth will be on a catastrophic, irreversible path. Mark my words, Stan, for the remainder of civilization there will be no better place on Earth to live than the Upper Peninsula of Michigan."

Stan's lips were pressed together, but his eyes were wide open. Only one word came to his mind. "Wow."

The word barely made it passed his lips. Stan was experiencing a state of euphoria that he hadn't felt since Lisa gave him unsolicited road head for the first time. A physiological cocktail of surprise and pleasure was causing a tingling sensation on his brain that made his eye lids heavy.

Realtors are trained early and often to make outlandish claims to stand out from the pack of realtors they're competing against. Stan's glazed eyes were still looking at Bianca as he thought about the absurd, but true claim, he could now market to all of his current and future clients: *Stan Zbikowski - the number one realtor in America's Best Place to Live.*

"As you're probably already imagining, once this study is published, the price of homes and land in the U.P. will increase significantly. But it would be a good idea not to talk about the study with anyone until after it's published," Bianca said quietly.

The bartender set the Bloody Marys on the table without saying a word. He hurried back behind the bar to answer the ringing rotary phone that was at least forty years old. Stan stirred his drink as he watched Bianca carefully remove the pickle and celery from her drink before taking a sip.

"Tell me something, Bianca. Why did you come back to Whisper Dunes to tell me this? You could've done it over the phone."

Bianca took another sip and said, "I wanted to see you. I miss sitting next to you at our favorite bar. I miss our conversations. Nobody ever made me laugh like you, Stan. I felt like I could talk to you about anything. In my experience, it's been incredibly rare to spend time with a man who's a good listener and slow to offer his opinion."

Bianca smiled at Stan. Not to be polite, but because she still had strong feelings for him. He took a few seconds, but Stan smiled back. She was hoping he'd say something, but he didn't. Bianca took another sip of her Blood Mary then said, "On the drive over here I must have seen at least three dozen yard signs that read: STOP THE ROCKET. What's up with that?"

Stan sighed before taking a long sip from his Blood Mary. He knew Bianca would be furious if he told her that multiple space companies wanted to build a rocket launch spaceport on the shores of Lake Superior. But he decided to tell her everything that had been going on in Whisper Dunes since she moved back to Montreal, and sure enough he was right. Bianca was so upset she struggled to find the right words to express her anger. Overwhelmed with the terrible news, her emotions got the best of her and she started to cry. Stan tried to convey empathy with a gentle head tilt while he watched Bianca wipe away her tears. She regarded Stan, and said in a frustrated tone, "Is it Space D?"

"Don't know for sure, but I've heard rumors that Space P, Space V, Space Q, and Beige Origin all want to build a rocket spaceport on the site."

Bianca pounded her fist on the table. "We can't let this happen!"

Stan nodded in agreement. He tried to comfort Bianca by pointing out that over the past century many ambitious real estate development proposals had failed to break ground in the U.P. In the late 19th century, a wealthy real estate developer who made his fortune building highly flammable wood structures in Chicago turned his sights to the Upper Peninsula with plans to build the next great American city. He quickly abandoned his plans when it became clear that the wilderness in the U.P. couldn't be tamed. After he became one of the most powerful men in America, Henry Ford made several attempts to develop summer villages for wealthy people along the Lake Superior shoreline, but failed. In the Upper Peninsula, the hilly, rugged, wilderness had always defeated ambitious men armed with money and bulldozers.

Bianca was still shaken and just couldn't comprehend how the most beautiful natural environment on Earth could be compromised by a space company. In hopes of providing Bianca with some peace of mind, Stan ordered another round of Bloody Marys then told her what happened in the town back in the summer of 1891. Frederick Law Olmsted, best known for designing Central Park in New York and Jackson Park in Chicago, arrived in the Upper Peninsula a few months after receiving an invitation from the civic leaders of Marquette County. Frederick was hired to turn Presque Isle Park into a hospitable outdoor haven where the growing population could congregate and enjoy the outdoors. Presque Isle Park is a 323 acre densely forested peninsula, just a mile north of downtown, that cuts into the crystal clear waters of Lake Superior. Frederick Law Olmsted, the most respected and sought after landscape architect in America, had already developed plans to transform

Presque Isle Park, but after spending the day walking through the park he met with the civic leaders of Marquette County and told them, "Don't touch it." To their credit, the civic leaders of Marquette County followed the advice of Frederick Law Olmsted and didn't touch Presque Isle Park.

Bianca was moved by the story. Her shoulders dropped and she looked a bit more relaxed as she finished the rest of her drink. Bianca sat upright in her chair and looked at Stan for a moment. She wished they could spend the day together but realized that he was eager to get back to the office.

"I still have a few weeks left on my lease. I wanted to experience Whisper Dunes one last time as a resident."

Stan looked uneasy as he sipped his Blood Mary. Bianca's head tilted forward as she kept her eyes locked on Stan. "I was hoping we could hang out, at least one night," she said in a sweet tone.

"I don't think that's a good idea."

Bianca moved her eyes away from Stan for a moment as her sweet demeanor vanished. Her eyes narrowed but didn't blink as she looked over Stan. Bianca finally said, "Have you ever spent the night with someone, knowing that you'll never see them again?"

Bianca's piercing stare forced Stan to close his eyes for a moment. He slowly rubbed the bridge of his nose before he shook his head.

"Well, you know where to find me if you change your mind," Bianca said as she stood up.

Bianca and Stan looked at each other for a long moment before Bianca turned and slowly walked out of the bar. Stan stared blankly at the jukebox in the corner. "Oh, boy," he mumbled to himself. He finished the rest of his Bloody Mary, put a twenty-dollar bill on the table, and walked out of the bar with his head lowered.

A white Chevy Malibu, clearly a rental, was cruising down a recently paved road. The posted speed limit was twenty-five, but the Malibu was going forty-five. The car slowed as the road curved dramatically to the right, but sped up as soon as the road straightened. To the right were hills covered with tall pines trees, and to the left, a mere fifty yards from the road, was the

Lake Superior shoreline. The driver of the Chevy Malibu, Neal Lomax, was in his late fifties and dressed in a seersucker suit. This was Neal's first trip to Whisper Dunes and he seemed impressed with everything coming into view as he continued down the scenic road. He smiled at the site of a bald eagle flying over the shoreline. The driver side window was down about halfway and Neal could feel the wind off Lake Superior getting stronger. He took a deep breath as a burst of cool air blew into the car.

A short, skinny woman in a white swimsuit coverup was attempting to cross the street with her two young boys. Excited at the sight of the beach, the boys ran ahead and safely crossed the street. The woman, who was pulling a wagon packed with beach toys, tried to catch up but the Tonka dump truck fell off the wagon and landed in the middle of the street. She was about to grab the dump truck, but froze at the sight of a distracted driver heading straight for her. The woman sprinted across the street as the Chevy Malibu rolled through the stop sign. Neal's eyes diverted back to the road as soon as he heard the sound of his car running over a metal, Tonka dump truck. Neal gasped and said to himself, "What in God's name was that?"

The woman screamed, "Drive like your kids live here, asshole!"

Neal glanced in the rearview mirror and saw the attractive mom giving him the middle finger. He looked embarrassed as he turned up the classical music and pressed down on the gas pedal.

The Chevy Malibu drove past a finely crafted wood sign that read: **Welcome to Whisper Dunes - Est. 1859.** Staked into the ground just past the sign were a dozen handmade signs that read: **STOP THE ROCKET!**

A group of six moms, with baby strollers in between them, were sitting at a long wood table on the porch of an 1880's Victorian home that had since been converted into a coffee shop and bar called, The Crib. The moms sipped their coffees and happily chatted away, but their demeanor quickly changed as they watched Neal's Chevy Malibu blow through the stop sign. The mom who was breastfeeding yelled, "That's called a stop sign, you dumb fuck!"

The mom wearing a Northern Michigan Football sweatshirt yelled, "Where'd you learn how to drive?! Cooking school?!"

The heavy-set mom in pink yoga pants yelled, "Go back to Milwaukee, asshole!"

The Chevy Malibu continued down a tree lined street that had modest, one-story homes on both sides. The classical music from Neal's phone was briefly interrupted by Siri, who told him to make a left at 4th Street in point-two miles. Neal couldn't help but notice that most of the homes had signs in their front yards that read: LAKE SUPERIOR IS LIFE! STOP THE ROCKET! A curious expression crossed his face as he muttered to himself, "Stop the rocket? What rocket?"

Neal looked impressed as he slowed down to admire St. Peter Cathedral, located at the end of the quiet street. The imposing sandstone cathedral, with a twin bell tower, looked like a cathedral you might expect to see while walking down a narrow, brick paved-street in a small town in Italy or France.

Neal continued driving up the street, passing more modest homes before he turned right onto a busier street. The Chevy Malibu passed the Marquette County jail, which was next door to a dive bar called Breakers. Across the street from Breakers was the Upper Peninsula Children's Museum. Neal, clearly perturbed, shook his head and said, "Jesus...haven't you people ever heard of a city planner?" As Neal's eyes returned to the road, he was forced to slam on the brakes. His car stopped a foot from the cross walk line, just as two stay-at-home dads desperately pulled their strollers toward the curb.

"Watch where you're going, dick weed!"

The other stay-at-home dad yelled, "Open your eyes!" He then threw his half-full coffee cup at the windshield.

Neal's face turned bright red as he sheepishly offered an apologetic wave. The two dads slowly pushed their kids in the strollers to the other side of the crosswalk. Neal slowly drove away as soon as he saw that the strollers were safely on the sidewalk. He rolled down the driver side window all the way and turned up the classical music in hopes of lowering his blood pressure. In the distance, the street looked like it would run right into Lake Superior.

Neal passed by a beautiful park with unobstructed lake views. A wooden hand made sign stood at the entrance of the park. The sign read: **South Beach Park - Adopted by the Electricians Local Union 1070.**

Neal headed north on Front Street and drove past a brew pub that operated out of a newly constructed building. Across the street, in a one-story brick building, a new wine bar was getting ready to welcome the afterwork crowd. Just a block up the street, two-dozen people were waiting for table to open up for lunch at the most popular establishment in town. The Vierling Restaurant & Harbor Brewery, which first opened its doors in 1883, was still located in the same two-story, red-brick building, right next door to Elizabeth's Chop House.

Neal saw that the light was red at the intersection of Front and Washington Street, and wisely slowed the car down before coming to a complete stop. Neal marveled at the building on the corner. The Savings Bank Building was one of the most architecturally significant buildings in the Upper Peninsula. Completed in 1891, the meticulously maintained rectangular building had a five-story front facade and seven stories in the rear. The ashlar stone on the first two floors initially caught Neal's eye, but he seemed more impressed as he tilted his head and stared at the rest of the building. Each floor still featured the original round corner windows, and on top of the flat roof, the building's iconic three-sided clock tower dominated the skyline.

Neal turned left onto Washington Street and seemed somewhat disappointed by what he saw. A nice afternoon crowd ducked in and out of the charming shops. Most of the adults were dressed in casual summer clothes that they'd probably had in their closets for well over twenty years. Neal turned down the music and said to himself in an angry tone, "Oh, come on...hasn't anyone ever heard of J. Crew around here? Christ almighty. It looks like everyone's headed to a Pearl Jam concert."

An unexpected, happy memory passed through Neal's mind like a lighting bolt. He smiled, thinking back to the night he saw Pearl Jam's first ever show at Madison Square Garden. Neal recalled exactly where he was standing in MSG that night: seven rows from the right side of the stage. He still had the guitar pick Mike McCready tossed to him. Back then, Neal worked for *The Village Voice* and had a very different point of view compared to the one he had now. He used to believe that, regardless of what you did for a living, careerism warped your moral code and sense of integrity. For a time, Neal really believed he'd be an independent journalist for the rest of his life. But Manhattan is a very expensive place to live, and an easy place to be miserable if you don't make a certain amount of money each month. So Neal decided that it was okay to try and make as much money as you possibly can. Four years after that incredible night at Madison

Square Garden, Neal had two closets filled with Brooks Brothers suits and shirts, and was quickly moving up the ladder at *Forbes*.

Neal made a right onto Third Street and headed north up the busy street. He drove past Snowbound Books, three coffee shops, Bellini's Pizzeria, and five bars. This three block stretch of Third Street was popular with the students at Northern Michigan University. The main campus was located about two miles northwest of downtown, but a lot of students lived off campus near Third Street.

Neal perked up when he laid his eyes on an old-fashioned ice cream shop on the corner. He found a parking spot, the only open spot on the block, and parallel parked his Chevy Malibu. He glanced at his driver side mirror, saw that no cars were coming, and exited the Malibu. Neal smiled and waved at an older couple he passed on his walk toward Marge's Ice Cream Parlor. In the front window of the ice cream parlor Neal saw a familiar sign: STOP THE ROCKET!

Neal sat at a small corner table in the ice cream parlor, enjoying a banana split. In between bites he scanned the wall across from him, which was filled with framed photos featuring customers over the years. The bell above the front door chimed as a customer entered Marge's. Neal's attention quickly turned to the latest customer. It was clear to Neal that this customer was unlike any of the other customers in the shop. For starters, he radiated a certain arrogance that would help him fit in at a country club, but at Marge's Ice Cream Parlor it made him stand out like a hardcore environmentalist who made his fortune trading oil futures. His close-set eyes seemed to be on high alert, waiting until an unsuspecting person got close enough so that his dark eyes could sparkle once again with mockery. Dressed in an expensive black suit with an open collar, the man was just shy of six feet, thin, and had a dark tan, as if to announce to anyone who cared that he didn't believe in sunscreen. Neal didn't think he looked like the type who hung out at the beach so the tan was likely the result of golfing everyday, or frequenting tanning salons. His phone was pressed to his ear as he approached the counter.

Charlie, the friendly, attentive, sixteen-year-old boy behind the counter, flashed a nervous smile. He was painfully familiar with this particular customer. "Good afternoon, Mr. Houston. Would you like your usual, sir?"

Hubert Houston nodded but didn't make eye contact with Charlie. If you asked Charlie, or any other person who'd ever encountered Hubert Houston, they would all say that he was the biggest asshole that they'd ever met. The only thing he was interested in, besides money, was his opinion of himself. He had no regard for anyone's well being, or rules of any kind. In fact, he rooted openly for the abolishment of all financial regulating agencies, the Consumer Protection Bureau, and the Environmental Protection Agency. In the divorce papers, his ex-wife stated that she believed every person started their life with a moral compass, but Hubert set fire to his moral compass before he was old enough to vote.

Hubert was born and raised in Whisper Dunes. His father used his inherited wealth to invest in real estate, and eventually became the largest land and property owner in the Upper Peninsula. Hubert hated his father, but was terribly close to his mother, who died while he was away at college. He moved back to town six years ago after spending most of his thirties in New York City, where he worked for a large hedge fund. Now forty-eight, Hubert ran his own hedge fund, although if you asked most people in town they believed he just managed all the money his daddy left him.

Charlie quickly scooped out a huge ball of cookie dough ice cream from the carton, plopped it into a waffle cone, and handed it to Hubert, who said, "Put it on my tab."

Charlie smiled politely. "No problem, Mr. Houston. Have a great day."

Hubert's eyes widened as he stopped in his tracks. He flashed a mean look at Charlie. "Don't ever tell me what to do."

Charlie's eyes squinted with confusion, but he didn't look intimidated. Hubert loved to intimidate people, but as he turned to leave he could tell that he had failed to intimidate the sixteen-year-old ice cream scooper. Charlie looked relieved as Hubert exited the shop.

Having watched the encounter unfold, Neal was both upset and curious. He had lived in New York City for many years and encountered thousands of assholes. He had interviewed some of the biggest assholes working on Wall Street and in corporate America, but this asshole he just watched berate a young man serving ice cream had a different air about him. He was a different breed of asshole than even Neal was used to seeing. Neal's curiosity got the best of him so he decided to approach Charlie.

Charlie had encountered Hubert on many occasions. He had learned to brush off any obnoxious thing that came out of his mouth and not let Hubert ruin his day. Neal stood in front of Charlie, not hiding the fact that he was clearly bothered by the encounter. Charlie smiled politely and said, "Everything okay with your banana split, sir?"

"Ah, yes. It's excellent. Sorry for the blunt question, but who was that jerk?"

Charlie looked surprised by the question. "Mr. Hubert Houston. The richest guy in town. He owns half the buildings on this street alone, including this one."

"The Mr. Potter of Whisper Dunes," Neal said in a soft tone.

Charlie's dad made him, his older sister and younger brother watch, *It's A Wonderful Life*, every Christmas, which is why Charlie smiled confidently and nodded in complete agreement.

"This is my first time visiting Whisper Dunes. It's a lovely, lovely town. But tell me, what's the deal with all the Stop The Rocket signs posted everywhere?"

"Some space company wants to buy a bunch of land along Lake Superior to build a rocket spaceport. Pretty much every person in the U.P. is against it. There's like a protest every week."

A wrinkle formed between Neal's eyebrows as his wide-open eyes remained locked on Charlie. "Any idea which space company?"

"It's one of the big ones," Charlie said.

"Space P?"

"No, not Space P."

"Space Y?"

"No, I don't think so."

"Space T or A?"

"No, never heard of those space companies."

"Beige Origin?"

"Nope."

"Space D?"

"Yes! Space D. They want to build the largest rocket spaceport in the Midwest."

Neal flashed an uneasy smile before he wiped his mouth. "I see." He couldn't help but think, how did he or anyone else at *Forbes* not know that Space D was looking to build a rocket launch spaceport in Whisper Dunes?

Neal politely regarded Charlie and said, "Appreciate your time, Charlie. Thank you for the excellent banana split, and keep up the good work."

Charlie was clearly touched by the compliment. He nodded and smiled. "Thank you for coming in today, sir."

Hubert entered his black convertible as he aggressively licked his ice cream cone with the same intensity as the only single guy at a bi-sexual orgy. He had purchased the BMW 8 Series Convertible at the beginning of summer even though he already owned two other luxury convertibles. Like a wealthy banking executive, who still moonlighted as a high price hooker on the weekends, Hubert had only one mission in life: to find ways to make as much money as possible. And he never forgot what his first boss on Wall Street liked to tell him on a regular basis: *what's the point of being a money grubbing whore if you're not going to flaunt your wealth?*

Still on the phone, Hubert finally responded to the person on the other line. "Don't pick up again if he tries calling you. Understand?" He suddenly became furious as his ice cream cone slipped out of his hand. "Son of a bitch! I just dropped my fucking ice cream cone!"

Hubert licked his sticky ice cream fingers as if he would never taste ice cream again.

"I want you to come by my place tonight. Eight sharp. I have an idea that I think will provide a clear-cut solution to this problem. By the way, did you send the video to your special friend? Very good. See you at eight. Oh, and wear that slutty dress I bought you…No, the red one."

5

Neal Lomax walked up the steps that lead to the Whisper Dunes Town Hall building. Listed on the National Register of Historic Places since 1975, the three-story red-brick building was raised on a sandstone foundation, and the tiled mansard roof with a cupola gave the building a European look. Although the outside of the impressive building had been well cared for, the interior was a different story. Even the office of the mayor of Whisper Dunes was in need of a major update. But the mayor was known for pinching pennies and had no current plans to waste taxpayers' money on addressing the much needed repairs inside the Town Hall building.

Mayor Russell Tillinghast had not made a single update to his third-floor office since becoming mayor of Whisper Dunes, thirteen years ago. He wouldn't even pop for a new window air conditioning unit after the old one broke during his first summer in office. Russ had lived his entire life in the Upper Peninsula and didn't think anyone needed to waste money on an air conditioning system. Hot days were still fairly rare in the U.P., although Russ would be one of the first to admit, the last two summers in Whisper Dunes had been hotter than normal.

Russ sat hunched over in his high-back green leather chair as he worked on making a fishing lure. The massive oak desk he was sitting behind had been in the same spot for nearly a hundred years. The mayor was slight in stature, with bushy white hair and calloused hands, the result of fishing around 300 days a year since he was a teenager. The mayor had a calm, friendly demeanor and was respected by just about everyone in Whisper Dunes. The mayor, known by everyone in town as Mayor Russ, was approaching seventy but could easily pass for being sixty. Russ's chewed up pencil was on a yellow legal pad near two fishing lures he had just made during the course of his afternoon phone calls.

Russ refused to join online video meetings. He had never used a computer in his life, and only used his flip phone for emergencies. There were only three ways to directly contact Mayor Russ. Through his office phone, through his office fax machine, or by mailing him a letter. Russ conducted all city business with face to face meetings, or over the phone from his office. He also made a point to reserve one hour in the afternoon, Monday through Wednesday, to receive phone calls from concerned Whisper Dunes residents. The residents were usually polite to Mayor Russ as he patiently listened to their complaints or bold suggestions, but not always.

The receiver of the thirty-year-old Nortel office phone was pressed to his ear as he started work on another fishing lure. Whoever was on the other end of the phone line did not have the mayor's full attention.

The dated wood paneled wall to the right of the mayor's desk was covered with photos of Russ either fishing or holding up a trophy he won at a fishing competition. Behind Russ's desk were dusty shelves filled with fishing trophies and six books: *The Bible, The Old Man and the Sea, Fundamentals of Municipal Finance,* and three books on public speaking. Above the top shelf, a five-foot-long Chinook salmon was mounted to the wall. Hanging on the wall near the door was a framed painting of a sailboat on rough waters. Below the painting was a small wood plaque. Engraved on the plaque was a quote, *Smooth Seas Do Not Make Skillful Sailors - African Proverb.*

Some people are lucky enough to discover at a young age what they truly love to do. For Russell Tillinghast it was fishing. When he was seven his grandpa took him fishing near the Marquette Harbor Lighthouse. Despite spending six hours on a terribly cold spring day and catching only one fish, Russ was hooked. He would eventually develop into a highly skilled angler. Unfortunately, Russ's love for fishing would result in his first and second marriage ending in divorce.

Russ nodded while listening to the long-winded person on the other end, but it was clear he was more interested in perfecting another fishing lure than listening to the caller. "Stan, you've known me for a long time. You know damn well that I firmly support the right to protest, but Lisa still needs to file for a permit before she tries to lead a rally through downtown. Otherwise, legally speaking, the town's liable should something happen during the protest. Hey, while I got you on the line, in hopes of saving our taxpayers a few bucks, we're planning on financing the 4th of July fireworks this year with private donations. Can I mark you down for five thousand? Come on, Zibs! You're the number one realtor in town, you should be my top donor."

Carol, a tall, heavy-set woman in her late forties, entered Russ's office. She could care less that Russ was on the phone. "The fax machine's busted again," Carol said in a raspy voice. She was once a very attractive woman. Carol had a tendency to remind her latest suitor that she had been voted homecoming queen a few years back. But the smoking and drinking had finally caught up with her and stripped away her good looks.

"Okay, thanks, Carol. I'll fix it after lunch."

"Also, there's a guy here who wants to see you. I think he said his name was Neal, but he doesn't have an appointment."

Russ looked a bit tense as he regarded Carol's expressionless face. "Neal from the County Auditor's Office?"

"No, he said he's with *Forbes*."

Russ's eyes widened with disbelief. He leaned back slowly in his chair as he stared at Carol, who still didn't seem to appreciate the situation. Russ had never gotten used to the fact that Carol habitually delivered mundane messages with a sense of urgency in her voice, while usually delivering high priority messages in a lackluster style that sometimes tricked Russ into questioning the importance of the message. But Russ was clearly not doubting the importance of this message. He took several deep breaths as he tried to control his emotions, but the shot of adrenaline was causing Russ to get antsy in his chair and he finally blurted out, "*Forbes* magazine?"

"That's what he said. He could be lying, but he seemed pretty legit to me. He's wearing a sharp looking seersucker suit. Definitely not from around here."

Russ forgot that Stan was holding on the other line until he glanced at the receiver in his right hand. "I'm sorry, but I'll have to call you back, Stan."

Russ quickly hung up the phone. He took a deep breath and exhaled as he leaned forward in his chair. He had a look on his face that Carol had never seen before. Russ was giddy but hyper nervous, like a very smart, yet very poor kid holding an unopened letter from the dean of admissions of an Ivy League school. Russ knew he would soon discover why a man from *Forbes* was waiting outside his office without an appointment, so he decided to treat himself and allow his mind to consider the best case scenario. Russ's facial expression made it clear to Carol that this was an important moment. Russ allowed himself about thirty seconds to embrace the fantasy scenario before he shook his head and stood up from his chair.

Russ began to clean up his desk. Instead of helping, Carol just stood there in silence. She actually looked amused while Russ frantically cleaned up his desk. He then moved over to the wall and straightened some of the photos. Carol said with a grin, "I'm guessing you have at least five minutes to spare for this fella?"

Russ opened up the closet door and started to unbutton his tight-fitting short sleeved shirt. "Give me two minutes, then send him in. And offer him some coffee."

"Coffee pot's empty."

"Dammit. Then offer him a water or a Diet Coke."

"We don't have Diet Coke. We have R.C. Cola and organic juice boxes."

"Just offer him water and tell him I'm wrapping up a call with the Governor and I'll be with him shortly. Then count to 180 and send him in."

Carol nodded and hurried out of the office. Russ changed into a light blue collared shirt and quickly buttoned it up before putting on a navy blue sport coat. He then put on a blue and red striped clip-on tie, grabbed a pair of brown loafers from the back of the closet, and sat back down in his chair. He took off his hiking boots and slipped on the loafers. The Mr. Rogers-style clothing transition was complete.

Russ picked up a red and white mint from the bowl on his desk and popped it in his mouth. He then grabbed the air freshener bottle from his bottom desk drawer. Russ walked over to the other side of the desk and lightly sprayed the two chairs before he moved back behind his desk and put the air freshener back in the drawer. Russ sat in his chair and tried to get his emotions under control. He had no idea who was about to sit across from him and that made him nervous. He rested his head on the back of the chair and closed his eyes. Russ thought about what his mom liked to remind him when he was growing up. *Sometimes, good things happen to good people.*

Neal Lomax sat across from Russ in a chair made of cheap fabric. Neal had a smug smile on his face as he watched Russ slowly rub his right hand over the next issue of *Forbes*. Russ was in a deep state of wonderment as he continued to stare at the cover. Neal thought to himself that Russ looked like a teenage boy staring at a *Playboy* magazine for the very first time. A heavy tear escaped Russ's eye and slid down his boney cheek as he tightened his grip on the magazine. The cover read: *Whisper Dunes is America's Best Place to Live*. Russ finally took his eyes off the magazine cover and kindly regarded Neal. "I feel if I let go of the magazine, I'll suddenly wake up from this wonderful dream."

Neal forced a smile and nodded before he took a sip from his can of R.C. Cola.

"I'm sorry, would you like a glass for your R.C.?"

"No, thanks. Your town is now is a very elite club, Mr. Mayor. Things will never be the same around here after we release that issue."

Russ finally opened the magazine and found the page where the cover story began. He started to read out loud. "Nestled on the southern shores of Lake Superior, the town of Whisper Dunes is the best place to live if you never want to worry about experiencing extreme weather events for the rest of your life." Russ seemed like he wanted to keep reading, but decided to close the magazine. He looked excited as his gaze landed on Neal. "What a great opener!"

"One of our senior writers wrote the piece. Believe me, Mr. Mayor, that article will lead to an intense global conversation on climate havens."

Russ nodded at Neal then moved his eyes back to the cover. He took a long, slow breath through his nose in an effort to slow down his racing mind. "Good Lord...I never imagined Whisper Dunes would ever be included in a global conversation."

"Yes, hard to believe...I understand," Neal said. "But get ready, Mr. Mayor, because pretty soon Whisper Dunes will be the most talked about town in America, and soon after, you'll be on the global stage."

Russ remained overwhelmed with disbelief, not sure what to say next.

"Please understand, Mr. Mayor..."

"Call me, Russ. Please."

"Okay. Russ, when this issue comes out, life for everyone in Whisper Dunes will change. In a few weeks, the national media will invade and start asking a lot of questions."

Russ tried to hide his uneasiness as he glanced at Neal. "What kind of questions?"

Neal gulped down the rest of his R.C. Cola before he stared at Russ. "Do the folks up here believe in global warming?"

Russ slowly exhaled through his mouth as he leaned forward and lowered his elbows on the desk. "Well, when you live in an area that gets an average of 165 inches of snow each winter...you're going to have a few folks who find it hard to believe that the Earth's warming."

Neal let out a long whistle. "That's a lot of snow."

"People who live in Whisper Dunes embrace the snow like the people down south embrace humidity. Heck, we probably have more winter festivals than we do summer festivals."

Neal set his R.C. Cola can on Russ's desk then casually leaned back in the chair while he crossed his legs. "Every year the same magazines name the same towns to their best place to live list. So this year, we decided to go left when everyone continues to go right. We said, lets be radical for once and make are pick based on only one criteria: the best climate haven in America. We were in the process of interviewing a bunch of climate scientists, who all had their own opinion on the best climate havens, but then one of our senior editors got wind that an important study on the best climate haven in the world was going to be published this year. We tracked down one of the climate scientists behind the report and she told us that the best place to live on Earth for the remainder of civilization will be anywhere in the Upper Peninsula."

Russ's wide eyes stared at Neal in disbelief. He slowly tilted his head to the right and said in a low voice, "No, shit?"

Russ leaned back in his chair, but the excitement was too much and he quickly leaned forward again. "I've been trying to get the town council to increase our marketing budget for years so we can put together a professional looking commercial that'll introduce us to the country as a great climate haven. But they keep telling me that Duluth, Cleveland, and Buffalo have already planted their flags as America's top climate havens," Russ said. He took a deep breath then exhaled as he usually did after getting worked up and talking too fast.

"Well, it's likely that Duluth, Cleveland, and Buffalo will be three of the largest cities in America by the end of this century, but they don't have the charm and beauty of Whisper

Dunes. And they certainly don't have thousands of acres ripe for expansion the way the Upper Peninsula does. The climate scientists we talked to said that the most valuable land in America is right here in the Upper Peninsula."

Russ slowly nodded and said, "I've been told many times that the Great Lakes will be the most valuable asset on Earth by 2050."

"Probably sooner than 2050."

Russ regarded Neal for a good ten seconds before he said, "Why did you settle on Whisper Dunes? There's a number of lovely towns up here. Why not just say, the Upper Peninsula is America's Best Place to Live?"

"We considered doing that, but Whisper Dunes is the largest and prettiest town in the Upper Peninsula with plenty of space to welcome climate migrants. You have good schools, an entertainment district...you've got a nice university."

"Climate migrants?"

You know, people looking to escape hellish living environments caused by heatwaves, hurricanes, droughts, wildfires, etc."

"Of course," Russ said with an uneasy look. It was clear his mind was wandering as he tried to comprehend the idea of Whisper Dunes becoming a safe haven for climate migrants. Russ suddenly had a nervous pit in his stomach, like a man who just boarded a plane with his mistress and discovered that his mother-in-law was sitting behind him.

"Mr. Mayor, when *Forbes* names a town, America's Best Place to Live, on average, home values in that town increase by nearly eighty percent."

Impressed, Russ let out a long whistle. Neal leaned forward in his chair and said, "But because Whisper Dunes is being selected solely on the issue of climate change, I think home prices will increase by roughly 300 percent within the next year."

"Wow. What about the cost of land?"

"Any land near Lake Superior will be considered some of the most valuable land in America."

"And to think that we were jumping through hoops trying to get the Midwest Craft Brew Festival up here in hopes of boosting fall tourism."

Neal smiled as he shifted in his chair.

"When does the issue come out?"

"Next month."

Russ suddenly appeared emotional again as he looked down at the cover. He sighed deeply, trying to stave off more tears. "Boy this is a big deal...a big, big deal," Russ said with a feeling of incredible pride. "I feel like everyone in this town just won the lottery."

"Do you have a press secretary, Russ?"

Russ looked caught off guard. He said sheepishly, "No, I have a regular secretary. She comes into the office two, sometimes three days a week, but I can ask her to come in on Fridays if needed."

Neal looked a bit concerned as he regarded the mayor.

"I'm known for being extremely frugal when it comes to spending taxpayers' dollars, so hiring a press secretary is probably going to make people in Whisper Dunes scratch their heads."

"Like I said, Russ, life for everyone in Whisper Dunes will change once the issue is released. You have to understand, the media has a way of making their presence felt. You need to prepare for their arrival."

Russ was no longer willing to hide his concerns. He reached down and pulled out a half-full bottle of bourbon from the bottom drawer of his desk. He set the bottle on his desk then, from the drawer, grabbed a glass that hadn't been washed since his first wife left him, twelve years ago. He poured a little bourbon in the glass and took a sip before he allowed his gaze to meet Neal's. "The thing of it is, the folks up here aren't known for embracing change. Between you and me, I'm a bit worried about how they're going to handle the media attention."

"Well, you're going to have to get them to warm up to the idea that they now live in America's Best Place to Live. Life in Whisper Dunes will change for everyone."

"Would you like some bourbon?"

"No, thank you."

"I don't usually drink before supper time, or on weekdays, but this news calls for a celebratory drink," Russ said just before taking another sip.

"I had the chance to walk around town earlier and I was impressed by how engaged people were with one another. Nobody seems to be addicted to their smartphones up here."

Russ flashed a friendly smile and said, "I've always said, show me a town with horrendous cell service and I'll show you a town filled with kind, thoughtful people. Of course, that's not to say we don't have a few bad apples rolling around town. But most folks who live in the U.P. still understand that the human experience is all about spending time with family and friends. My friend, Stan, likes to say, attending a key party after church is more acceptable in these parts than communicating via social media."

Neal let out a chuckle as Russ continued. "Most people in the U.P. are shielded from the spying empire in Silicon Valley because of the remoteness and dense forests. In fact, a lot of homes in the U.P. still don't have internet access. *Yoopers* tend to behave a little differently than your average bear, simply because they haven't been exposed to social media's mind control content."

Neal regarded Russ with a serious look that made Russ shift uneasily in his chair. "Mr. Mayor, our choice to break from conventional wisdom and crown Whisper Dunes, America's Best Place to Live, will beget a lot of media attention. I know I've already mentioned this, but I just want you to be prepared when all the cable news outlets and podcasts personalities flock to Whisper Dunes. You're going to receive a lot of media scrutiny over the next year."

"What's there to scrutinize?"

"First, they're going to come here looking to celebrate Whisper Dunes, but when they see those Stop the Rocket signs all over town, the media will start asking blunt questions."

Russ's eyes narrowed as he leaned back in his chair. He looked uneasy as his glazed eyes moved from Neal to the open window to his left. He stared at the American flag blowing in the wind for a moment, which helped calm his nerves.

"Mr. Mayor, without a press secretary, the national media will quickly turn your life into a living hell. When the national media finds out that Space D wants to bulldoze 5,000 acres of coastal forest land in America's Best Place to Live in order to build a rocket spaceport...you can bet your ass that they'll have some tough questions for you."

"How do you know about the rocket spaceport?"

"The nice kid who scoops ice cream at Marge's told me. Eventually, the Stop The Rocket campaign will become the focus of their reporting."

Russ nervously rubbed his left index finger over his upper lip. He regarded Neal and calmly said, "Well, I look forward to their questions. I've got nothing to hide."

6

The Whisper Dunes high school gymnasium was packed with over 2,000 people. Everyone in the gym was paying close attention to the tall man with the shaved head standing behind the podium. Sitting at a long table behind the podium was Mayor Tillinghast and four officials from the Michigan Space Association. Two uniformed state police officers stood about twenty feet from the speaker, John Pauley, who was dressed in a custom tailored black suit.

Stan and Lisa sat together in the second row. Lisa was busy reading through the M.S.A. pamphlet she received at the door. The thin pamphlet contained a few details on the economic impact the rocket launch spaceport would have on Whisper Dunes, while offering no evidence of the claims. Stan was holding the same pamphlet, but his eyes were looking at Randy, who was sitting in the front row. Stan was struck by how nervous Randy seemed. He kept fidgeting in his chair while biting his thumbnail, like a guy waiting for his STD test results after spending a week in Dallas for a work convention.

Stan tried to think back to the last time he saw Randy this tense. Nothing came to mind, except for the time Stan invited Randy to play in a charity golf outing at Timberstone. Stan remembered, with a smirk on his face, how Randy almost fainted when he told him on the tee box of the eighteenth hole that they needed to birdie the hole in order to win a ten-thousand-dollar bet. Stan had made the bet with the other twosome, Dutch and Gary, while Randy was pissing in the woods on the 2nd hole. Stan and Randy started drinking two hours before the round began, and it showed. They both double-bogeyed the first hole so Stan knew he'd have no problem convincing Dutch and Gary to take the bet. The best ball format took some pressure off Randy on the final hole, a long Par 4, but as he was lining up his eight-foot putt for birdie he pissed himself. He sank the putt, but refused to speak to Stan for a month.

John Pauley was overweight and bald, but spoke into the microphone with a certain unabashed confidence that made him look and sound like a seasoned politician who had mastered the art of deception. John said, in a booming voice, "It has been the Michigan Space Association's sole mission for the past four years to turn Michigan into the first space state in the Midwest. M.S.A. has been in serious discussions with multiple private space companies to build a rocket launch spaceport right here in the beautiful town of Whisper Dunes. Believe me when I say this, every space company we've met with has expressed incredible enthusiasm for developing a spaceport in Whisper Dunes. Currently, there are only thirteen spaceports in the United States. The Michigan spaceport will be used primarily to host vertical launches, through which rockets carrying satellites would be sent into low-Earth orbit. Big tech companies would pay a per launch fee to transport their payloads into space."

An angry man in his mid-forties, sitting in the third row blurted out, "How much you plan on charging those companies to dump their rocket shit into Lake Superior!?"

John looked like he was ready to respond but before he got a word out, Lisa and hundreds of other people started to repeatedly chant, "Protect Lake Superior! Stop the rocket!"

John barely reacted as the gym erupted in the chant. The crowd continued with their chant for over a minute, but John was unfazed. He looked as if he was trying to remember what he had for breakfast. The crowd finally reached their lung capacity and John calmly continued with his presentation. "Economically speaking, the rocket launch spaceport will be a home run for Whisper Dunes. At least 700 well paying jobs will be created from this spaceport. Keep in mind, the spaceport will also be used to send satellites into space that support the development of autonomous cars and trucks by providing data for GPS capabilities. The spaceport will also improve the health and wellness capabilities for anyone who lives in the Upper Peninsula."

Most of the people in the audience looked puzzled by this last statement. The man seated next to Stan turned to his wife and said, "Is he fucking high?"

For the first time all evening, John looked a bit unnerved. "Folks, there's no denying that a lot of good is going to come from this spaceport," John said as his eyes moved from an angry looking woman in the front row.

A man in the third row, who was wearing a tweed flat cap, stood up. He was holding a pen and notebook, and looked to be in his early forties. "Scott Powers, reporter with *The Mining Journal.* How big will the rockets be?"

John looked relieved to get an easy question. "Good question, Scott. The rockets used at this spaceport will be similar in size to the Firefly Alpha—the new two-stage, satellite rocket that is approximately 95 feet in length."

Scott looked concerned as he glanced at his notebook. He then looked right at John and said, "Ten seconds into the Firefly Alpha's debut launch, it exploded over the Pacific Ocean."

John's tense eyes did not blink as he reached for the bottled water on the podium. He took a long sip while everyone in the audience looked very curious as they waited for Scott's next question. Scott regarded John without any expression on his face and said, "Seeing that these rockets have a twenty percent failure rate, will the entire population of Whisper Dunes have to evacuate before every rocket launch?"

"That is highly unlikely, but I can assure you that the safety of everyone who lives in Whisper Dunes is our number one priority. People need to understand that new launch technologies are in development, and in the very near future I think the spaceport will have access to electronic propulsion systems, which will significantly decrease any negative environmental impact to the region," John said in an uneven tone.

"Last question," Scott said. "Why hasn't the Michigan Space Association shared any information from the taxpayer funded feasibility study on the economic benefits and safety risks that come with a rocket launch spaceport?"

John clenched his jaw as he pondered the best way to answer the question. He looked down and took another swig from his bottled water. John then gripped the podium stand with both hands. He looked discouraged as his gaze finally met Scott's piercing eyes. Just as John adjusted the microphone, a naked woman in her early twenties, likely a college student, came running from the side door and stopped in front of the podium. John actually looked relieved for the moment. A few people gasped in shock, but most of the audience acted like they knew she was going to show up. The naked woman held up a large sign over her head that read: STOP THE ROCKET!

Knowing her time was limited, she quickly said, "The noise from the rockets will trigger wildlife migration and turn Lake Superior into a dump for rocket fuel and satellite debris! No region in the country has been protected and preserved better than the Upper Peninsula! And no Great Lake has been protected better than Lake Superior!"

Most of the audience stood up and cheered loudly.

"Billionaires, suffering from extreme boredom and crippling insecurity, are obsessed with launching metal penises into the Earth's atmosphere just so they can have a reason to post photos on social media! We can never allow bored billionaires to shoot off rockets over Lake Superior! We only have one planet! Despite what that nut job from Space D says, humans will never be able to live anywhere but here on Earth! Fuck the oligarchs!" yelled the naked woman just before two police officers finally approached her. The crowd cheered loudly in support as the woman stood still with her head high.

"Okay, you said what you needed to say, now we have to arrest you," said the bigger of the two cops. The other cop carefully grabbed the woman by her wrist and led her toward the side door as the crowd gave her a standing ovation. A dozen people started chanting, "Stop...the...rocket! Stop...the...rocket! Stop...the...rocket!" Almost everyone in the gym joined the chant. "Stop...the...rocket! Stop...the...rocket! Stop...the...rocket!"

As the chanting continued, John calmly walked toward the table behind the podium, grabbed his briefcase, and headed for the nearest exit. Mayor Tillinghast watched as the three men sitting next to him angrily stood up and followed John out of the gym.

Stan and Lisa, both naked, relaxed in their hot tub, which was located on the back deck of their home. It was close to midnight and the temperature had cooled off considerably since hitting eighty-three earlier in the afternoon. Their backyard was very private and overlooked a forest, which consisted mostly of pine trees. The only light in the backyard was coming from the hot tub.

Stan sipped from a tumbler of gin and tonic then passed it to Lisa for a sip. "A guy who gets rattled like that after just a few questions is hiding something," Stan said.

"He said the spaceport is going to create over 700 jobs, but had absolutely no proof to support that claim," Lisa said.

"Yeah, that's a total bullshit number."

"Those assholes have been conducting the feasibility study for over two years and have provided no evidence for any of their numbers. And what the fuck? Feasibility studies don't last two years. Something dirty is going on behind the scenes."

Stan looked at Lisa as he slowly nodded. "Yeah, I think you're right."

He took a long sip from the tumbler before he looked into Lisa's eyes. "Like a plastic surgeon who owns a bunch of tattoo parlors and even more tattoo removal clinics, there's an unapologetic conflict of interest attached to this whole thing."

Lisa let out a big laugh. Stan used to make Lisa laugh all the time in their early years together. She didn't laugh as much as she used to, but God knows Stan still tried. When he was able to make Lisa let out a big belly laugh Stan felt like the greatest husband in the world.

"Whoever owns the 5,000 acres is fully convinced they're going to sell all that land to a space company," Stan said.

"We have to try and prove that just one of those bullshit projections from the feasibility study is a lie. If we can do that, then there's no way the zoning commission will rezone the proposed site for the spaceport," Lisa said before she took another sip from the tumbler.

Stan stared at Lisa, admiring her beautiful face. He smiled and said, "I love it when you get filled up with passion and rage. You are one sexy mama."

Lisa flashed a sexy smile before kissing Stan. After about ten seconds, she pulled away and said, "Why don't you ask Randy if he knows anything about when the study is going to be released?"

"Okay, but I've already brought it up with Russ, and he said my guess is as good as his."

The Town Hall building wouldn't be filled with workers for another two hours, but Russ was already sitting behind his desk reading a letter. His eyes squinted as he carefully read. He continued reading as he sipped his coffee. Whisper Dunes was written in yellow cursive on the dark blue mug. He looked concerned as he picked up a pencil and wrote a few notes on his yellow legal pad.

Randy knocked on the open door and entered. "Morning, Mr. Mayor," Randy said cheerfully.

"Morning, Randy."

"You wanted to see me?"

"Have a seat."

Randy sat in one of the two chairs in front of Russ's desk.

"How's your float looking for the parade?"

"Looking good. Just need to put the finishing touches on it."

"Good. Okay, let's get right to it then."

Russ handed Randy the letter he was reading and said, "A few concerned residents want to know why the Marquette County Planning Commission still hasn't scheduled a public hearing. It's been almost a year since a request was filed to amend the Marquette County Zoning Ordinance so that it prohibits a rocket spaceport from being constructed."

Randy shrugged in attempt to play it cool before he looked at the letter.

"The planning commission has tabled the issue at their last two meetings because they said they're still waiting for a response from their attorney," Russ said in a frustrated tone.

"Well, that should be expected, sir. The current county zoning laws have no language that mentions, or even relates to rocket launch spaceports."

"Without the zoning change, the proposed rocket launch site will probably be breaking ground by next year."

Randy nodded and said, "You're probably right."

"The Stop The Rocket campaign has collected well over the required one-thousand signatures needed to request the hearing. I want you to get to the bottom of this and make sure this hearing is scheduled before the end of July."

Randy's lips were nervously pressed together as he nodded. "I'm on it."

Randy dropped the letter on Russ's desk. "Anything else?"

"Yeah, as a matter of fact there is."

Randy struggled to hide is growing discomfort.

"I just received a package that piqued my interest. Based on the postmark it arrived almost two weeks ago, but Carol just got around to giving it to me."

"What was in the package?"

"A letter from our friendly Canadian neighbors threatening to sue the state of Michigan and Whisper Dunes if we go forward with the spaceport. Apparently, the spaceport would violate the Great Lakes Water Quality Agreement. Along with the polite, threatening letter, the package also included the completed feasibility study on the economic and environmental impact of the spaceport," Russ said.

Randy tried hard not to convey any emotions but Russ couldn't help notice his regular morning cheerfulness disappear from his face. The mayor opened his desk drawer and grabbed the 200-plus page report. Randy flinched at the sound of the thick report being dropped on the front edge of the desk.

"I didn't know the study was complete. Who sent you that?"

"The package came from the office of Environment and Climate Change Canada."

"Is that an official government office?"

"Yeah, they're equivalent to the Environmental Protection Agency. Except that the Canadian version of the EPA seems to actually care about the environment."

Randy crossed his legs as he shifted uneasily in his chair. "Have you read it?"

"No, God no. The last time I tried to read a feasibility study my vertigo quickly kicked in and I ended up in the hospital with a concussion. According to Carol, I fell and hit my head on the corner of the desk. I don't remember any of it."

Randy looked relieved as he exhaled softly.

"You know, it's been well over two years since the Michigan Space Association announced their plans for a feasibility study, which was completely financed by Michigan taxpayers' dollars. So how do you think Canada's Environmental bigwigs got their hands on this report before my office did?"

"I don't know, sir, but I'll look into it," Randy said.

The mayor looked at Randy for a good five seconds before he said in a patient tone, "I want you to analyze that report very carefully and give me a full summary by next Friday."

"You got it. But regardless of what the feasibility report says, I don't think anyone can deny that the spaceport will be a huge tourism draw. It would be the first spaceport in the Midwest, which will bring our town some national media coverage for the first time ever. Mark my words, Mr. Mayor, folks from all over the Midwest and beyond will travel up to the U.P. on a monthly basis, even in the dead of winter, to watch rockets launch over Lake Superior."

Russ looked puzzled as he met Randy's gaze. "That's surprising to hear, Randy...considering your wife and closest friends are firmly against the spaceport."

"I'm just trying to see the issue from both sides, sir. At the end of the day, I just want what's best for this town. Granted, my wife would kill me if she knew I wasn't one hundred percent behind the Stop the Rocket movement."

Russ looked conflicted as looked out the window. He considered whether or not to tell Randy the big news. He had not planned on telling anyone for at least a few days. Russ clasped his hands together and regarded Randy. He conveyed a serious look that Randy had never seen before. Russ's eyes got wide, then narrowed, then got wide again as he leaned forward his chair and rested his elbows on the desk. "What I'm about to tell you, will change the future of Whisper Dunes, along with the lives of every single person who lives here. Not just for the foreseeable future, but for the remainder of civilization."

Having no idea what Russ was about to reveal, Randy's eyes were wide with anticipation and his back was full of sweat. The door suddenly burst open and Carol entered, to Russ's dismay. "Morning, guys," Carol said cheerfully as she handed Russ a white paper bag. "Stopped off at Babycakes. Got you a cinnamon roll and a Bavarian cream donut."

Russ looked excited as he peeked in the bag. "Lovely, lovely. Thank you, Carol." Carol exited the office but did not shut the door behind her. Russ shook his head with annoyance. There was no telling when Carol might barge in again so he got up and locked the door.

Randy kept his eyes on Russ as he eased back in his chair, grabbed the cinnamon roll from the bag, and took a big bite. Randy was growing impatient as he watched Russ slowly chew. "Sir, you were saying."

Russ, unable to help himself, took another bite from the cinnamon roll. He then put it back in the bag and used his right thumb to wipe the corner of his mouth. "Nobody in this town knows what I'm about to tell you, not even Stan," Russ said.

Randy looked anxious as his eyes remained wide open.

"After the Independence Day parade, I'm going to get up on the stage and make a very important announcement."

"What are you announcing?"

Russ licked the last of the cinnamon from the side of his mouth. He then smiled and said, "*Forbes* has named Whisper Dunes...America's Best Place to Live."

Randy was clearly in a state of bewilderment. "Holy shit! Are you serious?"

Russ nodded slowly. "It took me a full twenty-four hours to comprehend and appreciate the gravity of the situation."

"Unbelievable. I had no idea we were even in the running for America's Best Place to Live."

"Neither did I," Russ said.

"This is huge."

"It's bigger than huge," Russ said, trying to think of something clever. "It's huge times ten."

Randy looked overwhelmed as his mind continued to race. He took a deep breath and quietly exhaled while his mind raced through different thoughts and questions. But there was one question at the forefront of his brain. *How will this affect the spaceport project?*

7

Bud Clancy, a sharply dressed man in his mid-nineties, proudly wore his World War II Veteran hat as he raised the American flag up the flag pole. The fifty-foot flag pole was located in the middle of Ellwood A. Mattson Lower Harbor Park. The wind off Lake Superior was almost non-existent so the flag did not move as it was raised slowly up the pole. A short man in his early eighties stood in front of the flag pole. He played "The Star-Spangled Banner" on his trumpet while over three thousand people looked on.

Mayor Tillinghast stood in the front row with his right hand placed over his heart. Most people in the crowd had their right hand over their hearts, but some had their eyes closed and their heads bowed. Some people just smiled as they admired the American flag, and more than a few people looked drunk despite that it was only five minutes past 9 a.m. The trumpet player hit the last note of "The Star-Spangled Banner" just as the flag reached the top of the pole. The silent crowd suddenly erupted into loud cheers.

Sirens blared from a hook and ladder firetruck as it slowly cruised east down Washington Street, which extended through the heart of downtown. The annual Whisper Dunes 4th of July parade had officially started. Three firefighters, each holding a red Solo cup filled with beer, stood on the back of the firetruck smiling and waiving at the adoring crowd. Both sides of the street were packed with a mix of families and raucous parade goers. It was clear that some folks had started partying way too early on this warm, sunny Independence Day.

Everyone in the crowd was wearing patriotic clothing and cheering loudly as the parade cruised down Washington Street. This was a day Whisper Dunes residents looked forward to all year long, and each resident had their own special way of celebrating, without fear of judgement by their neighbors. As the first of three firetrucks inched down Washington Street, all the kids cheered with excitement. Dozens and dozens of kids sat on their dads shoulders waving their little American flags proudly.

A 1959 silver Corvette convertible, carrying the Parade Marshall, followed behind the three firetrucks. The Parade Marshall was a stout man in his late seventies, who proudly wore his Vietnam Veteran hat. The Veteran had a big smile on his face as he waved enthusiastically at the cheering crowd.

The Parade Marshall car was followed by five Whisper Dunes police motorcycles, which were followed by five Whisper Dunes police vehicles and the Marquette County S.W.A.T. truck. Following behind the S.W.A.T. truck was the high school marching band, playing "America the Beautiful."

Not far behind the marching band was over two hundred kids who looked thrilled to be riding their decorated bikes in the parade. As the last of the bikes made their way down Washington Street, a long line of floats started to roll down the street. Most of the floats were decorated with either a patriotic theme or a movie theme. A remarkable float designed like a U.S. aircraft carrier stood out to the cheering crowd. The crowd cheered even louder when they spotted the fighter jet float, followed by a tank float and a submarine float. The movie themed floats were almost as impressive, but the ones that really stood out were: *The Wizard of Oz, It's A Wonderful Life, Jaws, Star Wars, Caddyshack, Top Gun, The Princess Bride, The Great Outdoors, Home Alone, A League of Their Own, Dumb & Dumber, Toy Story, The Birdcage, The Big Lebowski,* and *The Royal Tenenbaums.*

The Stop the Rocket float received the loudest cheers, in part because a very attractive woman, wearing a patriotic blue bikini with white stars, was sitting on top of a rocket made out of cardboard. Following the Stop the Rocket float was a pirate ship float. A large sign hung on the back of the float that read: **Happy Independence Day! From the Zbikowski Real Estate Group.** Bruce Springsteen & The E Street Band's "No Surrender" blasted from the speaker located at the front of the float. A smoke machine was pumping out smoke, which briefly provided cover for the people on the float. As the smoke started to clear, the crowd cheered when they saw Duane Murphy standing tall at the bow of the pirate ship. Duane was short, stout, and closing in on fifty. But his excellent pirate outfit, along with the real sword he held above his head, made him look like a larger than life figure.

Stan, dressed in his best pirate get-up, emerged from below deck to cheers along with a few boos. Duane turned and faced off with Stan, who was wearing an eye patch. Randy, also dressed as a pirate, drove the float while taking puffs from his cigar. Randy's two pre-teen daughters and Stan's three pre-teen boys, all dressed like pirates, threw candy to the crowd. Stan took a step toward Duane then pulled out a sword from his back case. Duane took four steps toward Stan and the sword fight began.

Stan forced Duane to back pedal onto the plank as the sword fight intensified. The crowd seemed to be rooting for Duane as he fought off Stan and forced him off the plank. Duane turned to the crowd and yelled, "This...is a day...for America!"

The crowd cheered wildly as Duane raised his arms up and down. Caught up in the moment, Duane took one step too many and lost his balance. The crowd groaned in horror, but Stan grabbed the back of his white puffy shirt and saved Duane from going overboard. The crowd cheered in relief while Duane took a bow. Grateful, Duane wrapped his arms around Stan before kissing him on the cheek. "Thanks a million, pal," Duane said. "I owe you one."

"Can you give me a month to pay up?"

"Fuck no!"

"Two weeks?"

"Fine. But until you cough up the dough, I'm not taking any action from you."

"Fair enough."

Ellwood A. Mattson Lower Harbor Park was packed with parade goers enjoying the post parade festivities. A five-piece folk-rock band played "This Land is Your Land" while most of the crowd sang along. On the side of the stage, Mayor Tillinghast sang along by himself.

Next to the packed beer tent, ten people were competing in a hot dog eating contest, including Duane. After shoving a few more hot dogs into his mouth, Duane looked over at the guy next to him and realized that he was way ahead. Duane picked up the plate of hot dogs in front of him and tossed the hundred or so cold hot dogs into the crowd.

The street across from Ellwood A. Mattson Lower Harbor Park was blocked off to traffic. Front Street was crowded with kids and their moms, who were cheering on a group of Whisper Dunes firefighters as they competed in a water ball fight. Five firefighters stood about fifty feet apart from another group of five firefighters while the two teams sprayed their hoses at a large, yellow, weighted ball that was suspended ten feet in the air on a one-hundred-foot-long wire.

Water sprayed all over the place as the firefighters tried to push the ball across the line. A hundred kids stood nearby cheering on the firefighters. Also cheering on the firefighters were some cute moms, along with at least two-dozen single girls in their twenties and thirties. Most of them were standing close enough to the water ball fight that they were drenched. A few of the women were in bikini tops and kept getting looks from the firefighters.

About fifty yards down the blocked off street, a long line of kids waited for their chance to ride on one of the three firetrucks. The kids patiently waited in line, and not one of them was holding a phone or a tablet to distract their little minds. Instead, the kids were all engaged in friendly conversations. The only thing that interrupted their conversations was the sight of the firetruck pulling away with a group of twenty kids riding on top. The sirens started up and the kids smiled and cheered.

The crowd size in Ellwood A. Mattson Lower Harbor Park had increased from earlier in the day. Over five thousand people were now at the park enjoying the beautiful day. The band was on break so the stage was empty, but hundreds of people were singing and dancing as the John Mellencamp song, "Pink Houses," played over the speakers.

Stan, still dressed in his pirate outfit, entered the beer tent, which was packed with a wide variety of people between the ages of eighty and eighteen. But no one seemed to be having more fun than Father John Carey. A Catholic priest in his early fifties, Fr. Carey was visibly drunk, sunburned, and laughing his ass off while surrounded by a group of guys who seemed to appreciate his jokes.

Russ had been waiting by the steps that led to the stage for the past ten minutes. He looked nervous as he quietly rehearsed what he was going to stay once he stepped on the stage. He took a deep breath and walked onto the stage just as "Pink Houses" ended. Most people in the crowd didn't notice

Russ waving from the stage as he slowly moved behind the podium. Russ took another deep breath to calm himself then lowered the mic. With great enthusiasm he shouted, "Happy Independence Day, Whisper Dunes!"

About half the crowd responded with cheers while the other half continued on with their conversations. Russ decided he'd wait a half-minute in hopes that the rest of the crowd would stop talking and turn their attention toward him.

"Folks! Folks! I need everyone's attention for one shining moment," Russ said cheerfully.

Most people in the crowd, but not everyone, finally turned their attention toward the stage. Russ looked over the crowd with a proud smile on his face, but a tidal wave of emotions quickly overwhelmed him. For a second, he thought he would have to turn his back to the crowd in order to gather himself, but he was able to temper down his emotions just enough so that he could continue facing the crowd. With both hands on the podium, Russ took a deep breath and scanned the crowd.

"What a day for America! What a day for Whisper Dunes!"

The crowd responded with roaring cheers.

"After I was blessed with the honor of becoming the mayor of Whisper Dunes, I made a point to challenge all of you to do your part to make sure Whisper Dunes remains a wonderful place to live. Since becoming mayor, I know you've heard me often say, we have to be responsible to more than ourselves. It's that attitude that will help us preserve are wonderful town for the next generation."

Russ looked pleased as the crowd cheered. "You know, my dad, who lived his entire life in this town, would often tell me that I was lucky to be growing up in the best town in America. Not for one minute, did I ever doubt that Whisper Dunes is the best town in America. But it's not because of our unique geographic location, or the architecturally significant buildings, or our incredible public school system, or the fact that we live in a four season paradise, or that the largest body of freshwater on Earth happens to be in our backyard. No, the reason this is such a special town is because of the wonderful people who live here!"

The crowd cheered loudly to Russ's delight. He flashed a big smile and patiently waited for the crowd to calm down. As he surveyed the crowd, Russ realized this was a moment that he would remember for the rest of his life.

"Today, on Independence Day, I have a once in a lifetime announcement to make! Like most mayors in America, it's an announcement that I have dreamed of making!"

Because their curiosity had piqued, the crowd was almost silent as Russ stood tall before them.

"It is with incredible pride and joy that I stand before you, on the 4th of July, to announce that *Forbes* has declared Whisper Dunes...America's Best Place to Live!"

The crowd, hoping the mayor would give them a reason to go crazy, erupted into pandemonium. Russ pumped his fist in the air as people started exchanging high fives and hugs, but not everyone in the crowd looked happy about the news. In fact, dozens of folks looked pissed off. Some people were so disgruntled they threw their plastic beer cups toward the stage. One of the cups filled with beer nearly hit Russ in the head.

"What in the blazes? I saw that, Nancy! You're a city worker, for God's sake!"

A dozen more cups landed on the stage, followed by a few water balloons, and finally a large white bra. Two police officers rushed up to the stage and stood in front of Russ, who looked flabbergasted. Russ stared out at the crowd for a minute and saw mostly happy people congratulating each other, but he also saw some disappointed folks. He shook his head as he spotted an older couple yelling at a younger couple. Russ walked back toward the podium and stood behind the mic.

"Listen up! Folks, this is a big, big deal! For way too long, I know it seemed like the rest of the country forgot about our town, and every town in the U.P. But not anymore! Whisper Dunes is a very special place, and we are more than deserving of this title! We should all be happy by this news! Celebrate with your friends and family and neighbors! Celebrate this incredible moment in your own special way! But please, celebrate like your kids are watching!"

A large group of people were gathered near the stage, drunk and dancing wildly to "Run Around Sue." Duane put a beer bottle in the middle of the dance floor, and then he and his boyfriend, Hal, started to dance around the bottle. Soon, other people tried to do the same thing. A guy accidentally knocked the bottle over as he tried to spin his wife, which prompted Duane to kick the couple off the dance floor.

Fr. Carey had a big drunk smile on his face as he danced with a gorgeous brunette in a blue tank top and white skirt. Fr. Carey moved closer to the beer bottle, and as he tried a dance move he accidentally knocked the bottle over with his velcro sandal. The bottle shattered on the dance floor and Duane immediately kicked Fr. Carey and his dance partner out of the game.

Under a large maple tree, about fifty feet behind the stage, Russ stood across from an irate, Hubert Houston. The mayor calmly regarded Hubert, whose face was red from yelling for the past five minutes. "Stop saying this is a blessing, Russell! It's a fucking curse. The corporate media outlets are going to invade our town and mess things up for everyone. That's why people sit on their fat asses and scroll through social media all day long and watch cable news every fucking night. They're compulsively searching for bad news about someone's life being destroyed over a bullshit scandal. Mark my words, Russ, this title is going to bring nothing but negative heat to Whisper Dunes."

"Hubert, you've been drinking all day on an empty stomach and I think you're over reacting. You've always been hyper-focused on yourself, and only interested when good things happen to you. But what you don't understand is that a lot of good people in Whisper Dunes are going see their lives improve because of this title. This is a win-win for every resident in Whisper Dunes. I mean, how could it not be? Real estate prices are going to sky rocket. Our tax revenues will increase considerably. We'll be able to improve services and go forward with more public works projects. Our local businesses are going to be booming, and once the out of state developers make it up here, they'll discover that the majestic, untamed wilderness of the U.P. is unfuckable."

Hubert looked calmer now. He blinked his eyes a few times as he rubbed the tip of his nose. "What's not unfuckable are my delicate plans that need to work out in order to save the city and county pension plans. I think you understand what I'm talking about."

Russ suddenly seemed tense as he looked around to make sure no one was in earshot of the maple tree. He finally looked at Hubert and said, "You said the deal's going through and that the pension systems will be made whole again. Why would the *Forbes* title mess up your deal?"

"This town is going to be under a microscope for the foreseeable future," Hubert said as his face became bright red again. "Before the media even enters Whisper Dunes, the first thing they're going to see are a bunch of fucking signs that read: Stop The Rocket."

Russ folded his arms and lowered his head. He no longer looked optimistic. Instead, he seemed almost as dejected as Hubert looked.

"You've said it yourself many times, this is maybe the only place left in the United States where the human experience hasn't been ruined. Well, my friend, life as we know it up here in our four season paradise is going to be totally fucked."

A vein bulged out of Russ's forehead as he got in Hubert's face. "I didn't ask for this, Hubert! This wasn't something I was even aware of until just a few days ago. But I believe we've been given an incredible opportunity to turn our sleepy town into a great American city."

"Listen to me, Russ, if you want to remain the mayor of Whisper Dunes, a city you have publicly claimed is your first and only love, then you need to hold a press conference and renounce the *Forbes* title, as soon as possible."

Russ rubbed his forehead in frustration. "You don't understand. This is not just about Whisper Dunes being a great place to live, their decision was motivated by the most serious issue facing the world."

Hubert squinted his eyes in confusion.

"*Forbes* decided to name Whisper Dunes, America's Best Place to Live, because of a yet to be published scientific paper on climate change."

Hubert was so confused that his squinting eyes caused him to unknowingly smile.

"The study has determined that—because of climate change—the Upper Peninsula will be the best place to live on Earth for pretty much the remainder of civilization."

Hubert's face turned red again. He couldn't find a single word to utter, so he grit his teeth and crossed his arms. Hubert turned his back to Russ and looked out at Lake Superior, realizing that his plans could go up in flames.

8

Stan, still dressed in his pirate outfit, drove his golf cart as fast as it would go down a hilly road lined with pine trees. He spoke frantically into a walkie-talkie. "No, I'm not fucking with you. I just got done talking with Mayor Tillinghast. Whisper Dunes is not on a list of best places to live. Whisper Dunes is America's Best Place to Live! Based on one factor...climate change. Mark my words, Walter, this is going to be an international story. Alright, call me back when you get off the boat."

The golf cart came to a screeching stop in front of a three-story brick building on Front Street that was over a hundred years old. Stan chugged the rest of his beer then hopped out of his golf cart and ran toward the front door of the building. Just before he got to the door he tripped and hit the pavement hard. Stan glanced at the blood running down his right knee as he got back to his feet. Didn't look too bad, he thought as he pulled out his office keys from his pirate pants. He unlocked the door and hurried into the building.

Zbikowski Real Estate Group - Est. 2003 was painted on the glass door of the office suite. The office suite had an open floor plan, high ceilings, and six large steel casement windows that overlooked Front Street. Stan bought the building six years ago and was going to convert the first floor into a bar that only served pizza, and turn the second and third floors into apartments. But Duane convinced him not to go forward with his plans. So he moved his real estate brokerage firm to the top two floors and rented the first floor out to an accounting firm.

A dozen realtors stood behind their desks as they shouted into their phones. All of the realtors were dressed in their casual summer clothes, but one realtor really stood out. A tall, thin woman with long brown hair was wearing a navy blue string bikini and beach sandals while trying to convince a client to buy as much land near Whisper Dunes as possible.

The door to Stan's office was closed. Unlike his home office, this office was neat and decorated with the goal of impressing current and future clients. The first thing that stood out when entering the office was the massive desk. On the wall that Stan was facing were three motivational posters: *Grind, Hustle, Execute.* On the other wall were three framed pictures that his kids made him when they were younger. On the tidy desk was a framed family photo, along with several thick manilla folders and a large black binder filled with leads.

Stan looked impatient as he stood behind his desk thumbing through the black binder. The desk phone was pressed to his ear as he waited for someone to answer the call. Stan's eyes widened with intensity as soon as he heard a voice on the other end. "Marco, it's Stan. What's your cash position? Okay, then tomorrow morning, go down to the bank and get a home equity loan. Talk to my guy, Jimmy, he'll work with you. Call me after you speak with Jimmy."

Stan quickly pressed another button on his desk phone. "The secret's out, Yuri, Whisper Dunes is America's Best Place to Live. That's how the next cover of *Forbes* is going to read. As your realtor and dear friend, I'm advising you to buy now."

Stan pressed another extension button on his phone. "I don't care how leveraged you are, Rocco, you have to get into the Whisper Dunes market today! So get out of that negative head space and switch gears to buy mode."

Stan was now talking into his cell phone. "I don't think you truly understand how incredible this situation is, Billy. Okay, let me paint you a picture. Imagine you're holding a perfectly made Bavarian cream donut in one hand. Just as you take your first bite, your beautiful wife starts giving you an enthusiastic blowjob. Then, a few minutes into the amazing blowjob, you look at your other hand and realize you're holding a winning lottery ticket."

Stan pressed another line. "Thanks for holding, Matt. Of course I'll tell you when it's the right time to sell. That's my job! But I'm telling you this as your dear friend, unless someone shows up to your door with a check for ten million, don't even think about selling."

Stan pressed another line on his phone. "Thanks for holding, Molly. Let me make this quick, sink every penny you have into Whisper Dunes real estate. Do it! And let your neighbors see you do it!"

Stan pressed another line on his phone. "Hey, Jordan, happy Independence Day. What? Client my ass! You sold him one house five years ago that he's still underwater on. I'm just trying help a friend. That's the difference between you and me, your clients view you as a realtor and my clients view me as their friend, because I am their friend... fuck me? No, fuck you!"

Stan pressed another line on his phone. "Sorry, Reggie, I got cut off for a minute. No, you don't understand, in a month it'll be too late. I don't care where you get the money. Rob a bank, ask your ex-wife...Reggie, the clock is ticking. In a few months those vultures from Wall Street will try to buy every parcel of land in the U.P. Ever single private equity whore and hedge fund slut will be trying to buy up blocks of houses at a time...my friend, you'll be quickly priced out of the Whisper Dunes market and I don't want to see that happen. You mean too damn much to this community. A year from now, I don't want to hear that you had to move away from the only town you've ever lived in. Reggie, you know I love you. So listen to me, please. You won't regret it. I guaran-fuckin-tee it!"

The parking lot of Breakers Roadhouse Bar was packed on what turned out to be another beautiful starlit night in Whisper Dunes. Lenny Trubisky stood alone in the poorly lit parking lot. He leaned back against his work van and lit a cigarette. His left thumb was covered in a bandage, forcing him to hold the cigarette with his right hand. He took a drag, thinking about what he might say if he bumped into Denise. Earlier in the evening, Lenny had no intention of going out. But after he took two Vicodin and downed four beers, he changed his mind. Lenny had already initiated his blackmail threats to Denise over the phone, four days earlier, which he now realized was a poor choice. But because he had never blackmailed anyone before, he wasn't too hard on himself. While he was getting his thumb stitched up, Lenny made the decision that he was going to blackmail Denise. He thought about calling her again to set up a meeting place, but after thinking it over, decided that catching her off guard was the best move. He had considered surprising Denise at her pilates studio, just as she was wrapping up a class, but he also liked the idea of bumping into her at a crowded bar. Lenny stared nervously at the side door as he took a long drag from his cigarette. He tossed the cigarette to the pavement as he walked slowly toward the side door.

Duane and Stan, both drunk, were singing karaoke on the small stage. Most of the people in the bar were having a ball dancing while Stan and Duane took turns singing verses from "Last Night," by The Traveling Wilburys.

Randy, one of the few semi-sober people in the joint, made his way from the bathroom toward the crowded horseshoe bar. He bumped into a woman he knew and twirled her around as they both sang the chorus. Just seconds after the song ended, Stan and Duane started singing a crowd favorite, "Man on the Moon" by R.E.M.

Denise walked through the front door of Breakers and stood still for just a moment as she looked over the crowd. Whenever Denise entered a room her glance seemed to register everything in a sudden inclusive flash, like a photographer's lens capturing a group photo. She kept her eyes straight ahead as she moved with ease through the crowd until she was standing at the end of the bar.

She looked incredible in her white and navy blue striped summer dress. Of course, Denise could be wearing a dress made out of garbage bags and still look stunning. There were two-dozen people standing around the bar waiting for a drink, but Denise remained patient, knowing she'd get her drink before all the other waiting customers. Denise didn't make eye contact with any of the men who kept glancing at her because her attention was focused on the stage. She was clearly amused watching Stan and Duane sing the second verse together. Just what she needed to escape the anxiety that had been flooding her mind since she received that call yesterday from Lenny. A relaxed smile appeared on her face as she distracted herself with a fun thought. *What would it be like to spend the night with Stan? I bet he's a good fuck.* It wasn't the first time this particular thought popped into her head. Denise had always had a crush on Stan. He was sweet to her when she first moved to town, and was one of the few guys who didn't hit on her when they bumped into each other at a bar...or a coffee shop, or the supermarket, or the library.

The bartender finally set a glass of house Cab in front of Denise, but she didn't notice because her eyes were still on Stan. "Want to start a tab, Denise?" asked the bartender.

"Yeah."

Denise slowly sipped her wine. The smell of cherries and black pepper took her mind back to that night last autumn when she bumped into Stan and Lisa at Zephyr's wine bar. She recalled how happy they looked, which made Denise a bit envious. She hadn't been in a serious relationship since college, and she sometimes fantasized about being married and having kids. Sometimes when she was all alone in her apartment, Denise would go so far as to fantasize about snuggling with her kids on the couch while they watched an animated movie. She never shared these thoughts and desires with anyone, because she didn't have anyone in her life to share them with. The life she chose did not allow for close relationships built on trust and love.

Even before moving to Whisper Dunes, Denise held out hope that she might finally meet a good man one day, who would never know about her complicated past. But her aspirations to meet her future husband hit a road block when some poor financial decisions forced her to put her plans on the shelf and find a solution to her serious money problems. Shortly after moving to Whisper Dunes, Denise came across a unique opportunity that would allow her to escape the crippling debt and start a new life. Everything was going according to plan until she received that call from Lenny.

Denise took a long sip from her wine glass as she pondered the difficult position she found herself in. Like a brilliant thoracic surgeon, who put herself through medical school by working as a call girl, Denise understood the importance of being discreet. Like blackmail, keeping secrets was an art form to her. Denise took great pride in guarding her secrets. She never once thought she'd make a mistake that would leave her vulnerable to being blackmailed. But after she swallowed the last of the wine in her glass, Denise finally asked herself a blunt question. *How the fuck did I allow myself to be blackmailed by Lenny Trubisky?*

Denise's glazed eyes were unknowingly staring at the bottles behind the bar as she thought about Lenny's possible motives for blackmailing her. She didn't know much about the man except that he was a thrice-divorced, unlicensed plumber, and if the rumors were true, a fairly successful womanizer. Denise recalled that during the past four years, she had only bumped into Lenny a few times around town, and each time he'd give a nod and a sheepish wave. Denise wondered if Lenny was not the person he made himself out to be to everyone in town.

She was deep in thought until the bartender set another glass of Cabernet in front of her. She nodded and said, "Thanks, Frank."

Fr. Carey, whose face was badly sunburned, bumped into Denise's shoulder just as she raised the wine glass to her natural full lips. "Oh, shoot! I'm sorry, Denise," Fr. Carey said. He had some competition, but Fr. Carey was likely the drunkest person in the bar. Funnily enough, instead of slurring his words, the drunker Fr. Carey got the clearer his pronunciation became. Fr. Carey, standing about ten inches from Denise's face, relieved himself with a burp.

"Hey, Denise, I got a dandy of a joke for you. What's long, green, and smells like bacon?"

Denise shook her head. "No idea."

"Kermit the Frog's fingers."

Fr. Carey started to laugh loudly just as the bartender handed Denise a napkin and another house Cabernet. She actually looked a bit offended. "You're disgusting."

"Oh, I'm sorry. I forgot that atheists don't have a sense of humor."

Denise picked up her fresh glass of wine and headed toward the dance floor.

Fr. Carey pointed at the middle-aged bartender and said, "Hey, Frankie! How about a Dewar's on the rocks from the best bartender in America's best place to live?"

Everyone at the bar cheered loudly to Fr. Carey's delight. "Okay, but that's your last one, Father," Frankie said.

Fr. Carey waved his right hand at him and yelled, "Oh, fuck you, I'm not driving."

Denise stood at the edge of the dance floor watching people dance wildly. She was going to leave, but the sight of Stan singing made her smile. She even felt the tension in her neck alleviate for a moment. The crowd erupted as Stan and Duane started singing the Meat Loaf tune, "Paradise by the Dashboard Light." Denise's eyes were on Stan as he moved around the stage like a wild man. She had started to relax enough to shake her hips, but she stopped shaking as soon as she got a whiff of cigarette smoke. Lenny snuck up behind her and leaned close enough so he could whisper in her ear. "I enjoyed watching your home movies. You are one talented woman, Denise. But blackmailing is a serious crime."

Denise slowly turned around to find Lenny looking right at her. She glanced at his bandaged thumb before they locked eyes. "More than a few interesting names in that little red book of yours," Lenny said with a cocky grin.

She finished the last of her wine then handed the glass to Lenny. He seemed uneasy as he watched Denise walk slowly toward the side door. Lenny set the wine glass on a high table that was already littered with empty beer bottles and walked toward the front door. He figured Denise would be waiting by his car so he stopped in the bathroom. He didn't haven't to piss that bad, but he was becoming increasingly nervous and thought that a quick piss might ease his nerves.

The parking lot was still filled with cars, but remained dark and quiet. Denise and Lenny stood between a white mini-van and Lenny's work van. Denise was uneasy even a bit scared, but didn't show it as Lenny looked her over. He grinned and finally said, "So, the pilates studio is just a way for you to get the guys interested in your special services?"

"No, my face and body are how I get guys interested in my special services. I teach pilates and yoga classes because I like getting paid to move my body in mysterious ways."

Lenny laughed as he grabbed a cigarette and lighter from his back pocket. Denise was clearly disgusted by the smell of the cigarette lighting up a few feet from her face.

"I think it's cute that you kept a diary of your sexual encounters. I didn't read every entry, but a few really stood out. I couldn't believe that one encounter you had with Judge Michaels at the Ritz-Carlton in Milwaukee. Holy smokes...did that really happen?"

Denise looked into Lenny's eyes and calmly said, "Lenny, you need to return everything that was in the shoebox back to me...before something bad happens to you."

Lenny was dumbfounded at how calm Denise looked. Mostly because of the nervous feeling in his stomach, he started to laugh out loud. "What are you going to do? Choke me to death with those pilate thighs?"

Denise's eyes narrowed on her expressionless face. "What do you want, Lenny?"

Lenny took a long drag from his cigarette then said, "One hundred grand. In cash."

Denise did not allow herself to convey any emotion while she stared into Lenny's eyes for what seemed liked a minute. She nodded slowly and finally said, "Okay. But you're going to have to give me some time to come up with the cash."

Lenny stared off in the distance as he took another long drag from his cigarette. "Being the nice guy that I am, I'll give you two weeks sugar tits. I get back from Florida on the 20th. Meet me in the church parking lot on the 20th at 10 p.m. with the dough."

Denise could no longer remain without expression. A look of bewilderment appeared on her face. "You're going to Florida in July? Jesus Christ, what's wrong with you?"

"Hey, it's cooler than Texas," Lenny said in a defensive tone. "Just make sure your tight, little ass is in that church parking on the 20th at 10 p.m."

"Fine, but I'm going to need that other thing you found in the box...now."

Lenny's gaze finally landed on Denise's wide eyes. He shook his head and said, "Sorry, but that belongs to me until I get my money."

Denise's emotionless face showed no hint of disappointment.

"I'll return everything that was in the shoebox once I receive my hundred grand. Understand?"

Denise's body remained perfectly still as she quickly considered her options. Lenny looked Denise over, thinking she was about to say something, but she didn't say a word. Lenny flashed a cocky smile and said, "Don't you worry, Denise, your secrets will still be safe with me after I receive the hundred grand."

Denise didn't blink as she watched Lenny get into his white cargo van. She glanced at the driver side of the van, which read: *THE PIPE MASTER: 24/7 Emergency Plumbing 906-270-6900.* The van sped out of the parking lot and quickly disappeared down the dark two-lane highway. Denise slowly pulled out her phone and dialed a number that was not in her contact list.

9

A glow-in-the-dark golf ball rolled toward the cup on the 10th green of the Potawatomi Country Club. Stan pulled the pin out of the hole just before the ball stopped two inches from the cup. He yelled,"Nice putt, Kevin!"

"Thanks, pal!"

It was forty minutes past midnight, but Stan and his buddies were only half way done with their round of golf. Stan had been sneaking onto Potawatomi Country Club and playing night golf since he was a teenager. As he got older, trespassing on the private golf course and playing golf in the middle of the night had gotten trickier to pull off, but Stan and a few of his buddies from childhood had refused to give up their favorite past time.

Stan pulled a beer from his pocket and cracked it open before he yelled, "Whose putt?" The golfers were all drunk and stumbling around the green. One guy was pissing in the sand trap and another guy was lighting a long joint. The only thing illuminating the pitch black green were the lights coming from the golf carts and a high-powered flash light. Most of the holes were carved out in the middle of a vast forest, and this particular hole was surrounded by giant oak trees. "Brian, I think it's your putt," Stan said.

Everyone watched as Brian stood over his glow-in-the-dark golf ball, which was about thirty feet from the hole. One of the other golfers shined his high-powered flash light on the hole while pissing on the green. Brian putt the ball and it miraculously sank into the hole. Stan and the other golfers erupted into loud cheers. Stan jumped high and gave Brian a high-five before the other highly inebriated golfers tackled him to the ground.

The only guy who didn't charge Brian was Bob, who was busy using his marijuana joint to light four bottle rockets, which were nestled in his empty beer bottle. Three bottle rockets shot up directly toward the sky, but one flew just above Stan's head, forcing him to dive to the ground.

"What the fuck, Bob!" Stan yelled.

"That wasn't supposed to happen! Sorry, Zibs!"

Billy, the shortest guy in the group, was in disbelief as he stared at something in the distance. "Holy moose balls!"

The guys all turned and looked behind them. The two-story clubhouse, located on a dune high above the first fairway, was on fire. The fire was flaming out of the ground-level windows and looked to be spreading fast through the clubhouse, which was built with white pine timbers from a nearby forest over a hundred years ago.

"Oh, fuck!" Stan said. His drunk eyes were wide open as he rested his hands on top of his head.

"Someone call 911!" Kevin yelled.

"I'm sure somebody else already did," Bob said. "Come on, we still got six holes to play."

Sirens from multiple firetrucks could be heard in the distance.

The sun was rising over Whisper Dunes on what was already shaping up to be a very eventful July 5th. A 2003—light blue—Chevy Silverado sped northbound on Front Street. On this particular morning, Whisper Dunes' Main Street looked a bit like Bourbon Street the morning after Fat Tuesday. Mayor Tillinghast had a gut feeling the partying would get out of control. So shortly after he made the announcement he called, Stu Rafferty—Director of Streets and Sanitation—and told him that the post 4th of July cleanup would require a bigger crew than normal. But because the Streets and Sanitation crew wouldn't be starting their cleanup efforts until seven, the downtown streets were still a mess.

Mayor Tillinghast sped westbound down Washington Street, but didn't seem to notice as his Chevy Silverado drove over hundreds of beer cans and Solo cups. The reason Russ didn't seem to notice the messy street was because his mind had been overwhelmed with an agonizing thought ever since he got off the phone with the Fire Chief. In fact, even before Russ hung up the phone, the possibility that someone set fire to the clubhouse crossed his mind. As he sped through town, he became more convinced that the crime of arson had been committed. His felt sick to his stomach as he considered how the national media would respond. Maybe he should follow Neal's advice and hire a press secretary, he thought. Part-time, anyway. As his truck sped through a red light Russ asked himself, *how do you even go about hiring a press secretary?*

Russ's thought process was broken when he nearly hit the only vehicle he'd come across this early in the morning—a city bus. Russ offered the bus driver an apologetic wave before he made a left at the next street. The Silverado sped down a residential street until Russ noticed something up ahead, which caused him to abruptly stop his truck in the middle of the street. Russ hurried out of his truck toward a man passed out in his own front yard. Russ turned the hose on and sprayed the man, who immediately woke up from his drunken slumber. "What the hell you doing, Russ?"

"I didn't want your five young kids waking up to find you passed out on the front lawn. Go clean yourself up, Malcolm," Russ said. Before the guy could say thanks, Russ was already back in his pickup truck.

The Fire Department's quick response had saved the Potawatomi Country Club from being completely burned down, but nearly half the clubhouse had been destroyed by the fire. One hose line, manned by three firefighters, was spraying a section of the clubhouse that had been destroyed and was still smoking. Another hose line, manned by four firefighters, was spraying a small section of the clubhouse that was still on fire. Four fire trucks, two ambulances, and five police cars were parked in the members-only parking lot. Because it was near the end of the firefight, most of the first responders were standing around, sipping coffee and bullshitting with each other.

Russ's Chevy Silverado sped up the steep drive that led to the members-only parking lot. He parked next to a black, unmarked police suv and quickly exited his truck. Russ took a few steps toward the clubhouse before he stopped and froze. He stared in disbelief at the burning clubhouse. "Oh, dear God," Russ said to himself. He looked upset as he walked quickly toward the burning clubhouse. The anger was building with each step, and prevented him from seeing the firehose a few feet in front of him. Russ tripped over the firehose and fell to the ground. Nobody seemed to notice and Russ quickly bounced back to his feet without realizing that he'd cut his right knee. Russ slowed down his stride as he got closer to the fire. He stopped about thirty yards from the burning clubhouse. His eyes started to water because of the smoke. Russ, still in a state of bewilderment, placed his hands on top of his head and stared at the burning clubhouse. Overwhelmed with smoke, Russ started to cough as he took a few steps back and gathered himself.

"Look at what these cocksuckers did!"

Russ turned around to see Hubert quickly approaching. His face was red and full of rage. Russ looked confused as he regarded Hubert. "You know who started the fire?" Russ asked in a measured tone.

"I have a pretty good idea."

"How do you know it was arson?"

"It's called trusting your gut, Russ. I'll give you my Range Rover if the Chief determines the fire wasn't premeditated arson."

Hubert stared at the destroyed clubhouse for a what seemed like a minute. He started to get emotional as he continued staring at the ruins. "My grandfather was one of the founding members of this club. My parents used to host my birthday party here every summer. Christ, I had my bachelor party here and my wedding reception," Hubert said as a tear escaped his eye.

Russ folded his arms and stared at the clubhouse with a blank look on his face. "What makes you assume it was arson? The clubhouse was built over a century ago. Could've been an electrical fire."

Hubert clenched his jaw in anger as he slowly moved his eyes away from the burning clubhouse and toward Russ. Hubert's piercing eyes finally met Russ's gaze. "According to Stan Zbikowski, a private country club is nothing more than refuge for the one percent, and it should be burnt to the ground," Hubert said.

Russ took a deep breath and nodded as he exhaled. "I do recall Stan saying that at a town council meeting last year. I also recall that his speech was slurred, the likely result of having one too many pops at his favorite watering hole before staggering into the meeting."

Hubert was clearly annoyed with Russ. "Oh, so if you're intoxicated that exonerates you from threatening to burn down a private country club?"

"No...I'm just..."

"Zibs, Daugherty, Murphy...they're all going down, and I'm the one who's going to burn their fucking soap box and piss on the ashes."

Mayor Tillinghast looked uneasy as he scratched his chin. He turned his attention to the firefighters, who were still trying to extinguish the flames burning in the pro shop. "Like a lot of residents over the years, those guys have all publicly expressed a strong desire to force the country club to change its offensive name. But I don't believe that gives you the right to accuse Stan or any one of those guys of committing arson," Russ said.

Russ could feel Hubert's cold eyes staring at him, but kept his focus on the firefighters for the moment. Russ finally turned his attention back to Hubert, who was staring at the mayor with his signature look—intense eyes, and clenched jaw. His jaw was clenched so hard saliva was starting to drool out the corner of his mouth. "So, if you're a fishing buddy with the mayor you don't have to worry about being investigated for arson," Hubert said. "Is that what your saying?"

"If the Fire Chief actually rules it arson, then I will urge him to follow any and all leads. But for all we know, Hubert, this could be the result of old wires, or a fireworks mishap."

Hubert took a step closer toward Russ, tilted his head inches from the mayor's face and said, "You can tell your boy, Zbikowski, and his cronies that I'm prepared to spend an obscene amount of money to guarantee that those assholes never get to live long enough to see Potawatomi Country Club change its name."

Russ didn't say a word, didn't even nod as he stared at Hubert without any expression on his face. Hubert finally turned his back to the mayor and started to walk toward his black BMW convertible. Each step was louder and angrier than the last. Hubert got into his car, put on his two-thousand-dollar Louis Vuitton sunglasses, and sped out of the parking lot.

The Fire Chief, Mike Albers, approached Russ with a cigarette dangling from his lips. "Morning, Mr. Mayor," Mike said before taking a long drag from his cigarette. Mike was around sixty, bald, and walked with a limp, the result of a rugby injury back in high school.

Russ nodded and gave Chief Albers a friendly smile. "Morning, Mike. So, what do you think?" Russ asked in a somber tone.

Mike took another drag before flicking his cigarette to the ground. "Too early to know for sure, but my gut tells me it was arson."

Russ looked deflated as he put his hands on his hips and took a deep breath. He exhaled then glanced up at the sky and said, "Oh, boy." Russ regarded Mike and finally said, "Is there any chance the fire was the result of an electrical issue?"

Russ tilted his head to the right as he held out hope that Chief Albers might respond with a maybe. "Russ, until the investigation is complete, I can't say with absolute certainty what caused the fire. But right now, all evidence points to arson."

Russ nodded respectfully and mumbled, "Okay." He turned to watch the firefighters as they continued to fight the fire.

"The one thing I do know for sure...the timing of this fire is going to get people talking. You don't need to be told this, but the rumors in this town are going to spread like wildfire...no pun intended."

Russ's wide eyes stared at the burning clubhouse as if he was searching for an answer in the smoke and flames. Mike lit another cigarette before he gave Russ a sympathetic look. Trying to mask his deep concerns, Russ's eyes narrowed as his gaze met Mike's. "The media is going to have a field day with this story," Russ said. "But I don't want that to deter you from doing your job. If it is arson, just make sure you do everything in your power to find out who did this, and for God's sake do not talk to the media."

Mike nodded before taking a long drag from his cigarette. Russ's eyes once again scanned the fire damage to the clubhouse. He closed his eyes for a few seconds and slowly shook his head. Russ couldn't help but suspect that a conspiracy had already been set in motion to destroy the reputation of his beloved town.

Stan was hungover, but tried hard to focus on the drawing of a gorilla that his youngest son had recently made him. Stan smiled as he continued to look at the picture on his desk, realizing that his son was a really talented little artist. The receiver to his landline phone had been pressed against his ear for at least a minute. While he waited for a voice on the other line, he slowly sipped coffee from a mug that featured a blue outline of Lake Superior, with every shoreline town labeled.

"Greek, its Whale. Put me down for two dimes on Cleveland and a dime on the over," Stan said in a groggy voice.

He was about to place one more bet but was distracted by his cell phone vibrating on the desk. The name on the caller ID prompted Stan to hang up the landline and answer his cell phone. "Hey Randy...What?! Oh, that's total bullshit! I was on the 10th green when the fire started. There's no way I, or anyone I was with could have started that fire. Who told you that God damn lie?"

The morning sun lit up Duane's large, boho-style kitchen. The kitchen was the only room in the house that truly accentuated Duane's carefree personality. A cigar dangled from Duane's lips as he stood over the stove making scrambled eggs. He tossed some cut up bell-peppers into the scrambled eggs then continued stirring. Duane took a sip of his coffee then turned to Stan and Randy and casually said, "Hey, sometimes a coincidence is just a coincidence."

Randy and Stan sat across from each other at the kitchen table. They exchanged a look full of doubt just before they both took a sip from their coffee cup. A big picture window was about two feet above the dark green table, allowing for the fresh cut daisies to get plenty of sunlight. "If that's true, then that would make this event the biggest fucking coincidence in the history of the Upper Peninsula," Stan said.

"Less than twelve hours after Russ made the big announcement, the oldest country club in the Upper Peninsula mysteriously started on fire. Coincidence or not, it's only natural that people are going to spread rumors," Randy said.

"Coincidences are like assholes, everyone's got one and they stink," Duane said.

Stan and Randy exchanged a funny look before Stan glanced at Duane and said, "No, you mixed that one up, buddy. Excuses are like assholes."

Duane laughed and shook his head as he realized his mistake. "What a dope. I'm sorry guys, I was up way past my bedtime last night. Duane's a little tie-tie this morning."

Duane walked over to the table holding the frying pan. He scooped a pile of eggs with the spatula and dumped a portion on Randy's plate then Stan's plate. "I gotta tell ya, I'm having a hard time believing that it was arson. I mean, in this town, if you don't want anyone to know about it, you don't do it," Duane said before dumping the rest of the eggs onto his plate.

Randy and Stan both looked a bit more relaxed as they considered the possibility that it wasn't arson. Duane set the frying pan on the stove then put his cigar in the glass ashtray next to the bowl of apples. Finally, Duane sat down at the table across from Stan and started shoveling eggs into his mouth.

"Well, the clubhouse was built in the early twenties. I guess its plausible to think that it could've been an electrical fire," Randy said.

Duane looked across the table at Stan while he took a long sip from his coffee cup. Stan struggled to hide his growing discomfort. He turned his attention to the eggs on his plate and picked at them before finally shoving a forkful into his mouth. "Well, as likely as that scenario might be, there's a bigger issue that we haven't discussed yet," Duane said.

Randy regarded Duane and said, "What's that?"

Duane let out a long sigh as he leaned back in his chair. "Stan, you've said on more than one occasion that you'd like nothing more than to watch the country club burn to the ground."

With a mouthful of eggs Stan said, "Wait, you just said you don't think it was arson."

"I think it's unlikely that the fire was intentionally started, but it's easy to understand why most of the rumors flying around town are implicating you as the arsonist."

Duane and Randy both stared at Stan for an uncomfortable moment before he finally said, "For the tenth fucking time, I did not set the clubhouse on fire."

"That's a relief," Duane said.

"You guys have known me for a long time...you know I'm all talk."

Randy and Duane both nodded in agreement.

"My mother and her sisters were the first ones to try and get those assholes to change the name of the country club. That was back in the seventies. Obviously, we've tried for years to no avail, and I guess that might make us targets for now. But I would bet you anything that Houston is the one behind the rumors," Stan said.

"God, I hate Hubert Houston," Duane said with a mouth full of scrambled eggs.

"He's the absolute worst. I'd invite a rabid wolverine covered in shit into my home before I invited Hubert Houston," Stan said.

Randy took a sip of his coffee then glanced at Duane then Stan. "I read recently that there's been a number of suspicious fires at country clubs where declining membership threatened to bankrupt the club."

"Well, I know for a fact that the club was dying for new members," Duane said.

Stan's eyebrows raised as he looked at Duane. "How do you know that?"

"I had a summer fling with a member before I started dating Hal. Here's another fun fact, the country club doesn't pay any property taxes."

"Who were you banging?" Stan asked.

"He's a private equity hot shot from Milwaukee. No one you know."

Randy looked uneasy as he glanced at Duane. "Do you want to do something about that dagger in your pants?"

"Oh, sorry about that. I snorted a little too much Cialis last night. The dragon's gonna be up for awhile."

"Huh. I've never tried that before," Stan said as he casually sipped his coffee.

"Oh, you should. You'll feel like a cocksure race horse. Just be careful though, if you snort too much you'll probably have to seek medical treatment."

A befuddled expression appeared on Randy's face. "Can we get back to the issue at hand?"

Stan looked defensive. "None of us had anything to do with the fire, and if you hear any cocksuckers out there spreading rumors, you look them in the eye and threaten to sue their ass for slander."

"Hey, as a cocksucker, I take offense to that," said Duane.

Stan looked embarrassed. "Sorry, that was rude."

"I'm just kidding. I know how much you like using that word when you're pissed. So do I."

"Listen, emotions are already running high in this town, and until the accusations die down, I suggest you lay low, Stan. You should think about getting out of town for awhile. Take the family on a nice vacation for the rest of the month," Randy said.

"Are you on smack? This is my busy season, no way."

Hal Vaughn entered through the kitchen door holding a bag of groceries. "Morning," Hal said jovially.

Hal was taller than Duane and about ten years younger. Duane looked excited to see his boyfriend and the two embraced with a long kiss.

"Oh, I hate your cigar breath. Smells like a walrus's butthole in there."

"Hey, my old man and my grandfather smoked a cigar every Saturday morning. You should be thankful that I only smoke one on the first Saturday of the month."

"Yeah, I thank my lucky stars," Hal said in a mocking tone.

Randy gave Hal a friendly smile, "Hey, Hal."

"Morning, Randy."

As Hal locked eyes with Stan his smile quickly faded away.

"Hiya, Hal."

"Fucky you, Stan."

"Hal, we've been over this. Being gay doesn't give you the right to add a y to any word you want."

Hal grabbed a sausage link from the frying pan and tossed it at Stan, who caught the link with his left hand and took a bite. "Thank you."

Hal remained aggravated as he started to put away the groceries.

"Are you still mad at me for that joke I told at your birthday party?"

Hal shot a pissed off look at Stan. "Of course I am! It was offensive!"

"Your mom and sister laughed."

"Oh, they're both drunks, they'll laugh at anything."

Duane walked over to the coffee maker and filled up his mug.

"Well, for what it's worth, I'm sorry, Hal. It was a poorly timed joke, and if I wasn't highly inebriated I'm almost certain I wouldn't have told it at your birthday party."

Just as Duane was about to take a sip from his coffee mug, he looked through the window above the sink and froze in disbelief. His wide eyes continued looking out the window before he finally muttered, "Oh, shit."

A Whisper Dunes police suv had just pulled up and parked in Duane's driveway. Chief Ray O'Malley, who was sixty-two but looked like he could still bench press three hundred pounds, exited the driver side door. A few seconds later officer Dave Alcocks exited the passenger door. Officer Alcocks was thirty-five, fit, handsome, and walked with the confidence of a man who's lived his entire life on the same block. Officer Alcocks married his high school sweetheart and lived just a few houses down from his childhood home, where his mom still lived.

Both officers were in their navy blue uniforms and sporting aviator sunglasses. Officer Alcocks followed closely behind Chief O'Malley as they walked toward the narrow two-story house that needed a paint job and a new roof. They were walking so slowly, it was almost as if they weren't sure whether they were at the right house. O'Malley glanced at the lawn that was in desperate need of a mow. He removed his sunglasses, turned to Alcocks and said, "Are you sure this is the right house? I thought you said Duane's rich?"

"Oh, he's loaded. He just happens to be one of those unusual dudes who lives way below his means."

Duane stepped away from the window and started to breathe heavily. "O'Malley and Alcocks are walking toward my front door," Duane said.

"Oh, shoot! Should I hide the coke, sweetie?" Hal asked.

Duane thought for a fews seconds then looked at Hal. "Yeah, you better."

Hal sprinted down the basement stairs. Stan looked upset with Duane. "I thought you were drug free?"

"I am, two years this November, but I had like ninety grand worth of coke still hidden in shoeboxes when I finally gave up that nasty habit. I don't know about you, but I don't know anyone who's ever flushed ninety grand down the toilet."

Randy looked frustrated as he glared at Duane. "I'm pretty sure O'Malley didn't come here this morning to try and find the coke hidden in your shoeboxes."

"Yeah, you're probably right," Duane said before taking a long sip from his coffee mug.

"Guys, I don't know why they're here, but we have nothing to fear because we did nothing wrong," Stan said. "Except for Duane purchasing high quantities of cocaine. But if I may echo Randy, I'm almost certain O'Malley isn't here to make a coke bust."

Randy was sweating bullets and his nostrils flared with each deep breath. Stan was quick to notice Randy's nervous demeanor. "Randy, you okay?"

Randy wiped the sweat from his forehead before nodding. "Fine."

Stan didn't look like he believed Randy, neither did Duane. Stan finally said, "Anything you want to tell us before O'Malley and Alcocks come in here and start asking a bunch of questions?"

"Nope."

"Then why are you sweating like an aging bull fighter with a bad case of gout?" Duane asked.

"Because your spicy eggs and the strong coffee are starting to do a number on my stomach."

"I'm sorry, but Hal likes his eggs Cajun style. If you gotta use the toilet, I'd use it now before we get hauled off to the station. I don't know if you've ever used a jail toilet before, but I have. Lets just say, I'd rather take a bath with my eighty-year-old mother."

"Wait, why would they bring us to the station?" Stan asked in a nervous tone.

"I think we might be suspects," Duane said.

10

Stan sat slouched in the metal chair in the small interrogation room. Bored out of his mind, he stared at his fingers as they tapped slowly then quickly against the metal table. He'd been alone in the room for almost an hour and was desperate for a glass of water. The good news for Stan, he had plenty of time to think about exactly what he would say to O'Malley once he finally entered the room. Stan was thinking, even when you're sitting in a cold, windowless, police interrogation room, waiting to be grilled with tough questions, it's a good feeling knowing that you have nothing to hide. He was completely at ease, excited even for the line of questioning to start. As he stared at the white cinder block wall, Stan thought about how his dad would occasionally remind him the importance of handling each fucked up situation in life with integrity. A bad situation will always fade away, but a bad choice could haunt you for the rest of your life. Stan put his hands behind his head and took a relaxed breath. The relaxed feeling was suddenly upended with a new thought that immediately changed his demeanor.

Stan considered the possibility that O'Malley had questions for him that were not related to the fire. He looked uneasy as he stared at the ceiling. He started to run through a list of other potential reasons he was sitting in the police interrogation room. *Did the cops finally discover Fr. Carey and his brother's psilocybin mushroom farm?* For the past few years, Stan and Lisa had occasionally purchased mushroom capsules from Fr. Carey and his brother. Fr. Carey liked to remind his customers that he was no different than monks who brew their own beer to support themselves and their local communities. Monks have been brewing their own beer since the Middle Ages, and as far as Fr. Carey was concerned, he and his brother were following in the footsteps of the monks, and the community of Whisper Dunes was better off for it.

Growing more concerned, Stan rubbed his fingers through his hair as he considered the possibility that Chief O'Malley might ask him to wear a wire to help bring down Fr. Carey's magic mushroom business. Stan stared at the door to the interrogation room, which made him panic more. He closed his eyes and worked on his breathing in hopes of taming his nervous energy. He wiped the sweat beads from his forehead, took a few more deep breaths, and stared at the white walls of the room. The white walls took him back to the first and last time he was arrested. It was the night before his twenty-second birthday and he was on a date with Lisa. It was only their second date and the night was going well until they bumped into some of Stan's friends. They started doing shots and before he knew it, he and Lisa were hammered. Stan thought hard, but couldn't remember what the guy said to Lisa, but it upset her and Stan didn't hesitate to defend her. He hit the guy twice in the face and watched him fall backwards and land on the pool table. That was the last night Stan drank tequila, the last night he punched someone, and the last night he slept in a jail cell.

The door to the interrogation room finally opened and in walked officer Alcocks, who sat across from Stan without saying a word. Stan was visibly intimidated as Alcocks's cold eyes stared him down. Alcocks really seemed to be focused on perfecting his intimidating stare, so much so that Stan wondered if Alcocks would even notice if he walked out of the room.

Chief Ray O'Malley entered the interrogation room with a cup of coffee in his right hand and a yellow legal pad in his left hand. O'Malley gave Stan a friendly nod before sitting in the chair next to Alcocks. "Sorry about the wait, Stan."

"No, problem, Chief."

"Just got off the phone with the Fire Chief."

Alcocks looked annoyed to see Stan ease back in his chair, and casually lower his clasped hands onto his belly. To Stan's great relief, it was clear to him that O'Malley and Alcocks were only interested in talking to him about the fire.

"Albers confirmed with one hundred percent certainty that it was arson."

Stan feigned an upset look. "Boy, that really burns my ass," Stan said. "The last thing this town needs right now is a fucking arsonist on the loose."

Chief O'Malley regarded Stan for a good thirty seconds, thinking that Stan was hiding something. O'Malley had interrogated thousands of suspects in the past thirty years, and knew the key was to make the person bored, then you intimidate them before you get them to relax. "Coffee, Stan?" Chief O'Malley asked in a friendly tone.

"I'd love some coffee. Thank you."

Chief O'Malley gave officer Alcocks a look, which prompted him to quickly exit the interrogation room. Stan watched O'Malley lean forward in his chair and slowly lower his elbows on the metal table. Stan was looking at O'Malley, but the Chief's hard look made him uncomfortable so Stan started to move his eyes back and forth between O'Malley and the cinder block wall. O'Malley had perfected his tough stare back in Detroit. He was promoted to a homicide detective in the Detroit Police Department one month before his thirty-second birthday. After all those years on the job, O'Malley still relished being in the intensely uncomfortable environment of an interrogation room. He loved the challenge of getting the person sitting across from him to reveal something they didn't want to.

"I'm fully aware that before I took over as Chief, the Whisper Dunes Police Department had a reputation for letting well-known residents off the hook for committing all sorts of infractions."

"I'm sorry, Chief, but what kind of infractions are you referring to?"

O'Malley's eyes got wide as he gave Stan a serious look. "After I was sworn in as Chief, I decided to patrol at night for my first month on the job. First night, I bust a guy for drunk driving. I get to the driver's side window and see an open bottle of vodka in the cup holder. I told him that's illegal and he said, since when? Do you know who that guy was?"

"Fr. Carey?"

O'Malley took a few seconds before he said, "Yep. Now, I've learned to accept that folks up here just don't like to follow certain laws. I've become more tolerant of the drunk driving on the weekends, and the underground gambling rings, and the occasional bar brawl, but when someone sets fire to the oldest members-only country club in the Upper Peninsula...well, my friend, I can assure you that the man responsible for this crime will be sent to prison for a very long time."

Chief O'Malley kept his steely eyes fixed on Stan, who shifted uneasily in his chair. Alcocks re-entered the room holding a plastic cup of coffee and a bottle of powdered coffee creamer. He handed Stan the cup of coffee and the powdered creamer. Stan nodded and said, "Thank you, Officer Alcocks."

Alcocks sat back down and watched Stan pour way too much powdered creamer into his cup. "Can I get a mixing straw?"

"Nope," Alcocks said.

O'Malley and Alcocks looked amused watching Stan use his thumb to stir his coffee. "Listen, you guys know me, and you know that I would never do anything to screw up my real estate business, or embarrass my family. I don't know who did it, but I didn't start the fire. And if my lawyer was here, I'm sure that he would remind you both that I attempted to call 911 to report the fire, but I couldn't get a signal," Stan said.

"Statistics show that most arsonists have a habit of calling 911 to report a fire that they started," Alcocks said dryly.

"That is total bullshit, Alcocks! I was a criminal justice major before I dropped out of Northern, so don't waste your time trying to intimidate me with facts you cooked up while taking a bath."

"Before you dropped out of Northern?" Alcocks asked. "I thought you were kicked out for banging the daughter of one of your professors."

"That's not true. I dated his daughter for a few months before I started sleeping with his wife."

Chief O'Malley shook his head and gave Stan a disapproving look.

"I was nineteen and getting aggressively hit on by the hot mom of the hot girl I was dating, whose dad, slash husband happened to be the department chair of the criminal justice program. I was in a lose-lose situation. Professor Smith eventually found out and got me kicked out of Northern. What can I say? Not everyone's destined to graduate from college."

Stan stiffened in his seat. He no longer seemed intimidated by the hard looks he kept getting from O'Malley and Alcocks. A secretary entered the room and placed a can of Diet Barq's Root Beer in front of O'Malley and a can of 7up in front of Alcocks.

"Thank you, Mable," said O'Malley and Alcocks at the same time. Mable quickly left the room, shutting the heavy steel door behind her. Alcocks cracked open the can of 7up while keeping his eyes on Stan. O'Malley tried not to smile as both Stan and Alcocks remained committed to their pugnacious disposition.

Stan glanced at Alcocks and said with a grin, "Surprised you didn't ask for a straw. You look like a straw guy to me."

"Well, you look like an arsonist to me," Alcocks said.

"Stan, four months ago you appeared at the Town Council meeting and said, and I quote, country clubs are nothing more than a refuge for the one percent, and they should be burnt to the ground. End quote," Chief O'Malley said dryly.

Stan casually crossed his legs then took a long sip from his cup of coffee. "Listen Chief, I had a few drinks at the Iron Bay Tap Room before the meeting started, and I really don't remember saying that...but if you said I did, then I'm sorry. I certainly didn't mean that."

"Well, I guess somebody heard you, Stan, because more than half of the Potawatomi Country Club is now a smoking pile of ash," Alcocks said.

Stan looked at Alcocks before taking another sip from his coffee cup. "For years, people in this town, starting with my mother, have been trying to force the club to change their name. I know for a fact that the leadership committee at Potawatomi Country Club has gotten hundreds of letters over the years, threatening all sorts of things if they didn't change their name. I'd bet you my brand new Denali that at least some of those threats included burning down the clubhouse," Stan said.

"Rest assured, Stan, we will be pursuing all leads in this case, but right now we're focused on you and your pals, Duane and Randy," Chief O'Malley said.

"Before we brought you in for questioning, we did a little research and came across one nugget of information that really stood out," Alcocks said.

Stan rubbed the bridge of his nose while keeping his wide, dry, eyes on Alcocks.

"We discovered that your Occupy Wall Street chapter is still operating as a not-for-profit entity, despite the fact that particular movement flamed out over a decade ago," O'Malley said.

Stan blinked hard then rubbed his left eye as if he had an eyelash stuck in there. He conveyed a certain nervous, defensiveness, which caused him to speak quicker than he normally would. "Full disclosure, we closed up our chapter before the movement even ended," Stan said. "I was never interested in the idea of starting an Occupy Wall Street chapter, but a former Whisper Dunes resident, Brody Banks, convinced Duane to get behind the movement and before you knew it we were hosting Occupy Wall Street meetings in the basement at Breaker's once a month."

O'Malley said in a curious tone, "Why did you close up your chapter?"

"Because we were sick of taking orders from the domineering hipsters in New York. They were only interested in their ideas, so we broke away from the movement."

O'Malley and Alcocks exchanged a look that made Stan's hand shake a bit as he took a sip from his coffee cup. He quickly thought about other areas of his past that these two may have been looking into.

"According to the not-profit tax ID number connected to your Occupy Wall Street chapter, just last year you guys purchased an ATV, two snow mobiles, and a 1996 winnebago," Chief O'Malley said. "Interesting purchases for a supposedly defunct Occupy Wall Street chapter."

Stan closed his eyes, rubbed the bridge of his nose, and took a deep breath. He finally opened his eyes as he leaned back in his chair. "I don't have a good answer, Chief. Why don't you go back to asking me about the so-called arson fire?"

Alcocks leaned forward in his chair and cracked his knuckles. "Are you and your boys Walter White-ing it in your Winnebago?"

Stan, clearly confused, squinted his eyes as he crossed his arms. "What the hell does that mean?"

"Are you not familiar with the television show, *Breaking Bad*?" Alcocks asked.

"I only watch sit-coms, and erotic thrillers."

"Stan, are you cooking meth in your Winnebago?"

"No! What kind of fucking question is that? I'm a successful realtor and property owner, why would I sell drugs? Wait, is that what the show's about—cooking meth in a Winnebago?"

"Yeah, pretty much," Alcocks said. "Great show."

"So, you admit that your Occupy Wall Street chapter is still active," O'Malley said.

"No, I don't admit that. We're not an active Occupy Wall Street chapter, but it was a real headache to do all the paperwork to legally dissolve our chapter, so we decided to transition into a community social club. Think of us as a local Boys & Girls club for adults."

Alcocks laughed as he shook his head in disbelief. Chief O'Malley looked at Stan with suspicious eyes, which only increased Stan's defensive mindset.

"We've made a commitment to volunteer our time and treasure in order to give back to the town we love so dearly. So far this year, members of our group have completed over 200 community service hours."

"Court ordered?" O'Malley asked dryly.

Stan actually looked offended as he regarded O'Malley. With a nervous energy in his voice, Stan said, "We rebuilt the stairs at a popular public beach, we donated new basketball hoops with glass backboards to the park district, and we paid for the repairs to the church bell tower. We're also organizing a half-marathon this October to raise money for the Humane Society. Oh, and we wrote the first check to support the Stop the Rocket campaign."

Alcocks and O'Malley pretended to look impressed. Alcocks let out a long whistle right before O'Malley said, "Well, you had me fooled? Based on the paper trail your little not-for-profit entity left behind, I thought you guys were just using your Occupy Wall Street chapter slash Boys Club to hide your illegal profits from gambling, and God knows what else."

"Do I need a lawyer?" Stan asked. He started to consider the possibility that he might be spending the night in jail.

O'Malley leaned toward Alcocks and whispered into his ear.

"Why does your not-for-profit entity own a condo in Myrtle Beach?" Alcocks asked with a judgmental grin.

"Our accountant advised us on that purchase," Stan said as he casually wiped away the beads of sweat on his forehead.

"Relax, Stan. I have no problem with your cute little scheme to avoid paying taxes. I'm not an IRS agent. I'm the Chief of Police of a peaceful community that was just named America's Best Place to Live. But if I find out that you set fire to the country club, then, brother...you are going down," O'Malley said in a measured tone.

"I did not set fire to the country club! Check the fucking surveillance cameras!"

Alcocks and O'Malley exchanged an uncomfortable look.

"The Potawatomi Country Club has no surveillance cameras on the property. All members are expected to abide by some bullshit, prep school honor code," Alcocks said.

Stan was clearly disappointed as he shook his head. "Since the beginning of time, wealthy, powerful people have tried to convince everyone that wealth is synonymous with ethics and honor. Trust us, while we find someone to blame who can't afford a good lawyer."

Chief O'Malley grinned, his way of letting Stan know that he agreed with him.

"Were you aware that Duane stole a can of gasoline from the basement of the firehouse yesterday morning?" Alcocks asked.

Overcome with surprise and fear, Stan slowly tilted his head to the right as beads of sweat, once again, covered his forehead. "I really think it would be best if I had a lawyer present," Stan said.

Duane was escorted into the interrogation room by a young officer. The Cialis was clearly still in his system because his erection had not subsided one bit. O'Malley and Alcocks both did double takes of Duane's erection as he slowly walked toward the chair and sat across from them. Bewildered, O'Malley glanced at Alcocks then shook his head as he regarded Duane. "Well, this is a first. I guess we can start by addressing the six-inch lizard in the room," O'Malley said.

Duane looked deeply offended. He leaned forward and squinted his eyes as he stared at O'Malley. "The fuck you say? It's eight and a half inches. If you don't believe me, Chief, go fetch a ruler!"

O'Malley and Alcocks both looked dumbfounded. They exchanged a glance. Both were unsure about how to proceed. O'Malley leaned back in his chair, folded his arms and said, "Duane, you've had an erection since we picked you up. Why?"

"I snorted a little too much Cialis last night. I tried hard to avoid performance enhancing drugs for as long as I could, but I'm not a young player anymore," Duane said with no hint of embarrassment.

Alcocks looked at Duane like he didn't believe a word that had come out of his mouth so far. "Eight and a half inches my ass," Alcocks said as he shook his head.

Duane popped up out of his seat and started to unbuckle his belt. In a panic, Alcocks pulled out his gun from the holster and pointed it at Duane. "Don't you fucking do it, Duane! Don't you do it! I swear to Christ I'll blow it off!" Alcocks screamed.

Chief O'Malley got between them and forced Alcocks to put his gun away.

Duane yelled, "Get a fucking ruler!"

"Control yourself, Alcocks! Jesus, man. Duane, buckle up and sit your ass down!"

Duane and Alcocks were both breathing heavily as they finally sat back down.

"You guys usher me away from my home while I was having a lovely breakfast with my lover and my two close friends, and drag me into this cinder block closet and insult me. Is this how you did things in Detroit, O'Malley?" Duane asked.

O'Malley decided not to respond. Instead, he began to walk slowly around the room with his hands behind his back. "Roughly fourteen hours before somebody set fire to the Potawatomi clubhouse, you stole a large can of gasoline from the basement of the firehouse," O'Malley said.

Duane folded his arms tightly and stared at the wall in an effort to hide the fact that he had suddenly become nervous.

"Duane, any reason you stole enough gasoline from the basement of the firehouse to burn down a large structure...like the Potawatomi clubhouse?" O'Malley asked.

"Listen, there are a lot of rumors flying around town right now. Personally, I think you guys should be looking deeper into that story about Larry Sullivan and Mark Pollard."

"What about them?" Alcocks asked

"Apparently, after there round of golf on the 4th of July, they got shitfaced and eventually got kicked out of the clubhouse bar. Later in the evening, multiple guys saw them in the locker room at the club, trying to light their farts on fire with a hundred-dollar lighter," Duane said with a straight face.

O'Malley didn't take the bait, but Alcocks allowed himself to crack a smile.

"Duane..." O'Malley said.

"How rude can you be?"

O'Malley and Alcocks exchanged a confused look before they focused their eyes back on Duane. "You invite me in here for questioning and you don't even think to offer me a cup of coffee, or a cigarette? What did I do to be treated with such disrespect? I've lived in this town for twenty-eight fucking years. I donate every year to local charities, pay my property taxes on time, and even though I can afford to live almost anywhere, I continue to call Whisper Dunes home."

Chief O'Malley glanced at Alcocks, who reluctantly stood up and exited the room. "Cream, no sugar, and I'll smoke whatever you got," Duane said.

Duane and O'Malley stared uncomfortably at each other for what seemed like a minute. "Okay, O'Malley, I'll answer your question. I recently donated a 65-inch tv to the firehouse, and I stopped over yesterday morning to make sure it was working properly. I also dropped off four-dozen donuts from Babycakes. As I chatted with the guys for a few minutes I happened to ask Chris if I could borrow some gasoline for my generator, which I was bringing over to Stan's party later that day," Duane said calmly.

"Why did you bring a generator to Stan's party?"

"To power the amps, man. Stan hired an incredible John Mellencamp cover band."

O'Malley wrote down some notes on his yellow legal pad. Duane tried to read what O'Malley was writing but gave up after a few seconds. He started to tap his fingers on the metal table, but stopped once O'Malley locked eyes with him. "Where do you have Stan and Randy holed up?"

"That's none of your business."

Duane looked uneasy as his eyes darted around the room before they landed back on O'Malley. "I get it. You're playing hard ball with me, while Alcocks tries to dulcify Randy and Stan in hopes they get a bad case of diarrhea of the mouth. But let me warn you, Randy is about as interesting as listening to four guys talk about golf, just after they finished playing golf. But he's a steel trap. The only thing you're going to hear from him is how much he loves his wife and two daughters."

O'Malley showed no emotion as Duane reached down to his crotch area and made a few adjustments. "As for Stan, he's one of the most successful realtors in the Upper Peninsula for a reason. He'll tell you exactly what you want to hear, even though it's total bullshit."

Randy looked uneasy, almost frightened, as he sat across from officer Alcocks in a makeshift interrogation room in the basement of the police department. "Ask my wife, we don't even own a grill because I'm so terrified of fires," Randy said.

"You were born and raised in Canada, is that correct?" Alcocks asked in a suspicious tone.

Randy's nose made a snorting sound as he sat up straight in his chair. "I'm a proud dual citizen of Canada and the United States. I love both countries with everything I've got."

Alcocks' suspicious eyes narrowed as he stared down Randy. "Let's say your wife was kidnapped, and the only way to guarantee her release is to burn a flag. You have a choice, you can burn an American flag or a Canadian flag...which one you choosing?"

Randy looked at Alcocks like he was the dumbest person in the world. "I'm a fucking lawyer, Alcocks. I know not to answer hypothetical questions, ever."

"Did Stan ever discuss with you his plans for burning down the country club?"

"No, because he didn't have plans to burn down the country club. He made those comments about burning down the country club when he was drunk and agitated. Like myself and Duane, Stan had nothing to do with the clubhouse fire."

Alcocks stared at Randy with his signature cold look for nearly thirty seconds before he said, "Where were you last night between midnight and four a.m.?"

Randy casually reached for his coffee cup and took a sip in hopes of conveying a sense of calmness. "In my home, sleeping."

"I see. I assume your wife can corroborate that statement?"

Randy took another sip of coffee before he nervously licked his lips. His eyes finally settled on Alcocks' gaze. "Apparently, I snore like a grizzly bear so we sleep in separate bedrooms."

Alcocks nodded before writing down some notes on his pocket notebook.

Duane remained calm and defiant as he sat across from O'Malley. "Are you sure, Chief? Happy to do it," Duane said.

"You can't order pizzas for the entire department, Duane."

"Oh, I forgot it was a crime in Whisper Dunes to be nice."

Alcocks entered the interrogation room holding a cup of coffee. He set the coffee in front of Duane and took a seat next to O'Malley. Duane looked pissed off as he glanced at the coffee. "There's no cream in here," Duane said. "And where're my smokes?"

"Duane, I have an eye witness who claims you groped the breasts of four different women at Stan's 4th of July party," Alcocks said.

Duane looked incredulous as he squinted his eyes and leaned forward in his chair. "It's called dirty dancing. They made a movie about it," Duane said. He looked uneasy as O'Malley and Alcocks continued to stare at him. "I'm a gay man! That's like arresting two heterosexual men for exchanging fist bumps. It's ludicrous! Why don't you be useful, Alcocks, and get me some fucking creamer?"

O'Malley rubbed his forehead in frustration while Alcocks wrote down a few notes in his pocket notebook. "After your Occupy Wall Street chapter flamed out, you guys kept your not-for-profit status but decided to turn your Occupy Wall Street chapter into a social club. Is that correct?" O'Malley asked.

"That's correct."

"Whose idea was that?" Alcocks asked.

"Listen, we're just a harmless social club. We meet once a week to drink some beers, shoot the shit, and exchange information on the games we plan on betting that week."

"So, it's essentially a gambling ring?" Alcocks asked.

"I'm not answering that question."

"Who would you say is the leader of the group?" O'Malley asked.

Duane hesitated before he finally said, "Stan."

"Stan said that your main purpose is to do volunteer work and raise money for community based projects," O'Malley said.

Duane was clearly caught off guard. "Oh yeah, we do a shit load of volunteer work."

"Stan also said that you guys have been financing the Stop The Rocket campaign," O'Malley said.

"Yep. That's been are main focus for the past year. I think I speak for every resident of the U.P. when I say, I don't want to see rockets shitting debris and pissing fuel into Lake Superior."

"Just for the record, your Occupy Wall Street chapter, which ruffled some feathers around town back in the day, is no longer in operation. Is that correct?" Alcocks asked.

"That's correct, and while I'm making statements for the record I've only been to New York City once and I was nowhere near Wall Street."

Duane sipped his coffee and immediately stuck out his tongue in disgust. "Jesus Christ, this is the worst cup of coffee I've ever tasted. I want some fucking creamer, right, fucking, now," Duane said.

O'Malley and Alcocks both looked befuddled as they stared at Stan with their mouths agape. "You were playing golf at midnight?" O'Malley asked.

"That's right. We teed off around eleven and wrapped up around two. Seven people can verify my alibi."

"How can you play golf at night?" Alcocks asked.

"Glow-in-the-dark golf balls. It's a blast. You should try it."

"I don't golf," Alcocks said. "I'm a cop, not a real estate broker."

O'Malley glanced at Alcocks then Stan and quietly said, "I golf."

"Really, since when?"

"I started about two years ago. I usually just hack it up at the driving range."

Alcocks looked surprise as he regarded O'Malley, who was staring closely at the bruise on Stan's forearm.

"Pretty nasty bruise you got there. How'd you get it?"

"I was sitting in the back of the cart when Matt drove too close to a ball washer pole. My forearm hit it square."

Looking uneasy, Stan licked his lips a few times, sensing that neither Alcocks or O'Malley believed him.

Alcocks flashed another frosty look at Stan. "Are you a member of the Potawatomi Country Club, Stan?"

"No, no I'm not. I refuse to become a member until the club changes its name. But I've been sneaking onto that course since I was thirteen. Why stop now?"

"After you finished golfing, did you go anywhere near the clubhouse?" Alcocks asked.

"No. We started the round on the third hole and ended on thirteen. Just like we always do."

"Were you or any of the golfers sober?" O'Malley asked.

Stan thought to himself for a moment. "I don't know if he was legally sober, but Bob was in pretty good shape."

Alcocks wrote down some more notes while O'Malley kept his eyes on Stan.

"If my rock solid alibi isn't enough, then go get a cue tip and I'll give you my DNA. I have absolutely nothing to hide. I have a showing at one so we need to wrap this up. Big client, can't be late."

Duane looked calmer now as he took a long drag from his cigarette. A large bottle of powdered creamer was next to his empty coffee cup.

"Where were you between midnight and 4 a.m.?" O'Malley asked.

Duane took another long drag before flicking the ash into his coffee cup. "I was bent over a riding mower in Eileen Nolan's garage," Duane said in a casual tone.

Neither O'Malley or Alcocks could hide their uncomfortable look. "You were having intercourse?" Alcocks asked.

"Is that what you and your wife call it?"

"Watch it."

"Yes, we were intercoursing."

"For four hours?" O'Malley asked.

"No, God, no. I'm pushing fifty, got a bum knee, and I'm a recovering coke head. I get light headed after about twenty minutes of doing the polka dance. I don't know what time it was exactly, but Eileen Nolan happened to walk in on us, so we wrapped things up and joined Eileen, Frank, Ron, and Betsy in the hot tub. We ended up walking home around two, two-thirty.."

Duane watched as O'Malley wrote more notes on his legal pad. "I don't know if this helps guys, but on the walk home Hal and I were almost ran over by a big black truck. I don't know my cars, but Hal's a real gear head and he swears it was a newer model Chevy Tahoe," Duane said.

O'Malley's wide eyed gaze met Alcocks's flabbergasted look.

"Did you or Hal get a look at the license plate?" O'Malley asked.

"No."

"What about the driver?" O'Malley continued, "Did you get a look?"

"Afraid not. The windows were tinted."

11

Russ sat behind his office desk with a big smile on his face. The receiver to his desk phone was pressed to his ear as he rocked slowly in his chair. The smile was still on his face when Carol entered the office. "We're low on xerox paper, toilet paper, and coffee creamer. I'm gonna make a run to the market," Carol said.

Russ put his hand over the phone speaker and said, "Don't forget to put the change back in the petty cash drawer."

Carol nodded and gave Russ a thumbs up before she exited his office.

Russ removed his hand from the phone speaker and said, "Thank you. That's just wonderful news. Absolutely incredible. This will be such a huge thrill, not just for the folks who live in Whisper Dunes, but for everyone who's lucky enough to live in the U.P. And I'd just like to mention, I have been a huge fan of *Good Morning America* since the Joan Lunden, Dave Hartman era."

Russ leaned forward in his chair and wrote down some notes on his yellow legal pad. He then dropped the pen on the legal pad, leaned back in his chair, and said, "Oh, mark my words, we'll be camera ready. I can guarantee that. When the *GMA* bus rolls into Whisper Dunes, we'll be ready to impress the velcro-strapped sandals off of every one of your viewers," Russ said with a certain confidence he wasn't used to conveying. "And just to put you at ease, we've got some experience hosting V.V.I.P.'s. Well, there's V.I.P.'s and there's V.V.I.P.'s. We've hosted both here in Whisper Dunes."

It was a chilly summer night and a light breeze was flowing through the screened door that led to the Zbikowski kitchen. It was getting too chilly for Lisa so she shut the door before walking over to the kitchen island. Near the edge of the marble countertop was a bottle of Pinot Grigio. Lisa uncorked the chilled bottle then moved over to the kitchen table and sat across from her friendly neighbor, Deacon Terry Lutterbach. Two wine glasses were already on the table and Terry filled them both up.

"You know, I've been a Deacon for almost eight years now and I've counseled many different couples, which is to say I know when a married couple has a real shot at saving their marriage, and sadly, I know when divorce is inevitable."

"Stan and I aren't looking to go to couples therapy. We tried it a few times and it was a disaster."

"Fair enough, but you deserve to be happy, Lisa, and from what you've told me it seems clear that your husband has lost his way. I think it's entirely possible that he's no longer interested in meeting your needs. And that's a problem."

At first, Lisa looked like she agreed with Terry, but then suddenly became defensive. "Terry, I am not comfortable with you criticizing my husband, or discussing our relationship. Stan has his flaws, and I have mine."

Terry gave Lisa a respectful nod then sipped his wine. "I'm sorry. Listen, I'm not perfect either, but what does separate me from most men is that I don't hide from my mistakes, or my true feelings. I'm a man of conviction and action."

A very uncomfortable look appeared on Lisa's face as Terry eyed her while taking a long sip of wine. He slowly crossed his legs and Lisa's comfort level plummeted as she spotted a small gun strapped to Terry's ankle.

"Jesus Christ, Terry, why do you have a gun strapped to your ankle?"

Terry actually looked offended as he regarded Lisa. "Please, don't take the Lord's name in vain."

"Why is there a fucking gun strapped to your ankle?"

"Just exercising my second amendment right, Lisa. It's our God given right to bear arms. I never leave home without at least one weapon on me."

"I hate guns. You can't be in my house with a gun on you."

"Have you ever touched a gun before?"

"No."

Terry flashed a smooth look full of cockiness that Lisa had never seen before.

"Do you want to touch mine?"

Lisa and Terry both looked startled as the back door suddenly opened. Stan entered and immediately became overwhelmed with rage at the sight of his wife sitting across from Deacon Terry. But before Stan could get a word out, Lisa stood up and warmly greeted her husband with a passionate hug. "Oh my God, Stan. Where were you? I've been trying to call you for the past six hours."

"Hey, Stan. Glad to see you're okay. I was praying for you."

"What the fuck are you doing in my house, Terry?"

Both Lisa and Terry were clearly unnerved. So much so that Stan thought they looked like they were hiding something.

"For Christ's sake, Stan, he's a Deacon!"

Terry's bottom lip started to quiver. He was clearly offended that Lisa had yet again taken the Lord's name in vain. Terry composed himself, stood up, and politely nodded at Lisa. "Thanks for the excellent Pinot Grigio, Lisa. Really appreciate your design ideas for my basement. Good night to you both," Terry said.

Terry hustled out the door as Stan gave him a hard look. "Good night, Terry," Lisa said.

"Go fuck yourself, Terry," Stan said.

Stan slammed the door and turned the bolt lock. As he turned around, Lisa stood up and got right in his face. "Why are you so upset with Deacon Terry?"

"Because he's a professional womanizer."

"What!?"

"I did a little research on are friendly neighbor, Deacon Terry. After he sold his dating app—*Lets Grab Coffee and Flirt*—for big bucks, he moved out of Grand Rapids and became a Deacon. Why? So he can manipulate naive and vulnerable women into becoming fuck buddies."

Lisa looked overcome with emotion. She grabbed her wine glass from the table and finished off the wine before regarding Stan. "Where have you been? I was really worried."

"I was down at the police station for the past eight hours."

Lisa's eyes got wide as she looked at Stan in shock. "Oh, my God. Why?"

"Chief O'Malley had a few questions for me regarding the fire at the country club."

"Does he think you actually started the fire?"

"He kind of did, until my alibi checked out. I'm all cleared. They even apologized for wasting my whole fucking day."

Lisa pressed her lips together as she quickly became emotional. She looked like she might cry, but she closed her eyes, took a few deep breaths and was able to stave off the tears. Stan's back was to her as he searched the fridge for a can of beer. By the time he got his beer and turned toward Lisa, her emotions had calmed a bit. Lisa was looking right at Stan as he leaned his butt against the counter and cracked the beer open. She noticed how tired he looked as he sipped his beer.

"I've been sick to my stomach all day. I called you fifty times. Nobody at the office knew where you were. Then I went snooping in your office and found a check made out to cash for twenty grand."

Stan looked embarrassed. He had trouble meeting Lisa's gaze until his embarrassed look was replaced with a defensive look. "Oh, so every time I can't find you that gives me permission to snoop around your closet?"

Lisa took a step closer toward Stan and softly said, "I was really worried about you."

"I'm sorry, Lisa, but I had no idea I was going to spend my entire day answering questions at the police station."

"I found another check made out for twelve grand. I honestly thought you were lying in a ditch with your legs broken."

"I owe money to Duane, not a mafia loan shark. Do you honestly think Duane would break my legs? He's one of my best friends!"

"Stan, gambling is a sickness and you need help."

"No, it's a leisure activity. Like racquetball or woodworking."

"I want you to see someone."

"You first."

"I'm serious, Stan. Your gambling could lead us to financial ruin if you don't quit soon."

"That is total bullshit! I'm the number one realtor in the U.P. and if I want to blow off some steam by gambling my walking around money, that's my decision. Last year, I was up around sixty g's for the year, and this year I was up almost eighty g's before I hit a bad string of luck."

Lisa let out a frustrated sigh then closed her eyes for a moment. Stan couldn't help but notice that Lisa looked like she was saying a quick prayer. Long before they got married, Lisa knew that Stan was going to be hard to tame. But to his credit he had made an effort, on occasion, to change his ways. What made it easy for Lisa to forgive Stan, even when he wasn't seeking forgiveness, was the fact that he was a good dad and had a kind heart. He rarely spoke about it, but Lisa knew that Stan would often volunteer at living communities for people with special needs. Stan didn't just volunteer, he became friends with the residents. He would take them out for lunch on their birthday, he would take them to concerts, and even though he was a Bears fan, Stan once rented a skybox at Lambeau Field and took a big group of his friends to watch the Packers home opener. As her prayer ended, Lisa reminded herself once again that she was going to stay with this man for the rest of her life.

"Please, listen carefully. I don't ever want to see that scumbag in our house again. Understand?"

Lisa took another step toward Stan and leaned her face a few inches from his. "Don't you dare talk to me like I'm your girlfriend. Understand?"

"Well, you show me some God damn respect and stay away from Deacon Terry. I don't ask for much, Lisa. I can't even remember the last time I asked for a blowjob."

"Two days ago."

Looking worn out and frustrated, Stan closed his eyes and sighed. "I've had a long day, and I don't want to go to bed angry. Marriage rule, number one."

"That's not marriage rule number one."

"Well, it should be."

"Imagine how wonderful our relationship would be if you followed all the other marriage rules?"

Dejected, Stan watched Lisa fill up her wine glass and hurry out of the kitchen. He was about to follow her, but decided to stay put as soon as he heard his phone ring. Stan pulled the phone out from his front pocket and saw **Mayor Russ** on the caller ID.

Stan and Russ were seated in handmade Windsor rocking chairs on the front porch of Russ's two-story log cabin.

The eighty-year-old cabin was built on a ridge deep in the forest. Stan and Russ both had their eyes focused on the clear black sky that shimmered with stars. It was an incredible sight they had been admiring since they were youngsters. No one from the U.P. even tries to describe what the sky looks like on a clear night when the moon and the stars fill the sky over the Upper Peninsula. There are no words to describe it, but *Yoopers* are not shy about telling their friends, who don't live up here, that they'll never forget a night of stargazing in the U.P.

Stan's eyes remained locked on the sky as he reached for his glass of bourbon and took a sip. A shotgun and a bottle of bourbon were on the wooden table between Russ and Stan. Realizing his glass was empty, Stan finally took his eyes off the sky in order to carefully pour some bourbon into his empty glass. He then filled up Russ's glass half way.

"I guess it shouldn't be a surprise, but not everyone is excited about our town being named, America's Best Place to Live," Russ said.

Stan slowly sipped his bourbon as he stared blankly at the sky. He finally said, "I don't know many people in this town who embrace radical change, or any change for that matter."

Russ had a sheepish look on his face. "I went fishing this afternoon...when I got back to my truck the windows were smashed, and on the front seat was a note wrapped around a fish."

Stan did not hide his concern as he regarded Russ. He shook his head slowly to try and convey some sympathy. "What kind of fish?"

"A brook trout."

"What did the note say?"

"A lot of swear words mixed in with a warning that if I don't tell *Forbes* to pick another town, I won't live long enough to defend my South Shore Spring Shootout fishing title."

"Jesus," Stan said. He looked dazed as he stared at the glass of bourbon in his hand. He took a deep breath and exhaled loudly. Stan and Russ both sipped from their glass of bourbon at the same time while they continued rocking slowly in their chairs. Stan focused his attention back on the sky and found the Big Dipper while Russ stared straight ahead at the thick forest. After he took another sip from his glass of bourbon, Stan looked perturbed and suddenly stopped rocking. He glanced at Russ, whose faraway look indicated he was thinking about something.

"That's strange," Stan said. "Why not select a more intimidating fish? Like a northern pike, or a walleye."

"I was thinking the same thing."

Stan and Russ continued rocking in their chairs for a quiet minute or two. The awesome views usually helped both of them do some deep thinking, but not tonight. They were both thinking, but struggling to figure out a plan for the best way forward. It was clear that major changes were coming to Whisper Dunes, like population increase, which would require intelligent city planning. But there were also many unknown factors that the town would eventually have to deal with, and this made Russ very nervous. The deep thinking allowed Russ to finally understand the purpose of public-relation firms and consulting firms. He realized that these firms allowed you to escape accountability for tough decisions you had to make in a moment of uncertainty and chaos. As he continued to rock slowly in his chair, Russ was quick to remind himself, under no circumstances would he use taxpayer money to retain the services of a P.R. or consulting firm. Even if it was crystal clear that one of these types of firms could help him get re-elected mayor.

Stan stopped rocking in his chair and finished the rest of his bourbon. "It might be awhile before we find out who started the fire, but it's an isolated crime that will soon be forgotten. You just can't allow yourself to get sucked into all the drama surrounding the event."

Russ sipped his bourbon slowly while looking at the stars. He finally turned to Stan and said, "Someone has already gone to the extreme to embarrass our town. I'd be lying if I said I'm not afraid of what they plan on doing next."

"Russ, you've always handled tricky situations with a steady hand and a great deal of integrity. That's why you've been elected mayor four times. But now you're the mayor of America's Best Place to Live, and some people are hoping that you fail. Nobody loves a fall from grace story like the media. They just need a little dirt. Once they get it...they'll go to great lengths to manufacture a shitstorm," Stan said.

Russ nodded and quietly said, "That's what I'm most worried about."

"This is an incredible moment in our town's history. But most folks around here aren't going to be quick to embrace the major changes that are coming. Remember when my investment group tried to open a Hooters? I woke up to silicone boobs on my lawn for a month."

Russ sighed as he watched Stan pour a little more bourbon into his glass. "I actually received death threats, signed by people I know," Stan said before taking a sip.

"I was already feeling a great deal of pressure with the upcoming zoning board vote, but I know the pressure of the job will only get worse once the national media comes to town."

Stan regarded Russ for a moment then said, "I think it would be a good idea to delay the vote until after Labor Day."

"The zoning commission has already rescheduled the vote four times. It's time for them to make a decision."

Russ picked up his glass of bourbon, but before it reached his lips, the glass slipped out of his hand as he nervously reacted to the sound of something moving quickly through the forest. The glass shattered on the porch floor a second before Russ grabbed the shotgun off the table. He stood up and aimed his weapon at another mysterious sound coming from nearby.

"Relax, it's just a wolf pack."

Stan watched Russ slowly lower the shotgun. With his eyes still focused on the forest, Russ eased back into his rocking chair. He placed the shotgun on his lap and started slowly rocking.

"You've lived in this town your whole life, Russ. You know enough not to take threats from a few pissed off people, seriously. You have to face facts. Some folks in this town are upset and there's nothing you can do about that, but most of the folks in Whisper Dunes are just a little uneasy about the future. It's your job now to keep them informed with any and all changes coming until they stop fearing the future."

"I've always been sympathetic to every concern vented my way, and that's not going to change. But whether they like it or not, the folks of Whisper Dunes are going to have to embrace change...starting next Friday."

"What's happening next Friday?"

Russ took a swig of bourbon right from the bottle. "*Good Morning America* is coming to Whisper Dunes," Russ said.

Stan was clearly surprised to hear this. He stopped rocking in his chair and looked at Russ. "Wow, *GMA*...Really?"

Russ was getting excited thinking about it, but tried his best to keep a blank expression on his face. "They want me to give a walking tour of the town while someone interviews me."

"Look at you. That's great, Russ."

"I'm already nervous sick about it. I hate talking on camera."

"Come on, you'll knock it out of the park."

Russ looked sick to his stomach as he thought about what it would be like standing in front of the *GMA* cameras and the bright lights while trying not to flub his response to a straight forward question.

"But let me give you some advice. Order all bars to close that day, and tell the *GMA* producers ahead of time that you won't answer any questions pertaining to the proposed spaceport, or the Stop the Rocket campaign...or any questions about the country club fire."

Russ looked at Stan and nodded in agreement before taking another sip from the bottle of bourbon. "It's strange," Russ said softly.

"What's that?"

"Climate change is the reason Whisper Dunes was named America's Best Place to Live, and it's the reason for the changes coming our way...yet it's still hard to imagine anything in this town ever changing," Russ said.

Stan ruminated on the mayor's words for a minute.

"Change can be hard. Lisa has been trying to get me to quit gambling since before we were married. I want to quit, but just can't seem to do it."

"Both of my wives tried to get me to quit fishing, but we know how that turned out."

Stan regarded Russ who was staring at the enormous blue spruce at the edge of the forest. "My dad liked to say, Whisper Dunes is the place where time stands still," Stan said.

Russ's gaze finally met Stan's. "My dad liked to say the same thing."

12

Randy and Duane sat across from each other in Randy's screened in porch, which was attached to the back of the house. It was a sunny but chilly morning, and Duane and Randy were both wearing fleece jackets. On the left breast of Duane's navy blue fleece jacket it read: Bellini's Pizza in red cursive.

Randy looked like he hadn't slept in a few days. He slowly sipped his coffee while staring through the screened porch with a faraway look.

Duane removed the long celery from his glass so he could take a sip from his Bloody Mary. Duane was relaxed and trying to stay upbeat for his friend's sake. Duane regarded Randy and saw a face full disbelief, as if he couldn't understand how he got into this situation. Not unlike a guy sitting all alone in the back of paddy wagon on a Friday night.

"What about your nosey neighbor? Mrs. Duncan had to have seen you get home," Duane said.

Randy's eyes were glazed over as he slowly shook his head. "She was out of town."

Duane grabbed the celery salt from the coffee table and added some to his Bloody Mary while he thought about other options that might help Randy with his alibi problem. Duane looked frustrated as he took a sip from Bloody Mary. "Shit, man. Without at least a hint of an alibi, people are going to keep spreading bullshit rumors about you."

Randy rubbed his forehead then closed his eyes. After a few seconds he opened his eyes to find Duane staring at him. Randy leaned back in his chair, exhaled loudly and said, "Why would anyone think that I'm an arsonist? I'm a lawyer for God's sake."

"Guilt by association. Once Houston knew he couldn't blame Stan he went after us, Stan's best friends. If I didn't have a rock hard alibi I'd be in the same boat with you, buddy."

"I was sleeping in my bedroom. The only thing I'm guilty of is that I don't share a bed with my wife."

Randy chugged down the rest of his coffee while Duane walked over to the drink cart and poured more vodka into his glass. Duane then added a little more Bloody Mary mix to his drink before sitting back down on the wicker chair. "Listen, I know it's none of my bees wax, but why do you and Vivian sleep in separate rooms?"

"She likes to watch television before bed and I like to read."

"That's a good reason."

"We've been sleeping that way for a few years now."

"Do you guys still fuck?"

"Oh, sure. At least once a week. Usually in my bed."

Duane sipped his Bloody Mary then said, "Well, if for some reason you're charged with arson, I will shell out whatever it takes to make sure you have an above average defense attorney."

"I've been an attorney for twenty years, Duane. I know a couple of good defense attorneys who would be happy to defend me pro-bono."

"Well, in case they decide to charge you, I'll take care of the bill."

Randy looked pleasantly surprised. "Really?"

"I own twenty-eight Bellini Pizza locations. I'm loaded."

"I thought you just had the two locations."

"I used my bookmaking profits to expand rapidly in the last four years in the event of the next recession. A great pizza joint is recession proof, baby."

"You've been driving the same car and living in the same small house since I've known you. What the hell do you spend all your money on?"

Duane sipped his Bloody Mary then said, "Mostly super PACS, environmental causes, homeless shelters for humans and dogs, oh, I also provide gap financing to several start-up cannabis companies. But at the end of the day, I live well below my means. Occasionally, I like to treat myself to an all-inclusive vacation, usually to Costa Rica."

"Look alive!" Stan shouted from seemingly out of nowhere. Startled, Duane tipped back in the wicker chair and spilled his Bloody Mary all over his fleece jacket. "Jesus Christ, Stan!" Randy shouted. "You scared the shit out of us."

"Sorry. I'm just so jacked up. The *Good Morning America* bus was just spotted passing the Cedar Motor Inn. They'll be here in twenty minutes. It's showtime, boys!"

Duane picked himself back up off the ground. He had a smile on his face as he looked at Randy then Stan. "This is so fucking exciting. God, what if they want to interview me?"

"They might. In that case, you better change," Stan said.

Duane unzipped his fleece, revealing a Bellini's Pizza t-shirt. "Lets go!" He tossed his fleece on the chair and hurried out of the screened in porch.

The *Good Morning America* bus cruised along Michigan State Road 28 at about twenty miles above the posted 55 m.p.h. speed limit. The wide open four-lane highway was lined with trees, mostly evergreens, and this section of the road was virtually empty of cars. The bus passed a group of ten cyclists just before passing a billboard. The billboard featured an add for Zbikowski Realty Group. The left half of the billboard showed a photo of Stan flashing his million dollar smile. The right half of the billboard read: **Whether Your Buying or Selling, Stan's the Man! Call the #1 Realtor in America's Best Place to Live, today! 906-928-ZIBS.**

The *GMA* bus cruised a few more miles before passing another billboard that read: **STOP THE ROCKET!**

Malcolm Ciccone sat upright in the chair across from Russ's desk. Five minutes after Russ arrived in his office that morning, Malcolm showed up unannounced and requested a sit down meeting. For the next thirty minutes, Russ sat patiently while listening to Malcolm's concerns. The well-dressed man, who was in his early eighties, spoke with passion, and at times his voice got choked up with emotion.

"Mr. Mayor, I strongly believe that the title bestowed on Whisper Dunes will set a curse in motion that will be damn near impossible to reverse. Everything we love about this town will be bulldozed by developers...the historic buildings, the homes, and the trees. I beg you to reject this bafflegab title of America's Best Place to Live," Malcolm said.

Russ regarded Malcom with kind eyes. "Malcolm, you are one of the all-time great residents of Whisper Dunes. You're a true historian and conservationist who has done more for this town than I have, and I've done a helluva lot. I believe everything happens for a reason, and I believe in fate. Malcolm, you know as well as I do that it was only a matter of time before the world discovered Whisper Dunes."

Looking defeated, Malcolm slouched in his chair as he stared blankly at Russ. "Nobody cares how much you know, until they know how much you care," Russ said with a smile. A smile slowly appeared on Malcom's face as he sat back upright in his chair.

"You introduced me to that Teddy Roosevelt quote during my first campaign."

Malcom slowly nodded. "That's right. My father was fond of that quote. He believed intelligence was meaningless without compassion."

"Trust me, Malcolm, I will always put the interest of Whisper Dunes residents over any outsiders. The sea might get a little choppy around here during the next year or so, but I will do my very best to navigate our town through the chop."

"A smooth sea never made a skilled sailor," Malcolm said with a gentle smile. Russ nodded and regarded Malcom, trying to convey respect with his look. "It's people like you, Malcolm, who make this town such a wonderful place to live."

Carol looked frantic as she bursted into the office. "The *Good Morning America* bus just pulled up," Carol said before catching her breath. Russ tried to remain calm, knowing Malcom was gauging his reaction. But before Russ said anything, he couldn't help but notice that Carol was wearing a much sexier outfit than normal. Russ and Malcolm both stood up at the same time.

"Thank you for your time, Mr. Mayor. Good luck today."

"Thank you, Malcolm. It's always a pleasure to spend some time with you. Let's try and grab dinner next week."

"Yes, that'd be great."

Russ waited for Malcom to exit the office before he grabbed the sleeveless, blue fleece jacket hanging over his chair and put it on. "What do you think?" Russ asked as he zipped up the fleece jacket.

Carol took a moment to look him over. She smiled and said sweetly, "You look good, Russ. Real sharp. What about me?"

Russ glanced at Carol and thought she really did look nice. He was, however, tempted to tell Carol that her outfit was a tad inappropriate, especially for a big event like today. But instead he smiled and said, "You look lovely, Carol."

Carol smiled as she rubbed her hand gently over the top of Russ's hair to try and push down a few hairs that were sticking up. "I just wish we didn't have to deal with this cold front," Russ said.

"Cold front or no cold front in July, the toothpaste is out of the tube, Mr. Mayor. *GMA* is here to shine their bright lights on America's Best Place to Live. This is a great day for Whisper Dunes. The whole country is watching."

"That's the spirit, Carol. Now, if we can just get the rest of the folks in town to embrace your mentality."

"They'll come along eventually."

"I hope you're right."

Carol followed Russ out of his office, through her office, and down the poorly lit hallway. They both walked with a bounce in their step, but Carol looked uneasy. "I just hope that nothing goes wrong today," Carol said.

As Russ looked at Carol she couldn't remember ever seeing him convey such confidence. "I truly believe that Whisper Dunes is a town of destiny, and nothing can get in the way of this great moment," Russ said. "Sometimes good things happen to good people. Don't ever forget that."

The *Good Morning America* crew moved quickly to set up the cameras and lights in front of the Whisper Dunes Town Hall. The wind had calmed down a bit but the temperature was still in the low sixties. Everyone in the crew was wearing hooded sweatshirts or light jackets as they worked to get the lighting and camera angles just right. *GMA* host, Lucy Campbell, stood still as an assistant powdered her nose. Lucy seemed frustrated as she stared at her phone.

"Fuck me, I still can't get wi-fi," Lucy said.

"Me neither," said the assistant.

Russ stood about ten yards from Lucy, patiently waiting for the interview to begin. He had a nervous expression on his face as he watched the gaffer use a light meter to get the lighting just right. Despite his nervous stomach, Russ watched the production crew do their jobs with great interest.

Russ was suddenly overcome with a jolt of tingly nerves as he heard one of the producers shout, "Okay, Lucy, we're ready to roll."

Lucy, who stood at five-six, waited as her assistant sprayed hair spray all over her long blonde hair. "Ready, Mr. Mayor?" Lucy asked in an energetic tone.

"You betcha," Russ said. He flashed a nervous smile and gave Lucy a thumbs up just as his stomach filled up with butterflies.

The camera operator pointed his camera at Lucy as she moved closer to Russ. The boom operator stood behind the camera operator. "3...2...1...We're rolling!" said the producer.

Lucy flashed her camera ready smile then raised the microphone closer to her mouth and said, "The beautiful town of Whisper Dunes is the largest city in the Upper Peninsula of Michigan. Set on the southern shores of Lake Superior, the area is often described as a grand force of nature luxury."

Lucy glanced at Russ then looked back at the camera. "As beautiful as Whisper Dunes is, like the rest of the Upper Peninsula, it's unfamiliar to most Americans. A mystery town even, so we thought we'd reach out to someone who knows this town like the back of their hand. Folks, we're in for a real treat, because today we have with us Mayor Russ Tillinghast. Mayor Russ is a lifetime resident of Whisper Dunes and the long-time mayor."

Russ's nervous smile caused him to speak in a higher tone not at all consistent with his normal voice. "It's an honor and a pleasure to be with you, Lucy, and I'm very excited that you and your incredible crew have decided to spend the day in Whisper Dunes."

"Mr. Mayor..."

"Please, call me, Russ."

"Russ, can you give are viewers a quick overview of your town's incredible natural surroundings?"

Russ nodded and smiled before allowing himself a quick breath. "Well, Lucy, Whisper Dunes is blessed to have the largest and cleanest freshwater lake on Earth right in our backyard. Lake Superior is so large that it has its own weather system. And for your viewers who haven't visited the U.P., it's important to know that Lake Superior is surrounded by hilly terrain and dense forests. In fact, eighty-four percent of the land in the Upper Peninsula is covered in forests, which is why we have the cleanest air in America. And because of Lake Superior, we have not experienced any drought over the past 150 years. Climate scientists have confirmed that because of Lake Superior and our unique geographic location, the Upper Peninsula of Michigan is completely shielded from every type of natural disaster."

Lucy looked intrigued. "Wow. That is absolutely incredible." Lucy glanced back at the Town Hall and said, "Now, Mayor Russ, I know you mentioned off camera that you wanted to briefly tell us about the architectural significance of your Town Hall building."

Russ flashed a much more natural smile. He looked at ease now, even confident. "Our Town Hall building was designed by John Lloyd Wright, son of Frank Lloyd Wright, one of America's most famous architects. JW, as his father affectionately called him, designed our Town Hall building back in 1925. During his remarkable career, John Lloyd Wright only designed three public buildings, all of which are still standing today. The Whisper Dunes Town Hall, as well as the Town Hall and public grammar school in Long Beach, Indiana, which is where he lived and worked for most of his career."

Lucy nodded as she flashed her beautiful smile. "Fascinating."

"And here's a fun fact I think your viewers will appreciate —in hopes of inspiring young architects, John Lloyd Wright invented Lincoln Logs, which were inducted into the National Toy Hall of Fame in 1999," Russ said.

"I did not know that. What a remarkable fun fact."

The production crew followed Lucy and Russ as they walked through the farmers market, which was set up in the parking lot across from Town Hall. Around fifty farm stands were set up in the crowded parking lot.

"Lucy, this is one of the largest organic farmers markets in Michigan, with vendors coming from all over the state and as far away as western Minnesota," Russ said. Because he was concentrating a little too much on his made for tv smile, Russ didn't see the apple on the ground up ahead. Before Lucy could respond, Russ stepped awkwardly on the apple and took a bad spill on the asphalt pavement.

"Oh, no, are you okay?" Lucy asked. Officer Alcocks suddenly appeared in front of Russ and helped him to his feet.

"Oh, I'm fine. Thank you, Officer Alcocks. You can cut that out, right?"

"Yes, of course. Do you need to take five or do you want to keep going?"

"I'm good, let's keep rolling."

"Great, ready when you are."

Russ took a deep breath as he wiped his brow and tried to bend his cut knee a few times, which caused Russ to wince in pain. He took another deep breath and a smile returned to his face as he and Lucy continued walking through the farmers market. Russ waved cheerfully at some folks standing off camera then looked at Lucy and said, "The people of Whisper Dunes have always believed that hospitality should be extended rather than advertised. Yes, we're a haven for outdoor lovers, always will be, but Whisper Dunes has quietly been developing an incredible dining and nightlife scene over the past decade. Through a community effort, we have revitalized our downtown, creating a nexus of fabulous dining options, a thriving entertainment district, and an emerging outdoor fashion scene. Oh, and we have zero crime to speak of. Folks come from as far away as Chicago, Detroit, Milwaukee, and Minneapolis to experience a memorable weekend in Whisper Dunes. And not just in the summer months. We have a four season paradise up here and get visitors all year long."

The production crew followed Russ and Lucy as they walked through a vineyard set on 200 acres of rolling hills. The wind had picked up a bit and Lucy was now wearing a heavier jacket. She flashed her pretend television smile as she walked close to Russ. "This is the second most profitable winery in the state of Michigan," Russ said.

Lucy stopped to take in the incredible view from the top of the hill. She'd been to many beautiful locations around the world, but she truly seemed impressed with the unique landscape of Whisper Dunes. "It's absolutely amazing. We're in the Upper Peninsula of Michigan, yet I feel like we could be in Napa Valley."

"Last year, *The Northern Sun Winery* and *Threefold Vine Winery,* ranked higher than the vast majority of vineyards in Napa and Sonoma Valley."

"That's incredible."

"Because of global warming, in the next few years most environmental experts think that Michigan will overtake California as the number one wine producing state in America."

Lucy's television smile vanished from her face. She looked concerned as she regarded Russ. "The Intergovernmental Panel on Climate Change has warned that the climate crisis is doom impending, with less than a decade left to act before it's too late. Now, despite your town's charming main street, and zero crime to speak of, and good schools, and beautiful location on the shores of Lake Superior, a spokesman for *Forbes* clearly stated that the only reason they selected Whisper Dunes as America's Best Place to Live is because of a five-year study conducted by a group of highly respected climate scientists. Their peer-reviewed paper, that could be released as early as next month, emphatically concluded that Whisper Dunes, and really anywhere in the Upper Peninsula, will be the best place to live on Earth for the remainder of civilization," Lucy said in a measured tone.

Russ's nervous, deep breathing, was picked up by the mic attached to his collar. He licked his lips, tried to relax his jaw, and forced a smile. "Wow," Russ said as he tried to come up with a more thoughtful response. "Listen, I'm no scientist, and I don't know a whole lot about climate change, but I do believe that all of us who are lucky enough to call Whisper Dunes, or any town in the Upper Peninsula, home, can proudly say that we live in the safest and most stunningly beautiful environment on Earth."

Lucy's smile did not return as her eyes remained locked on the mayor. "Since arriving in Whisper Dunes, I've run into hundreds of climate change advocates as well as many climate change deniers. Two of the largest parks in your town have seen climate change advocates from all over the country set up makeshift camps, which you have neither supported nor denounced. Just yesterday, CNN published a poll that states that forty percent of Whisper Dunes residents don't believe in climate change."

Russ folded his arms as he tried hard to keep the slight smile from disappearing from his face. "Well, as I've said before, when you live in a town that averages 165 inches of snow each year, you're going to have some folks who have a hard time believing in global warming. I mean heck, last Mother's Day we got five inches dumped on us."

"Do you believe in climate change, Mr. Mayor?"

Russ could no longer hide his growing discomfort. His eyes narrowed as wrinkles appeared across his forehead. Russ nervously licked his top lip as he struggled to make eye contact with Lucy. "Look, I'm not a climate scientist. I'm a lifelong resident and the proud mayor of Whisper Dunes. Our town has the cleanest air and water of any town on Earth, and not for one second have I, or any resident of Whisper Dunes, taken that for granted."

Lucy's piercing eyes closed slightly as her gaze remained focused on Russ. "Yes or no, Mr. Mayor, do you believe in climate change?"

Russ lowered his head for a moment as he took a long, deep breath. He forced a slight smile as his gaze finally met Lucy's cold stare.

"It's been said, you're not a real fisherman unless you've been divorced at least twice. Both of my ex-wives can vouch for the fact that I spend more time on Lake Superior than probably any resident in the U.P. and from my point of view...the climate in the Upper Peninsula has never been better. But unfortunately, the same can't be said for most places on Earth."

Lucy's smile slowly returned as she looked over Russ, who was clearly depleted of energy and in need of a chair. She turned to her producer and said, "I think we can use that."

Lucy walked out of the shot and toward her assistant, who handed Lucy a fresh cup of coffee. Russ looked around but no one was paying any attention to him.

"Can I please have a water break?"

"You've got five minutes, Mr. Mayor! Get whatever you need," shouted one of the producers.

The crew filmed Lucy and Russ as they stood on the beach. They were about five feet from the Lake Superior shoreline, and behind them were rows and rows of tall evergreen trees. The massive beach was empty on this chilly day. Lucy stared at the coastline in awe. "Just stunning."

"The fact that Whisper Dunes has nearly seven miles of beach on the southern shore of the world's largest freshwater lake is just icing on the cake, Lucy."

Russ bent down and picked up a handful of sand. "Here, open your hand," Russ said. Lucy opened up her hand and Russ dropped some sand in her palm. "If our incredible sandy coastline wasn't enough, I think it's worth mentioning that the only other place in the world where you'll find this type of sand is in Las Tijeras, Chile."

Lucy smiled and nodded her head as if she actually cared about this fun fact. A large wave broke suddenly on the shoreline and splashed Lucy and Russ. "Mother fucker!" Lucy screamed at the top of her lungs. The assistant came running towards Lucy with a blanket in her hand.

Russ's face contorted into a look of painful astonishment. "I'm sorry about that, Lucy. You know, two days ago it was eighty-five degrees in Whisper Dunes. The day before that topped eighty."

With the blanket wrapped around her, Lucy approached her producer and said, "Screw the beach shot. We're running behind schedule anyway. Let's go downtown."

Lucy and Russ walked down a sidewalk on Front Street. The opposite sidewalk was packed with people watching the segment being filmed. The street was blocked off for an art show that spanned two blocks. In the background of the shot, Duane and Hal were both licking ice cream cones while walking hand in hand. They stopped and pretended to be excited to check out a painting of a lighthouse. Standing next to them were Lisa and Stan, who were both holding a glass of wine while admiring a painting of a sunset over Lake Superior.

Lucy abruptly stopped, which caught Russ off guard. "This segment will probably be cut, so just give us a quick overview of your art scene and then we'll move on," Lucy said, looking bored.

Russ nodded and looked at the producer for direction. "Should I go now?"

The producer flashed a thumbs up and said, "Ready when you are Mayor Russ."

"Okay, so this is the Whisper Dunes Arts District. We host a number of different events and festivals on this street throughout the year, including our famous winter carnival. The first Friday of each month is when we shut down Main Street and turn it into a street festival that gives all of our local artists a chance to show off their latest work."

Lucy's face lit up with an enthusiastic smile. "What a great idea! That sounds so fun."

"One of the other nice things about our First Friday event is that it gives folks the chance to really take in and appreciate the buildings. Downtown Whisper Dunes has a tremendous inventory of historical architecture, dating back to the 1870's. Back then, the iron-ore mining boom led to a building boom in downtown. Most of the buildings erected during that time and well into the 1920's were built of locally quarried red sandstone."

"Do you have any buildings downtown that are famous for one reason or another?"

"As a matter of fact, we do. Just a few blocks over is the Marquette County Courthouse. Built in 1904, it's where many scenes from the 1959 legal thriller *Anatomy of a Murder* were filmed. Adapted from the John Voelker novel, the movie starred the legendary Jimmy Stewart. Hanging on the wall at The Vierling Restaurant is a signed photo of Jimmy Stewart standing on the top step outside the courthouse. According to my parents, Jimmy dined at The Vierling every night when he wasn't filming."

Russ was walking a few steps ahead of Lucy and didn't see her turn back and flash a frustrated look at her producer. Lucy held up two fingers with her left hand then slid her right thumb across her throat. She turned and faced Russ just as he came to a stop in front of Donckers Restaurant & Candy Shop. Lucy looked almost annoyed as an excited smile beamed from Russ's face.

"What do we have here, Mayor Russ?"

"This is Donckers Restaurant & Candy Shop. Family-owned for over a century. This was President Obama's first stop during his visit back on February 10th, 2011. He shook hands with everyone inside and could not have been any sweeter. Later that day President Obama delivered his—'Win the Future'—speech at Northern Michigan University."

Lucy looked pleasantly surprised to hear this. "That's amazing. I had no idea President Obama visited."

Russ, with a faraway look, was clearly thinking about that special day. He finally shook his head and smiled. "I still pinch myself thinking back on that day. Still sorta stunned that I got to hang out with President Obama for an afternoon. He even gave me a ride in his limo. Pretty sweet."

Unsure about what other surprises Russ might have up his sleeve, Lucy's attention was back on the mayor. The six-story, brick building up ahead caught Lucy's attention. "Mayor Russ, how about that beautiful building on the corner?"

"Do we have time for a quick story?"

"Yes, I think so. Lets hear it."

Lucy followed Russ until they were standing in front of the building. "Now here we have the one and only, Landmark Inn." Russ's face lit up as he stared at the handsome building. "The Landmark Inn is a triple A Diamond-rated hotel that opened in 1930."

Russ turned to gauge Lucy's reaction, but she looked like she was quickly losing interest.

"Any notable guests stay here over the years?"

"Yeah, a few. Back in July of 2002, The Rolling Stones stayed at the Landmark Inn."

Russ had Lucy's attention now.

"The Rolling Stones played a show in Whisper Dunes?"

"No. They came here to celebrate the life of an Upper Peninsula legend, and one of its favorite sons, Royden Walter Magee."

Lucy's attention was heightened now. She wanted to ask, who was Royden Walter Magee? But she could tell Russ was just getting warmed up with his story so she refrained from interrupting the mayor.

"But to Mick, Keith, Charlie, Ronnie, and Daryl, and everyone in the Rolling Stones family he was known simply as 'Chuch.' His story is pretty remarkable. 'Chuch' was a shoe salesman turned rock-club manager. One night he met Ronnie Wood in Detroit, and the rest is rock n' roll history. 'Chuch' was the beloved road manager for the Stones for nearly thirty years before his sudden death. When 'Chuch' wasn't touring the world with the Stones he lived a humble life on a farm just outside of town. Everyone in town loved 'Chuch' and he loved them right back."

Russ started to get emotional. He bowed his head for a moment in hopes of regaining his composure. He took a deep breath, cleared his throat and finally regarded Lucy, whose wide eyes were staring at Russ with astonishment.

"I wasn't mayor then, but I still got to meet Charlie Watts. What a gentleman. An absolute class act. Before the funeral, instead of stopping off at one of our town's popular bars, the Stones spent the day at our public library. In fact, Keith Richards, an avid reader and book collector, still donates books to the *Peter White Public Library* every year."

Russ's emotions were getting the best of him. His voice started to crack just as he said, "I betcha that's one Rolling Stones story that you and your viewers haven't heard before."

Lucy, with her mouth agape, slowly shook her head. Russ looked up at the street sign as if he'd just realized something. "Now this is interesting, right now we happen to be at the intersection where the world's first traffic light was installed," Russ said proudly.

"That is interesting," Lucy said. It was clear she was still thinking about the Stones and 'Chuch.'

"A little fun fact, the investor of the traffic light, Leslie Haines, was born not far from Whisper Dunes."

Lucy had a faraway look as she flashed a smile, but not because she gave a shit about the traffic light guy. She had been a Stones fan since high school and had seen the band in concert a dozen times. Lucy still fantasized from time to time about spending the night with Mick Jagger. Her eyes drifted back to the Landmark Inn as a new fantasy quickly took hold of her. It was like a movie scene was now playing in her head. It was July 2002, and Lucy was sitting at the end of the bar in the Landmark Inn on a hot night. Mick Jagger suddenly sat right next to her and told her how sexy she looked in her summer dress. Lucy paused the scene in her head as she heard Russ's voice getting louder. She still had a job to do, but she smiled slightly, knowing she'd return to her little fantasy scene later in the evening when she was alone in her bed.

The cameraman focused the camera just on Russ as he continued talking about the library. "A number of our residents work as telecommuters, and they like to set up their mobile offices in their cars, which they park in the library parking lot in order to take advantage of the library's internet hotspot. You have to understand that most folks in the U.P. don't get high speed internet service because of the rugged, hilly, remote landscape."

"So it sounds like Whisper Dunes residents aren't tethered tightly to technology."

"That's true, but we do have a very reliable social network platform in the Upper Peninsula, called bars."

Lucy and Russ walked through an Irish garden that was in the middle of a ten acre park—about a hundred yards from the shoreline of Lake Superior. The cameraman gave Lucy a thumbs up. "Okay, go ahead Mr. Mayor," Lucy said. She looked very bored as she glanced over the beautiful garden.

"This is our award winning Irish garden, which was dedicated last year in honor of the tenth anniversary of Ennis, Ireland being named our sister city."

Lucy faked a smile as she took a few steps toward the Easter lilies. "Son of a bitch!" Lucy yelled. She looked down at her right high heel sandal, which was covered in dog shit.

"What's wrong?" Russ asked.

Lucy looked furious as she dragged her heel across the grass. "What kind of asshole lets his dog shit in an Irish garden and doesn't pick it up?"

"I'm terribly sorry, Lucy. Want me to start from the top?"

Lucy started to walk away while dragging her right heel along the grass. "I'm breaking for lunch. We'll film one more segment, then we're getting the fuck out of here."

Russ looked upset with himself, thinking that he could have prevented the unfortunate incident from happening. He put his hands on his hips, took a deep breath and exhaled loudly as he watched Lucy step into a waiting black Chevy Suburban. The crew crammed into a white Chevy cargo van while the Chevy Suburban sped away. Russ was all alone now in the Irish garden. He couldn't help but think how dog shit in the Irish garden was bad karma. He felt a little better knowing that the footage would not be used, but this was not a good way to transition into the last filming location of the day. In Russ's mind, the last filming location was the most important.

He decided to hit the reset button and head over to Togo's for a coffee and his favorite sandwich. On the walk over to Togo's, Russ said a prayer and became more hopeful that filming at the last location would go without a hitch.

Russ rode his mountain bike down a dirt path in the county forest preserve. Lucy followed behind on her mountain bike while the crew filmed from a trailing golf cart with off-road tires. Russ slowed down and stopped his bike at a scenic spot overlooking a wooded valley. Lucy stopped her bike a few feet from Russ's bike, and waited for the cameraman to hop off the golf cart before she flashed her signature television smile.

"Members of the Ojibwe, Odawa, and Potawatomi tribes maintained villages across the Upper Peninsula for thousands of years. This whole area was once home to tens of thousands of Native Americans. Just up ahead, you'll see a beautiful tribute to the great Potawatomi leader, Chief Pokagon."

"Incredible. Can't wait to see it."

Russ got back on his bike and took off down the dirt trail. Lucy got on her bike and trailed about twenty yards behind Russ while the crew on the golf cart trailed another twenty yards behind Lucy.

Lucy happened to glance to her right and couldn't believe what she saw. She closed her eyes in disbelief for a second then looked to her right again. Lucy was in complete shock and almost lost control of her bike. "Holy shit!" Lucy screamed.

She squeezed the breaks on her bike hard, creating a thick cloud of dust that almost caused the crew to crash the golf cart into a huge oak tree. Russ was still riding his bike down the dirt trail with a relaxed smile on his face until he saw what Lucy was looking at.

"Oh, my God!" Russ shouted. Two seconds later his front tire hit a huge rock on the trail and he flipped over the handle bars, landing hard on his right shoulder.

Lucy didn't even bother to acknowledge Russ lying in pain on the dirt trail. Instead, she ran toward the dead body floating in the shallow creek. "Please tell me you're getting this!"

Both camera operators were following closely behind Lucy as they pointed their cameras at the dead body, which was stuck in a large beaver dam. The body was partially floating above the water. An arm and a leg were tangled in the dam and the face was clearly visible.

Russ held his right arm in pain as he jogged toward Lucy and the crew. "Turn those cameras off! I mean it! Turn 'um off!" Russ yelled.

He suddenly became quiet as he recognized the person floating face up in the creek. "Oh, no," Russ said in a barely audible tone. He entered into a state of bewilderment that he had never experienced before. Russ's wide, moist eyes stared at the dead man for at least a minute before he looked up at the cloudless blue sky.

13

Whisper Dunes Police Officer Trent Burrish, who looked close to forty, and Officer Clayton Wilson, early thirties, worked quickly to create an investigation perimeter with crime scene tape. Nearby, Officer Ned Hughes, late forties, walked slowly over dead leaves as he carefully searched the ground for clues. Ned was in plain clothes and wearing a blue nylon windbreaker with W.D.P.D. in yellow on the back. Ned stopped in his tracks as he spotted something under a few leaves. Excited, he picked up a stick and moved the leaves around until he was staring at a shotgun shell casing. Ned knew immediately that this was left behind by a hunter, not the murderer, but still decided to put the shell casing in an evidence bag.

Chief O'Malley and Officer Alcocks, both wearing gloves and waterproof boots, were carefully examining Lenny Trubisky's dead body. The body was still face up in the shallow creek and stuck in the beaver dam. It was supposed to be O'Malley's day off, and when he got the call he was just about to hop on his motorcycle for a scenic ride to Whitefish Point. He was the last to arrive on the scene. The first thing he did when got to the scene was order Officers Wilson and Burrish to increase the size of the crime scene perimeter. Before he put on gloves and waterproof boots to examine the body closer, O'Malley noticed the bandage wrapped around Lenny's left thumb—his entire right arm was above water and stuck in the well-crafted beaver's dam. He had yet to tell anyone, but O'Malley knew that Lenny's body had been dumped into the creek from a different spot. He thought it was likely that Lenny floated down stream for at least half a mile before getting stuck in the beaver dam.

"A twenty-two right behind the ear at very close range," Chief O'Malley said as he stood up. Alcocks looked stunned as he watched O'Malley turn around and take a long look at the hilly forest surrounding them. O'Malley's eyes narrowed, thinking maybe the killer was watching them from afar. Not the first time O'Malley got that feeling while working a murder scene. He knew that some killers enjoyed watching the cops investigate the scene as a form of entertainment. For a second, O'Malley actually thought that he saw someone hiding behind a huge oak tree, but it was just a deer.

"Russ told the *Good Morning America* folks that it was a hunting accident."

"Not a chance. I'm afraid Lenny was murdered."

Alcocks was clearly perturbed as he looked over the body. "How in the hell is it possible to sneak up behind someone in the middle of the forest and shoot them directly behind the ear?"

Chief O'Malley continued to scan the area. He stopped spinning around and held his gaze steady on a path that went to the top of the hill. Alcocks patiently regarded O'Malley while the Chief continued to stare at the top of hill as he thought through a couple different scenarios.

"Lenny wasn't murdered here."

Alcocks looked in the same direction where O'Malley was looking. "Where was he murdered?"

"Chief Albers said the fire at the country club started in the mechanical room. I'm pretty positive that's where Lenny was shot."

Alcocks slowly nodded. "Yeah, I can buy that."

O'Malley took a step toward Alcocks and said quietly, "Whoever shot Lenny wanted to eliminate all evidence at the murder scene, so the killer set fire to the clubhouse before disposing of Lenny's body in the creek."

"Do you think there was more than one person involved?"

"Yeah, I think so," O'Malley said.

Alcocks was clearly befuddled. He slowly rubbed his chin while staring wide-eyed at the beaver dam. He glanced at Lenny then looked at O'Malley and said, "But why did they dump his body in a creek? They went through all that trouble to destroy the evidence at the murder scene...then they just dump his body in a shallow creek. Doesn't make a lot of sense. Unless..."

"They wanted the body to be found because they knew how much it would embarrass our town," O'Malley said. "Is that what you were going to say?"

Alcocks nodded. O'Malley's blank stare moved from Alcocks to Lenny. He exhaled deeply through his nose then stepped out of the creek and walked toward an area where only

Alcocks would be able to hear him. Alcocks stepped out of the creek and walked in stride with O'Malley, patiently waiting for the Chief to speak. O'Malley finally said quietly, "I thought about that possibility, and I'm sure in the coming weeks that's what some people will want to believe. I don't know though..."

It was clear to Alcocks that O'Malley was struggling to sort through conflicting theories. "I'm not positive, but I don't think the guys who killed Lenny were familiar with the area," O'Malley said.

Alcocks looked unsure as he scratched his neck. "You really think they were outsiders? Like a murder-for-hire deal?"

"It's possible. Lenny was shot behind the ear at point blank range, that much is certain."

"Okay, but what the hell was Lenny doing in the clubhouse in the middle of the night?"

Chief O'Malley regarded Alcocks for a long beat. "Responding to a bogus emergency plumbing call."

Alcocks looked upset with himself that he hadn't considered this scenario. He vividly recalled the freezing night he had to make an emergency call to Lenny after a pipe burst in his basement. "Wait, but then doesn't that mean the guys who took out Lenny were likely members of the Potawatomi Country Club, and not members of a hit team?"

"Maybe...maybe not," O'Malley said.

O'Malley stopped walking and stared off into the distance for a moment before he regarded Alcocks. "A professional hit team would've had no problem getting inside a country club. Especially one built over a hundred years ago and with no security cameras. The club was closed when Lenny arrived. One of the guys could've easily posed as the building maintenance manager and guided Lenny into the mechanical room."

Alcocks nodded in complete agreement.

"There's no question that Lenny was set up," O'Malley said with a tinge of anger in his voice. "Whoever killed him, planned to shoot in the clubhouse. But I don't think they planned to dump his body in a shallow creek that runs through a nature preserve popular with bikers and hikers."

Alcocks looked confused as he shook his head. "So, Lenny's reputation as a reliable emergency plumber was how he was lured to the country club. But who the fuck would've had the motive to hire a hit team to murder Lenny? It just doesn't make any sense. He was drinking buddies with half the town."

O'Malley removed his sunglasses then scratched the back of his neck and said, "From what I gathered, he was an awfully talented womanizer."

"A womanizer? Yes. A talented womanizer? That's up for debate."

"Didn't Lenny have an affair with Russ's second wife?"

"I think he just had an affair with Russ's first wife. But he openly dated Russ's second wife after she divorced him."

O'Malley, clearly intrigued with these facts, rubbed his chin as he tried to convince himself that there was no way Mayor Tillinghast had anything to do with Lenny's murder. Officer Freddy Soller's voice came over O'Malley's radio. "Hey, Chief, it's Freddy. I just uncovered two sets of foot prints. One pair's at least a size twelve."

Alcocks couldn't help but flash an excited grin. He looked at O'Malley for a reaction, but his face was devoid of any emotion as he spoke into his radio. "Good work, Freddy. Where you at?"

"About a mile north of you guys. The footprints are just a few yards from the creek."

"Take a photo of each footprint at a ninety degree angle. We're hustling your way now."

Russ, with his right arm in a sling, stood in front of the door to the *Good Morning America* bus. Lucy, desperate to get on the bus, was losing her patience. "That man was the victim of an accidental hunting accident. End of story," Russ said in an angry tone.

"No, I'm pretty positive that man was murdered in America's Best Place to Live."

"Even if that's true, that area is located in unincorporated Whisper Dunes. So technically, he was not murdered in America's Best Place to Live. Plus, it's illegal to air footage of a murder scene."

"How do you know that was the murder scene? He could've been murdered somewhere else then dumped into the creek."

Russ looked to be in physical pain, or maybe he was just sick to his stomach. Lucy couldn't tell, but she could tell that he was growing more desperate by the minute. Russ decided to revert back to his normal, friendly demeanor. He said in a gentle voice, "Lucy, if you air that footage, Whisper Dunes will be ridiculed from coast to coast. It will be a permanent black eye on this town. Please, I beg you, don't show your viewers something they don't want to see."

"Mr. Mayor, whether we decide to air the footage or not, you can't cover up a murder investigation."

Russ looked like he was on the verge of great emotion as different scenarios played out in his head. "This is what you people in the media game live for...to manufacture, manipulate, and eventually exploit a fall from grace story."

Lucy looked like she completely agreed with Russ. She smiled and said, "Mayor Russ, everyone loves a sensational story, and this is a once in a lifetime sensational story that wouldn't be believable if it weren't true. And I'm going to be the one to break it to the world."

Russ looked defeated as he took a long, quiet breath through his nose. His glazed eyes stared at Lucy as she boarded the bus. She stopped and turned to give Russ one final look. "Yes, this will be a huge embarrassment for Whisper Dunes. No denying that. But frankly, it doesn't matter how many people are murdered in Whisper Dunes, thanks to climate change. As the Earth continues to warm at a rapid rate, people will be flocking to Whisper Dunes and every other town in the Upper Peninsula for the remainder of civilization. You could open a whorehouse across the street from a day care center, and property values in this town will still rapidly rise through the stratosphere."

Russ didn't allow himself to comprehend Lucy's opinion. His sad eyes watched her disappear inside the bus. The door closed and Russ, in a great deal of pain because of his separated shoulder, watched the *Good Morning America* bus speed out of the gravel parking lot. A cloud of white dust engulfed Russ, but he didn't bother to move. He stood alone in the gravel parking lot, wondering if this was just the beginning of a proverbial shitstorm.

Chief O'Malley sat behind the desk in his office with a curious expression on his face. Officer Alcocks and Officer Soller stood on the other side of the messy desk. "We sent photos of both sets of foot prints to a forensic podiatrist in Detroit, and he said that the perpetrators were clearly wearing anti-tracking shoes," Soller said.

O'Malley looked disconcerted as he slowly leaned forward and grabbed his coffee mug. He took a long sip from his coffee mug as he seriously considered the possibility that Lenny may have been murdered by a professional hit team. Then again he thought, it's not that hard for someone to purchase anti-tracking shoes. Especially in the U.P., which has tons of shops that sell outdoor gear.

O'Malley looked at Alcocks and said, "What about the tire tracks?"

"BF Goodrich, all-terrain T/A KO2 tires. A tire most likely found on a Chevy Tahoe," Alcocks said. "Or a GMC Denali."

O'Malley looked perturbed with Alcocks.

"A black Chevy Tahoe is awfully similar to a black GMC Denali," Alcocks said. "And do you know who recently leased a brand new black GMC Denali?"

Officer Soller had no idea, but O'Malley did.

"Stan Zbikowski," Alcocks said.

"Everyone knows that Stan's alibi checked out, Alcocks," O'Malley said. "He's no longer a person of interest."

"I'm just saying, wouldn't hurt to bring in Duane's boyfriend and have him prove to us that he knows the difference between a Chevy Tahoe and a GMC Denali."

O'Malley shut his eyes tightly as he rubbed his forehead in frustration. "Anything else?"

"Yes, sir. We located Lenny's plumbing van," Soller said.

O'Malley perked up in his seat. "Where was it?"

"Parked in his driveway."

O'Malley didn't hide his concerned look. "Do we have a search warrant yet for Lenny's house?"

"Not yet. The judge is fishing right now in northern Canada, but he said he'll do his best to fax over the search warrant today," Alcocks said.

"There's something else, Chief," Soller said.

"What's that?"

"I should've told you this earlier, but I pulled over Lenny for speeding on June 28th."

O'Malley's eyes narrowed with intrigue as he leaned back in his chair.

"I clocked him going fifty-two past Marge's Ice Cream Parlor. I gave him a warning because he had a bloody towel wrapped around his thumb and was trying to get to the E.R.," Soller said.

"What happened to his thumb?"

"He didn't say and I didn't ask. But he was in his work overalls, so I just assumed he cut it while on a job somewhere."

"That explains the stitches and the bandage on his thumb," O'Malley said. "How was his demeanor?"

"He looked frazzled and worked up about something."

"Think he got into a fight with someone?"

"Maybe. I didn't see the thumb but the towel was soaked with blood. I think it's more than likely he cut it with a knife at a job site. When people around here get into fights it usually involves their fists and nothing else."

O'Malley tried to reimagine the sequence of events in his mind. He said, "Okay, so he cut his thumb with maybe a saw or a knife at a job site. He then got into his work van, and was speeding to get to the E.R. when you pulled him over."

Soller looked to be wavering as he thought back on the encounter. "Lenny was heading north when I pulled him over, the opposite direction of the hospital."

O'Malley regarded Soller for a few seconds. "So, you don't think he was actually headed to the E.R.?"

"Now that I think about it, no, I don't think so."

"How do you explain the stitches on his thumb? He didn't do that himself," Alcocks said.

O'Malley stared at the wall to his left, which was filled with framed photos of his police days in Detroit. Looking at photos from years past tended to help him think.

"I'm sure he ended up going to the E.R. but when I pulled him over I think he was speeding to get home," Soller said. "I remember now, on the passenger seat was an orange Nike shoebox. I glanced at the box long enough to see that it wasn't a brand new shoebox. I have no idea what was in the shoebox, but my gut tells me it wasn't a pair of sneakers."

Chief O'Malley was deep in thought as he looked back at the wall of photos, thinking about what could've been in that shoebox. O'Malley stood up from his chair, looked at Soller, and gave him a nod of appreciation. "Nice work, Freddy. Lets get that warrant and go check out Lenny's place. Who knows, maybe we'll get lucky and find that shoebox."

Stan was cruising in his golf cart down a residential street lined with tidy one-story homes. He stopped the golf cart in front of a lemonade stand that was being operated by two ten-year-old girls. Both girls smiled cheerfully at Stan and said, "Hi, Mr. Zbikowski."

"Hi, girls," Stan said cheerfully. "I'll take a big cup today."

One girl handed Stan a red Solo cup with lemonade, while the other girl received a ten dollar bill from Stan. He flashed a friendly smile and said, "Thank you, very much. Have a great day!"

"You too! Thanks for your business!"

The girls waved at Stan as he started to drive away. He suddenly had to steer his golf cart to the far right and stop on someone's lawn while three Whisper Dunes police suvs sped by with their lights on, but their sirens off. Stan, clearly curious, decided to follow the police cars.

Lenny's A-frame cabin was surrounded by evergreen trees and set about two hundred yards from the street. A long dirt driveway led to the small house. Three police suvs were parked on the side of the country road, close to the entrance of the driveway. Before they made there way inside, O'Malley and the officers examined the dirt driveway for tire tracks. They found evidence of tire tracks that they were certain would match the tire tracks they found near the forest preserve—BF Goodrich, all-terrain T/A KO2 tires.

Lenny's work van was parked in front of the detached garage, about twenty yards from the house. Officer Burrish was taking high-resolution photos of the tire tracks while another officer was carefully casting one of the tire tracks. Two other officers were dusting the inside of the Lenny's van for prints.

Chief O'Malley and officer Alcocks were looking around the messy kitchen. The entire house had been ransacked.

Nothing destroyed, but every drawer had been opened, every couch cushion and mattress had been looked under. The intruders were obviously desperately searching for something in Lenny's home. An officer was dusting for prints in the living room while a half-dozen officers continued to search the place for clues.

On the faux-wood kitchen counter, four different kitchen design magazines were opened up. Officer Alcocks, with gloves on, thumbed through one of the magazines. "Looks like Lenny was getting ready to spend some serious dough on a new kitchen," Alcocks said. He continued to thumb through the magazine while O'Malley started to thumb through another kitchen design magazine.

"Awfully expensive taste for a thrice divorced plumber," O'Malley said drily.

Alcocks peeked over at the page O'Malley was looking at and let out a long whistle. "Oh, I like that backsplash."

"Nah, I prefer an old-fashioned subway tile backsplash."

Alcocks shook his head, clearly disagreeing with the Chief. "I like subway tiles in a bathroom, not in the kitchen."

"No, mosaic tiles are meant for a bathroom, subway tiles are meant for a kitchen," O'Malley said with strong conviction.

Stan casually entered through the front door and strolled through the kitchen, catching both Alcocks and O'Malley off guard. Alcocks yelled, "What the fuck are you doing here?"

Stan couldn't help notice Alcocks and O'Malley were holding interior design magazines. "I didn't know you two had an interior decorating business on the side," Stan said with a grin. "Well, I heard a rumor, but I guess I just didn't want to believe it."

"Get the fuck out of here, Stan!" Alcocks said.

O'Malley and Alcocks both sheepishly dropped the magazines back on the counter. Stan took out his wallet and flashed his P.I. badge before he started snooping around the kitchen. Alcocks looked dumbfounded while O'Malley seemed more perturbed than surprised. "Since when are you a P.I.?" O'Malley asked.

"Congratulations, Stan, you have a fake P.I. badge. What else are going to brag about, that you can jerk off with Vaseline?"

Stan looked defensive as he tossed the badge to O'Malley. "It's not fake. I got my P.I. license after the real estate market shit its pants in '08'."

"Good for you, Stan. But if you don't leave right now I'm going to arrest you for interfering with a murder investigation," O'Malley said as he tossed the badge back to Stan.

Stan looked emotional, but O'Malley clearly didn't buy the act. "Lenny was like a brother to me. I was the best man at two of his three weddings. I owe it to him and the entire town of Whisper Dunes to use my investigative skills to aid your investigation."

O'Malley exchanged a confused look with Alcocks before he regarded Stan. "Have you ever worked a murder investigation before?"

"Yeah, as a matter of fact I have."

"Oh really? What was the name of the deer?" Alcocks asked with a straight face. "Or was it a moose?"

Stan acted like he didn't hear Alcocks. "Four years ago I was hired by an anonymous person to investigate the suspicious death of an old man up at McComb's Corner. The cops said the man shot himself inside his fishing shanty, but the case was later ruled a homicide."

"Did you help solve the murder?" O'Malley asked.

Stan looked around the living room before finally regarding O'Malley. "After both checks bounced, I lost interest. But I followed up with the sheriff recently and he said the case was still open."

Alcocks looked at Stan with suspicious eyes for an uncomfortable ten seconds before he finally said, "When was the last time you saw Lenny?"

Stan tilted his head back as he thought for a moment. Alcocks and O'Malley stared at him with impatient gazes. "We went fishing about a month ago, just the two of us. That was the last time I saw him."

"Was he acting his normal self when you guys were fishing?" O'Malley asked.

"Yeah, nothing out of the ordinary. Didn't seem bent out of shape about anything. We fished for about four hours, had a few beers, and just chatted away."

"What did you guys talk about?" Alcocks asked.

"The only thing that sticks out is that Lenny was talking quite a bit about, Erin...Hubert Houston's ex-wife."

O'Malley raised his eyebrows and said, "What about her?"

"Lenny was dating her. I know that he started sleeping with her while she was still married to Hubert. After the divorce she moved to Florida but still made frequent trips to Whisper Dunes to see Lenny."

Alcocks, with his arms folded now, looked bewildered. "Lenny was banging Erin? I just can't picture that."

Stan nodded and said, "Lenny had a real fetish for divorcees. He fooled around with both of Russ's ex-wives, and at least a dozen other divorcees that I know about."

O'Malley shook his head, still struggling to believe that Lenny was such a successful womanizer.

"Yeah, I knew that," Alcocks said. "For some reason, Lenny was irresistible to women over the age of fifty."

"Was there anything going on in his life that would suggest he was in danger?" O'Malley asked.

Stan didn't hesitate as he regarded O'Malley. "No, nothing that I know of."

Alcocks gave Stan a hard look that strongly suggested he didn't believe him. Stan could feel Alcocks' eyes on him, which was why he kept his eyes steady on O'Malley, who was conveying a relaxed demeanor in hopes that Stan would get comfortable and maybe give away some information he didn't want to.

"Did Lenny sleep with both the mayor's wives while they were still married to Russ?" O'Malley asked.

"Not that I know of, but there was a rumor he was having an affair with Russ's first wife while they were still married."

Alcocks stared at Stan for another uncomfortable ten seconds or so before he said, "Did Lenny ever sleep with your wife?"

Stan's eyes narrowed as his nostrils flared up with rage. He scratched his left nostril with his thumb as a reminder to stay cool. "No," Stan said in a measured tone.

"He ever make a pass at your wife?"

Stan clenched his jaw as he shook his head.

Alcocks, with his arms still folded, took a few steps toward Stan and said, "Your good buddy had a reputation for working in the bedroom with a big stick and a loose tongue."

O'Malley shot Alcocks a look as if to say, *how do you know that?*

"Think your wife ever had the hots for Lenny? Maybe just a little curious to see what all the other women in town were raving about?"

Stan, looking like he wanted to hit Alcocks, took a step toward him and said, "I would not have been friends with him if he made a pass at my wife."

O'Malley glared at Alcocks, which caused him to seal his lips for the time being.

"Did Lenny ever do any plumbing work for you?"

"Yeah. In fact, the last time I spoke with him was on the morning of June 28th. He was supposed to spend the day installing new shower heads in all my rental units. I asked him if he wanted to golf on July 5th, but he said he had to pack because he was planning on traveling to Florida to spend a few weeks with Erin. He told me things were getting serious with her."

O'Malley and Alcocks both had curious expressions on their face as they regarded Stan. O'Malley said, "Did Hubert know Lenny was dating his ex-wife?"

"Not sure...probably."

"One of my officers pulled Lenny over on June 28th. He said that Lenny had cut his thumb really bad and was headed to the E.R."

"Yeah, Lenny, called me as he was driving to the E.R. He was attempting to install a shower head at Denise's apartment when he cut his thumb."

O'Malley kept a blank expression as he glanced at Alcocks, who did not hide his surprised look. Alcocks looked like he wanted to say something but didn't.

"Was Denise at home when Lenny was working on the shower head?"

"I don't know."

"Did Denise know ahead of time that Lenny was coming to her apartment to replace the shower head?" O'Malley asked.

Stan looked like he was trying to remember. "Lenny was supposed to replace the shower heads like two months ago. I think I emailed all my tenants back in March about my plans to have new shower heads installed in the units, but getting Lenny to do the job was a pain in the ass. I should've sent a reminder email to my tenants that Lenny was coming to install new shower heads, but I didn't."

O'Malley and Alcocks both looked pleasantly surprised to hear this information. O'Malley had another question he wanted to ask, but was interrupted by Fr. Carey, who suddenly barged into the kitchen. O'Malley, Alcocks, and Stan were dumbfounded as they stared at Fr. Carey, who slapped both hands on the counter as he tried to catch his breath.

"Jesus Christ," O'Malley said. "What are you doing here?"

"Did you ride your bike over here?" Alcocks asked. "I'm not doing mouth to mouth on you if you keel over. Don't want to get drunk on the job."

Fr. Carey finally got his breathing under control and said, "Is it true about, Lenny?"

"Afraid so," O'Malley said in a soft tone.

With his left hand resting on his hip, Fr. Carey slapped his right hand on the countertop. "Son of a bitch!"

In pain, Fr. Carey rubbed the palm of his right hand on his right butt cheek.

"I'll bet any of you ten grand that the arson fire and Lenny's murder are connected," Stan said.

Fr. Carey's face became contorted into a weird looking, curious expression. He looked at Stan then O'Malley. "Holy cow...I didn't even think about that, but you're right. They've got to be connected."

Alcocks gave Stan another hard look. "Well, considering that your good pal Randy still hasn't produced an alibi for his whereabouts on the night of the fire..."

"Fuck you, Alcocks! You know damn well Randy didn't start the fire!"

Fr. Carey actually looked sad as he put both hands on the countertop and lowered his head. He stared at one of the kitchen design magazines on the countertop then shook his head in disbelief. Fr. Carey was clearly looking at the cover photo depicting an ultra-modern kitchen. But it wasn't clear to O'Malley, Alcocks, or Stan whether Fr. Carey was staring at the photo because he was interested in the ultra-modern kitchen design, or because he was attempting to conceal his fragile emotional state.

"This whole situation makes about as much sense as updating an old A-frame cabin with a sleek modern kitchen," Fr. Carey said. He finally lifted up his head, but didn't look at anyone in the kitchen. Instead, he glanced at the messed-up living room and said, "Who would go through the trouble of murdering, Lenny? Granted, I haven't seen him at a single mass in six years, but overall the man was a class act."

O'Malley and Alcocks both looked confounded. "Class act? Father, the man was a serial womanizer," Alcocks said.

"Be that as it may, I'll remember him fondly for his generous spirit. I had to call him a couple times a year to fix the church's old plumbing system. Never charged me once. Not one dime."

Fr. Carey looked at Stan. "Oh, that reminds me. The annual church golf outing is next month and none of you golf junkies have signed up yet. It's our most important fundraising event of the year. Stan, are you sponsoring the 18th hole again?"

Stan glanced at his watch. "Shit, I gotta run," Stan said as he hurried out of the house.

"Say hello to Lisa for me," Alcocks said with a snarky grin.

"What's his hurry?" Fr. Carey asked.

"Hey, if your wife looked as good as Lisa Zbikowski, you'd be running home every chance you got to try and tickle her belly from the inside," Alcocks said.

"Completely uncalled for, Alcocks," Fr. Carey snapped. "Why don't you turn your attention from fantasizing about extra-marital affairs and focus on this murder investigation? The first forty-eight hours of a murder investigation are crucial."

Alcocks gave Fr. Carey an elbow to the shoulder and said, "Lighten up, Father. You know I love rubbing in the fact that you can't sleep with women."

Fr. Carey gave O'Malley then Alcocks a serious look. "I fully expect to see both of you purchase a foursome for the golf outing."

O'Malley nodded a few times and said, "Of course, Father. Wouldn't dream of missing the outing. What kind of car did you get for the hole-in-one prize?"

"Fully loaded Explorer."

"Nice."

"I don't golf and I'm agnostic, so I won't be attending," Alcocks said with a straight face.

Fr. Carey let out a long sigh. He then looked around the house to make sure the other officers weren't close enough to hear. Fr. Carey took a few steps toward O'Malley and said softly, "I don't know if this information will help, but in the past two years there's been an uptick in the number of confessions revolving around infidelity. Many men, and a few women, have confessed to me that they committed adultery. Lot of first timers, too. You can always tell when it's a first-time cheater confessing, because they cry their eyes out and choke on their snot."

O'Malley and Alcocks exchanged an uneasy look. O'Malley finally regarded Fr. Carey and said, "Doesn't that violate some sort of Holy Oath?"

Fr. Carey conveyed a very serious look as he stared at O'Malley for a good ten seconds. "I don't let my vows get in the way of my support for law enforcement."

Fr. Carey extended his right fist toward O'Malley, who reluctantly bumped it, and then to Alcocks who also exchanged a fist bump. "Back the blue," Fr. Carey said. "I'll be praying for you fellas. May God guide you in your quest to find Lenny's killer. I know I speak for everyone who lives in Whispers Dunes when I say, we're all counting on you."

O'Malley and Alcocks both looked to be in a daze as they watched Fr. Carey stroll out of the house. O'Malley let out a sigh of relief as soon as he heard the front door close. O'Malley and Alcocks glanced at Soller as he came down the stairs from the second-floor loft bedroom. He was clearly frustrated as he approached O'Malley. "We checked everywhere, Chief. No orange shoebox in the house or his van."

O'Malley did not look surprised. "Somebody was here looking for it. Maybe they found it, maybe they didn't. But I think it's safe to say, that shoebox did not belong to Lenny."

"What's our next move, Chief?" Alcocks asked.

"We need to find out where Lenny discovered that shoebox. Once we do that, I'm hoping we'll get a better idea of what's in the box."

Alcocks regarded O'Malley. "What are the chances Lenny found the shoebox in Denise's apartment?"

O'Malley scratched the itch behind his right ear then said, "I'd say the chances are pretty good."

14

The St. Mary's church parking lot was empty, except for the two cars parked in the last row. The back of the parking lot was bordered by a chain link fence that stretched nearly a hundred yards. On the other side of the fence was a vast forest. The late afternoon sun rays were penetrating the forest, creating a beautiful nature scene that looked like something Bob Ross would've imagined as he painted. Standing between the 1990 white Porsche 944 and the 2023 black GMC Denali were Stan, Duane, and Randy.

Stan sipped on a bottle of beer while flipping bratwurst on his portable charcoal grill. Randy and Duane both took big bites from their bratwurst while Stan continued his story about what happened earlier in the day at Lenny's cabin. Duane, wearing a t-shirt that read Cockburn Island on the front, didn't bother to wipe the mustard from the corner of his mouth as he took another big bite. While still chewing he said, "When you say ransacked, do you mean like there were important papers from drawers and filing cabinets all over the place? Or did the intruders just want to piss on his rug and break shit? You know, like in *The Big Lebowski*."

"I don't think Lenny owned a filing cabinet, but yes, there were papers and random shit all over the floor. It was clear somebody was looking for something," Stan said while flipping the brats.

"What do you think they were looking for?" Randy asked before taking another bite from his brat.

Stan seemed a bit paranoid as he glanced out at the empty parking before his eyes landed on Randy. He took a long sip from his beer bottle then said, "I don't know. But I know this...on June 28th, Lenny was installing a new shower head at one of my rental properties. He called me around noon and said he cut his thumb really bad and was headed to the E.R."

"Whose apartment was Lenny in when he cut his thumb?" Duane asked. He delayed wiping the mustard from the corner of his mouth because he was so intent on hearing Stan's response. Randy also looked very intent on hearing Stan's response, but neither Stan or Duane recognized that Randy was nervous. Before Stan said anything he pointed to the corner of Duane's mouth, which prompted him to wipe off the huge wad of mustard.

Stan looked at Duane then Randy and finally said, "He was in Denise's apartment."

Duane looked pleasantly surprised as he took another bite from his brat. "I just love Denise. I know what you heteros think of her, and I get it, she has the most incredible body I've ever seen. But she's also the sweetest, most considerate woman I know. She reminds me a lot of my grandma."

Randy struggled to mask the nervous feeling in his stomach that was starting to make him sweat. Stan turned his focus to rotating the brats and Duane grabbed a bottle of beer from the cooler, so neither picked up on the fact that Randy was almost in a state of panic. Randy took a long swig from his beer bottle, but the beer only made his knotted stomach more upset. Stan used a long fork to pick up a brat from the grill and tuck it into his bun. "I'll tell you what I think...I think Lenny found something that he wasn't supposed to," Stan said.

"Like dope?" Duane asked. "Maybe a kilo of coke?"

Stan looked at Duane as he took a big bite of his bratwurst. "Maybe."

"Denise is sweeter than a slice of double chocolate cheesecake, but I know she likes to party."

"Yeah, she likes to party, but I don't think she uses drugs. She's a world-class pilates instructor," Stan said.

"Did you relay this to O'Malley?"

Stan nodded while he lathered some horseradish sauce on his brat. "Yeah."

Randy gave up on controlling his emotions and started to cry with a barely chewed bratwurst in his mouth. Stan flashed a grin and said, "I told you that Polish horseradish was spicy. I take a spoonful anytime I get a stuffed up with a cold. Clears my nasal passage in two seconds."

Duane looked impressed as he took another bite from his brat. "Isn't that your grandma's homemade recipe?"

"Oh, yeah. You can't get horseradish sauce that strong in a store."

"You should think about selling it," Duane said. "I guarantee you there's a market for unbearably strong, organic horseradish sauce."

Randy started to cry harder while struggling to chew the piece of bratwurst. Duane looked concerned. "Spit it out, Randy! Its dangerous to try and swallow when your emotional. Believe me, I know."

Randy grabbed his throat with both hands as he started to choke on the bratwurst.

"Oh, fuck!" Stan yelled. "He's choking!"

Stan was suddenly stricken with panic and didn't even make an attempt to help.

Duane spiked his brat to the ground, took one big hop step to get behind Randy, and started the Heimlich maneuver. Duane used all his might to repeatedly thrusts his fists into Randy's diaphragm. "Come on, you son of a bitch!" Duane screamed. "Come on, buddy! Relax, Randy! You're not gonna die! I'm behind you with everything I got!"

Clearly winded, Duane pumped his fists into Randy's diaphragm with everything he had, and the bratwurst was finally dislodged from Randy's throat.

Out of breath, Duane was almost too weak to stand. He extended his arm toward Stan for help. Stan grabbed him and helped Duane ease into the lawn chair. Stan then helped Randy sit down on the cooler. Randy's eyes were watery and he was panting. He looked desperate to try and regain normal breathing. He stood back up and started to walk around in hopes of getting his breathing under control.

"Thats it, Randy, walk it off, buddy," Stan said.

Duane's big, wide eyes stared out at the dense forest that was filled with sun rays. Exhausted, he took a deep breath and exhaled slowly out his mouth. He was replaying what just happened in his mind. For a few seconds, he thought he might lose his friend. Duane chugged down the rest of his beer then turned to Randy and said, "You okay, pal?"

Randy was standing still and staring out at the forest. His eyes had stopped tearing up and his breathing was under control. He nodded then looked at Duane.

"Thank you, Duane...You saved my life."

Stan handed Randy a napkin as he started to tear up again. Randy wiped the tears away then wiped away the mustard from the corner of his mouth. Stan grabbed two beer bottles from the cooler, popped the caps off with an opener, and handed one to Randy then Duane. Stan clinked his beer bottle with Duane's and said, "Nice work, buddy."

"I didn't realize how much strength you use up doing the Heimlich. I'm still light headed," Duane said just before sipping his beer.

Randy finally looked like he had control of his emotions. He took a deep breath and said, "Guys, I need to tell you something."

Stan and Duane could tell by Randy's tone that something was wrong. They kept their eyes glued on Randy. Feeling deeply embarrassed, he lowered his head and finally said, "I'm being blackmailed."

Stan and Duane both stared at Randy in disbelief. Unsure how to respond, they looked at each other, shook their heads, then looked at Randy. Stan finally muttered, "What?"

Duane's mouth was agape. "By who?"

Randy closed his eyes for a second. He then glanced at Duane and said very softly, "Denise."

Beer sprayed from Stan's mouth, just missing Randy. "Holy Christ! Are you serious?"

Randy was too embarrassed to say anything at the moment. Stan started walking in circles in order to get his emotions under control. Duane, however, looked a tad confused. "Surely you're not talking about Denise Lyons. The only other Denise I know is the barista at my favorite coffee shop. But why in the world would a college student, who works part time as a barista want to blackmail you?"

Randy put his hands on his hips as he regarded Duane. "I'm being blackmailed by Denise Lyons."

"Holy shit," Stan said in a soft tone. He looked like he needed to sit down. "I have so many questions, I don't know where to start."

Duane still didn't look like he believed Randy. "Denise Lyons, an elite pilates instructor and community activist, who also happens to be Stan's favorite tenant, is blackmailing you?"

Randy let out a frustrated sigh. "Yes."

Stan looked perturbed as he glanced at Duane. "She's not my favorite tenant," Stan said in a defensive tone.

"Why is Denise blackmailing you?" Duane asked. "You don't have any money."

"It's complicated," Randy said.

"Blackmailing usually is," Duane said.

"Somehow, she became aware that I have a copy of the yet-to-be-released feasibility study on the rocket launch spaceport. To quickly summarize, the feasibility study strongly recommends that the rocket launch spaceport not be built."

Duane shook his head in disbelief. "What a giant waste of money and time. Those assholes spent two and a half million dollars and two years to finally determine that launching shitting rockets over Lake Superior is a bad idea."

"The report states that the financial benefit to Whisper Dunes from the spaceport's operations would be equal to the addition of two fast food restaurants. Combined with all the environmental concerns, it's not hard to understand why the report strongly opposes the spaceport," Randy said.

"So, why does Denise care about this report?" Stan asked.

Randy looked at Stan with a blank expression and said, "Because it could cost her ten million dollars."

Stan's face was filled with dismay. He blurted out, "What? How?'

"So what does she want you to do? Burn the report? It's going to be released eventually to the public," Duane said.

"She's ordered me to do everything in my power to make sure Russ doesn't get his hands on that report before the zoning board meeting. If there's a tie, Russ has the deciding vote to amend the 5,000 acres so it can be developed into an industrial site."

Stan was in disbelief as he regarded Randy. "You're telling me that Denise, a pilates instructor and part-time community activist, is the one who owns the 5,000 acres?"

"No, someone else owns the land. Her job is to blackmail me and probably half a dozen other people in order to increase the chances that the land will be rezoned. So whoever owns the land can sell it to a space company. According to Denise, her partner has reached an agreement to sell the land for a hundred million dollars, ten of which goes to Denise."

With their mouths and eyes wide open, Duane and Stan both struggled to process the information. Stan and Duane shared a confused look before they regarded Randy. Stan finally said, "How exactly is Denise blackmailing you?"

Randy closed his eyes tightly and lowered his head in shame. He started to scratch the top of his head while Stan and

Duane stared at him with uneasy looks. It's not that he didn't trust Stan and Duane, but he had never told anyone what he was about to tell them. He understood how hard it would be for them to wrap their minds around the fact that Denise seduced him. If fact, he expected them to doubt his story. Never in his wildest dreams did Randy ever imagine he'd be important enough to become the victim of a well- designed, well-executed, blackmail operation. As his gaze met Stan's then Duane's, Randy realized that once he opened his mouth and told his two closest friends about his relationship with Denise, his life would never be the same. Stan and Duane both had the gift of gab, Randy thought, and it was possible at some point down the road that one or both of them could slip up and tell someone about his secret. Randy had intended to carry this deep, dark secret around with him for the rest of his life. But here was his chance to come clean and admit his terrible mistake to his two most trusted friends. By doing so, he thought he could start the process of forgiving himself. *It's now or never*, Randy told himself. He glanced at the forest before moving his eyes back on Stan and Duane. He finally said, "Denise seduced me, then secretly filmed us having sex."

Stan was so overwhelmed with shock that his entire body stiffened, but for some reason Duane acted like he didn't hear Randy. Duane put his right hand behind his right ear and said, "Come again?"

Randy looked relieved to finally share his secret. But Stan and Duane looked like they didn't believe him.

"It's a long story, so I'll just start with the most recent part. A few weeks ago, Denise emailed me a video of us that she secretly filmed."

"You really had sex with Denise?" Stan asked with an incredulous look stuck on his face.

"Yes."

Duane and Stan both looked at Randy, dumbfounded, trying but unable to visualize Randy having sex with Denise.

"She trapped me in her honey pot."

Stan slapped Randy's right shoulder. "You're not lying, are you?"

Randy shook his head ever so slightly. His sad eyes moved from Stan toward the forest.

"What's she like in the sack? I bet she's a real handful."

Duane looked upset. Unable to hold in his anger any longer he yelled, "You dumb, fuck! How could you cheat on

Vivian!? She's sweeter than peach cobbler. She's a wonderful mother, and holds down a full-time job."

"I thought you said Denise was sweeter than peach cobbler," Stan said.

Duane flashed an angry glare at Stan. "No, I said she's sweeter than a double chocolate cheesecake." Duane's angry glare moved back to Randy. "I'm sorry she can't find the time to sculpt her body like Denise does, every single day, but despite her busy schedule as a working mom I think Vivian's pretty darn cute."

Randy looked ashamed as he diverted his eyes away from Duane's judgmental stare. Randy closed his eyes and took a much needed deep breath. He opened his eyes to find Duane still staring at him. "You're a lawyer who makes less than six figures a year...she should be cheating on you!"

"I know," Randy said in a barely audible tone.

"I think what Duane means is, you and Vivian are one of the happiest married couples we know. So why would you risk losing your wife for a few cheap thrills in the sack with an incredibly gorgeous pilates instructor?" Stan asked. Immediately after asking that question, Stan realized that he probably would have done exactly what Randy did.

"Oh, shut the fuck up, Stan. You would've done the same thing, except you would've probably been the one to film it," Duane said.

Stan smacked his lips together and rolled them inward as he slightly nodded his head.

Randy looked emotional again. He took a deep breath and glanced at Stan then Duane. "I love my wife very much. I would do anything for her," Randy said. He tried to compose himself as he struggled with intense emotions. "What I'm about to tell you is top secret. I'm serious, I will burn your houses down if you repeat a word of what I'm about to say. Understand?"

Duane quickly put both hands over his mouth in shock. "Oh, my God, Randy...did you burn down the clubhouse?"

"No! Sorry, that was a dumb threat. Just forget about my veiled threat and promise me that you'll never tell anyone what I'm about to tell you."

"I promise," Stan said.

Duane raised his right hand. "I promise, Scout's honor."

"I didn't know you were a Boy Scout?" Stan asked.

"How do you think I learned the correct way to do the Heimlich?"

Randy, clearly annoyed, flashed a frustrated look. "Do you want to hear what I have to say, or not?"

"Sorry," Duane said in an apologetic tone.

"A few months ago, I bumped into Denise at Stucko's. I had a rough day at work and had just ordered my second whiskey sour when Denise happened to sit down on the bar stool next to me. She commented on how stressed I looked and patiently listened as I vented about my work issues. She's a great listener. It had been a long while since someone really listened to me. Before Denise left she offered me a free week of pilates classes at her studio. I thought, I'm twenty pounds overweight, what the hell. A little pilates might do me some good."

Duane and Stan, their eyes glued to Randy, were intrigued. Duane was eagerly bobbing his head forward and backwards as he waited for Randy to continue his story. The tension in his neck and shoulders had subsided and Randy started to convey his usual steady demeanor. He crossed his arms and allowed himself an easy breath.

"Two weeks later, I showed up to my first ever pilates class. It was brutal. I barely made it through. In fact, I thought about leaving half way through the class but considering she personally invited me, I thought that would be rude. After the class, Denise came up to me covered in sweat, flashed a big, sexy smile, and complimented my effort. I made a couple jokes at my expense then she invited me up to her apartment for a smoothie. I should've politely declined, but I quickly discovered that when Denise looks into your eyes and flashes that incredible smile of hers...it's impossible to say no. Soon as we got upstairs, she started asking me about the Stop the Rocket campaign while she made the smoothies. I rambled on about how even if the rocket launch site got approved, Canada will likely sue Marquette County to stop it from going forward. Then she asked me about the feasibility study. I lied and told her I hadn't read it. I remember there was an uncomfortable silence. I think she knew I was lying, so I thanked her for the blueberry smoothie and the free pilates session, and started to make my way toward the door. But she got between me and the door while blabbering on about the benefits of doing pilates everyday. Then...she spilled her smoothie on her t-shirt. She didn't say anything, she just smiled and handed me her smoothie. Then she took off her t-shirt, and suddenly the most beautiful woman I've ever seen was standing two feet from me, topless. It didn't seem real. I just stood there, dumbfounded, staring at her perfect breasts."

"Then what happened?" Duane and Stan asked at the same time.

"She slowly dropped to her knees and started going down on me."

Stan and Duane both looked stunned and aroused. Duane cleared his throat because his mouth had been agape for so long. Stan looked like he wanted to say something, but was only able to shake his head in disbelief. Randy was clearly upset with himself as he lowered his head.

"I didn't know what to do. I froze up. That has never happened to me before. I remember looking down at her and thinking, would it be rude if I asked her to stop? But she was so into it. The sound of her sucking and moaning completely hypnotized me. Honestly, I can't even remember where I finished."

Stan crossed his arms tightly and mouthed, "Wow."

"As I was driving home the realization of what happened finally started to sink in. I felt terrible. I actually had to pull my car over to the side of the road so I could throw up. I love Vivian very much and never once thought about cheating on her. She's perfect, why would I? That was the first time that I've ever cheated on my wife and it really shook me up. The next day, I went back to Denise's apartment to confront her and that's when she seduced me again. This time we spent the afternoon having sex."

Stan, his eyes wide-open, said, "Wow. What's her favorite position? I bet she likes to be in charge."

Duane looked furious with Stan as he turned toward him and said, "Jesus Christ, Stan. Randy fell victim to Denise's unavoidable honey trap. He's going to be scarred for life. The poor sap probably blacked out while she was screwing his brains out."

Randy's gaze met Stan's and he said, sheepishly, "Sex with Denise was a total blur. I couldn't keep up so she got on top and just dominated me."

Stan let out a long whistle and said, "Yeah, that's pretty much how I pictured it." Duane's face was contorted as he used quite a bit of mental energy trying to envision the scene.

"We only had two encounters before I ended it. The day after I told Denise never to contact me again, she emailed me the video of us doing it on her bed."

Stan looked perplexed as he said, "You never suspected that she might be filming your encounters?"

"No. I never once saw a camera or even her phone in the bedroom. Obviously she had a secret recording device somewhere. After she sent me the video I immediately went to her place to confront her, but she quickly made it clear that I was under her control now. She told me that I can't let Russ get his hands on the feasibility report before the next zoning board meeting. If I fail, Denise will send the video to Vivian, and my life will be over."

Stan remained in a state of bewilderment as he slowly shook his head. "What a vindictive broad," he said. "Boy, she had me fooled. I always thought Denise was a real sweetheart. She's adored by everyone."

"If you asked me about Denise ten minutes ago, I would've said she's sweeter than peaches soaking in a can of fructose syrup," Duane said.

"Boy, you really like your sweeter-than similes," Stan said.

Duane acted like he didn't hear Stan. "I just can't wrap my head around the idea that Denise would set up a honey trap to blackmail you, or anyone for that matter."

Randy sighed then took a sip from his beer. "Yeah, it was quite remarkable how quickly she switched from being so sweet and affectionate to cold and evil. I still can't get the image out of my head of her grinning at me as she threatened to ruin my life."

Stan regarded Randy closely and said, "Do you have any reason to believe that she might be blackmailing other guys in town?"

Randy took his time before he finally said, "Yeah. I don't have any proof, but just call it a hunch."

Duane looked distraught as he blurted out, "What?"

"Any idea who else?" Stan asked.

"None. Like I said, it's just a gut feeling."

Duane took a step toward Randy and said, "So, you're saying that Denise Lyons is running a sexpionage operation right here in Whisper Dunes? A.K.A.—America's Best Fucking Place to Live!"

"I didn't say that, but I think it's possible," Randy said.

Stan opened another beer and said, "Denise's got ten million bucks coming to her if a space company buys that land. I think it's more than plausible that's she's fucking and blackmailing at least a few guys in town, namely the old farts on the zoning board commission."

"God, I hate that word," Duane said.

Stan looked a bit confused. "Fucking?"

"No, plausible."

"Huh, I like that word," Stan said. "The big question is, who's Denise working for?"

Duane looked very concerned, even scared. "The guy or guys who murdered, Lenny? Who are probably also the same guys who burned down the clubhouse."

Stan's faraway look made it seem like he was considering this scenario. "Maybe."

"Could be someone local, but then again it could be some big shot out East or out West," Randy said. "All I know is that I wish I wasn't in this position."

Stan and Duane both looked like they felt bad for Randy. Not sure what to say, Duane put his hand on Randy's shoulder and gave him a sympathetic nod.

"You guys have known me for a long time. I would never do anything to hurt my wife or kids. Denise literally backed me into a corner and gave me a blowjob without my consent. Now she has the power to ruin my life," Randy said as he started to tear up. "My wife and kids are my entire life. I'm nothing without them. But if Vivian sees that video she'll take the kids and divorce my sorry ass. I know it."

Duane tried to comfort Randy by gently rubbing his back. Stan abruptly banged his fist on the hood of his GMC Denali in a fit of rage. "You blackmail one of us! You blackmail all of us!"

Randy looked a bit taken back.

"Fuckin A," Duane said loudly.

"You're an outstanding dad and a wonderful husband," Stan said. "And catching one hummer, and going a couple rounds on the mattress with a smoking hot pilates instructor doesn't change that fact...not one bit."

Randy took a deep breath. On the verge of tearing up again, he glanced at Stan and Duane. "Thank you."

Duane looked intensely serious as he put his hands on his hips. "What do we do now, soldiers?"

Stan had a determined look on his face as he glanced at Duane then Randy. "We will do whatever it takes to make sure Denise doesn't send that video to Vivian. But keep in mind, we're dealing with a savvy, very vindictive woman here. If we have any chance of beating her, we have to think like her. And starting right now, we need to watch each others back. Lenny found something in her apartment, and it cost him his life."

Duane rubbed his chin while a thought crossed his mind. He slowly shook his head. "God, it's so hard to picture Denise as a cold-blooded killer. A dynamo in bed? No. But a killer? She's such a fun, laid back free spirit. She single-handedly convinced the town council to ban plastic straws, create a butterfly habitat, and legalize topless bathing at the beach...all in the same year."

"Well, at the very least she's a cold-blooded blackmailer, who preyed on a sweet, sensitive, family man," Stan said.

"Hey, lets keep in mind that O'Malley was a highly respected homicide detective with the Detroit P.D. before he became the top cop in Whisper Dunes. I think it's only a matter of time before he figures out who killed Lenny," Duane said.

Stan looked uneasy as he considered an unlikely scenario. "Is it possible that Denise could have something on O'Malley?" Stan asked.

Duane and Randy both conveyed a look of doubt. "No way," Duane said. "Not, Chief O'Malley."

"I don't know. Denise has a very unique way about her...I feel like she has the power to seduce anyone," Randy said.

"Not me," Duane said proudly.

Randy stared at Duane. "Are you intrigued by the idea of receiving head from a blowjob artist?"

"Absolutely, " Duane said. He looked uneasy as he made a fist and bit his knuckles.

"Then Denise has the power to seduce you."

"Let's simplify and focus," Stan said impatiently. "All we need to do is find evidence that Denise is blackmailing people. With any evidence, O'Malley can get a warrant, raid her place, confiscate all her devices, and arrest her ass on the spot. Hopefully before Denise emails Vivian the sex video."

Randy took a sip from his beer before regarding Stan. "Because of what Lenny stumbled upon, whatever was in Denise's apartment that could link her to a blackmail operation has probably been removed."

"Yeah, you're probably right, but I bet we'll find at least one clue that leads us in the right direction," Duane said.

Stan looked to be in agreement with Duane as he took a big bite from his brat. "There's a huge attic above Denise's apartment. The only way to get access is from Denise's bedroom. I betcha she's hiding something up there."

"Only one way to find out," Duane said.

"What in God's name do you guys think you're doing?" Fr. Carey shouted from about thirty yards away.

The guys all quickly turned in the direction of Fr. Carey as he approached. "We were just gonna call you, Father," Stan said jovially.

"You're grilling brats on church property, fifty yards from my residence, and you don't think to invite me over?"

"I'm sorry Fr. Carey, that was an oversight on my part," Duane said.

"Where the heck did you guys learn your manners from?"

Randy handed Fr. Carey a bun just as Stan used the tongs to pluck the last brat off the grill and into Fr. Carey's bun. "Mustard or horseradish?" Duane asked.

"Mustard, please. I've tried Stan's homemade horseradish sauce before. Delicious, but it gave me the shits for two days."

Duane handed Fr. Carey a bottle of spicy mustard. He squeezed a liberal amount over the brat as he noticed Duane's t-shirt. "Cockburn Island. I've got the same shirt. Does it say, 'You'll Be Glad You Came' on the back?"

"Oh, yeah."

"I need to get back there. Beautiful place."

"Onions?" Stan asked.

"No, thanks," Fr. Carey said before he took a big bite. Fr. Carey glanced at Stan, then Duane, then Randy. "Three buddies grilling brats in the church parking lot while basking in the late afternoon sunshine. Let me guess, you're chewing the fat on the latest conspiracy theory surrounding Lenny's murder? I gotta tell you, the one about the oil execs hiring a hitman to take Lenny out in order to embarrass Whisper Dunes makes a ton of sense...a ton of sense."

"No, actually..." Stan said before getting cut off by Fr. Carey.

"Whatever you think happened to Lenny, just know that it goes deep. So before you guys go subscribing to a particular conspiracy theory, ask yourself this question, what if it's a conspiracy theory hiding the real conspiracy theory?"

The guys all looked very confused as they watched Fr. Carey stuff the rest of his bratwurst into his mouth. He casually grabbed a beer from the cooler then took the napkin out of Duane's hand and wiped his mouth. "Have a blessed rest of your day...and don't forget to be a blessing."

Stan, Duane, and Randy closely watched Fr. Carey as he walked back toward the church rectory.

"Is there any chance that Fr. Carey's in the middle of all this?" Duane asked.

"No. But I'm pretty sure he started that rumor about Lenny being murdered by a Baptist minister from Iron Mountain because Lenny slept with his wife and sister," Randy said.

Duane's curious eyes narrowed as he rubbed his chin. Stan looked at Duane then Randy and said, "I gotta be honest, that one is more plausible than most of the rumors I've heard so far."

Chief O'Malley walked with a cautious stride down the short, narrow hallway. He stopped in front of the only door in the hallway and remained highly alert. Since becoming a cop over thirty years ago, his heart always started to beat faster right before he knocked on a door. Regardless of whose door he was knocking on, O'Malley was always prepared to defend himself before his knuckles hit the door. His attentive eyes started to narrow with anticipation. He wasn't nervous, just intensely focused. He knocked twice on the apartment door then took a step backwards. Out of pure habit, O'Malley lowered his right hand until it was about an inch from his service revolver.

The door swung open and Denise was able to hide her surprise by flashing a warm smile. She was wearing a short, pink, silk robe that was loosely tied. Her left breast was almost completely exposed, but O'Malley didn't seem to notice because his eyes quickly moved from her hands right to her smiley face.

"Good morning, Chief."

"Morning, Denise."

"How can I help you?"

"I'm sorry to bother you, but I'd like to ask you some questions, if that's okay?"

Denise's friendly smile widened while she made no attempt to close up her robe. "Sure. Fire away. Oh, I'm sorry, would you like to come in? I can make you one of my famous smoothies."

"No, thank you. This will just take a minute."

Denise's smile slowly vanished as she folded her arms. "I'm sure you've heard by now about Lenny Trubisky."

Denise feigned a sad look as she kept eye contact with O'Malley.

"Just terrible. I barely knew him, but he seemed like a nice guy. It's so awful that people keep spreading these unfounded rumors about him. That's not the Whisper Dunes that I know and love."

"Yeah, there's already some really wacky stories out there."

"I don't believe any of them. I know some people around here love a good conspiracy theory, no matter how much of it is rooted in bullshit," Denise said. "But most of the people I know in Whisper Dunes don't spread unfounded rumors for fun, except for maybe Father Carey. What scares me though is that it won't be long before the national media starts reporting on the most entertaining rumors because they know that's what there audience wants them to do."

O'Malley nodded in complete agreement. In doing so he finally noticed Denise's left breast, which was barely hiding behind her robe. O'Malley's eyes got wide for a second, but he quickly narrowed his eyes as they landed back on Denise's face. "Stan told me that Lenny came by your apartment on the 28th to install a new shower head."

Denise closed her robe tightly then folded her arms while keeping her eyes firmly on O'Malley. "Yes, that's correct."

"Where you here when Lenny was installing the shower head?"

"Briefly. I let him in and then I went for a bike ride. I stopped off at the beach for a quick swim. When I got home Lenny was gone."

"Did Stan alert you that Lenny was coming over to install the shower head?"

"Yes. I bumped into him a few weeks ago at the beach. I was sunbathing topless, but that didn't stop Stan from coming over and saying hello. We chatted for a bit then before I jumped in the lake he casually mentioned that Lenny was going to be stopping over to install a new shower head."

O'Malley tried hard to keep a blank face as his gaze remained locked on Denise's gaze. But O'Malley started to look uneasy as he saw how comfortable Denise looked. Her sexy smile was actually causing O'Malley to lose his train of thought. Denise stood relaxed in her doorway, looking as if she was prepared to answer questions all morning. O'Malley had no choice but to allow his mind to recall the worst murder scene he ever saw. It was his second year as a Detroit homicide detective, and he only had to think about the horrific scene for a few seconds before his mind snapped back into focus. "When was the last time you saw Lenny?"

Denise acted like she was thinking about the question. She tilted her head up and ran her right thumb and index finger along the eighteen-carat gold necklace hanging low around her neck. Her eyes finally landed back on O'Malley and she said, "At Breakers, the night of the 4th. I happened to bump into him at the bar. We both said hello, and that was it."

"Did you two chat about anything particular?"

"No. I just said hi. Lenny was lit up like a Christmas tree. He could barely talk. I stayed at the bar and he stumbled away. Didn't see him the rest of the night."

O'Malley looked uncomfortable again, but not because Denise's nipples were clearly visible through the thin, silk robe. He squinted his eyes and rubbed the bridge of his nose before he finally said, "I'm sorry, Denise, but I have to ask...did you and Lenny ever have a romantic relationship?"

Denise looked surprised, even a little embarrassed. "No. God, no. Why would you even think to ask that?"

"It's come to my attention that Lenny was very sexually active in the community, and frankly I've been surprised to learn about some of his past relationships."

"That's news to me, Chief. Like I said before, I barely knew Lenny. Never even had a real conversation with the man."

O'Malley looked Denise in the eyes for a moment then offered a polite nod. "Thank you, Denise. I appreciate your time."

Denise smiled sweetly as she tilted her head ever so slightly to the right. "My pleasure, Chief. Don't hesitate to stop by again if you have any more questions. Now, if you'll please excuse me, I have to get ready for my next pilates class."

O'Malley smiled slightly as he started his walk down the hallway just as Denise shut her apartment door.

The oldest diner in town, which was last updated in the mid-70s, was practically empty. A few customers were quietly enjoying a late breakfast at the counter, but the booths were all empty except for the back corner booth. O'Malley sat across from Alcocks, who was scarfing down banana pancakes.

"You don't think she was telling the truth?" Alcocks asked with a mouthful of banana pancakes.

O'Malley slowly sipped his coffee. "I think she was being straight with me in regard to her relationship with Lenny. But she's hiding something."

"Everyone's hiding something, Chief."

"Denise told me that she ran into Stan at the beach a few weeks ago and he notified her that Lenny was coming over to install the shower heads. But I contacted all of Stan's other tenants, and they all stated that Stan never told them that they were getting new shower heads."

Alcocks looked surprised as he quickly wiped his mouth. "Have you talked to Stan yet?"

"Yeah. He said he bumped into Denise on the beach a few weeks ago, but because she was topless he can't recall any details of their conversation."

Alcocks nodded as he wiped syrup off his chin. "Yeah, I can see that. I was walking my dog on the beach last week and saw Denise paddle-boarding topless. Wow. Forgot where I was for a couple of minutes."

"Wasn't Denise the one who spearheaded the effort to legalize topless bathing?"

"Yeah. As soon as she got behind the movement, pretty much every gal in Whisper Dunes supported the movement. My wife and mom included."

O'Malley sipped his coffee, still trying to get the image of Denise in her loosely tied robe out of his mind.

"Did you read my report on Lenny's wake and funeral?" Alcocks asked.

"Yeah. Nothing stood out, huh?"

"No, not really. The wake and funeral were both well attended. Lenny didn't have any family, but he was the most trusted plumber in this town for over thirty years so he had a lot of pals. Stan gave a rambling eulogy, but I thought Fr. Carey's homily was pretty good."

"I saw in the report that Russ attended both the wake and funeral."

"Yep."

"Did the former Mrs. Houston make it to the wake or funeral?"

"No, didn't see her. From the time the wake started until it ended, there was at least one of our guys inside the funeral home. Nobody saw her."

"What about Hubert?"

"Nope."

"Denise?"

"No."

The pretty waitress, Grace, stopped by the table. "More coffee, gentleman?"

Alcocks shook his head before chugging the rest of his coffee.

"Please," O'Malley said. He watched Grace carefully pour coffee into his cup. "Thanks, Grace."

Grace looked around to make sure no one was close enough to hear. "Guess who I served breakfast to this morning?"

"Who?" O'Malley asked.

"Anderson Cooper."

Alcocks looked impressed. "No shit?"

"Yeah, he's in town to do some in-depth reporting. Super nice guy. Big tipper."

Grace took an uneasy breath as she looked around the diner again. She closely regarded O'Malley. "There's something else I wanted to tell you."

"Go ahead."

"I didn't think much of it at the time, but after I heard about Lenny I couldn't stop thinking about this customer who came in here on the morning of the 4th of July."

O'Malley and Alcocks were both staring at Grace with curious eyes.

"This strange looking guy came in here about an hour before the parade started. I guess strange isn't the right word. More like, big and scary looking. He sat quietly in this booth for about a half-hour sipping coffee. I asked him twice if he was ready to order and he just shook his head. While I was delivering an order to a nearby table, he suddenly bolted out of here and hopped into a black suv."

O'Malley was able to keep a blank expression while Alcocks flashed a curious smile. They exchanged a look, almost daring each other to ask the obvious question. O'Malley finally looked at Grace and said, "What kind of suv?"

"One of those obnoxiously big ones. It was black and the windows were all tinted."

"Was somebody else driving?" O'Malley asked.

Grace had to think about it for a few seconds before she said, "Yeah, the guy got in through the front passenger seat. As soon as he shut the door the car took off."

Alcocks showed Grace his phone. "Did it look like this suv?"

Grace looked closely at the photo on the phone. She shrugged and said, "Sort of."

Alcocks showed the photo on his phone to O'Malley—a black 2023 GMC Denali.

O'Malley showed Grace the photo on his phone—a black 2023 Chevy Tahoe. "What about this suv?"

"Yes! That's it."

O'Malley gave Alcocks a dirty look.

"What did this guy look like?" O'Malley asked.

"Big white guy. A real muscle head. At least 6'2. Probably close to 240 pounds. He was wearing a black hat, a white golf shirt, and tan shorts, but he didn't look like a golfer. He looked more like one of those extreme sports jocks. In great shape, but with a permanent disgruntled look."

O'Malley gave Grace a friendly nod. "Thank you, Grace. This is very helpful."

"My pleasure."

Grace flashed a quick smile and walked away.

Alcocks took a deep breath and exhaled for what seemed like five seconds. "Now what?"

O'Malley leaned forward and set his elbows on the table. He looked frustrated as he glanced over Alcocks' shoulder. He stared at the painting on the wall depicting the Stannard Rock Lighthouse. A small gold engraved plate under the painting read: *The Loneliest Lighthouse in the World.* O'Malley finally met Alcocks' gaze. "I hate to admit it, but there's reason to believe that more than two people may have conspired to murder Lenny."

"I was afraid you were going to say that, Chief. Be that as it may, it's awfully hard to imagine that there's a conspiracy revolving around the murder of a thrice divorced, unlicensed plumber."

O'Malley nodded then went back to staring at the painting. "Well, right now all the evidence points to a major conspiracy."

16

A male reporter with CBS Evening News, dressed in jeans and a navy blue CBS News fleece jacket, stood on the sidewalk at the corner of Third and Front Street while the camera crew filmed his report.

"Here in Whisper Dunes, some residents that we talked to are already calling it the *Forbes* curse. Shortly after being named, America's Best Place to Live, this picturesque town on the southern shores of Lake Superior has been deeply shaken by the mysterious murder of a beloved community member. Rumors and conspiracy theories have been swirling around town, causing heated debates at local watering holes. But everyone seems to agree that the murder is linked to the mysterious fire at the nearby Potawatomi Country Club, which the Fire Chief has confirmed was arson."

A female reporter with ABC News stood near the Lake Superior shoreline as the wind started to pick up. She looked like she was enjoying the view, but snapped into action as soon as she saw the producer and cameraman give her a thumbs up. "Ready when you are, Alice."

"Scott, we've spent all day talking with residents and most of them admitted that this is the first time they've ever felt scared living in Whisper Dunes. Who murdered Lenny Trubisky? That's the burning question on everyones mind up here in America's Best Place to Live. The theories surrounding Lenny Trubisky's murder have ranged from well thought out and conceivable, to patently absurd."

A female reporter with NBC Nightly News stood in front of the camera crew. Fifty feet behind her was the bright red Marquette Harbor Lighthouse—the oldest structure in the county. "Earlier today, I spoke with the owner of Herb's Gun

Shop and he told me that sales have skyrocketed in the past week. Now, prior to the mysterious arson and murder in Whisper Dunes, the big controversy in town was the proposed site for a rocket launch spaceport. The controversial plan has seen strong resistance from the Stop the Rocket campaign. The grassroots campaign continues to gain steam and has gotten incredible support from many residents in Whisper Dunes and from folks all across the Upper Peninsula. We were told earlier today from a Stop the Rocket spokesperson that the campaign is starting to get support from people all over America as well as from people all over the world."

A male reporter for BBC News was reporting from outside Marge's Ice Cream Parlor. There was twenty people standing in line outside of Marge's, all of whom were watching the reporter as he spoke with a thick British accent into the camera. "Right now, there are three hotly debated issues in America's Best Place to Live: Will the zoning commission vote to rezone the proposed rocket launch site? Is climate change real? And finally, did the person who set fire to the historic Potawatomi Country Club also murder Lenny Trubisky?"

Russ held his briefcase tightly as he hustled up the steps in front of the Town Hall building. He forced a polite smile while a dozen reporters surrounded him. A reporter shouted, "Is it true that your first wife left you for Lenny Trubisky?"

Russ stopped abruptly on the steps and glared at the reporter. "That is absolutely false!"

He lowered his head and walked quickly toward the entrance while the reporters continued to crowd him and stick microphones inches from his face.

"Was your second ex-wife romantically involved with Lenny Trubisky at the time of his murder?" shouted another reporter.

"I can't speak intelligently about the romantic lives of either of my ex-wives," Russ said as he hurried past the reporters. A police officer was holding open the glass front door as Russ entered the building. A few reporters attempted to follow Russ inside.

"Get out of here, you bums," yelled the officer as he shut the door.

Russ stood behind his desk, chugging from a bottle of Pepto-Bismol. Carol watched him with a concern look. "Want me to get you a Sprite?" Carol asked.

Russ shook his head as he tossed the empty Pepto-Bismol bottle into the trash can. Feeling overwhelmed and exhausted, he slumped into his chair and stared aimlessly out the window. "What a nightmare."

"I didn't know your first wife left you for Lenny," Carol said.

Russ looked pissed off, but refused to take his anger out on Carol. He regarded her and said in a gentle voice, "She didn't. She left me because I spent all my free time fishing. I didn't deserve her."

"I was at my weekly rosary club last night, and someone suggested that you should denounce the *Forbes* title. I really think you should consider doing that, sir."

Russ leaned back in his chair and said, "I thought about that, but I think it'll just create more controversy and attract more nosey television reporters."

Carol took a sip of decaf coffee from her lipstick-stained mug. "Yeah, you're probably right. Before I forget, Chief O'Malley wants to speak with you. He said to stop off at the station on your way home tonight."

Russ nodded before glancing at the document on his desk. "Tell him I'll be there at six sharp."

"Okay. Lastly, what do you want me to do with all the television people who keep calling and demanding an interview with you?"

"Just hang up, unless it's someone with NBC Nightly News. I'm still considering doing the Larry Holt interview, but haven't made up my mind yet."

"Roger that," Carol said. She shut the door as she exited the office.

Russ wheeled his chair around so he could face the photos on the table behind his desk. He stared at a photo of him and his dad on a fishing boat for a good minute before slowly closing his eyes. Different thoughts entered Russ's mind while he remained perfectly still in his chair. He thought back to some of those memorable moments on the fishing boat, just him and his dad. Anytime he got to go fishing with his dad, Russ knew he was going to receive some pearls of wisdom. Not on how to become a better fisherman—Russ's dad never spoke about fishing when they got on the boat. The advice Russ received from big Russ was meant to help him deal with life situations that tend to sneak up on you and knock you down. One piece of advice was repeated often: Be patient and stay calm. No one can catch a fish when they're angry.

Russ finally opened his eyes, but his mind was still racing while he searched for an answer to help him get through this difficult situation. *A situation that may get worse before it gets better*, he thought. But he reminded himself that Whisper Dunes *will* need someone to step up and defend this town and its residents against the media outlets, who will race to exploit this comically dramatic situation that had already put Whisper Dunes on the national and international news cycle. Russ understood that the aim for all the talking heads on cable news, social media, and podcast shows was exactly the same...to milk this crisis for as long as they can in hopes of picking up new viewers and listeners.

Russ's eyes landed on a photo of him and his mom on the day he was sworn in as mayor of Whisper Dunes. She died a year after Russ began his first term as mayor. She was a talented woman, who had dreams, but never got the chance to follow them. It was Russ's soft spoken mom who would remind her only son from time to time—don't react, respond.

Chief O'Malley's spacious office had recently been cleaned. The only window in the first floor office gave the Chief a nice view of St. Peter Cathedral. His wife had offered to decorate the office for him but he declined. He did, however, allow her to put a potted plant in the corner next to the book case she bought him. Near the end of his great run with the Detroit Police Department, Nellie encouraged Ray to become a reader in hopes of staving off Alzheimer's, the disease that slowly ended his dad's life. Nellie liked to remind her husband that reading the back of a shampoo bottle is better for your brain than staring at your phone all day. To Nellie's surprise, Ray took her advice and it wasn't long before he became an avid reader. Prior to Lenny's murder, O'Malley had been knocking out a book a week, usually crime fiction, but not always. Based on Nellie's strong recommendation, Ray had recently started reading poetry for the first time in his life. Nellie loved Maya

Angelou, so Ray had been reading her beautiful poems for the past month. He'd even memorized a few.

Hanging on the knotted pine wall panels, behind his massive oak desk, were five different watercolor pictures of the American Flag. Each painting was framed and hung in a precise way. The pictures looked like they were painted by his grandkids. On the wall left of his desk were a dozen framed photos of his wife, kids, and grandkids. On the wall right of his desk were a dozen framed black and white photos of O'Malley with his friends and partners from his days with the Detroit Police Department.

O'Malley sat calmly in the black leather chair behind his desk, patiently listening to Russ share details about his troubled marriages. What stood out to O'Malley was how Russ took all the blame for both his marriages failing, despite the fact that both his wives cheated on him repeatedly with multiple men, including Lenny. But Russ had yet to mention this fact, which O'Malley found odd, instead he blabbered on about his regrets as a husband. O'Malley could see that his friend was extremely vulnerable at the moment so he made an effort to convey a sympathetic look.

"I've known you for a long time, Russ. Never once did you mention to me that your first or second wife was cheating on you." O'Malley said in a soft tone. "Nobody should have to deal with the collapse of their marriage alone. You suffered through two rough divorces, man. It's not healthy to shoulder all that pain."

Russ looked ashamed as he glanced at a photo on the wall before his sad eyes landed back on O'Malley. "It's not something that I've ever felt comfortable talking about. I was embarrassed. I don't know," Russ said, shaking his head. "For some reason I never had the urge to talk to anyone about the fact that both my wives turned me into a cuckold. Not even a shrink."

Russ was getting emotional and for a second O'Malley thought he might start balling. "Well, you're talking about it now," O'Malley said.

Russ took a deep breath and was able to gain control of his emotions. He calmly looked O'Malley in the eyes and said, "The media has turned me into a murder suspect. I have no idea how to respond."

"You're not a suspect in Lenny's murder. You're just unlucky in love. You want to give a big fuck you to the media, and all those assholes on social media? Don't respond. Don't give them one fucking word."

Russ nodded slowly and even allowed himself to crack a smile. O'Malley kept his gaze on Russ while he glanced at each photo on the wall. Finally, he looked back at O'Malley and said, "I knew my first wife was cheating on me with multiple men, but Sue never told me with whom and I never asked. I can't deny that I was a lousy husband, so I never really took offense to her infidelities."

"That's total bullshit, Russ. I know plenty of bad husbands, you were not a bad husband."

"Well, once Sue found out I was shooting blanks I think that gave her permission to play the field."

"Did she have a relationship with Lenny?"

"I don't know...probably. As for Tammy, I did become aware that she was cheating on me with Lenny. I confronted her once and she denied it. Six months later, Tammy left me. I also suspected that she was having an affair with Hubert Houston, but I have no evidence of that and never confronted Tammy or Hubert."

O'Malley shook his head in disgust. He clearly felt bad for Russ, but understood why some people had started rumors linking him to the murder. Russ's glazed eyes were looking over O'Malley's left shoulder.

"Tomorrow, I'm going to send out a press release that clearly states that you are not a suspect, nor were you ever a suspect. But the rumors surrounding your involvement in Lenny's murder will likely persist until the media finds another sensational storyline to stroke."

Russ regarded O'Malley for a long while until he finally said, "Do you think I should resign?"

"No, I don't. Whisper Dunes needs you captaining our ship. You've done nothing wrong. Keep doing your job, dammit."

Russ looked encouraged, even focused as he nodded.

"I want to assign you round the clock security."

Russ shifted uneasily in his chair as his eye lids lowered.

"You okay with that?"

Russ looked down at his clasped hands then glanced at O'Malley. "Yeah, I'm okay with that."

"Between you and me, your life could be in danger."

Russ barely reacted because he'd already considered this possibility.

"Hell, I could be in danger at this point. As we continue the investigation, I'm becoming more and more convinced that the motive behind Lenny's death is much more complicated than I initially thought."

"I see. Is there any truth to the rumor that the producer behind the most popular murder-mystery podcast is somehow behind Lenny's murder?"

"No, I'd stop believing that one. But you better believe that every media outlet in America is looking for ways to exploit this highly sensational story...a story even they couldn't dream up."

"Do you have any credible leads yet?"

"All I can tell you at this point is that there's credible evidence that suggests at least two people, and probably more, conspired to murder Lenny."

Russ stared at O'Malley in total disbelief. "I don't understand. Why would multiple people conspire to murder a thrice divorced plumber?"

"I can't discuss an ongoing investigation with you, but I can confirm that your former wives weren't the only married women Lenny slept with."

The breakfast rush had ended two hours ago and the diner was nearly empty, except for an old couple sitting at the window booth, and Stan and Randy, who were sitting in the back booth. Stan sipped his coffee while Randy looked at his watch. Randy was clearly agitated as he glanced at the entrance then at Stan. "Where the hell is he?"

"Duane said he's coming. Relax. He'll be here."

Stan and Randy both sipped their coffee, which seemed to be getting worse with each sip. They both cringed as the sour taste lingered on their tongues. Stan took another quick sip, as if the coffee might somehow taste slightly better. He puckered his lips in disgust and said, "This is the worst cup of coffee I've ever had. What the hell's going on back there?"

"Yeah, I can't drink this."

Stan spotted Grace behind the counter and waved her over. Grace looked sleep deprived as she walked slowly over to the table. "What, Stan?" Grace asked.

"Was this coffee made from reused grounds?"

"Why do you ask?"

"Because the coffee taste like possum piss."

"Add some more creamer."

"Half and half isn't going to do the trick today, Grace. If it's not too much trouble can you brew us a fresh pot?"

Grace let out a long sigh. The kind you release at work after you've been up all night with your fussy newborn baby. She looked at Stan for a few seconds, then pulled up her t-shirt and popped out her huge left breast from her nursing bra. Stan and Randy watched in awe as Grace picked up Stan's cup of coffee and squeezed breast milk into the cup. She then calmly placed the cup in front of Stan who, along with Randy, looked bewildered as they stared wide-eyed at Grace's huge left breast.

"Would you like some breast milk with your coffee, Randy?"

"No, thank you."

Grace placed her left breast back into her nursing bra and pulled her t-shirt down. "My shift is about to end and I need to run home so I can feed my baby. If you need anything, just ask Frank."

Stan politely nodded as he raised his coffee cup in appreciation. "Thank you, Grace. And congratulations on your newborn baby. May God bless you and your precious angel."

Grace couldn't tell if Stan was being sincere. She forced herself to smile ever so slightly and said, "Thank you."

Randy and Stan watched Grace walk behind the counter, grab her purse, and exit the diner. "I didn't know she had a baby," Randy said. "She looks great."

Stan nodded as he sipped his coffee. "She's a single mother with two jobs and still trying to get her law degree. Pretty impressive."

Stan took another sip from his coffee cup as Randy looked on.

"How is it?"

"Not bad. It's sweeter and creamier."

Randy took a quick sip from Stan's cup. "Oh, that is sweet."

Stan grabbed his cup before Randy could take another sip.

"Who's the father?" Randy asked.

"I don't know."

Stan slowly leaned forward and whispered, "About a year ago, Lenny told me that Grace was sleeping with Houston, because he was the one paying her law school tuition."

Randy rolled his eyes in disbelief. "Bullshit. I don't believe that for a Sacramento second."

"Why would Lenny lie about that?"

"Because Lenny was a drama mama, who loved doubling down on a rumor."

Stan nodded in agreement with Randy. He took another sip from his cup and then said, "Lenny got that crazy rumor from Erin."

"Erin who?"

"Erin Houston. Hubert's ex-wife. Lenny had been dating her for the past year. I know for a fact that they started fooling around while she was still married to Houston."

Randy leaned forward in disbelief. "Are you serious?"

"Lenny said things were getting hot and heavy. He told me that he was planning on moving to Florida, part-time."

Randy looked at Stan for a fews seconds before he said, "Is it possible that Hubert killed Lenny? Or hired someone to kill him?"

"He's the only truly awful person I know. Of course it's possible. That piece of Wall Street shit is capable of anything."

Stan reacted to his phone vibrating with a text message. He pulled the phone out of his pants pocket and read the text. "He's here. Let's go."

Hal was driving a U-Haul cargo van. Stan and Randy were in the back changing into dark gray jumpsuits. Duane's voice came through the speaker on Hal's phone. "Are you sure she doesn't have a secret security alarm?"

"No, she does not have a security alarm in her apartment. None of my tenants do," Stan shouted from the back of the van.

"She's led me into her apartment on more than one occasion and she never accessed a security alarm," Randy said as he zipped up his jumpsuit. "But obviously she has hidden cameras."

"Yeah, but I bet she only uses them when she's fucking someone in her bedroom," Stan said.

"Roger that," Duane said. "Her last pilates class of the day ends in five minutes. Once she leaves for lunch I'll send the text. Over and out."

17

Duane, with binoculars pressed to his eyes, stood still in his second-floor master bedroom. The white venetian blinds were open just enough so that he could see through the window. An unlit cigarette dangled from his lips as he stared across the street at the red-brick, two-story apartment building. The day Denise moved into the second-floor apartment, Duane walked over with a dozen assorted donuts from Babycakes Bakery and introduced himself to his new neighbor. They became fast friends. One time, they drove to Chicago and boarded a flight to Paris without any luggage, on a dare. It was Christmas Eve and they ended up spending a week in Paris, just the two of them. But the relationship eventually cooled after Duane started dating Hal, who thought Denise was a bad influence on him. Hal once walked into a bathroom at a Halloween party to find Duane snorting several lines of coke off Denise's tits. After that night, Duane made a point to stop hanging out with Denise. They were still friendly to each other, but as Duane stared at the first-floor pilates studio he tried but couldn't remember the last time they hung out together.

On the desk in Duane's bedroom was a nearly empty donut box from Babycakes, a pack of Camel cigarettes, a freshly poured cup of coffee, and a walkie-talkie. Duane was still in his bathrobe but he looked like he'd been up since sunrise. Stan's voice came over the walkie-talkie. "Falcon to Grasshopper. Over."

Duane quickly picked up the walkie-talkie. "Falcon here. Over."

"Has the black widow departed the cave? Over."

"That's a negative, Falcon. Pilates class ended twenty minutes ago but she's still in the building. Over."

"Roger that. Over."

Duane finally lowered the binoculars as he reached for his cup of coffee. He took a long sip from his coffee cup then lit a cigarette before getting back into position. Duane pressed the binoculars to his eyes and stared at the entrance to Denise's apartment building. A minute or two passed and Duane became bored again. He moved the binoculars until he was looking at the park to the right of Denise's building. He looked excited as he spotted a blue jay perched on the branch of a birch tree. "Hey, a blue jay! Looks like the mamma. Beautiful."

The blue jay flew away but Duane tried to track the bird through his binoculars. He looked left, then up, then down, then to the right before Denise suddenly came into view. "Oh, shit."

Duane watched as Denise got into her yellow Jeep Wrangler and sped away. He set his binoculars on the desk and picked up his walkie-talkie. "Grasshopper to Falcon. The black widow has left the building. I repeat, the black widow has left the building. Coast is clear. Over."

Stan's voice came over the walkie-talkie. "Roger that, Grasshopper. We are en route. Over."

Duane grabbed the last donut from the box and took a big bite as he stared out the window. He began to ruminate on the question, *is this a good idea?* Probably not, he concluded. But when you live in a small town, it's fun to do something out of the ordinary every now and then. Even if that something is breaking into someone's apartment and searching through their belongings. Duane couldn't help but feel a bit bummed that he was watching from the safety of his home while Stan and Randy did the dirty work. But someone had to be on lookout. Duane took a moment to consider how crucial the position was to the operation. He smiled, knowing the operation wouldn't be possible without him...the lookout guy.

Duane kept his eyes wide open in anticipation of Randy and Stan being dropped off in front of Denise's building. While he patiently stared through his window, waiting for Stan and Randy's arrival, Duane considered something that gave him chills. *The last guy to go into Denise's apartment found something that cost him his life. Is it possible that Stan and Randy could be murdered next?* Duane wanted to stop thinking about this scenario, but couldn't. He looked nervous as he grabbed what was left of the last donut and stuffed it into his mouth.

The U-Haul cargo van pulled up in front of Denise's apartment building. Randy slid open the door and jumped out, followed by Stan. In addition to wearing grey jumpsuits, they were both wearing black baseball hats, booties over their shoes, black gloves, and N95 masks. The cargo van pulled away as Stan and Randy quickly made their way to the front of the building. Stan removed a set of keys from his pocket and unlocked the wooden-framed glass door. Stan held open the door and Randy entered the building with Stan following close behind.

Duane was looking through his binoculars, which were pointed right at Denise's apartment building. He lowered the binoculars and said softly, "Be careful, guys."

Stan unlocked the two deadbolts and slowly opened the door to Denise's apartment. Stan entered first as he put the keys in his pocket. Randy slowly closed the door behind him and then turned the top deadbolt lock. Stan and Randy shared an uneasy look as they both seemed unsure about what to do next. Stan started to remove his mask.

"Leave it on! There's a very good chance she's got hidden cameras all over this place," Randy said.

"Yeah, you're probably right. I'll start out here, you start in the bedroom," Stan said as he readjusted his mask. Randy walked quickly toward the bedroom, almost as if he knew exactly what he was looking for. Stan looked around the open kitchen, which led to a large living room. The place was immaculate. The kitchen counter was clean and clutter free except for a smoothie recipe book, which was right next to the blender. Stan looked through a few drawers then walked over to the hallway closet.

He opened the hallway closet door with caution. Inside was a small washing machine next to a small dryer. On top of the washing machine was a laundry basket filled with dirty clothes. Stan looked through the laundry basket and came across yoga pants, t-shirts, socks, and panties. He closed the hallway closet door and moved to the living room. For some reason, Stan thought the living room seemed bigger than he remembered. He had only been inside the apartment once since Denise moved in over four years ago. Stan and Lisa attended a little cocktail party she hosted to celebrate the opening of her pilates studio. Stan moved around the room, looking for a hidden camera, but he quickly convinced himself that the room was camera free.

Stan walked over to the small desk in the corner. On the desk was a coffee cup filled with black and blue pens, an Olympia SG3 typewriter, a spiral notebook, and a book: *Elmore Leonard's 10*

Rules of Writing. Stan looked curious as he picked up the notebook and opened it. On the first page was a poem written in cursive. Stan read the first two lines then started to flip through the notebook. Most pages were filled with random notes that Stan couldn't read because the cursive handwriting was so bad. He set the notebook down exactly where it was on the desk and pulled open the desk drawer. It was empty except for an old photo of Denise and a good-looking man in his forties, maybe fifties. Denise looked to be in her early twenties in the photo, which was taken at a crowded restaurant. Stan stared at the photo and said, "Who's that asshole?" He put the photo back in the drawer and walked toward the bedroom.

Stan walked into the master bedroom to find Randy carefully examining Denise's walk-in closet. "We may not have much time left, let's get up to the attic," Stan said.

"Just give me another minute."

Stan stared at the king-size bed and his mind was immediately flooded with dirty images. He shook his head and tried to focus on the task at hand. He glanced at Randy as he was searching through a drawer. "Find anything interesting?"

"Not yet."

Randy, on his hands and knees, started to look through each of the five shoeboxes on the floor. He opened the first four boxes to find that they just contained expensive high heels. The last box was an orange Nike shoebox. Randy opened it and found that it only contained a pair of brand new running shoes.

Stan was distracted by all the sexy dresses hanging up in Denise's closet. "God, she's got panache."

Stan followed Randy out of the closet and into the bathroom. "What was she like in the sack?"

Randy ignored Stan as they entered the bathroom. "Come on, we're best friends. You can tell me."

"She's very strong."

"Did she rough you up?" Stan asked with a sheepish grin. "I bet she's into role playing."

"Stan, this woman has threatened to destroy my life. Please stop asking me questions about her."

"Fair enough."

"Just know this, letting Denise take me upstairs for a smoothie will always be the biggest mistake of my life."

"Biggest mistake of your life? Come on, she made you a delicious smoothie and gave you a magical blowjob. That's like sitting in the passenger seat of a stolen Ferrari as it speeds along the Pacific Coast Highway at sunset. You didn't steal the Ferrari. You did nothing wrong, except enjoy the once-in-a-lifetime ride."

Randy glared at Stan. "Did you forget why we broke in here?"

"I'm sorry. You're right."

Randy looked through the drawers under the double sink while Stan opened the shower door. He looked perturbed seeing that the old shower head had not been replaced. For some reason, Stan had envisioned that Lenny replaced the shower head then went to the E.R. to get his thumb stitched up. Stan opened the closet door and froze in disbelief. On the top shelf were four boxes of condoms, two bottles of organic lube, two bottles of sweet almond body oil, and six tubes of chapstick. On the shelf below was a pink dildo, a double-ended glass dildo, a magic wand vibrator, two pairs of handcuffs, a whip, and four scented candles.

Stan continued to stare in disbelief. "Look at this."

Randy quickly moved next to Stan. His mouth and eyes opened wide as he looked over the items on the shelves. Randy looked at Stan and said, "I told you I'm not the only guy stuck in her honey pot."

"This doesn't necessarily prove Denise is blackmailing other men. Just proves she has a very high sex drive. You should see our master bathroom closet. It looks pretty similar to this, minus the box of condoms and the double-ended glass dildo."

"You and Lisa have a pink dildo in your bathroom closet?"

"Actually, it's black," Stan said sheepishly. "It only comes out of the closet for special occasions."

"Good to know."

"She ever bring her toys out when you were over?"

Randy shook his head. "Nope."

"You gotta face facts, buddy, a high sex drive is the best way to get through six months of winter up here," Stan said. "Why do you think Lisa and I never get the winter blues? Because we like to ski and go ice fishing? No! Because we bang all winter long."

Duane was still looking through his binoculars, except his binoculars weren't pointed at Denise's apartment building. They were pointed at the park next to Denise's building, where four shirtless men in their twenties were playing a game of two-on-two basketball. If the binoculars had been pointed at the apartment building, Duane would have just seen Denise park her Jeep in front of her building, hop out with an iced coffee in her hand, and enter through the front door.

Stan and Randy were carefully searching the bedroom for a hidden camera. The bedroom was tidy and spare of any clutter, which actually made it harder to determine where Denise might be hiding cameras. Randy walked over to the only painting on the wall and removed it, but quickly hung it back up when it was clear there wasn't a camera behind the painting. Stan opened the nightstand drawers while Randy checked the TV-stand cabinet.

"There's no sign of a secret camera anywhere," Stan said. "She must have been recording with her phone or maybe a mini-HD camera. You can hide those things anywhere."

Randy looked defeated as he rested his hands on his hips.

"Did you two do it anywhere else besides the bedroom?"

"No, everything happened on the bed. She's old-fashioned that way."

Stan glanced up at the ceiling hatch, which was located just outside the walk-in closet. "Time to check the attic."

Stan pulled the small ladder out of the closet and set it up under the ceiling hatch. Randy and Stan suddenly froze as they both heard footsteps walking up the creaky wooden steps to the apartment. "Oh, no," Randy said.

Stan quickly pulled out his walkie-talkie and spoke in a quiet, yet panic-stricken voice. "Caterpillar to Grasshopper..."

"You're Falcon," Randy whispered.

"Falcon to Grasshopper. Have you spotted the black widow? Please tell me she's not walking up the stairs right now. Over, you fuck."

Duane looked annoyed as he finally pointed the binoculars at Denise's apartment building. Stan's panic-stricken voice came over Duane's walkie-talkie again. "Come in Grasshopper. Do you read me? Over."

Duane spotted Denise's empty Jeep parked in front of the building. He gasped and said, "Oh, shit!"

He dropped the binoculars and grabbed his walkie-talkie. "It's Grasshopper! Abort mission! Get out of there now! Over!"

Randy started to panic as Duane's voice came over the walkie-talkie again. "I repeat. Abort mission! Over."

Stan quickly pulled himself into the attic. He then lowered his hand to pull up Randy. "Grab my hand."

"It's too late. Save yourself."

"Okay. Put the ladder back in her closet and hide. I'll text Duane. He'll think of something."

Stan gave Randy a thumbs up just before he closed the ceiling hatch. Fear radiated through Randy's body at the sound of Denise's keychain jangling as she unlocked her apartment door. Randy put the ladder back in the closet. He considered for a moment that he should hide in the closet, but became overwhelmed as he considered his other hiding options. He heard Denise walk into the kitchen. Running out of time to make a decision, he ran out of the closet and slid head first under Denise's king-sized bed.

Denise, holding her iced coffee and some mail, pulled out one of the two stools under the kitchen island and sat. She sipped on her iced coffee while looking over her mail. All bills and a red envelope, the address written with a black Sharpie. No return address. Denise opened the letter to find a cheap birthday card. She opened the card and read the hand written note. *Still have not located your special shoebox. This is a major problem. Need to discuss this issue further with you. I'll be in your neck of the woods on Friday. Think of a good place to meet.*

Denise's eyes were still on the card. She looked uneasy, thinking about her next move. She sighed in frustration, ripped up the card, and tossed it in the trash can underneath the sink. Denise walked slowly toward her bedroom while staring at her phone. She entered her bedroom and tossed her phone on the bed. She then stripped off her clothes, grabbed her phone, and walked into the bathroom. Denise sat on the toilet and started to pee while playing Wordle on her phone.

Randy, lying perfectly still on his back under the bed, looked somewhat relaxed as he listened to Denise pee. He closed his eyes and slowed down his breathing in hopes of calming himself.

Stan was sweating like a coal baron watching his only daughter marry a guy who works for Greenpeace. The attic was hot, but the sweat dripping from his forehead and back was mostly because Stan was panicking like a Swiss banker who just discovered his pregnant mistress works for the I.R.S. With his cell phone pressed to his ear, Stan looked through the small circular window as he waited for Duane to answer. Stan mumbled to himself, "Pickup...pickup." Stan ended the call and quickly typed a text message: *This is Falcon. I'm stuck in the attic and Caterpillar is stuck under the black widow's bed. This is now a rescue mission. Over.*

Duane paced frantically around his bedroom as he read Stan's text message. An idea suddenly popped in his head and he stopped pacing the bedroom. Thinking about the idea for about a minute, he finally said to himself, "Yeah, that might work."

Randy heard water start to fill up the bathtub. A few seconds later he saw Denise's feet walk toward her bed then vanish as she hopped onto the bed. Johann Sebastian Bach's, "The Well-Tempered Clavier," started to play loudly from the portable speaker on the nightstand. Randy listened to the beautiful music for about a minute before he thought he heard a buzzing sound, which sounded an awful lot like a vibrator. He closed his eyes again, almost as if he was trying to meditate. A crazy thought crossed his mind as he focused on breathing very slowly. Randy started to imagine what Denise might do if he rolled out from under the bed and surprised her. *Of course she'd scream, but then what? Would she shoot me with the gun I once saw in her nightstand? Or maybe we'd lock eyes for a while then Denise would try to fuck me. Or maybe she'd scream, punch me in the face a few times, and then try to fuck me. Yeah, that's probably what she'd do.*

Denise was reading *The Poems of Emily Dickinson,* while being soothed by her vibrating neck massager. She was lying on top of the covers, totally relaxed, until she was interrupted by her cell phone ringing. She checked the caller ID - **Restricted**. Denise looked uneasy as she considered not answering the phone. After the fourth ring she turned off her vibrating neck massager and the music before answering her phone.

"Hello."

All Denise heard was someone breathing heavily. Then a very deep voice said, "I know what you did. Meet me at the library in thirty minutes...or I'm going to the cops with the evidence. I'll be in the mystery section."

Denise's eyes got wide as she struggled to gulp down the sudden lump in her throat. "Who is this?"

"Be there in thirty minutes, or I'm going to the cops."

Denise took a deep breath through her nose. As she exhaled through her nose, a confident tone returned to her voice. "You have no fucking idea who you're dealing with, do you?"

"Oh, you bet your sweet little ass I do. I'll see you at the library in thirty minutes."

"What will you be wearing?" Denise asked in a calm voice.

"Don't worry about it. You'll know me when you see me. Don't be late."

Denise slowly set the phone down as her eyes narrowed. She could barely blink her eyes. She looked to be in shock, as if she just saw a ghost. She had a feeling in her stomach that she hadn't felt in many years. The last time she experienced this gut-wrenching feeling, she was a sophomore at the University of Pennsylvania. It was late October and she had just finished her last class of the day. When she got back to her apartment she was shocked to find a man and a woman, whom she had never met before, sitting on her couch. After a discussion that lasted just over an hour they left, and Denise's life would soon change forever.

Just a moment ago she was completely at peace, but now, the sick feeling in her gut was getting worse and she thought she might have a panic attack. Denise looked like she wanted to cry, but she didn't. Instead, she got out of bed, walked into the bathroom, and lowered herself in the bathtub for a quick soak before her impromptu meeting.

Duane was clearly on edge as he paced around his bedroom. He rubbed his fingers through his thick, brown hair. He continued to think about his next move, but that only caused him more distress. Duane looked out the window then started stretching his hamstrings. First his right then his left, but stretching his hamstrings only increased his heart rate. He took a few deep breaths then reached for his coffee cup and gulped down the rest of the coffee. He then grabbed the binoculars off the table and got back into position.

Stan looked out the attic window, desperately trying to convince himself that Duane would be able to execute the rescue mission. Based on their discussions over the years, Stan had faith in Duane's problem-solving abilities. But as Stan thought about it more, he didn't have much proof that suggested Duane was a great problem solver. On more than a few occasions, Duane had bragged to Stan about being a great problem solver, but he rarely, if ever, cited any examples. As he continued to sweat profusely, Stan started to brace for the likelihood that he would be stuck in the hot attic for awhile. Stan started to scan the attic in hopes he might find something that could occupy his time. But there was nothing in the attic except for some old paintings and a dozen storage boxes. In addition to the heat, the dust was also getting to him. Stan had to sneeze but used all his might to hold the sneeze in, which made his eyes tear up. Despite his teary eyes, Stan perked up at the sight of Denise's Jeep speeding down the street. He moved his hand to his chest and breathed a sigh of relief.

Duane kept his binoculars on Denise's speeding Jeep until she was out of sight. He then picked up his walkie-talkie and said, "This is Grasshopper. The black widow has left the building. The coast is clear. Over."

Stan's voice came over Duane's walkie-talkie. "Roger that. Nice work, Grasshopper. Over."

Randy remained perfectly still under Denise's bed even though he was almost certain she was out of the apartment. While under the bed, Randy had reflected on the last few years of his life. Because what else are you supposed to do while hiding under your seducer's bed?

It seemed like a lifetime ago that he had sex with Denise on the very bed he was now under. Randy had forgotten most of the intimate details of their two encounters on the bed. He considered this to be a sign. A sign that he was still in love with his wife. He could no longer remember anything specific from his encounters with Denise because he wasn't present when she was going down on him, or when she was on top of him. Randy suddenly looked disturbed as one memory crept into his mind. He couldn't help but think about a very specific moment when Denise was on top of him, slowly moving up and down. Randy remembered the exact moment when a few beads of sweat slid down from one of Denise's perfect breasts—for the life of him he couldn't remember if it was the left or right breast—and dropped in his eye. Randy recalled how the stinging in his eye prompted him to close both eyes for a few seconds. When he finally opened his eyes, the hard nipple from Denise's left breast was less than an inch from his stinging eye. *That means the sweat must've dripped down from her left breast*, Randy thought.

Randy closed his eyes tightly in frustration. He was upset with himself, and desperate to shed this memory from his mind. Maybe he should tell Vivian about the affair, he thought. He'd feel better, but it would be hard on her and give her more than enough reason to end the marriage. But Randy had never known Vivian to be a spiteful person. She was always quick to forgive, and ready to move past life's problems. Yes, the passion had slowly faded away, but their love for each other was still strong. Their marriage could survive the affair, Randy thought, but he knew that it would change the dynamic of their marriage forever.

"Randy! Let's go!"

Randy turned his head to the left to find Stan on his hands and knees looking at him. He slid out from underneath the bed and Stan helped him to his feet.

"You okay?" Stan asked.

"Yeah. Where's Denise?"

"Gone for now. Somehow, Duane got her to leave."

Stan and Randy hurried to the front door and quickly exited Denise's apartment. Stan shut the door and quickly pulled out his master key to lock the door. As they hustled down the hallway towards the stairs, Randy asked, "Find anything in the attic?"

"No. Nothing up there except old paintings and boxes of clothes that belonged to former tenants."

Randy let out a disappointed sigh. "Well, that was a complete failure."

"I'm sorry, buddy, we tried. I'm afraid she's still got you by the balls, but don't worry, we'll figure something out."

18

Denise's Jeep pulled in front of the Peter White Public Library. Completed in 1904, the massive library was built with Indiana limestone on a slightly sloped hill overlooking Front Street. The library happens to be directly across the street from the Landmark Inn, a boutique hotel where The Rolling Stones stayed when they came to town to attend the funeral for Royden 'Chuch' Magee—their longtime road manager and dear friend.

Denise cautiously got out of her Jeep. She remained vigilant as she walked up the steps and toward the main entrance of the library. She was wearing black sunglasses so the sunlight reflecting off the Indiana limestone didn't bother her. Her eyes were wide open and her head kept turning from left to right. She stopped abruptly and spun around, thinking someone might be following her. There was no one behind her, or to her right, or to her left. In fact, there was no one even sitting on the steps that lead to the library. This was strange, Denise thought, considering it was a beautiful summer day. There were always at least a few bookish kids reading on the steps whenever the weather was nice, but not today for some unknown reason. Denise continued slowly up the steps that lead to the library.

Denise was overwhelmed with paranoia as she walked through the lobby. Her sunglasses were still on, allowing her to closely eye everyone who came into view. Denise was usually noticed and gawked at wherever she went in Whisper Dunes, even at the library, which she visited at least once a week. But she didn't recognize the few people she passed and none of them made eye contact with her. Denise passed a small reading area that had two easy chairs in front of the fireplace and one long wooden table. It was in this room that Mick Jagger, Keith Richards, Charlie Watts, Ronnie Wood, and Darryl Jones spent a summer afternoon reading before attending "Chuch" Magee's funeral. There had been much debate over the years among the staff as to whether or not they should hang a plaque on the wall to commemorate the date The Rolling Stones spent the afternoon reading in the room. A plaque was ordered a few years back, but because the room was originally dedicated in honor of a longtime Whisper Dunes resident, who happened to be an outspoken teetotaler, the staff decided to hang the plaque in the employee break room.

Denise remained hyper observant as she walked slowly toward the mystery section. She headed down a deserted aisle. She made her way down two more deserted aisles before she heard the sound of a page being turned. Denise stood just a few feet from the aisle where someone was thumbing through a book. She spotted a person standing at the end of the aisle and froze. A book was covering the face, but it was definitely a man. Whoever it was had their nose buried in *"A" is for Alibi* by Sue Grafton.

Denise was nervous, but it didn't show as she walked slowly toward the man at the end of the aisle. She was about ten feet from him when he suddenly lowered the book. The man looked at Denise as she took off her sunglasses. She was about to hang the sunglasses on her black tank top, but decided to hold the sunglasses in her right hand in case she needed a weapon. Because her eyes had been on high alert and wide open since walking up the steps to the library, her eyes were dry, causing blurry vision for a few seconds. She didn't immediately recognize the man, who said, "Hello, Denise," in a low, deep voice.

Denise blinked her eyes a few times and saw Terry Lutterbach standing in front of her. He flashed a smile as she took a few steps toward him. Denise had no expression on her face as she looked over Terry. She was struggling to believe that Deacon Terry was the one who made the phone call. But there he was in front of her, the only person in the mystery section. As she thought back to the call, the guy did sound kind of like Deacon Terry.

"Welcome back to the mystery section. The last time I bumped into you here, I believe you were checking out a few Elmore Leonard books," Terry said.

"That's right. Good memory."

"Now Elmore Leonard was a fantastic writer, but I've told several of the librarians here that his books shouldn't be in the mystery section because he wasn't a mystery writer. He was a crime writer. Maybe the best ever."

Denise's blue eyes narrowed as she regarded Terry. "With it being such a beautiful summer day, I'm surprised you didn't want to meet on your boat."

Terry looked confused, so much so that he was unsure how to respond. He finally said, "I needed a break from the sun. My dermatologist told me I have to spend a full day inside for every two days outside."

"I see."

Denise and Terry stared at each other for an uncomfortable moment. Terry realized that she was content not saying a word. He watched Denise hang her sunglasses on her black tank top and noticed she wasn't wearing a bra. Terry glanced down at the book in his hands then looked back at Denise.

"Ever since I was a kid I loved going to the library and finding a quiet aisle to read in. But then you showed up in my aisle and I'm thinking, enough reading, let's get to know each other better over a few stiff cocktails. I'm buying."

Denise continued to have a blank expression on her face. She was looking Deacon Terry in the eyes, which seemed to make him uncomfortable. Denise finally said, "I thought that voice on the phone sounded familiar."

Terry tilted his head to the right as a puzzled expression appeared on his face.

"*'A' for Alibi*. Now that's a fun book," Fr. Carey said as he came down the aisle. "I read it on a cruise ship."

Denise and Terry both looked uneasy as Fr. Carey quickly approached. Denise was clearly annoyed as Fr. Carey moved right between them. Terry tried to pretend that he didn't smell alcohol on him, but not Denise. Her judgmental eyes met Fr. Carey's friendly gaze. "Do you normally have a few shots of vodka before coming to the library, Father?"

"Nah, that's from last night. My brothers came to visit. We were at Flanigan's until two. That reminds me, Terry, I still need to purchase beer for the golf outing. Can you call your beer distributor buddy and see if he can give us a good deal?"

"I'll try my best," Terry said jovially.

"What brings you to the mystery section, Fr. Carey?" Denise asked.

"Heading on a camping trip tomorrow and I need a good mystery book to cozy up with for the night."

Fr. Carey flashed a goofy grin. "Unlike you two, I'm only allowed to go to bed with a good book and a trusty flashlight. It's what we priests call an unapologetic threesome."

Fr. Carey elbowed Terry in the shoulder as he let out a laugh. "Truth be told, I'll probably be too exhausted to get into a book. We're going to be fishing from the crack of dawn until sunset, which means I'll probably just pass out by the fire. Last fishing trip I was on, I woke up to a black bear tossing my salad. I shit you not."

Deacon Terry forced out a laugh, but Denise didn't even smile.

"It's called a joke, Denise, lighten up. You may be a knockout, and a talented pilates instructor, and a community activist, but life will take on a whole new meaning once you finally develop your sense of humor."

Denise and Terry both looked uneasy and desperate to end the conversation.

"Well, I need to run. Have fun camping, Father. And don't you worry, I'll give my buddy a call and try to get a good beer deal for the golf outing," Terry said as he quickly walked away.

"Thanks, pal. In case I'm not back in town, can you cover for me and celebrate morning mass on Monday and Tuesday?"

"Of course."

"Terrific."

Fr. Carey flashed a friendly smile as he regarded Denise, who struggled to make eye contact with him. "What do you say, Denise? Do you have a good book recommendation for your favorite priest?"

"As a matter of fact I do. *Eleanor & Park* by Rainbow Rowell."

Fr. Carey flashed a curious look. "I'll give it a shot. Thanks, Denise. Oh, before I forget, can you volunteer to work the 9th hole for the golf outing? It's our biggest money-maker hole."

"You know you can count on me, Father."

"Bless your heart." Fr. Carey looked a tad uneasy as he regarded Denise. "You know, when it comes to personal choices I'm as liberal as a pregnant lesbian, but if it's not too much trouble, can you try and wear a bra this year?"

"I don't wear a bra when the temperature gets above eighty degrees."

"Okay, I respect that."

Denise flashed a smile and walked away. Father Carey squinted his eyes as he looked at the row of books in front of him.

The sun was starting to set on the Marquette Harbor Lighthouse. Painted red each spring, the lighthouse was located on a small, tree-covered peninsula that was surrounded by a rocky shoreline. The north winds had been blowing all afternoon and big waves were crashing onto the massive rocks. On most summer days, hundreds of locals and tourists visit the Marquette Harbor Lighthouse, but because of the strong winds there was no one outside the lighthouse, except for Duane, Randy, and Stan. The three bickering friends stood on a small patch of grass behind the lighthouse, taking turns pointing fingers at each other.

"Hey, I found a way to get your asses safely out of there, didn't I? So where's my fucking thank you?" Duane yelled.

"What if she recognized your voice?" Stan asked in an angry tone.

Duane looked perplexed as he put his hands on his hips. "There's no way she knew it was me. I talked really slow and used this deep, raspy voice. Come to think of it, I kind of sounded like Deacon Terry."

Randy, who was just as distraught as Stan, took a step closer toward Duane. "What if someone was actually in the mystery section when Denise got there? Their life could be in danger now!"

Duane rolled his eyes at Randy and said, "I think it's entirely possible that you've watched one too many episodes of *Murder, She Wrote.*"

"What are you talking about? I don't watch *Murder, She Wrote.*"

"Well, I do, and I can assure you that your imagination is getting the best of you right now."

"Well, I think it's more than plausible that somebody was in the mystery section when Denise showed up," Stan said.

"Stop staying plausible," Duane yelled. "I apologize for nothing. My rescue plan was a good one, and if you dipshits don't recognize that, you can forget about asking me to be your lookout guy, ever again."

"You still haven't told us how Denise got back into the apartment without you seeing her," Randy said.

"I drank way too much coffee and couldn't hold it any longer. Clearly, she got back into her apartment while I was in the bathroom."

"Bullshit! You probably got distracted by some toned guy jogging by in a pair of spandex shorts," Stan said.

"You son of a bitch!"

Duane lunged at Stan, but Randy was able to restrain him before he could throw a punch.

"Fuck you, Stan!

"You had one job! Watch the front door!"

"I did my job! If I made one mistake, it was drinking too much coffee!"

Duane took a long breath and looked up at the sky in hopes of calming his emotions. He looked at Stan and said, "I was in the can when I heard your radio call. I returned to my post, and after spotting Denise's Jeep, I immediately put my rescue plan in motion."

Randy and Stan both looked ashamed. Duane could tell that they believed his bullshit story. No longer in defense mode, Duane decided to attack. "Let's talk about you guys and your failure to find anything. If either of you had any balls you would've ripped the place apart. Had you done that, I bet you would've found some evidence that links Denise to Lenny's murder. At the very least, you probably would've found some evidence that blows the doors open on her blackmail operation. I told you guys before you went in, she's probably got a secret hiding place under the old floorboards."

"We asked you to join us, more than once, but you insisted on being the lookout guy," Stan said.

Randy looked emotional as he stared at Lake Superior. "I'm sorry, guys. I should have never dragged you into this mess. This is my problem, not yours. That was a desperate, stupid attempt to try and right my wrong. I screwed up, not you guys."

Duane looked sympathetic as he glanced at Randy. "You were seduced by an incredibly beautiful woman, Randy. It's not your fault. Hell, I would've even taken the bait just to see what all you straight guys are always raving about. By the time you realized you were stuck in her honey trap, it was too late. I could be wrong, but I really believe Vivian will forgive you. Maybe not immediately, but I think eventually she'd let you move back in."

Randy's eyes were watery as he continued to look out at the lake. He finally turned toward Duane and gave him a long hug. "Thank you, Duane. You're right, there's a chance she would forgive me. But I just can't bear the thought of breaking Vivian's heart. "

Stan put his hands on his hips as he lowered his head. He seemed upset with himself. He slowly raised his head up and looked at Randy. "I too know what it's like to fall under the spell of a beautiful woman, who wants to take you upstairs for a ride. It's exhilarating and terrifying at the same time," Stan said in a somber tone.

Duane and Randy both regarded Stan with curious looks on their face as Stan searched for the right words.

"Dr. Bianca Marquette, one of the climate scientists behind the big study that's about come out, tried to seduce me on multiple occasions."

"What in the..." Duane said.

"You knew about the climate change study?" Randy asked in disbelief.

"Not until very recently. We met one night about two years ago at Portside Inn, or maybe it was Rose's Dugout. Anyway, we started bumping into each other around town and before I knew it we were drinking buddies. Bianca told me she was a climate scientist, but never told me she was working on a study that was going to change the fate of our town forever. In fact, she lied and said she was a visiting professor at Northern. In addition to being a great conversationalist, she was gorgeous, as most French-Canadian women tend to be. I was mesmerized by her beauty, and despite the fact that I told her I was married, she always invited me back to her place after we had a few drinks together. I never took her up on the offer, not once. But one night she got hammered on espresso martinis so I drove her home. On the drive to her apartment she went on this passionate rant about the need for new ecosystems to combat the rapidly rising sea levels. I was so enamored with what she was saying that I was extremely slow to acknowledge her wandering hand. When I looked down, she was trying to give me a Western grip handjob."

Duane looked stunned as he rested his hands on top of his head. Randy, however, could feel Stan's pain. His lips tightly compressed as he tilted his head to the left and conveyed a sympathetic look.

"I hesitated at first, but eventually I brushed her hand away."

"Then what happened?" Duane asked.

"I pulled over to the curb and kicked her out of my car."

Randy flashed Stan an empathetic look and said, "I'm sorry that happened, Stan. A weaker man would not have done what you did."

Stan nodded, but still looked full of guilt.

"Did you tell Lisa?" Randy asked.

Stan slowly shook his head and said, "No."

"How do you know she's one of the climate scientists behind the study?" Duane asked.

"I met with her recently. Bianca fessed up who she really is and briefly discussed the climate study. She's getting ready to travel all over the world to promote the study, which states that the Upper Peninsula will be the best place to live on Earth for the remainder of civilization."

Duane looked at Stan suspiciously while shaking his head. "Seduced by a climate scientist...wow."

"She didn't seduce me. She came on to me. There's a difference," Stan said.

Duane crossed his arms and bit his bottom lip as he pondered Stan's claim.

"Now that I've got that off my chest, I owe you an apology, Duane. I was mad and didn't mean what I said about you being distracted by a jogger in spandex shorts. That was a stupid, thoughtless thing to say. I'm sorry."

Duane stared at Stan without any expression on his face. He finally shook Stan's hand and said, "Apology accepted."

The handshake turned into a hug. Stan then turned around and regarded Randy. "I know I told you earlier that you're powerless now and the only thing you can do is play by Denise's rules. But here's the thing, even if you do everything she says, Denise will have leverage over you for the rest of your life. That's no way to live, man. If I were you, I'd walk into Chief O'Malley's office tomorrow morning and tell him exactly what happened. Denise committed a serious crime when she blackmailed you with that sex tape. Of course, by doing this, you're also going to have to come clean with Vivian."

"I told you guys, I'm not the only one she's blackmailing. Stan, you saw what was in her bathroom closet."

"What was in her bathroom closet?" Duane asked.

"A lot of sex toys and a lot of lube," Stan said.

"Well, you can't have a lot of sex toys without a lot of lube," Duane said. "With that being said, I don't think that's proof Denise is blackmailing high profile men in this town."

"I know it's not exactly proof, but I have no doubt Denise used her honey trap to compromise some powerful people in this town, including a few cops," Randy said.

"You think she got to Russ?" Stan asked.

"No, not Russ. Being an asexual fishing nut is a superpower if you happen to be a politician."

Stan and Duane both sighed in relief.

"What about O'Malley?" Stan asked.

"Like Russ, O'Malley's incorruptible."

"Alcocks?" Stan asked.

"Maybe."

"O'Malley's a great cop. For all we know, he's already been secretly building a case against Denise," Duane said.

"Yeah, more reason to believe that I'd end up like Lenny if Denise found out I was talking to the cops," Randy said.

"So, what are you going to do then?" Stan asked.

"Why don't you just tell Vivian the truth? If she kicks you out, you can move in with me," Duane said. "Hal and I do nude yoga in the living room every morning, but other than that I think you'll find it to be a comfortable living situation."

Randy, thinking about the near future, became emotional as he stared at the different shades of blue on the surface of Lake Superior.

19

Stan pushed his grocery cart down the cereal aisle. His cart already contained six bottles of red wine, three cases of beer, and two bottles of vodka. He grabbed three boxes of a heart-healthy, wholegrain cereal from the shelf and tossed the boxes into the cart. He then pushed his cart to the end of the aisle and made a hard left. Up ahead, Stan noticed a pretty girl behind a sample table that was displaying six open bottles of wine. Stan did not hesitate to push his cart toward her. The pretty girl flashed a big smile at Stan and said, "Hi there, are you familiar with the Round Barn Winery?"

Stan smiled back and glanced at the eight sample cups of wine on the table. "I'm afraid not. What do you recommend?"

"The Round Bar Cabernet is my favorite, but we also have an excellent Merlot and some award winning red blends."

Stan picked up a sample cup of wine and chugged it down. "What is that, Zinfandel?"

"No, that's our Pinot Noir."

"No shit? You had me fooled."

Stan picked up another sample cup and chugged it down. "And this one?"

"That's our popular red blend."

"It's smooth. I like it."

"Would you like to try our award winning Cab?"

Stan licked the wine off his top lip and said, "Yeah, why not?"

She handed him a cup of the Cabernet. Stan sniffed the wine before shooting it down. He was clearly impressed. "Oh, that's terrific. I'll take three bottles of your Cab."

"Very good, sir."

Stan put a huge bag of dog food into his grocery cart and proceeded down the pet food aisle. His cart was no longer filled with booze and boxes of healthy cereal. Ten minutes earlier he was a mile from home when he realized that he forgot to buy the blue-cheese olives Lisa had requested. Shortly after returning to the grocery store, Stan glanced at the list Lisa gave him and saw that he had also forgotten to pick up dog food, bread, bananas, toilet paper, and tampons.

Stan spotted the condiment aisle and turned left to find just one person in the aisle. He hesitated before slowly moving down the aisle toward Denise. She was wearing a long summer dress, and focused at the moment on inspecting the jar of green olives in her hand. She didn't see Stan approaching because she bent down to check out a different brand of olives. Stan couldn't help but stare at Denise as she remained bent down, looking at different olive jars. Distracted by the images of Denise and Randy having sex that had just popped into his head, he slammed his cart into the front of Denise's cart. Frightened by the sound of the grocery cart crash, Denise dropped the jar of olives, which shattered all over the floor.

"Oh, shit! I'm sorry, Denise."

Denise was now standing erect. Her surprised eyes locked in on Stan, who looked embarrassed. Neither of them acknowledged the broken jar of olives. Glass and olives surrounded Denise's feet, which were only protected by sandals.

"You okay?"

"Fine. Quite a collision. Were you staring at your phone or my ass?"

Stan sighed and said, "Your ass."

Denise smiled as she stared at Stan for a few seconds. "You don't look so good."

"That's news to me."

You've got tired wine eyes."

"Oh, I'm not drunk. I just threw back a couple at the free wine-tasting booth."

"Have you tried the Round Barn Cab? It's excellent."

"Matter of fact I have."

Denise turned and grabbed another jar of olives from the shelf. Stan glanced at Denise's large purse, which was in the grocery cart surrounded by vegetables, blueberries, plain yogurt, and two bottles of vodka. He spotted Denise's phone in the side pocket of the white leather purse. Denise scanned the other green olive brands on the shelf as Stan glanced at her. "Is it dirty martini night at your place?"

Denise grabbed another jar of green olives from the shelf before she looked at Stan. She flashed a sexy smile and said,

"Good guess. Why don't you stop by tonight? My old girlfriend from college is visiting. She's a riot, you'll love her."

Stan let out a nervous laugh. "Sounds like it's gonna be a fun night. I'd love to stop over, but I promised the old ball and chain I'd take her out for a steak dinner at Elizabeth's and then over to Breakers for some Friday night dancing."

Denise's piercing blue eyes remained fixed on Stan's face as he nervously scratched his chin. She imagined, just for a brief moment, what it would be like to be married to a man who was excited to take her out dancing every Friday night.

"Well, maybe another time," Denise said with a hint of disappointment in her voice.

"Yeah, maybe. Hey, can you do me big favor?"

Denise flashed a coy grin and said, "Well, now that depends."

"I fucked up my back playing basketball with my kids the other night. Can you reach down there and grab me a jar of blue-cheese olives?"

"Sure. It'll be my good deed for the day, helping out an old man."

Just as Denise reached down to grab a jar of blue-cheese olives, Stan quickly grabbed her phone out of the side pocket of her purse and looked at the screen. MISSED CALL - HOUSTON (4). Stan slid the phone back into the side pocket of her purse right before Denise turned around and handed him the jar of blue-cheese olives.

"Thank you, Denise."

She winked her right eye at Stan and said, "I hope you think of me when you sip on that extra-dirty martini tonight."

"I don't drink martinis," Stan said as he placed the jar of blue-cheese olives in his cart. "Have fun with your friend tonight."

"Hey, why don't you come to my yoga sculpt class tomorrow at four? It's great for the back, and you're guaranteed to shed a few pounds."

"You know what? I might actually take you up on that offer."

"I hope you do. If you make it through the entire class without quitting, I'll treat you to a blueberry smoothie up at my place."

Stan felt his stomach get queasy while his knees started to shake. "No promises I can finish your class, but if I do, I'll be looking forward to that blue ball...blueberry smoothie."

Denise gave Stan a look that made his penis start to move. She started to push her cart down the aisle, but turned and said, "Hopefully I'll see you tomorrow."

Stan nodded, and despite his shaky knees, started pushing his cart quickly in the opposite direction.

The nighttime sky over the Upper Peninsula was clear, and the half moon and twinkling stars were providing the only light in the empty church parking lot. Well, not completely empty, there were two cars in the parking lot: Stan's black 2023 GMC Denali, and Duane's white 1990 Porsche 944, with vanity plates that read: *Go for Go.*

Stan, Randy, and Duane were standing between the two cars. Stan had Randy and Duane's full attention as he shared details of his chance encounter with Denise. "Just as she reached down to grab me a jar of blue-cheese olives, I got a good look at her phone in her purse. She had four missed calls from Houston," Stan said.

Duane and Randy looked more confused than surprised. Randy finally asked, "What do you think that means?"

"I think it means that Denise is mixed up with Hubert Houston."

"Think she's blackmailing him too?" Duane asked.

Stan looked at Randy. "Denise told you that she gets ten percent of the purchase price if her partner sells the 5,000 acres to a space company, right?"

Randy's eyes widened as he nodded slowly. "Holy...shit."

"So, Houston is the one who owns all that land?" Duane considered his question for a few seconds before he said, "Yeah, that makes sense."

Randy clenched his jaw in anger. "Hubert, fucking, Houston. How did I miss that? Of course Denise is working for the richest guy in the U.P."

Duane squinted his left eye and tilted his head to the right as he considered something. "I knew Denise didn't kill, Lenny. It had to be Hubert."

Stan's face was full of doubt as he shook his head. "No, I'm pretty sure the two of them conspired to murder Lenny. But Hubert's not one to get his hands dirty, so it's highly likely he hired someone to take Lenny out."

Randy looked like he agreed with Stan as he folded his arms. "Denise told me that Space D plans on paying one hundred million in cash for the 5,000 acres."

"Which is at least twenty million more than the land is actually worth," Stan said.

"I think Lenny came across some sensitive information about the deal at Denise's apartment," Randy said. "Denise told Hubert, and he hired someone to kill, Lenny."

"I fucking hate Hubert Houston," Duane said.

"What I'd like to know is how did Denise get mixed up with Houston?" Stan asked.

"Now that's a good question." Duane said.

"Did she ever mention his name around you?" Stan asked.

"No, never," Randy said.

Duane looked at Randy and said, "I gotta be honest with you. I really can't blame Denise for blackmailing you to keep that report hidden. If I had ten million bucks coming my way, and you had some way of preventing my big payday, I'd blackmail your ass."

Randy rubbed his eyes, trying to avoid eye contact with Duane for the time being.

"And I'm one of your best friends," Duane said.

"Fuck Hubert Houston, fuck Denise, and fuck Space D," Stan said. "We've got to find a way to stop them, or Whisper Dunes is fucked."

Stan took a deep breath as he tried to get control of his emotions. He took two steps back and put his hands on his hips.

"Take it easy, big guy," Duane said in a gentle tone.

"There's got to be some way to blow up the deal," Stan said with great intensity.

Duane regarded Randy for at least five seconds before he said, "There is a way to blow up the deal."

Randy, looking very uncomfortable, bit the inside of his cheek. He glanced at Duane then Stan before he allowed himself to take a deep breath.

"All Randy has to do is make that feasibility study public before September 1st, and then there's no way the zoning board can vote to rezone the land for industrial use," Duane said.

Randy hadn't blinked in over a minute, and the stress that was radiating through his body was starting to make his chest hurt.

"Of course, if Randy does that, Denise will send the sex video to Vivian," Duane said. He continued to keep his eyes fixed on Stan, as if Randy was nowhere near them. "Unless she has a remarkably forgiving heart, Vivian will divorce Randy, leaving him heartbroken and on the verge of financial ruin."

Randy closed his eyes tightly and exhaled through his mouth in frustration.

Duane looked like he felt bad as he regarded Randy. "I'm sorry, Randy. I didn't mean to be so matter of fact. I think there's a strong change that Vivian would find it in her heart to forgive you."

"I've already discussed this with you guys. I think there's a chance she'd forgive me, but it's guaranteed that her heart will be broken. I'll never be able to look her in the eyes again."

Duane gently rubbed Randy's shoulder and said, "You're right. There's got to be other ways to blow up the deal."

"Before we can blow up the deal, I think we need to figure out when the Denise and Houston partnership began. I've never once seen them in public together, nor have I ever heard any rumors about them hooking up," Stan said.

"Yeah, me neither," Duane said.

"Maybe they're not partners. Maybe Denise is blackmailing Hubert."

Stan's mind continued to race with different thoughts. He scratched his chin and glanced up at the sky. He then glanced at Randy and Duane. "Maybe you're right, Duane. Maybe Denise really is a kind, sweet natured woman. But a power hungry whore like Hubert Houston didn't see a kind and sweet woman. He saw a naive and vulnerable woman, who could be groomed and manipulated."

Randy and Duane both looked curious as they listened intently. Stan glanced at the dark forest before he looked at Randy. "I think it's entirely plausible to believe that Houston ordered Denise to seduce and blackmail you. And I think she blackmailed at least a few other people in this town at the behest of Hubert Houston."

Randy quietly pondered Stan's theory while Duane looked like he wanted slam his fist into Houston's face.

Duane's jaw was clenched so tight that it hurt when he said, "That doesn't surprise me one bit to find out that a country club scumbag like Hubert Houston is a pimp."

Randy looked genuinely confounded. "Why would a successful hedge fund manager moonlight as a pimp?"

Stan flashed a grin as he seemed amused with the thought that just popped into his head. "If Jack White has taught us anything, it's that you can't be a pimp and a prostitute too."

"Can't argue with the wisdom of Jack White," Duane said. "But if anyone is capable of being a pimp and a prostitute, it's Hubert Houston. He's a money-hungry, power broker, who's spent his entire adult life operating behind a velvet curtain. That cocksucker is capable of anything."

Stan and Randy both flashed a disapproving look at Duane.

"It's offensive when you guys say it, not when I say it," Duane said.

"Hubert Houston is the worst human being I've ever met," Randy said. "Yes, he's capable of anything, but I think you guys are underestimating Denise. She's very intelligent and a master at the art of seduction. She's more than capable of running her own blackmail operation without the help of Houston."

Duane folded his arms as his eyes narrowed. "Hubert Houston inherited millions from his dad's real estate empire before he allegedly became a hedge fund dipshit out in New York. Then out of the blue, he moves back to Whisper Dunes and starts managing other peoples' hard-earned money out of his dad's old office on Front Street. Do you know the first rule one must follow when convincing people to give you their hard-earned money to manage? Pretend you know what you're talking about. It would not surprise me one bit to learn that Houston's rinky-dink hedge fund is just a front for a prostitution ring that focuses on blackmailing high-net individuals like myself."

"I think that's plausible," Stan said. "Assuming that Houston is in serious debt, and desperately needs to raise some dough in order to cover his trading losses."

"Good evening," Fr. Carey said.

"Jesus Christ!" Randy gasped.

Because of the darkness and the intensity of the conversation, the guys did not see Fr. Carey sneak up on them. Terrified, Stan dropped his beer bottle on the pavement just as Duane clutched his chest with his right hand. Stan finally turned around and was first struck by the yellow eyes of a massive Irish Wolfhound, then by the orange glow from Fr. Carey's Cuban cigar.

"No, it's just me. A humble servant to our Lord Jesus Christ," Fr. Carey said before taking a long puff from his cigar. His beloved Irish Wolfhound growled, forcing Fr. Carey to tug on the leash. He then gently pet the dog's head.

"You guys are a little early. The first morning Mass doesn't start for another ten hours."

"Good timing, Father, just about to throw some brats on the grill," Duane said.

Fr. Carey looked suspicious as he glanced at Duane. "Oh, yeah. We're the brats? Where's the grill?"

"Dammit, I forgot the grill," Stan said.

"Want to know what I think?" Fr. Carey asked. "I think you three amigos stumbled upon some intriguing information relating to Lenny's murder."

Duane, Stan, and Randy exchanged uneasy looks.

"I don't know what you guys uncovered, but please, be careful," Fr. Carey said with the cigar wedged in the side of his mouth. "My gut tells me that the killer is among us in our beautiful town. If the killer isn't caught soon, I believe someone else will be murdered. Maybe even one of us."

"What makes you think the killer will strike again?" Duane asked in a nervous tone.

"Discovering sensitive information that could jeopardize someone's huge payday from a secret business deal is very dangerous."

Randy and Duane were shaken with fear, but Stan showed no emotion.

"It's true, we've discovered some information that has led us to develop our own theory, but my gut tells me you have some information that could help us out," Stan said.

Fr. Carey took another long drag from his cigar before looking up at the stars shining brightly over the Upper Peninsula. Stan, Randy, and Duane's eyes widened with great anticipation. Fr. Carey looked down for a second, as if he was trying to recall a specific conversation. Finally, he tilted his head up and stared at

Randy. "After you've been to bed with this woman...nothing else seems to matter."

The guys all stood in stunned silence, each with their mouth wide open, but nobody looked more shocked than Randy.

"I heard that in confession recently. And not the first time I've heard someone say those words."

Stan, Duane, and Randy all looked very uneasy. Stan and Duane exchanged a look while Randy kept his gaze on Fr. Carey.

"Father Carey, I don't want to tell you how to do your job, but I'm pretty sure you're not allowed to discuss what you hear in confession," Randy said.

Fr. Carey took a long drag from his cigar. "Well, sometimes, Randy, in order to catch a criminal you have to think and even act like a criminal."

Fr. Carey's eyes moved from Randy, to Duane to Stan. "You didn't hear it from me, but in the past few years there's been a massive increase in the number of adultery confessions I've heard, and not just men. More than a few wives have confessed to cheating on their husband...with a woman. A very, very, sexy woman."

"How do you know she's a sexy woman?" Duane asked.

"Not once has anyone mentioned her name during a confession, but on multiple occasions the confessor has described this woman's special features."

Stan, Randy, and Duane all looked to be in shock. For nearly a minute no one said a word. Stan watched Fr. Carey take a long puff on his cigar. "Do you have an idea of who this seductress might be?" Stan asked.

Fr. Carey nodded slowly and said, "When she's not conducting a pilates or yoga class, you can find this woman at the beach most summer afternoons...sunbathing topless."

Duane, Stan, and Randy all gave Fr. Carey an understanding nod.

"Do you think this woman killed Lenny?" Duane asked.

"I'm not certain of that. Although it's entirely plausible to think that."

"Lenny found something in her apartment he shouldn't have, and now he's dead," Stan said. "What do you think he found?"

Fr. Carey stared blankly at Stan. "No idea. But whatever he found clearly motivated someone to take his life."

Fr. Carey noticed that Randy looked to be the most shaken up. He gently put his hand on Randy's shoulder and said, "I'll leave you gentleman as you were. But it might be a good idea to wrap up your meeting. Someone might be watching, and I'm not talking about the Lord Jesus Christ our Savior."

Stan nodded respectfully. "Thank you, Father, for your divine wisdom. Always a pleasure."

Fr. Carey nodded as he took another drag from his cigar. "The golf outing's coming up and the number of people registered so far is lower compared to last year. It's the church's biggest fundraiser of the year. Do me a favor, guys, get the word out to your pals, okay?"

Randy nodded and said, "You can count on us, Father."

"Bless you."

The guys watched Fr. Carey and his Irish Wolfhound walk slowly toward the red- brick rectory behind the church.

"Great, now I'm going to have night terrors for a week because of that dog," Duane said. "What kind of dog is that anyway?"

"Irish Wolfhound," Stan said.

"That was the most terrifying dog I've ever seen in my life."

Randy looked uneasy as he slowly scanned the forest. "Do you really think someone is watching us?"

"I don't know, but it does kind of feel like it," Stan said.

Duane, Randy, and Stan all looked in different directions before exchanging nervous glances.

"Guys, we're in deep now. We need to be more careful going forward," Stan said.

"Why do you think Fr. Carey gave us that information?" Duane asked. "I mean I'm glad he did, but that was kind of strange."

"He knows what we're up to. He's just trying to point us in the right direction," Stan said.

Randy had a determined look on his face as he eyed Stan and Duane. "He expects us to do something with that information. You guys heard him, if you want to catch a criminal sometimes you have to think like one. Even become one."

Duane and Stan stared suspiciously at Randy.

"I'm going to break into Houston's mansion. If he and Denise are working together, I may find something I can blackmail Denise with," Randy said.

"Are you out of your mind?" Stan asked. "That's a terrible idea. Breaking into Denise's apartment was a total failure, and her place was easy to break into."

Randy sighed and lowered his head in frustration. Duane regarded him, empathizing with his dejected friend.

"I have no doubt you'd find something that would incriminate him and Denise, but there is no way to break into Houston's mansion," Stan said. "I guarantee you it has a top notch alarm system and cameras everywhere. It's impossible."

Duane's eye narrowed as he glanced at Randy then Stan. He had a look on his face that suggested he knew something they didn't. "Difficult, but not impossible."

20

Denise was hiking with Hubert on a rocky trail near the edge of the eastern shoreline of Isle Royale National Park—a rugged island in Lake Superior with no roads. Denise loved the fact that there were over 600 species of plants on the island, and Hubert loved the fact that it was more likely to cross paths with a moose or a wolf than another human being while hiking around the island. There was nothing but tall evergreens to their left and crystal clear water to their right. Denise and Hubert were so absorbed in their heated conversation that neither of them noticed that two great blue herons had just flown fifty feet in front of them.

"I betcha half the town knew my wife was having an affair with that asshole. Of course some people are going to speculate that I killed Lenny," Hubert said in a nervous, high-pitched voice. "But guess what? Lenny slept with both of Russ's wives and about fifty other married women in this town."

"Yeah, and that's why they're dozens of crazy rumors floating around town right now. Nobody knows what to believe," Denise said in a measured tone. "We can only hope more crazy rumors keep spreading, and as long as the media continues to report on every rumor they come across, the line between fact and fiction will remain blurred. All we need to do is stay calm and follow the plan."

Hubert stopped walking, which forced Denise to stop. "But the problem is O'Malley and his boys aren't distracted by the rumors. From what I've gathered, O'Malley already has a strong theory he's pursuing. The cops know Lenny was in your apartment. I'm sure they suspect he discovered something."

Denise looked defensive. Her eyes got wide and she contorted her face in a way that Hubert had never seen before. "Don't you dare blame me, Hubert. There's nothing I could have done to prevent Lenny from getting into my apartment. I had no idea that Stan hired him to change the shower head."

"I'm not blaming you. You're right, there's nothing you could have done. Just bad luck. But we can't deny the fact that a highly respected former Detroit homicide detective is now suspicious of both of us."

"Well, we both know I'm not going to jail. And if I were you I wouldn't worry too much because O'Malley's investigation isn't going to wrap up before the zoning board vote. You just might have to make your move to the Cayman Islands a little sooner than planned."

Denise started walking again, prompting Hubert to follow. "I think at some point O'Malley will get a search warrant to go through my apartment and studio," Denise said. "Tomorrow I'm going to move all my sensitive documents to your house."

"Yeah, that's probably a good idea," Hubert said as his shoulders slumped down. He put his hands in the pockets of his khaki pants. He looked more relaxed now as he glanced at the water.

"What about Randy?"

"He's held up his end of the bargain...so far. Russ is still under the impression that the feasibility report hasn't been completed," Denise said.

"Good. The zoning board meeting is coming up soon. We know we have at least two votes, guaranteeing a tie. Leaving it up to old Russ to break the tie."

Denise and Hubert continued walking along the uneven trail. There was nothing more to talk about so they both lowered their heads and got lost in their own thoughts. They looked like an unhappy married couple that just agreed to try couples therapy one more time, despite the fact that neither one had any intention of changing.

Hubert glanced at Denise for a second before his eyes looked back down at the rocky trail. For some reason, the thought of pushing Denise off the narrow trail just crossed Hubert's mind. He was upset with himself that he would even consider doing such a thing. He had never once considered killing Denise, most days he thought he was in love with her, but all of a sudden his mind was entertaining the idea of giving Denise a swift push off the trail. Falling onto jagged rocks and rolling into Lake Superior would likely kill her, he thought. But Hubert hated doing anything without a sure-fire guarantee. Besides, what self-respecting hedge fund manager would kill a valuable partner? In the hedge fund business you look for unique ways to double cross and steal from your partners and clients, but you don't kill them...well, not usually, anyway.

Before his dad finally allowed him to manage some of his fortune, Hubert worked for a large hedge fund in New York City. He didn't learn much except that running a hedge fund was mostly about fundraising, not investing. When someone has the ability to consistently raise money for your fund, you do everything in your power to keep that person at your firm.

He met Denise when he was living in Manhattan. They had a hot summer romance that ended when Denise moved back to Paris. But Denise made a point to stay in touch. She liked to trade stocks and commodities via multiple trading apps, and whenever Hubert got access to inside information he would usually share it with Denise.

Hubert never thought he'd see Denise again after he moved back to his hometown. So he was more than a tad surprised when Denise contacted him out of the blue one evening and told him she was moving to Whisper Dunes. She wanted desperately to start a new life in a small town that she was familiar with. When she was growing up, Denise came to the U.P. every summer to visit her grandparents, who lived in a small town just north of Whisper Dunes. After Denise made the move, she and Hubert made a point not to be seen together in public. But they also made a point to get together once a week to share a very expensive bottle of red wine and fuck. Usually at a hotel in Green Bay or Duluth, but sometimes at Hughie's mansion— Denise only called him Hughie after she downed a few tequila shots.

Less than a month after opening her pilates studio, Denise's daily classes were booked solid but her financial problems continued to worsen. She was on the verge of bankruptcy because of too many bad trades, that's when she decided to pitch Hubert on a unique partnership. Because she had always proved to be loyal and reliable, he agreed to give it a try.

After the partnership started, Denise stopped spreading her legs for Hubert and was all business. This was hard on Hubert because like every other man who had met Denise, he was in awe of her beauty and fantasized about her often. But Hubert respected her wishes and never even made a pass at Denise once the partnership began. Sometimes, maybe to tease him or maybe just to remind him of her talents, Denise would explain in great detail about why sex was the greatest of all art forms. Then she'd go into even greater detail about why no one is more powerful than a beautiful woman, who's educated and practiced in the art of deception.

At the beginning of summer their relationship became physically intimate again. It was Denise who initiated a night of passionate sex, and Hubert enjoyed every second of it, but very recently he started considering the possibility that Denise was setting him up for his eventual downfall. Hubert ruminated on the idea of pushing Denise to her death for another minute before he was distracted by a bald eagle hovering near the shoreline. Denise and Hubert watched in awe as the bald eagle dove straight down and fished out a northern pike. They tracked the bald eagle's flight until it disappeared into the island's dense forest, made up mostly of tall evergreen trees.

Hubert and Denise shared a quick look. Denise smiled first then Hubert flashed a smile before lowering his head and thinking—more like obsessing—over whether or not he could still trust Denise. He focused his eyes on the trail, which was getting rockier and harder to walk on. Hubert had never caught her in a lie before, but Denise was acting different. She always walked tall and usually looked him the the eye when they spoke, smiling with ease. But now she was walking hunched over and refusing to make eye contact. Hubert suspected that she might be hiding something from him. He knew though, if he started asking Denise tough questions and accused her of wrongdoing, he would give his most valuable partner more reason to double cross him. Without Denise, the one hundred million dollar land deal was not possible.

Stan sat behind his office desk in his worn leather chair, looking at photos on his desktop computer of a large house that needed a lot of work. A short woman in her late twenties knocked twice on the office door, which was open.

"Hey, Vicky. Come on in," Stan said cheerfully.

Vicky entered holding a Priority Mail Flat Rate Legal envelope. She handed the envelope to Stan and said, "This just arrived for you."

"Thank you."

Vicky walked out of the office as Stan looked at the large envelope. He set it on his desk and went back to analyzing the house on his computer screen. But his eyes slowly moved back toward the envelope. Normally, when Stan was focused on assessing a property he didn't let anything distract him, but the sheer size of the envelope made him think that whatever was inside might be important. Stan opened the envelope, reached inside and pulled out the contents: a one page typed letter and a silver house key. Stan looked curious as he squinted his eyes and quickly read the letter.

Lisa pedaled her mountain bike up the long driveway. She had planned on a five mile ride but ended up going ten miles. She cruised past Stan's Denali then her mini-van and stopped just shy of the garage. The garage door was open so Lisa walked her bike inside, but before she parked her bike by the other six bikes in the corner, she noticed a dozen fishing poles laying across six moving boxes near the door that led to the backyard.

Stan flipped over the eight burgers on his gas grill. Standing alone on his back deck, he took a long sip from his bottled beer then looked out at the forest. Not in a suspicious way —he was just enjoying the view. The sun was setting and the beautiful orange and pink rays had cut paths through the forest.

Lisa slid open the screen door and joined Stan on the deck. "Hi, honey," Stan said as he flashed a smile. "How was your ride?"

"Fine."

She walked over to Stan and planted a quick kiss on his lips. "Why are there a bunch of fishing poles and like two hundred *Playboy* magazines in our garage?"

"Just some things I inherited from Lenny," Stan said before letting out a muffled burp.

Lisa looked confused while Stan flipped the burgers.

"Lenny left me his fishing cabin on Goose Lake. Well, it's more of a shack than a cabin. There wasn't much in there except a few good records, a dozen excellent fishing poles, and a very impressive collection of *Playboy* magazines.

"Wow. Can't believe he willed you his cabin. I didn't realize he had a place on Goose Lake."

"Me neither. Just learned about the place today when I got a letter from his attorney. It was a bitch to find, especially considering there's no internet service within thirty miles of the area, but it's a gorgeous piece of property."

Lisa was thinking about something before her eyes landed on the grill. "Want me to make a salad?"

"Yeah, that'd be great."

Stan watched Lisa turn around and walk back into the house. Since they'd started dating, Stan rarely missed an opportunity to check Lisa out. He thought Lisa was more beautiful now than she was ten years ago, and she was really beautiful ten years ago. He smiled as he thought back to the days before they were married. On warm summer nights they would often take a midnight stroll on the beach and make out on the shoreline.

Stan stared at the sunlight cutting a path through the forest, wondering whether there might be a chance that Lisa would be up for a midnight stroll tonight. Perfect night for it.

The beautiful albeit explicit images that had just formed in his mind vanished at the sound of his phone ringing.

Stan pulled out the phone, checked the caller ID then answered. He tapped the speaker button as he turned the grill burners off. "Hey, Russ."

Russ's energetic voice came over the speaker. "I just got a call from Larry Holt's assistant. She said Larry wants to interview me. What do you think I should do?"

Stan moved the phone closer to his mouth. "Russ, if it was anyone else I'd say don't do it. But I'd be lying to you if I said I don't respect Larry Holt. Truth be told, I respect the hell out of that guy. Do the interview."

"I was hoping you'd say that."

"Just make sure you keep the focus on Whisper Dunes, and not on any of the bullshit rumors. Every time he wants to switch gears, you need to be prepared to swing the pendulum right back to America's Best Place to Live. Your talking points should only focus on the fact that Whisper Dunes is a beautiful four-season nature paradise, and that the town is home to incredibly kind, generous, and hard-working people. It's these people who make Whisper Dunes a great place to live and work."

"That's good. Hey, maybe I can stop over tomorrow and we can practice."

"Yeah, let's do it. But remember, Russ, you have to be discreet before and after the interview. Don't talk to anyone. Let Carol take all your calls. I'm serious. You need to be more discreet than a thoracic surgeon who put herself through med school by moonlighting as a high priced call girl. Understand?"

"Understand. Thanks, Stan."

"See you tomorrow, Mr. Mayor."

21

Randy sat with his two daughters around a small circular table, painted light blue, on the sidewalk outside of Marge's Ice Cream Parlor. Sophie and Zooey, thirteen and eleven, were both enjoying their blue moon ice cream cones while Randy was eating Mackinac Island fudge ice cream from a cup.

"How's the blue moon?" Randy asked jovially.

"Eccellente, Papa," Sophie said with a sweet smile.

"How about we take a walk to the Children's Museum after our ice cream?"

"Sorry, Dad, but I think we've outgrown the children's museum," Zooey said.

"No, don't say that. If that's true than that my means my two girls have grown up way too fast."

Zooey and Sophie shared a silly look before Zooey started speaking in Italian to Sophie. Randy watched with delight as his girls conversed in Italian. Zooey looked at her dad, smiled and said, "How about instead of the museum, we take a drive down to UPAWS?"

Randy stared at his ice cream while scooping some out of the cup. Sophie and Zooey closely eyed their dad as he took a bite.

"Come on, Dad, let's see if there's any puppies in need of rescuing," Sophie said.

Randy leaned back in his chair and sighed. His last dog ran away when he was fourteen. Randy swore he'd never get another dog again. But his daughters had been persistently asking to get a puppy for over a year now. Maybe it was time, Randy thought. He knew he'd eventually become the sole caretaker of the dog, but he also knew his girls would love having a dog in the house.

"You don't have to make any promises. We just want to take a puppy for a walk," Sophie said.

Randy bit down on the inside of his cheek before finally looking at his girls, who were both smiling in anticipation that their dad would say yes. The girls were fairly convinced he would say yes, but they started to have their doubts as Randy took his time to even make eye contact. He was staring at the brick building across the street when he finally said, "Okay."

Zooey and Sophie flashed big smiles as they both stood up and hugged their dad.

"Thank you, Papa," Zooey said in Italian.

"You're the best, Dad," Sophie said.

Randy's white Ford Explorer drove down a heavily wooded private road. Up ahead the girls saw a white and black sign attached to a red post that read: **Upper Peninsula Animal Welfare Shelter - upaws.** Randy saw a parking spot near the front entrance, and within two seconds of putting the car in park the girls opened the door and ran towards the entrance.

Sophie and Zooey, with Randy trailing close behind, walked down a long hallway that housed twenty kennels on each side. Behind the chain-link fence door of each kennel was an adorable mix-breed dog that was begging to be adopted. Sophie and Zooey spent a minute or two looking and awing over each dog. Randy stood behind the girls, watching each interaction with a slight smile on his face. Every dog, ranging in age from eight weeks old to eight years old, seemed to be screaming, *pick me! Pick me! Pick me!*

They finally got to the end of the hallway. Randy held the door open for the girls, but they were standing still, distracted by what they saw through the glass window. Randy let go of the door handle and looked through the window to see that Zooey and Sophie were staring at a woman giving a puppy a bath. The girls couldn't tell what kind of dog it was because of all the suds covering the puppy's face. Randy stood frozen in absolute shock. He hadn't looked at the puppy yet because his eyes were fixed on the woman bathing the puppy. For a moment, Randy thought about picking up his girls and running out of the kennel, but before he could make a move, Denise glanced at him. She was just as shocked, but quickly flashed a smile to hide her discomfort. Denise went back to bathing the puppy for about five seconds, but then turned her gaze towards the girls. Denise smiled and waved them into the grooming room. Without even turning to ask their dad, Zooey and Sophie burst through the double swing door.

Randy watched his girls approach Denise and the sudsy puppy, while still playing with the idea of running out of the dog shelter and hiding in his 2012 Ford Explorer. He knew his girls would eventually make their way back to the car. He'd tell them he was sorry, but that he had to take an important call from the mayor. Something he had done on several occasions, most recently while at Sophie's piano recital.

"Oh, my God! Look at this cutie pie," Sophie said. The girls were now standing directly across from Denise and the puppy. Sophie had a big smile on her face as she gently pet the puppy's head. The excited puppy started to wag her tail, which made Zooey and Sophie smile and giggle. Denise was about to say something to the girls, but pressed her lips together at the sight of Randy walking through the door. Because their dad was standing behind them, Sophie and Zooey did not see the fear on his face as he locked eyes with Denise.

"What's its name?" Zooey asked.

Denise smiled sweetly and said, "Nala. I'm just finishing up her bath then we can take her for a walk, if you'd like?"

Zooey and Sophie struggled to control their excitement while Randy looked like he might faint. "Girls, what about that boxer-mix in the first kennel you liked? I'll go ask that nice guy up front if we can take him for a walk."

"No, we want to walk Nala," Sophie said.

Zooey noticed the sweat on her dad's forehead. "Dad, are you okay?

"I'm fine, sweetie, just a little hot in here."

After drying the puppy, Denise led everyone into the playroom while making friendly chit-chat with the girls. As the girls finally got to play with Nala, Denise walked over to Randy in the corner and stood about a foot from his right shoulder. They stood in silence while watching Sophie and Zooey try to teach Nala how to sit and stay, without much luck.

Denise finally looked at Randy and said, "I think they like her. Honestly, she's one of the best-behaved puppies we've ever rescued. And come on, who doesn't love a lab-mix?"

Randy kept his eyes on the girls. "Since when do you work here?"

"I've been volunteering at UPAWS twice a week since before I opened my pilates studio. It's ten times better than therapy."

"Good to know," Randy said. He finally made eye contact with Denise. "I thought you might be following me."

Denise folded her arms without showing any expression. She and Randy went back to watching the girls play with Nala. "Have your girls ever had a dog?"

"No."

"They seem to me like they're ready to take care of this dog." Denise walked towards the girls and said, "Hey, would you girls like to take Nala for a walk?"

"Yeah!" Sophie yelled.

"Great! There's a nice park just down the street," Denise said.

Randy closed his eyes and let out a frustrated sigh. Denise looked sensitive to Randy's growing discomfort. "Relax, I just want to see how the girls do with her out in the open," Denise said. "There's a couple of things we look for to make sure the dog will be a good fit before you bring her home."

Denise grabbed the leash from behind the door, hooked it up to the puppy, and then handed the leash to Zooey. "Lead us out," Denise said with a smile. Zooey, Sophie, and the puppy exited the playroom, but Randy and Denise stayed in the room for another minute.

Randy glanced at Denise and said, "I didn't know that you had such a love for dogs."

"Well, we never took the time to really get to know each other. Honestly, you didn't strike me as the type of dad who would let his kids have a dog, much less a rescue dog. But I guess I was wrong about you."

Randy regarded Denise for a moment. He wanted to say something, but decided to keep his mouth shut. He followed Denise out of the playroom and down the long hallway. Randy and Denise exchanged a glance. Randy was caught off guard by how vulnerable Denise looked. "Back when I was growing up in Seattle, my mom and I used to volunteer at the animal shelter near our home every week. I quickly discovered that no matter how down you are, the dogs always find a way to cheer you up."

Randy regarded Denise. "I guess in your line of work, you need some cheering up now and then."

Denise watched the girls and Nala exit through the door at the end of the hallway. She finally said, "Yeah, sometimes."

"You weren't always a bad person, were you?" Randy asked in a gentle voice.

Denise regarded Randy, but she couldn't find the right words, so her lips didn't move.

"It's never too late to change your ways," Randy said. "I don't know how you ended up in this life, but you don't have to keep doing what your doing."

Denise put her head down as she pushed open the door at the end of the hallway and stepped outside.

The two acre park backed up to a forest filled mostly with sugar maple and red maple trees. A gravel walking path bordered the field that was covered in a mixture of tall green grass and purple wildflowers. The park was crowded with people, young and old, trying to get the most out of a summer afternoon. Randy and Denise stood in the middle of the field—about four feet apart from each other—watching Sophie and Zooey play with Nala. The girls were trying to teach Nala a few tricks, which was proving difficult because the three-month-old pup was only interested in chasing birds. Denise had a slight smile on her face and seemed at ease watching Randy's daughters having fun chasing Nala around the park. Randy, however, stood erect with a blank face. He was still struggling to believe that he was actually standing next to Denise while watching his girls play. A worst-case scenario that he had never considered.

Randy reacted to his phone ringing. He looked at the caller ID—Mayor Russ. Randy quickly walked away from Denise. He got about twenty yards away from her before he finally answered the call, which ended up only lasting a few minutes. Carol, without checking with Russ, had told a producer at *Good Morning America* that Russ would be happy to do a sit down interview. Russ wanted Randy's opinion on whether or not he should sit down for a one-on-one interview. Randy strongly advised him not to do the interview.

Denise's face was filled with joy as she continued to watch the girls play with Nala. She walked over to the girls and pulled a few puppy treats from the inside of her jacket. "Pretty good, girls, but the key to training a dog is patience, consistency, and treats," Denise said with a smile.

She handed a small milk bone to Sophie then another one to Zooey. "Now, you've got her attention so you can teach her anything."

"Sit, Nala," Zooey said. "Sit...sit."

Nala finally sat still to the girls delight. Zooey and Sophie both said, "Good girl." The girls exchanged a look then started running together to see if Nala would follow. She did for a few seconds before getting distracted by a butterfly.

"See if you can get her to stay for more than five seconds," Denise said. She watched with a big smile on her face as Sophie and Zooey spread out from each other, each with a treat, and took turns trying to get Nala to sit then stay. Denise's mind started to wander, imagining a life where she was a mother. It's a remarkable feeling when you find yourself in a present moment that suddenly matches with images you've only experienced through your imagination. Denise was perfectly still. She knew she was experiencing transcendence. One blink and it would be over. She had walked through many parks, on many beautiful afternoons, just like today, often imagining how she would spend a day at the park with her kids. Almost a minute had gone by and Denise had not blinked or taken a breath. But her transcendent experience ended as the sound of Nala's barking rang in her ears.

Denise still had a hard time accepting the person she had developed into. This was not the life she had imagined for herself. But certain people entered her life when she was young and vulnerable, and sent her down a path of their choosing. By the time she realized she was no longer in control of her own life, it was too late.

Denise was still smiling even though she had a sick feeling in her stomach. She watched Sophie try to get Nala to stay by using a stern, grownup voice. Nala started hopping around then took off toward the forest. Denise watched the girls run after Nala until something in the distance caught her eye. Her smile disappeared. She looked uneasy, even angry as her attention was now focused on the two men sitting on a park bench under an old maple tree. The men were deep in conversation and had no idea they were being watched at the moment. Denise's eyes narrowed as she stared in disbelief at Deacon Terry Lutterbach, who was in the middle of an intense conversation with Officer Alcocks. Denise put her sunglasses back on and casually pulled her black hoodie over her head so that it was covering most of her forehead. Denise turned her attention back to Sophie and Zooey as she thought through her next move.

Denise flashed a smile at Sophie and Zooey as they started to run toward her while Nala followed closely behind. "That was some impressive puppy training," Denise said.

"Thanks," Sophie said.

"Where did my dad go?" Zooey asked.

Denise actually had no idea where Randy was until she spun around and located him about forty yards away. "There he is," Denise said. She turned back around to find Zooey and Sophie looking right at her.

"We really want to adopt Nala, but I think we're going to need your help convincing our dad."

"Will you please help us?" Sophie asked in a sweet voice.

Denise regarded Sophie then Zooey and said, "Of course I will."

Denise bent down and put her hands on her knees so that she could look both girls in the eye. "I'm pretty confident I'll be able to convince your dad to adopt Nala, but you girls have to promise me you'll take excellent care of her."

Sophie and Zooey both flashed huge smiles and said, "You can count on us, Ms. Denise."

22

A tall woman in her early seventies stood on the covered front porch of the Nahma Inn. She hummed a tune to herself while watering the plants in the hanging baskets. Inside, the first-floor restaurant was packed with cable news reporters and one print journalist from *The Mining Journal*—the most widely circulated newspaper in the Upper Peninsula.

Randy, dressed in a light grey suit and holding a briefcase, walked up the porch steps. The woman watering the plants stopped and regarded Randy, almost as if she was expecting him. "Good morning, Randy," she said.

"Morning, Mrs. Campbell," Randy said cheerfully.

"Grabbing some breakfast?"

"Nah, just a coffee this morning."

"Careful. A lot of nosey news reporters in there."

"Thanks for the heads up."

Randy entered the restaurant as Mrs. Campbell went back to watering the plants.

On the second floor of the Nahma Inn, at the end of the hallway, was the Honeymoon Suite. Inside the Honeymoon Suite, Cynthia Rogers—a senior reporter for The Associated Press—stood in front of the antique oval cheval mirror. She had on a white robe and a bath towel was wrapped around her wet hair. Claudia's face was close to the mirror as she carefully applied lipstick—opulent red. She heard footsteps coming down the long hallway, but didn't react as she remained focused on slowly moving the lipstick over her plump lips. The sound of dress shoes walking on a thin runner that covered the old wood floor in the hallway grew louder. The footsteps then came to an abrupt stop. A few seconds later, two hard knocks on Cynthia's door startled her so badly that she smeared the lipstick across her cheek. Her neck turned toward the door but she didn't move her feet.

A manila envelope slid under the door. Cynthia remained perfectly still, staring at the envelope with great uncertainty. She listened to the fading sound of footsteps walking away from the door. Ten seconds of silence passed before Cynthia walked slowly toward the door and finally picked up the envelope. She opened it and pulled out a five by seven notecard. The handwritten note read: *Ask Mayor Tillinghast how much of the city's pension fund is invested with Hubert Houston's hedge fund.* Cynthia looked at herself in the mirror and smiled.

Russ stepped out of the side door of St. Christopher's Catholic Church. He walked slowly among a dozen local residents, who were chit-chatting as they left morning Mass. A young, fit-looking, Whisper Dunes police officer kept a close eye on Russ as he walked toward his pickup truck.

"Mr. Mayor, what I just don't get is why you can't stand in front of a camera and say that the people of Whisper Dunes unequivocally reject being designated America's Best Place to Live. Now, leave us alone," said a man who looked to be close to eighty.

"Why can't you say that?" Asked another man in his late sixties. "It sure would put this whole mess to bed a heck of a lot quicker."

"Guys, I hear you, and I'm not happy either about the way things are going. But that's just not a realistic option as this point," Russ said.

"I think what the mayor is saying is that the Preparation H gel is out of the tube, and there's just no way of putting it back in," said a tall man in his early seventies.

"Right now, we're at the mercy of the national media. They've created this narrative, and there going to keep building it up with as much drama mixed in as possible until they get bored reporting on the story. The fact is, they could be here for a while," Russ said. "We got to stick together. I promise, this storm, like all storms, will come to an end. And when it does, we'll be a better, stronger community."

Cynthia and her cameraman stepped out from behind a massive pine tree in front of the church. Russ was clearly caught off guard as Cynthia shoved a microphone in his face. "Mr. Mayor, how much of the municipal employees' pension fund is managed by Hubert Houston's hedge fund?"

Russ lowered his head, almost cowering, as he walked quickly toward his pickup truck. "This is a place of worship," Russ said angrily. "Have you no decency? I'd expect this from other outlets, but not from an AP reporter."

"Mr. Mayor, your city's employees have a right to know whether or not Houston Capital has mismanaged their pensions. Are you aware that Houston Capital is facing serious financial trouble?"

Russ tried not to convey any emotion but it was clear he was becoming frazzled. "Because of Houston Capital's bad trades, is the city of Whisper Dunes facing serious pension liabilities?"

Russ finally got to his pickup truck. He opened the door then turned to Cynthia and said, "Call me old-fashioned, but I don't speak to reporters on church grounds."

Cynthia and her cameraman watched Russ get into his pickup truck and speed away. The police officer hurried into the passenger side of a waiting Whisper Dunes police suv and the vehicle sped off, tailing the mayor's pickup truck.

Cynthia turned to her cameraman. "All you have to do is ask the questions and let the audience believe what they want. We just introduced a whole new storyline to this saga."

Russ sat at the kitchen table in his quiet cabin, reading a document. He did not seem distracted by the ringing coming from his cell phone and landline. Russ had become immune to the ringing sound over the last few weeks, but a loud knock at the front door caused him to quickly get up and grab the shotgun from his kitchen counter.

"Russ! It's Stan!"

Russ looked somewhat relieved, but still held his shotgun tightly as he walked toward the front door. "Any chance you were followed?" Russ asked before his hand reached for the door handle.

"No. I was extra careful."

Russ and Stan sat in the old rocking chairs on the front porch of Russ's cabin. It had been cloudy all day and a light rain started to fall just before Russ and Stan eased into the rocking chairs. The sun had started to set, but tonight, no one in Whisper

Dunes would get to see the sunset. A rare occurrence in the summertime. A bottle of bourbon and two glasses were on the small table between the rocking chairs. Russ's shotgun was resting on his lap. Stan filled up both glasses before he eased back into the rocking chair.

"I don't want to talk about it because it'll just make me more upset. But when this storm passes, and the waters finally calm, you and I are going to sit down and discuss the definition of discreet," Stan said.

Russ didn't even bother to nod. Deep in thought, his eyes were focused on a pine tree in the distance. "What I admire most about the natural world is its unflappable indifference to human inventions and human error," Russ said.

A puzzled look appeared on Stan's face as he regarded Russ. His eyes moved from Russ toward the forest. Stan thought that the worst thing he could do at the moment was talk. He slowly sipped his bourbon while staring at two blue jays, who just landed near the top of a tall birch tree.

"The only real bad thing about getting older is that you have less people in your life you can trust. At least that's been my experience of getting older," Russ said.

Stan took another sip of bourbon before regarding Russ. "How much of the city's employee pension fund does Houston manage?"

"Almost all of it," Russ said in a barely audible tone. "I don't know how he convinced the finance committee to let him manage all that money, but I always suspected he somehow blackmailed a few members of the committee."

"You're right to suspect that. Houston's blackmailing more than a few people in this town. His old man was known for doing the same shit."

Russ took a long sip from his bourbon, looked at Stan and said, "Hubert needs to sell his 5,000 acres to a space company in order to make his fund whole again. Without that hundred-million-dollar payday his hedge fund will go bust. If that happens, the city's employee pension fund will be wiped out."

Stan did not conceal his anger. "That mother fucker!" Stan yelled as he pounded his fist on the table. He finished the bourbon in his glass before regarding Russ, who could not bring himself to meet Stan's gaze. His eye lids were heavy as he stared out at the forest, looking forlorn.

"That means he'll continue to do everything in his power to force the zoning commission to rezone his 5,000 acres. We both know Houston has at least one or two zoning commissioners in his pocket. I think it's likely you'll be forced to cast the deciding vote on whether or not to rezone the land. If you vote to rezone the land, you'll be outcasted in the only town you've ever lived in, Russ. Your political career will be finished. Worse, you'll feel pressure to move far away from here."

Russ stopped rocking in his chair. His sad eyes finally met Stan's angry gaze. "Yeah, you're probably right. But I can't let the employee pension fund go bust."

"Tell your pals on the zoning board, not to vote to change the current zoning ordinance. I'll find a buyer who doesn't want to develop the land for a spaceport."

Russ looked at Stan like he was unhinged.

"Who else besides a space company is willing to spend a hundred million on 5,000 acres of forested land that's hard to build on?"

"Under the current zoning ordinance terms, the land can be developed for recreational use, which includes developing a resort of some kind. As long as it offers outdoor recreation."

"Do you happen to have a buyer already interested?"

"Not yet, but I have someone in mind."

Russ's uneasy expression was replaced with a curious expression as he regarded Stan. "Who?"

"Sir Branch Bradford," Stan said matter-of-factly.

Russ's eyes widened in disbelief. He had to lick his top lip in order to prevent his jaw from dropping. Russ stared at Stan, hoping that he would quickly elaborate, but Stan didn't say a word. "Sir Branch Bradford? The British billionaire?"

Stan nodded with confidence. "Yep."

"That's your solution, to sell the land to a British billionaire? Jesus Christ, Stan. Please tell me you're kidding."

"Just listen to me for a second. Unlike those jerk-offs, who run Space D and Beige Origin, Bradford is a space industry titan, who happens to be a hardcore environmentalist. I think he would jump at the chance to buy the 5,000 acres that has essentially been earmarked for Space D."

"Even if you're right, how the heck are you going to get in touch with Sir Branch Bradford?" Russ asked with a befuddled look.

"Hey, there's a reason they call me The Hammer," Stan said with a little too much confidence.

"Didn't you get that nickname in college because you slept with nearly every girl on the hockey team?"

"My nickname in college was Iceman. People started calling me The Hammer after I started my real estate business. Why? Because I'm a closer, Russ."

Stan's boastful self-description did not ease Russ's concerns. He gazed nervously at the cloud-filled sky before he finally looked at Stan. They stared at each other for an uncomfortable moment before Russ said, "Well, you can't hammer a nail that you can't find."

23

Over three thousand people were gathered in Ellwood A. Mattson Lower Harbor Park on a warm, sunny afternoon. Most people occupying the park had traveled to Whisper Dunes from all over the country to support the Stop The Rocket movement. Over eight hundred tents covered the park grounds. The first wave of protestors who arrived were very respectful to the locals and to the land they were occupying, but the latest wave of protestors acted like they were at Burning Man festival. Upon arrival, their outlandish behavior quickly upset most Whisper Dunes residents and the first wave of protestors. But the media couldn't get enough of them. During the past week, over a dozen media outlets had their reporters and camera crews set up around the park in hopes of catching all sorts of action to report on.

A camera crew walked through a row of tents. They passed a young couple in their early twenties standing outside their tent chatting with another couple in their early forties. The huge sign posted in front of their tent read: STOP THE ROCKET—DON'T REZONE! Across the way, a banner posted high above a tent read: OCCUPY WALL STREET IS BACK BABY!

The camera crew briefly filmed a woman and a man—both in their late seventies—holding a banner that read: JESUS CHRIST WAS A RADICAL LIBERAL.

The crew filmed three naked women in body paint—all in their late twenties— holding a banner that read: DON'T LET WALL STREET OCCUPY AMERICA'S BEST PLACE TO LIVE! A few tents over, a young couple held a banner that read: SPACE EXPLORATION IS AS POINTLESS AS TRYING TO COLLECT TAXES FROM A BILLIONAIRE.

A cable news reporter was reporting live from the eastern end of the park. Lake Superior was visible in the background, but so were dozens of partially nude protestors. The male reporter looked into the camera and said, "It's been said before that the U.P. is such an amazing place, that once you experience it, you'll never want to leave. Which explains why residents are more than a little unnerved at the sight of new protestors arriving in Whisper Dunes every day. Most protestors have been setting up makeshift camps around Whisper Dunes for the past two weeks, but the beautiful park I'm standing in, Ellwood A. Mattson Lower Harbor Park, is considered headquarters for the protestors. This beautiful park has always been a place for members of the community to gather for youth sporting events, family picnics, weddings, art festivals, summer festivals, winter festivals, and on summer nights it's a great place to enjoy live music. But for the past two weeks, the environment here resembles what you'd expect to see at a poorly organized music festival."

A PBS reporter had her microphone near the face of an irate man in his late fifties. The bearded man was wearing a tie-dyed Peace t-shirt and yelling, "This beautiful, peaceful town has been victimized by corporate owned media companies! Multiple media moguls conspired to put Whisper Dunes on the national stage with the sole intention of embarrassing this great town with a manufactured scandal!"

The crowd behind the angry man cheered loudly in support. A naked woman covered in pink, green, and yellow paint suddenly jumped in front of the angry man and grabbed the microphone. "Stop the rocket! Space exploration is the biggest waste of money anyone has ever spent on anything! We need to stop spending money on pointless space travel and start properly educating and feeding Americans! Who gives a flying twat how many planets there are!? The time has come to free Whisper Dunes from corporate greed and the media's power grip! But the only way that can happen is if we legalize psychedelic mushrooms!"

The crowd cheered as the woman started to dance wildly in front of the cameraman. The reporter signaled to the cameraman to stop filming and walked away just as the naked lady started to hula-hoop to the growing crowd's delight.

Houston stood in the middle of his large office with his cell phone pressed to his ear. The top floor office had beautiful views of Lake Superior, but Houston never took the time to enjoy the view. People like Hubert Houston didn't appreciate the natural world and could care less about a nice view. In his mind, anything that distracted him from making money should be avoided. Houston gripped his putter tightly while standing over a golf ball. He stared at the auto-return putting cup, twenty feet away. Hubert attempted his putt but badly missed the cup. Pissed, he banged the bottom of the putter against the hardwood floor.

"Want to know your problem, Russ?" Hubert shouted into his cell phone. "You continue to ignore my excellent advice. For example, I've told you for years to stop letting people bring their dogs to the 4th of July parade because people are sick and tired of stepping in dog shit on the parade route. Last year that chubby fuck, Sherry McManus, slipped on some dog shit and went down on a fire hydrant. Not only was the town on the hook for Sherry's dental work, you had to buy her a new pair of Donna Karan sandals."

Hubert was growing more frustrated as he missed another putt. "It's time for you to listen to me, Russ. I don't give a greasy fuck if it's a conflict of interest. You need to do whatever is necessary to convince Tad O'Toole that this is a once in a lifetime opportunity for our town to partner with one of the most innovative companies in the world."

Russ was seated behind his desk with the phone pressed to his ear while Houston continued to badger him. He was dressed nicely and had gotten a haircut the day before, but he looked like he hadn't slept in days. Russ didn't even notice that Carol had just entered the office. Ever since the media invaded Whisper Dunes, her attire had become increasingly sexier. Some would probably even categorize her attire as distasteful, even scandalous. But being that Russ was an ardent defender of the First Amendment, which he believed extended to a person's right to wear whatever they wanted to, Russ didn't say a word about Carol's fashion choices.

"The NBC News team is sending over a car. Should be out front in ten minutes."

Russ glanced at Carol and nodded. She smiled and exited the office while adjusting her bra.

"Hubert, I have to go."

A black Chevy Suburban cruised down Front Street. Russ, sitting in the second row bucket chair, looked nervous. He stared out the window, trying to collect his thoughts. Sitting in the other bucket chair was Shannon, a senior NBC News producer in her early fifties. Shannon was reading old texts on her cell phone while sipping coffee. Russ cracked the window and took a deep breath. The driver of the Chevy Suburban glanced in the rear view mirror. "Would you like me to turn the air on, sir?"

"No, that's okay. Just need some fresh air," Russ said.

Shannon glanced at Russ and smiled. "Don't you worry, Mr. Mayor, this will be the most fun you've ever had being interviewed. Larry likes to create a very relaxed interview setting."

"That's great to hear. Truth be told, I've always struggled with interviews."

"Oh, why's that?"

"One, I don't like to talk about myself, and I really don't like bright lights."

"Well, I'll tell our lighting tech to dim the lights as much as possible. We'll be outside, so that shouldn't be a problem," Shannon said with a smile.

The crew was busy setting up for the interview on a bluff that overlooked Lake Superior. It was seventy-eight degrees with no wind, but the heavy clouds were blocking the sun. Despite the request from Russ, the lighting technician had no choice but to use extra lights for the interview. Two wooden director chairs were surrounded by the bright lights, and two cameras were positioned so that the Marquette Harbor Lighthouse at the end of the peninsula could be captured in the shot.

It was almost 11 a.m. but the producers decided to delay the interview another hour, hoping that the clouds might disperse. Even with no sunshine, Lake Superior still looked incredible in the background, Russ thought. He sat very still in the makeup chair looking out at the calm water. He loved it when Lake Superior got this calm, it was like God hit the mute button. There was nothing to hear, or even smell when the lake was this calm.

Russ turned his attention to the hardworking crew. He looked fascinated as he watched the crew work. He tried his best to remain still in the chair as Deanne, the makeup artist, powdered his cheeks and his nose. "I took a nice long walk on the beach yesterday, and I was blown away by how different the sand felt on my feet," Deanne said cheerfully.

"The only other area in the world where you'll find that type of sand is on a small stretch of beach in Chile," Russ said with a friendly smile.

"Wow, that's incredible," Deanne said as she continued to dab some makeup on Russ. "I love how your town has preserved the coastline and not let a bunch of millionaires come in and build beach mansions."

"Well, there's a good reason for that. Back in 1908, a gorgeous tree-covered dune that rose high above the coastline was nearly flattened to make way for the town's first and only beachside mansion. A ten-thousand-square-foot Georgian-style home built by the Brentwood brothers for their mother."

Deanne had stopped powdering Russ's face, but her eyes were still focused on him as he seemed committed to finishing the story.

"The Brentwood brothers made their fortune in the corset business back in the late 19th century. They made their corsets out of a barn in Michigan City, Indiana, or was it Three Oaks, Michigan? Anyway, the company was barely getting by until the oldest brother got the bright idea to start manufacturing corsets with a softer feather-bone. By 1900 they were the largest corset company in the world."

Deanne faked a sincere look. "No kidding?"

"The brothers owned a lot of property in the U.P. and decided to build their mom one incredible mansion. But this was back before you needed permits to build anything. The town was furious that a dune was leveled to make way for this mansion, so an ordinance was quickly passed that prohibited homes from being built on sand dunes along the coastline," Russ said.

His relaxed smile quickly disappeared and he become visibly nervous at the sight of Larry Holt approaching. Deanne could tell Russ was uneasy. She smiled at Russ and said, "Don't worry, Mr. Mayor. Larry is one of the nicest people in the news business. A true gentleman."

Russ glanced at Deanne, smiled, and gave her an appreciative nod.

The mayor sat in a high-back director-style chair, five feet directly across from Larry, whose calm demeanor had not done much to relax Russ. Larry patiently listened to Russ, whose nerves were making him speak quickly, to the point where he was running out of breath near the end of his responses. "Here's a hard truth, since the beginning of time humans have been remarkably susceptible to the manipulation of facts. Social media companies continue to thrive because of this fact. Let me go a step further, social media companies are a direct threat to our beautiful democracy."

"Let's get back to the spaceport question, Mr. Mayor. Are you open to the idea of Space D building and operating a rocket launch spaceport just down the road from where you and I are sitting?"

"I have yet to review the feasibility study, which hasn't been released yet. So I'm not going to support or reject the spaceport until I have the opportunity to review the study. But regardless of this proposed project, or any other proposed project...I'm always in favor of what's best for the people of Whisper Dunes."

Larry regarded Russ as he casually wiped the sweat from his forehead. "Mr. Mayor, millions of people from around the world have signed an online petition begging the town of Whisper Dunes to reject Space D's plans to build and operate a spaceport on the shores of Lake Superior," Larry said in a measured tone. "Things have gotten so tense that Canada has threatened to sue the state of Michigan if your municipality approves the spaceport. Like so many other people, Canada's Prime Minister has expressed his fear that Space D will use Lake Superior as a dump for rocket refuse."

"I'd just like to mention that my office has been in touch with the Prime Minister's environmental team, and we've had some very positive conversations. I can assure you that the decision about the spaceport will not be made without consulting our neighbors to the north."

"Space D launches more satellites into space than any other space company. Currently, they have over 4,000 satellites in orbit. The other fear that most people have is that Space D already occupies most of the Earth's orbit routes. Once a carrying capacity of an orbit is maxed out, you block everyone from trying to compete in that market," Larry said.

"Listen, I'm not a space guy, Larry. I'm a politician and a fisherman, and above all I'm a proud member of the Whisper Dunes community. I will say it until I'm blue in the face, I only want what's best for the town of Whisper Dunes and for the entire U.P. region."

"Mr. Mayor, under the current township zoning ordinance, a spaceport is legally prohibited on the 5,000 acres that Space D has expressed interest in buying. In fact, there's no land anywhere in the Upper Peninsula of Michigan that's zoned to operate a rocket launch spaceport."

Russ allowed himself to take a deep breath. He shifted in his chair and looked a bit more confident. "Regardless of what happens with the spaceport," Russ said in a defensive tone, "Whisper Dunes is America's Best Place to Live. Period. We are surrounded by incredible natural beauty. We have the largest freshwater lake in the world in our backyard. We have the cleanest air of any place in America. We have a robust economy, great public schools, a top-notch university, a vibrant entertainment district, fabulous restaurants, almost zero crime to speak of..."

"Mr. Mayor, a well respected resident of Whisper Dunes was found murdered less than a week after an arsonist set fire to the Potawatomi Country Club. Most people believe that the two crimes are connected," Larry said. His narrow eyes remained locked on Russ while he patiently waited for a response.

"The speculation surrounding the murder and the fire is a case of perception creating its own reality. Being a long-time member of the media, you know that the prediction of a train wreck is intended to precipitate one."

Larry regarded Russ for a few seconds then said, "Is Whisper Dunes still one of safest towns in America?"

Russ did not blink as he leaned forward with great conviction. "You betcha, and I have the numbers to prove it." He pulled a notecard from the left back pocket of his khaki pants, glanced at it and said, "This year alone, there have have been four murders in Kennebunkport, Maine. Six murders in Newport, Rhode Island. Eight murders on Fishers Island in Florida, and a whopping seventeen murders in the Hamptons. It should be noted that at least eight of those Hampton murders have been linked to a serial killer, who's still on the loose."

Larry patiently allowed Russ to continue his defensive response. "Do you know how many murders we've had in Whisper Dunes in the past ten years?"

"No, I don't."

Russ slowly held up one finger. "One. Whisper Dunes is as safe as any town in America."

Russ eased back in his chair, looking happy with himself. Larry took his time and finally said, "The main reason that Whisper Dunes earned the title—America's Best Place to Live—is because the town is quite possibly the best climate haven in the world...according to a soon-to-be-released study by a group of highly respected climate scientists."

"I know I speak for everyone who lives in the Upper Peninsula when I say, we are very grateful that we get to live in such a beautiful place. Up here, we vigorously defend and preserve our natural resources, and it's understood by everyone who lives in the U.P. that your best days in life happen outdoors."

"Mr. Mayor, I know you've received a lot of hate mail from climate change deniers ever since *Forbes* made their announcement. Do you think it's possible that the person behind the arson and the murder is a radical climate change denier?"

Russ pressed his lips together and narrowed his eyes. He nodded slowly as his eyes remained focused on Larry. "Yes, I think it's possible. But I have no doubt that whoever committed these terrible crimes will be caught by the Whisper Dunes police force, prosecuted, and sent to prison for the rest of their life."

"You're up for re-election next year. Will you run again for mayor of Whisper Dunes?"

Russ turned his head slightly to the left and looked out at Lake Superior. He finally turned his attention back to Larry and said, "Teddy Roosevelt liked to say, nobody cares how much you know until they know how much you care. The people of Whisper Dunes know how much I care about them, and I think they'd like for me to remain in office as their mayor."

"Not everyone who makes their home in the Upper Peninsula believes in climate change. Do you believe in climate change, Mr. Mayor?"

Russ clasped his hands together as he leaned forward in his chair. "Yes...yes, I do. And I also believe that the Upper Peninsula of Michigan is without question the best place on Earth to live." Russ glanced at Lake Superior then turned around and looked at the hilly forest in the distance. "Take a look around, Larry, you're in paradise," Russ said jovially. "Mother Nature created a masterpiece up here."

Larry flashed a respectful smile before glancing at the lake. "It's incredibly beautiful. But how do you plan on protecting the residents of Whisper Dunes from hedge funds and private equity firms, who will no doubt try to buy up most of the land and homes in the area?"

"It's a good question. I'll tell you what I'm going to do— I'm going to get our town council to vote on a new ordinance that will ban hedge funds and private equity firms from buying residential or commercial property, or land in Whisper Dunes. I will also work hard to convince the other towns in the Upper Peninsula to do the same. I am one hundred percent committed to preserving the natural land here in Whisper Dunes, and all over the U.P. for the next generation."

Larry regarded Russ closely before he finally said, "Mr. Mayor, will that vote take place before or after the zoning commission's upcoming session? A crucial session that will determine whether or not the proposed spaceport site is rezoned."

Russ could not hide his uneasiness. He forced an awkward smile and finally said, "Most likely after."

24

The open floor office at the Zbikowski Real Estate Group was buzzing with realtors trying to close a deal. Of the twenty-eight cubicles, twenty were occupied with realtors standing behind their desks, spewing out real-estate jargon to their clients. All the clients were being pitched the same story—buy now, or you'll soon be priced out of the Whisper Dunes market.

Stan looked anxious sitting behind his office desk. The receiver to his landline phone was pressed to his ear while he obsessively squeezed a stress ball with his right hand. Stan's huge yellow Lab, Payton, was sleeping on a dog bed in the corner. "I'm asking for five minutes, that's it," Stan said with great eagerness. "Just hear what I have to say...please. Five minutes and not a second more."

Stan slowly rubbed his forehead to ease his headache while listening closely to the person on the other end of the call. Looking somewhat relieved, Stan stopped squeezing the stress ball. "I'll be there. Thank you."

Randy walked hand in hand with his wife, Vivian, along the shoreline of a secluded beach north of downtown. It was a perfect late summer day. Sunny, warm, and windless, which was why Lake Superior was unusually calm. So calm, it looked like glass. They had been walking for five minutes, maybe longer, without saying a word.

Vivian finally glanced at Randy and said, "I'm sorry for overreacting about the dog. I was just caught off guard. You're right, I think the dog will be great for the girls. God knows, they've wanted one forever."

"You had every right to be upset, Vivian. I should've at least given you a heads up that I was thinking about letting the girls get a dog."

She smirked and said, "I'm glad you didn't tell me. Because if you had, I would've tried to convince you not to get a dog."

Randy smiled just before he kissed Vivian. They continued walking quietly along the peaceful shoreline. Randy looked out at the water while Vivian carefully looked for beach glass. "I can't remember the last time I saw more speed boats on the lake than sailboats. It's kind of strange," Randy said.

Vivian glanced out at the water for a few seconds before looking at Randy. "Even without the wind, I'd still rather be on a sailboat."

Randy and Vivian locked into each other's gazes for a moment. "Yeah, me too," Randy said. "Just wish I could afford to get you a nice sailboat."

"Well, I prefer watching sailboats from the shore than actually sailing in one," Vivian said with a grin. Randy smiled back. He held her hand a little tighter as they continued walking down the shoreline.

"So, for our anniversary, it's in two weeks, in case you forgot," Vivian said with a smile. "I thought we could check out that winery in Traverse City we've been trying to get to for the past few years," Vivian said warmly.

"Yes! No more excuses. I'll get my mom to watch the girls and we're going to make a long weekend out of it. Let's do nothing except drink wine outside and snuggle and fuck inside, and maybe outside too."

Randy smiled as he watched Vivian laugh out loud. He planted a quick kiss on her lips. Randy and Vivian slowed their walking pace, as if they were both making an effort to savor this precious moment. Randy felt happier with each step in the warm sand, but the incredible feeling was suddenly replaced by the pain one feels when getting sucker punched in the gut. Randy struggled to breathe as he spotted a topless woman about fifty yards away. The topless woman was sitting in her reclined beach chair, reading a book. Her face was covered by a wide-brim straw hat, but Randy recognized the incredible body. The radiant, bronze skin, the long legs, the toned tummy, the perfect breasts...Randy didn't need to see her face. He knew who was sitting in the beach chair.

Vivian was still looking down at the sand in search of beach glass and had yet to notice the topless woman, or that her husband was in pain with discomfort. As they got closer to the topless woman, Randy's worst fear was realized when the woman removed her hat. He watched her slowly reach into her beach bag and pull out a pair of black sunglasses. Just before she put on her sunglasses, Randy locked eyes with Denise. She smiled slightly before putting her sunglasses on, but she didn't go back to her book. Instead, she reached back into her beach bag and grabbed a tube of sunscreen lotion.

Randy held Vivian's hand tighter. "Want to head up and grab a drink at Iron Bay Tap?"

"No, let's keep walking. I haven't found any beach glass yet."

"Honey, you know it's hard to find beach glass this late in the summer."

"I know, but it's been a while since we took a long walk together on the beach. Let's keep going. Who knows, maybe you'll get lucky."

Vivian looked at Randy with loving eyes before she gave him a deep kiss on the lips. "I'm really enjoying our day together. I don't want it to end," Vivian said.

"Me, too. I love you, Vivian."

Randy and Vivian looked straight ahead, and both saw Denise stand up and start applying sunscreen lotion to her shoulders. She then applied lotion to her neck before she lowered her hands and slowly rubbed lotion all over her large, firm breasts. Denise's tanned breasts were just a shade lighter than her silver-dollar-sized areolas.

Vivian didn't seem bothered by the topless beauty in the distance, but Randy felt a sharp pain in his chest as he inhaled through his mouth. Beads of sweat slowly appeared on his forehead.

"Is that Denise?" Vivian asked.

Randy looked in Denise's direction for a second before moving his eyes back toward Vivian's face. "Denise the pilates instructor?" Randy asked in a shaky voice.

Denise picked up her paddleboard and walked toward the water. Vivian looked over Denise's incredible body before glancing at Randy. His head was lowered and he was desperately focused on trying to find a piece of beach glass.

"God, what a body on her," Vivian said, without a hint of jealousy in her voice.

Randy acted like he didn't hear Vivian. Determined to find a piece of beach glass, his eyes remained locked on the sand.

He stopped in his tracks at the sight of a green piece of jagged beach glass. "I found one!"

Randy bent down as slowly as he possibly could. He finally picked up the piece of jagged beach glass and held it up in front of Vivian, like a proud child showing off their first ever trophy. He placed the beach glass into Vivian's left hand and watched her analyze the weathered piece of glass. She moved her left index finger over the round, smooth edges and stared at the dull green glass. Randy glanced toward Denise's direction and froze. She was walking toward him and his wife. Vivian's eyes were still fixed on the beach glass. But Randy, his eyes hidden behind aviator sunglasses, stared at Denise's big, beautiful breasts as she approached. He couldn't help it. If any person on planet Earth was standing where Randy was standing at that particular moment in time, they too would have been staring at Denise's bare breasts. The way the sun was glaring down on Denise's perfectly symmetrical, tanned breasts was absolutely mesmerizing. Like someone staring at an exceptional painting, Randy was in a trance as this living work of art moved slowly toward him and his wife.

"Oh, my God! I've been looking for beach glass all afternoon, but haven't found a single piece," Denise said with an excited smile on her face. "It's so hard to find beach glass towards the end of summer."

Randy remained in a trance but Vivian flashed a warm smile. "Oh, it's so hard. Thankfully, my stud muffin here got lucky," Vivian said with a smirk. She looked at Randy and said, "I can't remember the last time you got lucky on the beach."

Vivian gently elbowed Randy in his ribs as she shared a quick laugh with Denise. Vivian was completely at ease while she took a few seconds to look over Denise's body. Her eyes landed back on Denise's smiley face.

"Hey, I wanted to let you know I thought you had an awesome pilates session the other night," Denise said.

"Thanks. I was having trouble hanging in there at the end."

"The last ten minutes are always the hardest, but you finished strong," Denise said right before glancing over at Randy. "Feel free to bring this big lug next time. Doing yoga or pilates with your partner can be so beneficial for your relationship. Especially in the bedroom."

Randy felt his chest get tighter and his stomach cramp up. His hands started to tremble so he moved them toward his rear end. As the palms of his hands settled on the top of his chubby ass cheeks he was finally able to exhale.

Denise moved her eyes from Vivian to Randy. She knew that he adored his daughters and was an excellent father, but now she realized that he really did still love his wife. Denise could see the happiness behind Vivian's eyes, just like she saw the happiness behind Sophie and Zooey's eyes when they were with their dad. Randy had created a happy, loving family, and Denise decided right then and there that she wasn't going to destroy it. Randy was providing Vivian and his girls with a happy family life. The same life that Denise had once hoped for, but never had the chance to experience. She still desperately wanted what Vivian and Randy had, but deep down knew it was highly unlikely.

"What do you think, babe? Want to join me next week for a session?" Vivian asked.

Randy regarded Vivian with a slight frown.

"I'm sorry, but I gotta brutal schedule next week."

Denise flashed Randy a big smile and said, "I've got a couple spots open in my six o'clock class tomorrow night."

"Thanks for the offer, but I've got my weekly bridge game at the VFW tomorrow tonight."

"I didn't know you're a Veteran."

"I'm not, but my friend and bridge partner is."

"Well, in case you change your mind I'll keep two spots open in the front."

Randy politely nodded.

"That's so thoughtful. Thank you," Vivian said.

"Well, it was fun running into you guys. Enjoy the rest of your walk," Denise said.

Vivian smiled easily and said, "Thanks. Looking forward to the next pilates class."

"Have a good paddle," Randy said.

Randy and Vivian watched as Denise entered the water and quickly stood up on her paddleboard. They both looked impressed by how fast Denise was able to paddle away from the shoreline. It looked like she was paddling right toward the sun as it slowly set over Lake Superior. Vivian grabbed Randy's hand and they continued their walk along the shoreline.

A chandelier made of antique guns and spurs hung from the middle of Hubert Houston's office. The four-story grey stone building on Front Street was built in 1890. The enormous top floor office had been updated at least a dozen times, but the original wood-burning fire place had never been touched.

Hubert sat very still in his high-back leather chair behind his massive oak desk. The desk had originally belonged to his grandfather. The gold nameplate on the desk read: Hubert Hommediue Houston. Stan sat in the only chair across from Hubert. His relaxed demeanor, along with his ability to smile vanished as soon as he entered the office. The soft leather chair was low to the ground, and Stan kept having to adjust his position every few seconds to prevent his ass from sinking deeper into the chair.

"I can get you more than 100 million for your 5,000 acres," Stan said in a steady voice.

Hubert rested his folded hands on his pot belly as he continued to stare down at Stan. After almost a minute Hubert finally said, "I've already told the nice people at Space D that I'm going to sell them the land. They're going to build the largest spaceport in North America. It's going to be beautiful."

"I'm sure the renderings for the project look great, but once Space D finally realizes that the land can't be rezoned to suit their plans they'll walk away from the deal."

Hubert didn't change his expression. His cold, dark eyes stayed locked on Stan. "You seem awfully sure that the zoning commission has already made up their mind. But I know something you don't know," Hubert said with a cocky grin.

"Oh, what's that, Hugh?"

"Don't call me Hugh. It's Hubert. Understand?"

Stan was only able to bring himself to nod.

Hubert slowly reached for the cigar box on his desk and took out a Cuban cigar. "Cigar?"

"No, thanks."

Stan watched Hubert carefully cut the end of the cigar with a gold cigar cutter then slowly move the cigar toward his mouth. Stan looked disgusted as Hubert wrapped his fat lips around the perfectly rolled cigar. While Hubert took his time lighting the cigar, Stan glanced around the office. "Cozy office," Stan said in a mocking tone.

"This is where I do my best thinking," Hubert said. He tilted his head back, glanced at the ceiling, and blew a plum of smoke out of his mouth.

"Who decorated it?"

"My grandmother. This used to be my grandfather's office. Then my father took it over. My father taught me many things in this room."

Stan noticed a quote inscribed over the massive fireplace. He read it to himself. Amused, Stan decided to read the quote out loud. "'When you have somebody by the balls don't let go to get a better grip.'"

Hubert had a proud look on his face as he stared at the inscription above the fireplace.

"Who's that quote by?"

"My father," Hubert said.

"Didn't your father die in this office?"

Hubert nodded and said, "He dropped dead while screwing his secretary. Lucky bastard."

Hubert leaned back in his chair and took a long puff from his cigar. As much as he tried not to think about his dad, Hubert couldn't help but remember the ruthlessness his dad tried to instill in him. When Hubert was growing up he rejected most of his dad's teachings, and actually took pride disappointing him. But eventually he turned into the man his dad wanted him to be.

Stan looked amused as he watched Hubert walk over to the bar cart with his chest puffed out. He picked up a bottle of twenty-year-old bourbon and poured a small amount into his glacier-bottom rocks glass. Stan was not surprised to see Hubert's initials engraved on the side.

"Have you ever tasted really good bourbon, Stan?"

"Is there such a thing?" Stan asked, only half joking.

Hubert took a very slow sip of his bourbon before he walked back to his desk and eased into his chair. He took another painfully slow sip before looking at Stan. "My father believed that a man is whored by his friends and distinguished by his enemies."

"Well, if that's true then you are one distinguished gentleman," Stan said with a straight face.

Hubert actually cracked a smile before taking another slow sip from his glass. "You might find this hard to believe, Stan, but I've always admired you. You don't pretend to be anyone but yourself. You represent this town well."

Stan's eyes were wide now as he leaned forward. "Well, my dad liked to remind me that it takes a lifetime to build up a reputation, and only a moment to destroy it."

Hubert didn't seem to be paying attention to Stan anymore. He took another long puff from his cigar as he leaned back in his chair. He admired his Cuban cigar as he said, "I remember your father once told me that you were going to be a United States Senator one day. We had been drinking all afternoon at the club, but he meant it."

Stan's eyes drifted off of Hubert as he thought about his dad for a moment. His dad did have ambitious plans for him, but Stan never once heard his dad discuss politics, let alone political ambitions for any of his three sons. After Stan got kicked out of Northern Michigan University, his relationship with his dad became fractured. It still bothered Stan that he disappointed his dad. The last time Stan saw his dad smile at him was when he told him that he was going to be a grandpa for the first time.

Hubert's condescending eyes remained fixed on Stan. "Instead, you became a realtor."

"I have a passion for real estate. Always have."

"So do I. My real estate portfolio is larger than my ex-wife's ass."

"Okay, let's talk real estate. I can get you 150 million for your 5,000 acres, and you don't have to rezone the land. So please, let me broker the deal for you."

"I've already entered into an agreement with Space D. I'm going to sell the land to those space dorks, and that's that."

Stan shook his head in disbelief.

"Whisper Dunes will be home to the largest rocket launch spaceport in North America. People will come from all over to watch rockets launch over Lake Superior. Whisper Dunes will become the Cape Canaveral of the Midwest."

Stan looked dejected as he slumped in his chair. "You really believe that's going to happen?"

Hubert nodded as he sucked on his cigar. He blew a plum of smoke at Stan then said, "I plan on investing heavily in Whisper Dunes real estate over the next two years. Tell you what, Stan, if those sexy agents I hired have any trouble handling my load, I know where to find you."

Stan seemed to be pondering an idea as he stared blankly at Hubert, who flashed a smug smile just before finishing off the last of the bourbon in his glass.

"One more thing, Stan."

"Yeah?"

"If you and your beautiful wife ever need a *trois* for your *ménage*, give me a call."

Stan refrained from showing any emotion. He stared at Hubert for at least half a minute. Hubert laughed then said, "Sure you don't want a cigar for the drive home?"

Stan took his time standing up. For a second, Hubert thought Stan might leap across the desk and beat the shit out of him, which is why his right hand was gripping the handle to the desk drawer where he kept one of his many guns.

Stan's eyes narrowed as he regarded Hubert. He then turned around and exited the office.

Once again, Hubert found himself alone, sucking on his cigar.

25

The rear of the clubhouse to the Potawatomi Country Club no longer smelled like smoke, and even though it was still off limits to members, Houston had access to the windowless conference room on the second floor. It was the same room where his dad and grandfather used to conduct secret meetings that usually centered around illegal business dealings, or new ways to evade paying personal and corporate taxes. Sometimes the meetings were organized to discuss which political candidate to support.

Hubert sat at the head of the surprisingly short conference room table. Seated around the table were Burt Patterson, Joe Hackett, and Reggie Cooper. The men were all in their sixties and wearing dark green blazers with the Potawatomi Country Club logo on the right breast pocket. Only Reggie was smoking a cigar, which had filled up the small room with dense smoke, but nobody seemed to mind.

"The time has come for us to stand up to the sons of bitches who set fire to our beloved club. The same sons of bitches, mind you, who are now trying to undermine a once in a lifetime opportunity for our town to partner with Space D, and build something that has never existed in Michigan, or anywhere in the Midwest," Hubert said.

Burt, sitting the furthest from Hubert, leaned forward in his chair and said, "Hubert, based on the plans defined by the township master plan, building and operating a rocket spaceport anywhere in Marquette County is against the law."

Reggie calmly smoked his cigar, but Joe and Burt looked uneasy as they waited for Hubert's response. Hubert slowly leaned back in his leather chair. "You flaming fuck," Hubert said. His face was already bright red before he said, "You have no idea how to defend this town, Burt. If you truly care about Whisper Dunes, and if you're actually in favor of kicking all the radical nuts out of town, then you'll vote to amend my 5,000 acres."

Reggie didn't look intimidated, in fact he looked upset. "I'm a mother fuckin capitalist, but I also happen to believe in global warming. I've read the feasibility report, Hubert. I can say with certainty that there is no way I'm voting to rezone your land for industrial use."

Hubert stared at Reggie with a cold, expressionless look. Reggie, however, didn't flinch. He was probably the only man in the room who wasn't intimidated by Hubert. They had known each other since their days playing on the club's junior golf team. Hubert came from a much wealthier family, but Reggie was always far more popular. Hubert was always jealous of Reggie when they were growing up because he was the star athlete, who got good grades and had a pretty girlfriend. Reggie had always had the upper hand on Hubert, or at least he thought he did.

It seemed as if Hubert was about to say something, but Burt was quick to chime in. "You don't have the votes, Hubert, and you know it. I think it's time you find another buyer for the land. Someone who understands and respects zoning laws, and someone who has a vision to develop the property for recreational use," Burt said.

Reggie was behind the wheel of his Mercedes SUV, going thirty miles over the speed limit, when he reacted to his phone getting a text. He picked up his phone and opened the text to find that it was a video of him having sex with Denise in a hotel room. Reggie dropped his phone in shock and lost control of his steering wheel. He nearly drove his car off the two-lane highway, but regained control just before his tires hit the loose dirt off the shoulder. Reggie's eyes were wide and his knuckles were white as he steered his car back on the road. He was breathing heavily and sweating profusely while desperately trying to focus on the road. As it sunk in that he was now a blackmail victim, Reggie started to weep. He hit his hand on the steering wheel and screamed, "Son of a bitch!"

Over five thousand people were standing in front of the Town Hall building on a hot afternoon. A brutal heat wave had been affecting most of America for the past few days, but the brutal heat failed to suffocate the Upper Peninsula. Today's high would reach eighty-five before cooling considerably after sunset.

A warmer than usual August day in the Upper Peninsula, but not the kind of heat that was forcing most of the country to be imprisoned in their air-conditioned homes and offices.

During the past five hours, a very boisterous and patriotic crowd had gathered outside the Town Hall building. Along with at least one thousand American flags blowing in the gentle wind, there were at least one thousand Stop the Rocket signs being held up high by people from all walks of life. In front of the massive crowd, three hundred people were singing, "This Land is our Land," in perfect harmony.

Chief O'Malley stood shoulder to shoulder with a few of his men behind a row of barricades that were set up in the middle of the street. He had been directing his men since seven in the morning. They were told to be on heightened alert, but not to engage with an unruly protestor unless they commit a crime.

In the rear of the Town Hall building was a small parking lot. Parked next to the mayor's old pickup truck was Houston's black Range Rover. Duane's white 1990 Porsche 944 came speeding into the parking lot and parked illegally behind the Range Rover. On the dashboard of the Porsche was a sign that read: Bellini's Pizza - Delivery Driver. The driver side door opened and a pair of weathered white cowboy boots hit the pavement. Duane reached into the back seat and grabbed a navy blue blazer, which he put on over his blue Hawaiian shirt. He then took off his aviator sunglasses, put them in the inside pocket of his blue blazer, and walked toward the rear entrance.

The hearing room inside the Town Hall was packed with mostly Stop the Rocket supporters. Everyone had their eyes focused straight ahead on the six members of the zoning board committee, who were seated in their assigned chair on an elevated bench. Seated at the far right was Reggie Cooper. Burt sat next to Reggie, and sitting at the other end was Joe. Sitting between Houston's buddies were two women: Julie and Ann, both in their forties, and Ernest, who at eighty-three was the oldest person on the committee.

Watching from the front row was Russ, who was seated between Carol and Randy. All three looked very tense. Sitting two rows behind the mayor were Stan, Lisa, and Duane. All eyes were on Hubert Houston, who was standing behind the podium. He stood tall and looked calm, knowing that everyone else in the room was struggling with gut-wrenching nerves. The podium, with a plaque of the town seal front and center, was located in the open space between the six committee members and the packed gallery. Dressed in a very expensive suit, he removed the cordless microphone from the stand and gave it a few taps to make sure it was on. Hubert then moved the microphone close to his mouth and said, "Today...the real problem for Whisper Dunes is the future."

Almost everyone in the gallery looked very confused. Duane and Stan shared a look. Duane mouthed, "He must have snorted some bath salts."

Stan nodded in agreement as he pointed to his right nostril.

"Anyone who's ever spent time in Whisper Dunes knows that our town was the best kept secret in America. Now, thanks to *Forbes*, and a yet-to-be-released climate change paper, the cat's out of the bag. The whole world now knows that Whisper Dunes is America's Best Place to Live. But long before *Forbes* made that declaration, everyone in this room already knew that they were living in a remarkable town. Whisper Dunes has always been a beautiful, peaceful town, where crime simply didn't exist. Until very recently, I didn't know a single person who locked their doors at night. But our way of life in Whisper Dunes has been threatened by an arsonist and a murderer...and a bunch of nosey, disrespectful outsiders. I'm talking about the journalists and protestors who just want to cause chaos in hopes that people will pay attention to them when it's their turn to step on the soap box."

Dozens of people scattered throughout the two-hundred-seat gallery looked very interested in what Hubert was saying, but most people seated had already tuned him out.

"I was born in Whisper Dunes. I was raised here and I'll die here. Yes, I lived in New York City for a while, but one morning I woke up and realized that I left my heart in Whisper Dunes."

An older woman in the front row got the Tony Bennett reference and smiled. Hubert took a few steps toward the gallery and said, "I love this town more than any of you will ever know. I want nothing but the best for everyone who calls Whisper Dunes home. The future for Whisper Dunes is very bright, assuming we don't turn our backs on innovation and technology."

Hubert lowered his head for a moment to gather his thoughts. He wiped his forehead with the back of his right hand and then said, "Our way of life has been threatened. I strongly believe that the same people who set fire to our country club also plotted to murder Lenny Trubisky. And I have no doubt that these same people are heavily involved with the Stop the Rocket movement."

The gallery erupted in boos. Even Hubert looked taken back by the loud booing. He lowered his head as he waited for the booing to quiet down. There were still a few people booing when he said, "Like all movements to stop innovation and job creation, a few radicals have taken matters into their own delusional hands and have brought anarchy to Whisper Dunes. These radicals are a clear and present danger to all of us! We must stand up to them!"

Hubert turned around and looked at each member of the zoning board committee. He took a slow breath through his nose before turning back around to face the gallery. "Today, the members of the zoning board committee have an incredible opportunity to make a statement in the name of freedom and innovation! Today, the members of the zoning board committee have an opportunity to stand up to anarchists! These outside agitators continue to camp out in parks all over Whisper Dunes. I say it's time to send them packing! Today, the members of the zoning board committee have the power to rezone one of the most unique pieces of land in the world! If they make the right choice today, the global space industry will come to our town and create thousands of high- paying jobs and turn Whisper Dunes into a world class destination!"

The massive crowd in front of the Town Hall building was very quiet as they waited for word on the zoning board committee's decision. It was a sight that even the most senior news reporters had never seen before—over 5,000 people standing close together, and no one was making a sound. But the peace and quiet would not last long. The old wooden front door of the Town Hall building was pushed opened and a news reporter stepped outside. The man, in his early thirties, yelled, "Vote's in! They're gonna rezone the land!"

The crowd erupted in boos and screams. Chief O'Malley, along with all the other officers standing between the crowd and Town Hall, calmly stood their ground. O'Malley was the only officer not in riot gear. He watched a dozen guys surround a news van and try to tip it over. After a couple of attempts, they succeeded.

Inside the Town Hall zoning hearing, the booing had not stopped. Hubert looked frightened as he hurried toward the exit that was behind the committee bench. But he was forced to wait behind all six of the committee members as they were led through the narrow doorway, one by one under the watchful eyes of four county sheriff deputies.

Duane took off his left white cowboy boot and whipped it at Houston, barely missing his head. Houston turned to look at the gallery. All the angry faces scared him, which motivated him to cut the line ahead of Reggie and run down the hallway toward the rear parking lot.

Outside the Town Hall building, the chaotic behavior was spreading like wildfire. Two guys were using a metal baseball bat to break open a fire hydrant. But before they could bust it open, two Whisper Dune police officers in riot gear subdued them, put zip ties around their wrists, and led them into the paddy wagon. Down the street, the ABC News crew was recording a group of angry protestors throwing bricks at a CNN News van. Across the street, a woman and man in their early twenties were spray painting the NBC News van. But most of the protestors were too stunned to cause any trouble. Many were screaming, some were crying, but only a few had the desire to deface public and private property.

Houston sped out of the parking lot, but didn't get further then a block before someone tossed a brick through the windshield of his black Range Rover. The busted windshield only made him drive faster down the street, forcing protestors to sprint toward the sidewalks. Houston avoided hitting the protestors, but as his car turned right and sped up the street someone hit his rear windshield with another brick.

Russ stood behind his office desk, yelling into the phone. "No, we don't need the National Guard! Everything is under control. Our police force did an incredible job keeping the peace. Listen, I have lived in this town all my life. I know just about everyone, but I didn't recognize a single person in that crowd today. Frank, the only thing that means is that the zoning board committee will likely amend certain zoning restrictions surrounding the 5,000 acres. Personally, I still think they're only going to make changes that allow for recreational development. As of today, building a rocket launch spaceport in Whisper Dunes, or anywhere else in the U.P., is still legally prohibited."

Carol walked into the office but Russ quickly waved her away. She held up a piece of loose leaf paper that had something written on it. Russ squinted his eyes but couldn't read the note so Carol took a few steps toward him. His eyes got wide as he read the note—*Sir Branch Bradford is on Line 4. Should I take a message?*

26

O'Malley rocked slowly in his desk chair. He looked like he had just returned to his usual state of calmness after experiencing a day full of chaos. Sitting across the desk was officer Alcocks, who seemed relaxed as he sipped from his coffee cup. On the side of the cup it read F.B.I.—Female Body Inspector. A gift from his mom. Alcocks's dad passed away when he was a teenager, so his mom, God love her, tried to be both a good mother and father to her only son. She taught Alcocks how to rock climb, how to cook, how to manage finances...before prom she showed him how to use a condom properly with the aid of a small cucumber. Alcocks would never admit this to anyone, but he was a virgin when he met his future wife. He did, however, admit on numerous occasions that his mom was his best friend.

"That's the first riot I've ever been involved in where not a single officer or protestor was hurt. I don't think anyone even suffered a scratch," O'Malley said, looking more disappointed than surprised.

"I was shocked at how fast things calmed down. I didn't even get to use my pepper spray."

"Nobody got to use their pepper spray."

"That was like a forty minute riot," Alcocks said.

"If that."

"Is that even long enough to technically qualify as a riot?"

O'Malley shrugged his shoulders. "Good question. In my opinion, the chaos has to last at least sixty minutes for it to qualify as a riot. Of course, we've got every major news outlet in the country reporting on it, and they're already framing it so it looks like it was the biggest riot of the 21st century."

"But I'm sure none of the reporting will mention that the riot was actually incited by a reporter," Alcocks said.

O'Malley took a long sip from his coffee cup then leaned forward in his chair and said, "Switching gears, I want to search Lenny's house and office again."

"Soller and I did another search early this morning. Walked through his house, searched his work van again, his personal car, and his shitty office. We didn't find a single pair of Nikes or a Nike shoebox. There should be no doubt that the orange Nike shoebox Soller saw in Lenny's van belonged to Denise. For reasons still unknown, Lenny stole the shoebox from Denise's apartment and that's why he was murdered," Alcocks said in his usual confident tone.

O'Malley looked like he agreed with Alcocks. He pushed back his chair and rested his size twelve feet on the desk. "I've given this a lot of thought, and I still have no idea what may have been in the shoebox. What do you think?"

"Maybe drugs? Maybe a flash drive containing compromising photos or videos? It's anyone's guess at this point in the investigation. I say we go over to Denise's apartment and ask her why she thinks Lenny stole her shoebox."

O'Malley's eyes started to narrow as he rubbed his chin. "That's not one of your better ideas. In fact, that might be your worst idea of the year so far."

Alcocks was offended but didn't show it.

"If Denise becomes aware that we know Lenny took the shoebox from her apartment, we'll have absolutely no chance to find the shoebox ourselves."

"Chief, the chance of us finding that shoebox is close to zero. I think it's very likely Denise recovered the shoebox from Lenny's house before or after she whacked him."

"There's also the possibility she's still desperately searching for the shoebox as we speak. Regardless, if we ask her about the shoebox there's no telling what she'll do next. Frankly, I think it's a real possibility that she could flee the country."

"Yeah, maybe. But maybe she makes a mistake and walks into our trap."

O'Malley did not hide his confusion. "What trap?"

"Well, obviously we're going to have to create one, but I have some ideas."

"It's highly likely Denise played some role in Lenny's death, but she had help. I want to find out who else she's involved with before we start turning up the pressure on her. Understand?"

Alcocks nodded and said, "Alright."

A couple different ideas started to rattle around O'Malley's mind as he stared at a photo on the wall of himself, back when he was a rookie police officer in Detroit. "Starting today, we need to keep a better eye on Denise. You and Soller will be in charge of tracking her movements."

"You're not in Detroit anymore, Chief. It's awfully tricky to run surveillance on someone in a small town. Especially someone as popular as Denise."

O'Malley rubbed his right palm over his face in frustration before he looked back at the wall. This time he stared at a different photo on the wall and got a new idea.

Alcocks kept a respectful eye on O'Malley as he continued to stare at the photo. "You cooking up a plan, Chief?"

"Yeah, but you're not going to like it."

A cardboard sign was taped to the glass door of the local driving range. The sign read: *Due to consistently poor behavior on the range, a $50 dollar security deposit is required if you want to hit balls. Sincerely, Management.* The glass door swung open. Stan walked out of the pro shop—slash bar—and headed toward the driving range holding a bucket of balls and two clubs: a driver and a five-iron. It was only a few minutes past eight in the morning, but Stan looked like he had been up for awhile. It was sunny but chilly, and Stan was wearing a thick fleece. Only two people were swinging on the range at this hour. Stan glanced to his right and saw a heavy-set man he didn't know swinging from the last tee box on the right side of the range. Stan looked left and saw Chief O'Malley standing over his ball as he was about to swing his pitching wedge. He walked slowly toward the Chief, who hit two more shots before looking in Stan's direction.

"Morning, Stan," O'Malley said cheerfully.

Stan had to clear his throat before he said, "Morning, Chief. I didn't know you liked to golf."

"Just started playing for the first time when I moved up here."

Stan positioned his driver long ways behind his back. He started to stretch while watching O'Malley chip a few balls with his wedge. O'Malley stopped swinging and reached for his thermos of coffee next to his golf bag. He took a sip then regarded Stan. The serious look on his face made Stan uneasy. "Thanks for meeting me at this hour. I'm going to get right to it, Stan. What would you say to doing a little P.I. work for the department?"

Stan stopped stretching. Clearly bewildered, he finally made eye contact with O'Malley. "I should've had more than two cups of coffee this morning. Sorry, but I'm struggling to comprehend."

O'Malley watched Stan drop a few balls on the green turf.

"You told me you got your P.I. license during the great recession. Were you bullshitting me?"

"No. I'm a legit P.I."

"Good. Then I need you to keep a close eye on Denise."

Stan lost control of his driver on the backswing and it went flying into the soda machine. A puzzled expression appeared on his face. He tilted his head to the left a bit and said in an incredulous tone, "Why do you want me to follow Denise?"

"Because you're a realtor. You're supposed to be driving around all day. I don't think she'll get suspicious if she notices you following her. I want to know who she spends her time with, and where she hangs out when she's not at her pilates studio. And if possible, get a DNA sample."

"How the fuck am I supposed to do that?"

"If you see her toss something into a garbage can that she put her lips on, say a coffee cup, put on rubber gloves and use a plastic baggie to remove the item from the garbage. Easy."

Looking overwhelmed, Stan closed his eyes for a few seconds and rubbed his forehead. He opened his eyes to find O'Malley staring right at him.

"You think she killed Lenny, don't you?"

O'Malley looked around to make sure no one was in ear shot. He then stared at Stan with a blank face for an uncomfortable ten seconds.

"Some things you suspect, some things you guess, and some things you just know."

Stan watched O'Malley hit another ball before putting the wedge in his bag and grabbing his 3-wood. Before he took another swing he looked at Stan and said, "As of today, I have no proof of any wrong doing by Denise. In order to build a case against her, I need your help. Right now, we're trying to locate an orange Nike shoebox that Lenny likely stole from Denise's apartment. We're pretty positive the shoebox contained something other than shoes. If we find it we might be able to link Denise to Lenny's murder."

Stan's back stiffened and his eyes were wide open now, but he tried to play it cool. He scratched the stubble on his chin as he regarded O'Malley. "I think I might be able to help you, Chief."

"Good."

O'Malley swung his club and hit another nice shot.

"But if I help you, I want complete immunity for life from any driving infractions that I might get pulled over for. I also want assurance that you'll stop looking into the business dealings of our Occupy Wall Street chapter—slash—not-for-profit community support organization—slash—men's goodwill social club."

Stan waited patiently as O'Malley considered the deal. O'Malley took a few practice swings before he lined up the head of his brand new 3-wood behind the ball. He stared at the golf ball and finally said, "Deal."

Stan's black GMC Denali was traveling seventy in a thirty-five m.p.h. zone. The narrow, hilly road was lined with yellow birch trees on both sides. Stan slowed down and made a quick right turn onto a muddy dirt road. It was a bumpy ride for about fifty feet until the tires of the Denali started driving over gravel. Stan cruised down the gravel driveway for another two hundred feet before he hit the brakes and the Denali slid to a stop in front of Lenny's tiny fishing cabin. The cabin was set about forty yards from the shoreline of Goose Lake—a small lake surrounded mostly by evergreens. Stan exited the Denali and hurried toward the front door.

Stan burst into the only bedroom in the cabin, breathing heavily, and opened the door to the small closet. He knew what he was looking for and found it immediately. The orange Nike shoebox was on top of four dozen *Playboy* magazines, exactly where Lenny had left the shoebox. Stan looked nervous as he stared at the shoebox. Finally, he leaned down and carefully picked it up. He held the shoebox as if it contained something very valuable.

Stan took a deep breath as he continued to stare wild-eyed at the orange shoebox. He slowly removed the lid with his left hand while he stared inside the box without expression. Stan was confused because at first he really didn't understand what he was looking at. He dropped the lid, took a deep breath, and slowly exhaled with disappointment. On the drive over to the cabin Stan had convinced himself that the shoebox was filled with flash drives storing Denise's sex movies, and cash...lots of cash. He squinted his eyes until his eye lids were almost shut, as if this would help him understand what he was looking at. Stan's left hand finally reached into the shoebox and pulled out a stack of papers bound together. The stack was thick, probably close to 400 pages, and there were handwritten notes all over the title page. Stan walked over to the bed, sat at the edge, and started to read the manuscript.

Stan's eyes moved off the road and toward the passenger seat. His face filled up with frustration as he looked at the orange shoebox. Normally, Stan did his best thinking whenever he drove down a lonely country road. But instead of a clear mind he was overwhelmed with confusion while he struggled to make sense of the theory that Lenny was murdered for stealing the contents inside the shoebox.

Stan was not a big reader, and he had only read the first two chapters of the manuscript before he got confused and stopped reading. But regardless of what the book was about, Stan just couldn't understand why Lenny would steal it in the first place. Stan's eyes landed back on the road as he considered the likelihood that Denise killed Lenny for stealing the manuscript.

"Son of a bitch! Where did he come from?" Stan yelled. His eyes moved from the rear view mirror to the side mirror. A black Ford Explorer with red and blue lights flashing from the grill was following Stan's Denali. There was nowhere to pull over on the narrow two-lane highway, so Stan put on his flashers and slowed down as he looked for a place to stop.

Stan saw a weathered wood sign that read: **Carp River Falls Nature Preserve**. He turned off the flashers and turned on his right blinker just before slowly turning into a small parking lot. In front of the parking lot was an open grass field that led to multiple hiking trails. There were only six cars parked in the lot, but Stan made a point to park in the spot that was between two empty cars. He checked his rear view mirror to see that the black Ford Explorer had turned off the red and blue lights and was now parked about twenty feet directly behind his Denali. Stan reached for the orange shoebox and quickly hid it under the passenger seat before opening the glove compartment and pulling out his registration. Stan then rolled down his window and put both hands on the steering wheel.

Officer Soller exited the unmarked Whisper Dunes Police suv and walked slowly toward the Denali as he scanned the area for potential witnesses. Soller removed his sunglasses just as he got to the driver side door. He regarded Stan and said, "Boy oh boy, you were driving awfully fast back there. Late for an open house?"

Stan acted calm, maybe even a bit cocky. "For your information, Officer Soller, I'm on assignment for the Chief. Special operation."

Soller pressed his lips together to prevent himself from cracking a smile. "I see. That sounds very interesting."

Stan was clearly perturbed as he stared at Soller. "You think I'm fucking with you? Call Chief O'Malley."

Stan now looked anxious as Soller stared at him with a blank face. "Go ahead, call him," Stan said. "I doubt he'll share any details about my assignment, but he'll tell you that I have full immunity from any diving violations."

Officer Soller scanned the area again looking for witnesses. Not a single person was nearby. He pulled a pair of black industrial gloves from his back pocket, the same kind of gloves he would normally wear at a crime scene.

Stan became sick with fear as he watched Soller put on the gloves. "What are you doing? You gonna shoot me for speeding? I'm on special assignment for Chief O'Malley! Call it in!"

Officer Soller calmly regarded Stan. "I know. Your assignment is to follow Denise, and my assignment is to follow you."

Dumbfounded, Stan's eyes narrowed as he stared at Soller. Stan muttered, "What?"

Soller took another look around the area to make sure no one was keeping a watchful eye on him. "I'm going to need that orange shoebox, Stan."

Stan, with his hands still gripped to the wheel, nodded slowly. He reached under the passenger seat, grabbed the shoebox, and handed it to Soller. "For the record, I was planning on personally delivering the box to Chief O'Malley."

"When?"

"Right now," Stan said, lying through his teeth.

Soller held the shoebox with two hands. "This is prime evidence in the murder investigation of your friend."

"Yeah, well, I'm finding it awfully hard believe that Lenny was murdered for stealing a manuscript."

Soller looked confused. "A what?"

"Just open the fucking shoebox."

Soller opened the shoebox to find the thick manuscript. He shook his head in disbelief as he put the lid back on the box. "Just a box full of pages. Did you remove anything out of this shoebox?"

"Absolutely not."

Soller's suspicious eyes moved from Stan's face, which looked to be in heightened defense mode, and landed on a young couple walking toward their car.

"Chief O'Malley is convinced that Lenny was killed for stealing that shoebox. I just hope somewhere buried in those pages is evidence that helps you arrest the son of a bitch who murdered my friend," Stan said.

Soller turned his attention back to Stan. "If there was something else in this shoebox, say a flash drive, and you took that flash drive...you'd be in a lot of trouble for interfering with a murder investigation."

Stan's eyes did not divert from Soller's intimidating look.

"You know, Soller, a while back, there was a rumor that Denise was sleeping with more than one cop on the force. I sure hope she hasn't compromised some of the men who are sworn to serve and protect the good people of Whisper Dunes," Stan said. "Do you know who informed me that Denise was sleeping with a couple different guys on the force?"

Soller didn't blink as he slowly shook his head.

"Lenny."

Soller regarded Stan for an intense twenty seconds before he said in a soft tone, "Thanks for the shoebox, Zibs."

Stan watched Soller put on his sunglasses and walk back to his vehicle. Stan started his car and quickly pulled out of the parking lot as soon as Soller's vehicle was out of sight.

"That is total bullshit, Ray! Why would you tail me?" Stan asked in a desperate tone. "I thought we were on the same team."

Chief O'Malley sat calmly behind his desk while he cleaned his service revolver. Stan leaned down so he could put both hands on O'Malley's desk. "Am I a suspect?"

O'Malley finally set his service revolver on the desk and looked at Stan. "No, Stan, you're not a suspect. But I'm awfully curious to know, how did you gain possession of the orange shoebox a mere two hours after I told you about the significance of the orange shoebox?"

Stan eased into the brown leather chair in front of O'Malley's desk. He regarded O'Malley with nervous eyes and said, "That's a fair question. I received a key in the mail and a letter from Lenny's attorney stating that Lenny had willed me his fishing cabin on Goose Lake. I was surprised to learn this, especially considering I didn't know about the place. Lenny never once mentioned that he had a fishing cabin on Goose Lake. I went to the cabin just last week and had a look around. In the small bedroom closet I happened to notice an orange Nike shoebox on a stack of nudie magazines. I just assumed there was an old pair of shoes in there, and didn't bother to peak inside."

O'Malley was now paying careful attention. Even before he became a cop, O'Malley found it hard to trust anyone. He believed most people were compelled to lie when telling a story, but for the moment, O'Malley allowed himself to believe Stan's story.

"That shoebox and its contents had zero meaning to me until our little chat at the driving range."

"Did you read any of the manuscript?"

"Yeah. I read the first twenty pages then I got confused and started nodding off."

O'Malley leaned back in his chair and said, "I looked up the author, Weslie Addle. The only person that came up was a realtor in Indiana."

"Huh. There were so many handwritten notes on the title page I didn't even notice the author's name. I guess I just assumed it was written by Denise."

Stan and O'Malley both looked to be deep in thought as they stared blankly at each other.

"Why would Denise have in her possession an unpublished manuscript from an unknown author?" O'Malley asked.

Stan shook his head. "No idea. Maybe a friend of hers wrote it, and sent it to her for feedback?"

"That's somewhat plausible, but what prompted Lenny to steal the manuscript from Denise's apartment?"

"Maybe there was something else in the box...like a bunch of cash," Stan said. "That would've gotten Lenny's attention."

O'Malley slowly nodded. "Yeah, maybe."

"Chief, you said Officer Soller saw the orange shoebox in Lenny's van when he pulled him over. But you have no way to prove Lenny stole that shoebox from Denise's apartment...even though we both know he did. Assuming that Denise didn't write, *I killed Lenny*, somewhere on the manuscript, I don't think you have anything other than a shoebox full of pages."

O'Malley scratched the whiskers on his chin as he stared at the wall covered in photos. He was staring at a photo of himself in his patrol uniform, surrounded by his wife and two young kids. O'Malley let out a long sigh. He looked at Stan and said, "I think its best that I pour myself a cup of Joe, put on my reading glasses, and read the whole fucking thing."

Stan nodded. "Yeah, that's probably a good idea. Who knows, maybe you'll find a clue? Or at the very least it could be a fun read."

O'Malley shot Stan an intimidating look. "Not a word to anyone about the manuscript. Understand?"

Stan nodded then shifted uneasily in the chair. He always prided himself on being a trusted confidant to his family members and many friends. But what do you do when your close friend has been murdered, and you hold a closely guarded secret of another dear friend that just might help solve the murder? Stan contemplated the question for a minute before he said, "There's something I need to tell you, Chief."

27

Stan stood behind the bar in his spacious basement mixing a whisky sour. The fully finished basement had a pool table in the middle of the room. In the corner was an old jukebox that had been broken since Stan's 40th birthday party. An electronic dart board hung from the middle of the wall, a Father's Day gift from his boys. Mounted on the wall across from the bar were three, sixty-five-inch flat screen TVs. Hanging on the wall behind the bar was a wood carved topographical depth chart map of the Great Lakes.

Stan handed the whisky sour to Randy, who was sitting on one of the six bar stools, staring at Lake Michigan on the Great Lakes depth chart map. "Did Denise ever mention the name Weslie Addle to you?" Stan asked.

Randy thought for a moment, but the name meant nothing to him. He finally shook his head and said, "No. Why?"

"Lenny stole a shoebox from Denise's apartment that contained a manuscript written by Weslie Addle, titled, *French Poetry Majors Make The Best Spies.*"

It was obvious to Stan that Randy was curious about the manuscript. While Randy thought to himself, Stan grabbed a bottle of beer from the mini fridge under the bar and cracked it open.

"Good title," Randy said. "Is Weslie Addle friends with Denise?"

"I don't know. To the best of my knowledge, she's an unknown, unpublished author."

"What's the book about?"

"Couldn't tell you. I only read the first twenty pages before I started getting confused. In my defense, I'm not much of a reader."

"Can you tell me anything about the story?"

Stan glanced at the ceiling as he tried to remember. "Let's see...it was written in first person. The narrator's a woman, who's starting her junior year at an Ivy League school, I think

Penn. She has a boyfriend, but she may or may not be sleeping with one of her professors."

Randy stared blankly at Lake Huron on the map while he pondered the information for a moment. He glanced at Stan and said, "Did you google Weslie Addle?"

"Oh yeah. Only one person came up in the search. A realtor from Indiana."

"Where's the manuscript now?"

"Because it's considered evidence in Lenny's murder investigation, I gave it to O'Malley."

"How'd you get your hands on it?"

"I found it in a shoebox in the closet of Lenny's fishing cabin."

"I didn't know he had a fishing cabin."

"Me neither until I inherited it. It's up on Goose Lake. It was a bitch to find."

A puzzled expression appeared on Randy's face. He took a long sip from his whisky sour then said, "That's strange Lenny never told you about his secret fishing cabin. Especially considering his decision to will it to you."

Stan nodded in agreement. "Believe me, I gave it some thought, but still have no idea why he never told me about the place. I wouldn't be surprised if he used the cabin for his secret rendezvous. The only pieces of furniture in there were a king-sized bed and a chaise lounge. There's also an inflatable hot tub on the back deck. A nice one too."

Randy's puzzled look had not disappeared. "So Lenny stole an unpublished manuscript, written by an unknown author, from Denise's apartment, and O'Malley thinks that's why he was murdered?"

Stan took a long swig from his beer. "Yeah. Crazy, right?"

Stan and Randy both reacted to the sound of Duane heading quickly down the basement stairs. He caught his breath as he approached the bar. A look of excitement crossed his face as he said, "He'll do it."

Stan cracked open a bottle of beer and handed it to Duane. "Nice work, buddy."

Duane chugged half the beer then sat on the stool at the end of the bar. Randy was staring at Duane in disbelief. "How did you convince him to shut off the power? As an attorney, I can confirm that's highly illegal," Randy said.

"Because, not only am I an incredible lover, I'm also an incredible friend. Frank and I are still very close since I broke off the engagement. He'd do anything for me."

"But it's only been a year since you broke off the engagement. I'd still be pissed at you," Randy said.

"Well, he's not. And to prove it, he granted my request to cut the fucking power at Houston's house so we can bypass the security system and break in."

Randy was filled with doubt. "I still don't see how Frank can just cut the power to Houston's house on your request."

"He's the only V.P. at the power company who's an actual electrical engineer. He can do whatever he wants to," Duane said. "Believe me, if Frank says he's going to do something, he's going to do it."

Duane could tell both Randy and Stan were still skeptical. "What else do you guys want from me? A Western-grip handjob?"

Randy shifted nervously on the stool as Stan said, "You're right. Frank is a man of his word. The operation's a go."

Randy lowered his head, which was heavy with doubt and guilt. "I'm sorry, guys, but I think we should call it off. If we get caught, we're in deep shit."

"This was your idea!" Duane yelled.

"If the spaceport goes through, Whisper Dunes is in deep shit," Stan said.

Randy's sad eyes stared at his drink for a moment. He exhaled deeply before taking a long sip. Stan and Duane exchanged a frustrated glance. Stan then grabbed a manila folder from behind the bar and dropped it in front of Randy. He slowly opened the folder to find forty photos of the exterior and interior of Houston's stately brick mansion.

"I sold Houston his house almost six years ago. He hasn't done any renovations so these photos are up to date."

Randy and Duane flipped through the photos. "I like that backsplash in the kitchen," Duane said.

Randy looked at a photo of the wine cellar. There was a red circle on the photo.

"The wine cellar takes up almost half the basement," Stan said.

"Why's this back wall circled?" Randy asked.

"That's where the secret room is. That bottle of Zinfandel that's circled is actually a lever. Just pull it down and the door opens."

Randy and Duane both nodded. "Pretty cool," Duane said.

Randy still looked concerned as he glanced at Duane then Stan. "Even with access to the secret hiding room, the risk-reward is still out of whack."

Stan's nostrils flared as he took an intense breath. "We need to stop Houston from making the deal with Space D, and this is our only chance to do it. We live in one of the greatest natural wonders on planet Earth, and I'm prepared to break every law in the book to protect my hometown."

Duane stared down Randy. "I don't make guarantees often, but I guarantee we'll find something in his house that we can use to force Houston to kill the deal with Space D," Duane said. "Or, at the very least, we'll find something that will send his ass to prison."

Stan gave Randy a long, hard look. He finally said, "Are you with us, or not?"

Randy allowed himself to take a deep breath. "As a practicing attorney, no. As your best friends...yes."

Excited, Duane pumped his fist then said, "Frank has guaranteed me that he can keep the power off at Houston's house for approximately thirty minutes. Mass on the grass starts at five sharp, so I told Frank to cut the power right at five."

"Are you guys sure he doesn't have a backup generator?" Randy asked.

"Positive," Stan said.

"Stan, I want your ass at Mass on the grass to watch Hubert in case he leaves early for some reason."

"Roger that," Stan said.

"What if he decides not to go?" Randy asked.

"Don't worry, he'll be there. I bumped into that fucker this morning at Velodrome's."

"Oh, they've got the best coffee," Duane said.

"He apologized then he invited Lisa and me over to his house for a drink after Mass."

"What'd he apologize for?" Duane asked.

"Two nights ago he asked if he can join Lisa and I for a threesome. Right after he rejected my pitch to sell his 5,000 acres to someone who doesn't want to build a rocket spaceport on the land."

"I fucking hate Hubert Houston. I'm so glad we're breaking into his house. Even if we don't find any incriminating evidence, I'm going Doc Kimble on his house," Duane said with great intensity.

Randy and Stan both looked confused. "Doc Kimble...what does that mean?" Randy asked.

"Remember in *The Fugitive* when Doc Kimble breaks into the one-armed man's apartment?"

Stan nodded and smirked. He understood, but Randy was still confused.

"It's not until Doc Kimble fucks up the one-armed man's apartment that the cops start suspecting the one-armed man murdered Doc Kimble's wife," Duane said.

Randy looked upset now. "Dammit! That's a great idea! Why didn't you think of that when we broke into Denise's place?"

Duane was slow to respond. He glanced sheepishly at Randy. "It just didn't occur to me then. Denise is so sweet, and charming, and thoughtful, and inclusive, there was just no incentive to fuck up her place. Plus, she rents her place from Stan. I can't imagine a bigger fuck you to Stan then going into one of his nicer rental units and trashing the place."

Duane took a long sip from his beer bottle. Randy and Stan looked at each other as if to say—*I'm just glad Duane's on our side*.

Lisa and the kids had been sound asleep for a few hours, but Stan was in the dining room staring at his laptop. He read back the email he drafted. The subject of the email read: America's Best Place to Live—DON'T TOUCH IT. Stan shook his head in frustration as he pounded the delete tab eights times. He had been working on the email for nearly two hours in hopes that it would somehow get the attention of Sir Branch Bradford.

Stan started typing a sentence then stopped. He leaned back and read the sentence then reread it three more times before he read out loud, "'This land will be the jewel in your real estate portfolio, but more importantly it will allow you to be known as one of the great land conservationists of the 21st century. When Frederick Law Olmsted, the great American landscape architect, walked on this precious piece of land, back in 1891, the natural beauty of the land prompted just three words out of his mouth...don't touch it.'"

Stan looked pleased with himself. He typed some more before leaning back in his chair and reading out loud, "'This is a once in a lifetime opportunity to own and protect 5,000 acres of land, about half of which borders the largest freshwater lake on planet Earth. The land is currently zoned for recreation development. Modeled after, The Hole in the Wall Gang Camp, founded by Paul Newman, I have a vision where you create and finance a similar camp. Your camp would bring together kids with disabilities from all over the world and give them the chance to be kids...and raise a little hell. Pretty soon, firing rockets into space will be as easy and uninteresting as lighting off a bottle rocket. But by purchasing this land, you'll have the opportunity to create one of the best summer camps in the world. A camp that, over time, will have an ever-lasting positive impact on tens of thousands of kids. To be perfectly blunt, this should be a very easy decision for you. I am available 24/7 to answer any questions you might have. Best regards, Stan—The Hammer—Zbikowski.'"

Stan hit the delete button a few times. "'Best Regards, Stan Zbikowski.'"

28

Russ sat at the head of the conference table. Other than a few paint jobs, the only conference room in the Whisper Dunes Town Hall hadn't changed much since the building opened in 1895. The City Council members: five men and three woman, all over the age of fifty, sat at the long table looking concerned as they read the document in front of them. Russ fidgeted in his chair while he watched the group take their time going through the document.

Russ's chair creaked as he leaned forward and said, "Folks, we need to pass a new ordinance, A.S.A.P., that will make it illegal for any investment fund, including private equity, family offices, and hedge funds, from buying any type of real estate in Whisper Dunes. If we don't pass this ordinance now, at least half the residents of Whisper Dunes won't be able to afford to rent an apartment or house, and very few will be able to afford to buy a home."

The oldest man in the room, Leo Durocher, finished reading the document and leaned back in his chair. Leo was close to eighty but still fit as a fiddle. "I understand the reasoning, Mr. Mayor, but I will not stand in the way of capitalism. Not today, not ever. However, if the zoning commission does actually go forward and approve Houston's land for industrial use, then I might reconsider voting in favor of your proposed ordinance," Leo said.

Russ flashed a surprised look at Leo. He shook his head in disappointment then glanced around the room. "Anyone else want to close their eyes and shrug while private equity funds and hedge funds try to take over our town? Because that's what will happen if we don't vote now to protect the interests of every resident of Whisper Dunes. Almost half the population in Whisper Dunes is in the hospitality industry, living pay check to pay check. I'm in favor of building our tourism industry up, and I fully support development: new hotels, restaurants, a new marina, maybe a business park, a golf course community...hell

I'm even in favor of building a new airport. But we can't allow Wall Street banks, and hedge funds, and private equity weasels to come into Whisper Dunes and buy up all existing real estate."

Gail Roslyn, who was seated at the middle of the table, looked at Russ and said, "I fully agree, Mr. Mayor. We need to protect our residents, and we're running out of time to do it."

Lee Brown, a bearded man with glasses sitting across from Gail, regarded Russ. "Mr. Mayor, I appreciate you bringing this very important issue to everyone's attention, but first things first...what in the hell do you plan on doing with all those bums camping in Presque Isle Park, and Picnic Rocks Park, and Lower Harbor Park?"

Russ closed his eyes for a moment. He looked uneasy as he considered a response that would make everyone in the room happy. But before he could respond, Mr. Brown said, "My wife took our dog and two grandchildren for a sunset walk yesterday in Lower Harbor Park, and ran into a bunch of hippies doing nude yoga while blasting sitar music. This is Whisper, fucking, Dunes. Not a spiritual wellness retreat in Big Sur. We need to kick those assholes out of our parks, now!"

"I hear you and I want everyone to know I'm working on it," Russ said. "I'm in close contact with Randy Daugherty as he continues to navigate the legal hurdles surrounding the issue, and I think we're close to taking our parks back."

Over 3,000 environmental activists were mulling around their tent city in the middle of Presque Isle Park. The 323 acre forested peninsula, located just north of downtown, was one of the most popular destinations in the Upper Peninsula. But during the past month the public park had been occupied by protestors from all over the country, and even from countries as far away as Brazil and New Zealand.

On the outskirts of the forest that covered the middle of the park, the protestors had set up their community campsite in a grass field that led to a dozen or so hiking trails. Most of the protestors populating the campsite were hardcore environmentalists. But there was also a small Occupy Wall Street section, as well as a small group of nudists, who had become obsessed with Bellini's Pizza. This was evident by the stacks of Bellini's Pizza boxes surrounding their tents.

Dozens and dozens of American flags and state flags were flying outside the tents. Most protestors also had at least one sign posted outside their tent. *Stop the Rocket! Protect Lake Superior! Occupy Wall Street! Ban Social Media! Corporate Media is the Greatest Threat Against Humanity! Free the Nipple!*

A college-aged couple was making out in their open tent while a dude in his forties, who looked like he hadn't showered in over a month, sat nearby playing the bongos. A delivery driver arrived at the tent next door and handed a Bellini's Pizza to a naked couple who looked to be in their early thirties.

Nearby, a news reporter stood in the middle of a sea of people as he tried to finish his report. "An online petition opposing the rocket spaceport has just reached one hundred million signatures. The signatures are represented by Americans in all 50 states, the District of Columbia, Puerto Rico, and at least 44 other countries," said the news reporter. "Space D has launched more satellites than any other space company in the past year. And with over 4,000 satellites currently in orbit, Space D occupies most of the Earth's orbit routes. The company also has a history of blowing up rockets. One of many reasons the folks here in Whisper Dunes are so determined to stop the rocket spaceport. According to multiple reports, the spaceport could break ground on the shores of Lake Superior early next year."

A woman, who was taller than the news reporter, had to lean down a bit so she could speak into the microphone. "The only thing worse than a government monopoly is a private monopoly the government is dependent on," yelled the woman. The crowd cheered loudly as the woman took the microphone from the reporter and looked into the camera.

"Satellites control drones and missiles and critical images used for military intelligence! Satellites should not be controlled by private companies! And NASA should not rely on Space D for essential services!"

The news reporter got back control of his microphone. He looked frustrated as he took a few steps toward the cameraman. "The number of protestors flocking to Whisper Dunes has doubled in less than a week, and it's clear to this reporter that they're starting to wear out their welcome. It's also clear the protestors have no intention of leaving Presque Isle Park until they succeed in stopping the rocket spaceport from being built."

The woman tried again to grab the microphone from the reporter, not realizing that the cameraman had stopped filming.

"No, we're done here! And if you touch my microphone again, I'll have you arrested!"

The woman screamed, "Fuck you!" The crowd cheered as the reporter and the cameraman hurried back to their news van.

Denise and Hubert were laying next to each other in a hotel bed, naked and sweaty. Denise took a sip from a glass of water then leaned her head back against two pillows. Hubert put both hands behind his right hamstring, lifted his right leg in the air, and attempted to stretch.

"What'd that grizzly fuck Leo Durocher say?"

"He's willing to support the mayor's proposed ordinance to ban any corporation or L.L.C. from owning real estate in Whisper Dunes."

"Son of a bitch!"

Denise took another sip of water while avoiding eye contact with Hubert. Her glazed eyes were staring across the room at the black and white photo of a snow-covered sand dune.

"Nothing ruins a good business deal like an incorruptible politician," Hubert said as he got out of bed. He grabbed his white linen pants from the desk chair and put them on.

"He may not be corruptible, but Russ is power hungry just like every other politician. He'd do anything to remain mayor of Whisper Dunes for the rest of his life," Denise said.

"You're absolutely right. After Mass on the grass we're going to pay him a visit, together."

Denise had no expression on her face as she continued to stare at the picture on the wall.

"Stop by my house before Mass on the grass for a glass of wine. I have something I want to give you."

"Okay," Denise said softly.

"Oh, and bring some blow and a batch of your famous kale chips. I love those things."

Denise nodded just as her cell phone started to vibrate on the nightstand. She glanced at the caller ID—PRIVATE. She hesitated to answer, but finally pressed the green "accept call" icon. She put the phone to her ear and softly said, "Hello."

The caller slowly said, "I know what's in the orange shoebox. I think we have something to talk about. Meet me tonight in the church parking lot. Nine p.m. sharp."

Denise looked to be in a state of shock. She set the phone on the bed and then started to breathe slowly through her nose. Her head slowly landed back on the two pillows. Denise closed her eyes and started to think how to handle the situation.

"Who was that?"

"A cancelation for my hot yoga class tonight."

Hubert finished buttoning his shirt. He put on his navy blue sport coat before grabbing his keys off the dresser. "Good fuck session. I'll see you Saturday. Don't forget the goodies."

Denise watched Hubert exit the hotel room. She closed her eyes while laying motionless on the bed. After two minutes, she picked up her phone and dialed a number.

The hotel's main entrance glass doors slid open and out walked Hubert. He headed toward his new Bentley Continental GT with a bounce in his step. He had no idea that Officer Alcocks was taking photos of him from an unmarked Ford Explorer in the back row of the parking lot.

Alcocks, with a hat pulled down low on his face, watched the metallic-green Bentley speed away. Aided by his two friends in the Wisconsin State Police, Alcocks was able to track Denise to her favorite hotel in Green Bay. He was shocked when he saw Hubert get out of his Bentley and enter the hotel, but after sitting in his car for almost two hours, the shock faded away. O'Malley and Alcocks knew that Denise had a partner in crime, now Alcocks was certain he had just identified the other suspect in Lenny's murder.

Alcocks spent the next twenty minutes looking at a series of beautifully composed nude selfies his wife texted him earlier in the day. Something she did whenever she thought the stress of the job was getting to her husband. Alcocks was grinning as he went through the photos one more time. He was still grinning when he put the phone down on the passenger seat and focused his attention back on the hotel entrance. His eyes suddenly got wide as he leaned forward. Alcocks grabbed the camera and started snapping photos of Denise exiting the hotel through the sliding glass doors and walking quickly toward her Jeep Wrangler.

Alcocks sat across from Chief O'Malley, sipping coffee. O'Malley sat quietly behind his desk looking at the photos Alcocks took on the digital camera. O'Malley stopped looking at the photos and regarded Alcocks. "How long were they in the hotel room?"

"Two hours. Denise got to the hotel first then left about forty minutes after Houston left."

O'Malley leaned back into his chair and said, "What do you think?"

"In addition to being fuck buddies, I think Denise and Hubert conspired to murder Lenny."

Officer Soller barged into the office with a bounce in his step. He flung up his right hand, which held two pages of phone records. "I was finally able to subpoena the phone records from the country club."

O'Malley and Alcocks stared at Soller with great anticipation.

"An outgoing call was made from the pro shop on July 4th at 10:48 p.m."

O'Malley actually looked excited for once. "Who was the call made to?"

"Lenny's emergency plumbing number."

O'Malley quickly stood up and looked at Alcocks. "Get Judge Riley on the phone now. Tell him it's finally time to approve our search warrant for the club. And while you have him on the phone, tell him we need a search warrant for Denise's apartment. If he puts up a fight, tell him we've finally got strong evidence."

Alcocks looked uneasy as he regarded O'Malley. "When you say strong evidence, are you referring to the shoebox that contains an unpublished manuscript?" Alcocks asked.

"Yeah, but don't tell him that. Just say we uncovered a piece of evidence that could be the motive behind the murder."

Alcocks nodded and said, "Ten-four."

29

Stan drove his golf cart while sipping vodka lemonade from his blue tumbler. Lisa sat next to him sipping the same drink from her red tumbler. They were both wearing sunglasses and dressed in classy summer attire, suitable for an outdoor Mass. Stan gave his wife a long look. He was mesmerized by her natural beauty. "You know, you're more beautiful now than you were when we first started dating," Stan said. "And you were really hot back in college."

Lisa flashed a sheepish grin before taking another sip. She still loved it when Stan complimented her, even though most of the time the compliment was followed up with a request that was sexual in nature.

"The other night...I liked walking into Brendan's room to find you reading to him," Lisa said.

"I'm really trying to get all the boys to start reading more. I told them it's never too late to become an avid reader. At this point in civilization, books may be the only thing left to safeguard the human mind from the Silicon Valley mafia."

"You're right. You know what would be fun?"

"What's that?"

"Let's start a couples book club," Lisa said.

"Great idea! Let's do it."

Lisa flashed Stan a sweet smile before sipping her drink.

"How's your drink?" Stan asked.

"Refreshing."

Stan grinned and said, "Sure it's not too strong?"

"A little strong, but it's good."

The golf cart cruised down a quiet tree-lined street, filled with charming one-story homes. Stan was quiet for a minute before he regarded Lisa. He had planned on waiting until he had a few sessions under his belt before telling Lisa, but changed his mind while looking into her eyes. "I have my first session with my therapist next Thursday."

Lisa looked pleasantly surprised. Before she got choked up she said, "Really?"

Stan nodded while keeping his gaze on Lisa's growing smile. "I know you've been asking me to go for a while now, and I'm finally ready to rap with a shrink. I want to stop gambling, even if that means I have to stop drinking, and more than anything I want to become the husband you deserve."

Overcome with surprise and joy, Lisa's eyes became moist. Never in her wildest dreams did she expect Stan to give therapy a shot in hopes of becoming a better husband. She wrapped her left hand around the back of Stan's neck and kissed him on the lips. They continued to kiss while Stan kept one eye on the road, but the kiss ended when a splash of vodka lemonade landed onto his blue shorts.

"I'm proud of you, Stan. It takes courage to admit you need to make some changes. I'm going to make some changes too."

Stan smiled slightly as he rested his hand on Lisa's left kneecap. "I just want us both to stop taking each other for granted," Stan said. "I love you. You and the kids are the best thing about my life. You're all I care about."

Lisa smiled while considering an idea that just popped into her head. She was overcome with a tingling sensation as she allowed herself to embrace the idea. This was the kind of idea that normally popped into Stan's head, but it was in her head now. In the past, when an impulsive, adventurous idea popped into her head she quickly dismissed the idea. But not today. Her eyes glanced at the forest before landing on Stan. "If you recall, one of our first marriage counselors spoke about how important it is to seek out new adventures and sexual experiences as we get older," Lisa said.

Stan looked at Lisa with a curious grin. "That's right. I liked that marriage counselor. Why'd we stop seeing her?"

Lisa put her hand on Stan's inner right thigh and slid closer to him. She flashed a sexy smile and said, "There's a trailhead coming up. Why don't you take a detour through the forest?"

Stan checked his watch. "Honey, Mass starts in twenty-three minutes."

Lisa flashed a sexy smile and said, "Then we better be quick."

Hubert, his lips stained red, was cruising solo down a residential street in his tricked out golf cart. The metallic-green golf cart had off-road tires and a neon lighting kit under the cart. "Simply Irresistible," by Robert Palmer was blasting from the sound system while a different neon color glowed from under the cart every two seconds. Hubert stopped singing to take another swig of wine from his tumbler. He then reached into the plastic bowl on the bench seat and grabbed a few homemade kale chips.

"God, these are good!"

Hubert, munching on the kale chips, made a left at the stop sign. He bobbed his head as he cruised down a narrow street that ran parallel with the first hole fairway of the Potawatomi Country Club. Hubert's happy high suddenly vanished as his golf cart came to a stop. He turned off the music and his normal pissed-off look returned to his face while he was forced to wait behind at least two dozen decorated golf carts. One by one, the golf carts entered through the open gate and headed to the middle of the first fairway to search for a parking spot.

There was a makeshift altar set up about twenty yards from the front of the green. At least two hundred golf carts were already parked in front of the altar. In front of the golf carts were five rows of lawn chairs. About ten yards of grass was between the last row of lawn chairs and the first row of golf carts. There were twenty rows of golf carts parked in front of the makeshift altar. Each cart was decorated with an obscene amount of Christmas lights in preparation for the annual end of summer Venetian Night golf cart parade, which was scheduled to start thirty minutes after sunset.

Most of the people in the lawn chair section were standing and making small talk with their neighbors. Seated in a lawn chair in the first row, furthest one left of the altar, was Denise. She looked intrigued watching the two altar boys set up the altar. Denise had planned on wearing jeans and a cardigan sweater, but it was a warm evening so she chose to wear a white and navy blue striped summer dress that was probably a bit too tight for Mass. Even for a Mass taking place outside on the fairway of a golf course.

A white pick-up truck was parked across the street from Hubert Houston's red-brick Georgian mansion. G&G Contracting, Inc. was written in cursive on both doors of the truck. Duane, wearing a gray jumpsuit, sat in the driver seat. Randy, also in a gray jumpsuit, sat in the passenger seat. Gordon Lightfoot's, "The Wreck of the Edmund Fitzgerald" was playing on the radio.

"This is the first time I've ever missed Mass on the grass," Randy said, looking disappointed.

Duane's eyes remained focused on Houston's house. "We'll still be able to catch the Venetian Night golf cart parade...if everything goes as planned."

Randy and Duane both sipped from their coffee cups at the same time. A quiet minute passed before Duane said, "Did you know that Pope Francis was a bouncer?"

Randy looked curious. "Like a bouncer at a bar?"

"Yeah."

"When was he a bouncer?"

Duane's eyes narrowed as he scratched his chin. "I'm not sure. But I assume it was before he became a priest."

Duane poured coffee from his thermos into his cup as Randy checked his watch. Realizing that Randy was growing more nervous with each passing minute, Duane felt compelled to try and calm Randy's nerves.

"Have you seen *Narcos*?" Duane asked.

"Yeah, it was okay. I'll still take a multi-cam sit-com over a dramatic true-story any day of the week."

"Hey, I'm with you, buddy. Fun fact though, did you know that Escobar appeared on the *Forbes* billionaires list seven years in a row?"

Randy was clearly surprised to hear this. "No, I didn't."

"Don't tell me crime doesn't pay," Duane said.

"Well, he did eventually die in a hail of gunfire."

Duane took a long sip from his coffee cup. He then set the cup back in the cup holder and popped a stick of gum in his mouth. "I read that while he was on the run, he kept his daughter warm by burning over two million in cash," Duane said before his gaze met Randy's surprised look. "I thought that was sweet."

"Speaking of sweet, it was very nice of Hal's brother to let us use his work truck."

Duane nodded emphatically as he chomped on his gum. "Yeah, he's a nice guy. I told him I needed to use the truck to move some shit out of my storage locker. Thankfully, he bought it."

Randy curiously watched Duane take a small silver case out of his breast pocket. Duane opened the case, removed a Q-tip, and carefully stuck it up his nose to Randy's astonishment.

"What are you doing?" Randy asked.

"It's very difficult for me to blow my nose so I have to clean house with a Q-tip."

"Why can't you blow your nose?"

Duane rolled down the window and tossed the Q-tip out the window. "Back in the late 90's I developed a thousand dollar a week coke habit. With some spiritual guidance and a lot of willpower, I finally kicked my nasty little habit," Duane said as he gently rubbed the bridge of his nose. "But unfortunately, all that snorting led to a deviated septum, which makes blowing my nose a real chore."

Randy had an incredulous look on his face as he regarded Duane. "But you still drink...heavily."

Duane shook his head then turned his attention back to Houston's mansion. "I think giving up all bad habits at once is asinine."

A Whisper Dunes Police suv drove past about a hundred protestors standing outside the entrance gates to the Potawatomi Country Club. The protestors were holding signs that said: CHANGE THE NAME OF YOUR DESPICABLE CLUB! YOUR PLAYING GOLF ON STOLEN LAND! COUNTRY CLUBS ARE A REFUGE FOR RACIST ASSHOLES!

Chief O'Malley, Officer Alcocks, and Officer Soller walked through the burned- out locker room of the clubhouse as the general manager of the country club followed closely behind with suspicious eyes.

"Gentlemen, let me remind you, despite the appearance, this is still a very exclusive private country club. And I expect the three of you to conduct yourselves as respected guests of the Potawatomi Country Club."

O'Malley and Soller didn't bother to look at the snooty asshole because they knew Alcocks would take care of him. "Fuck off, Peter. This is a crime scene, where a murder and arson took place," Alcocks said. "This is our domain now, dickweed. Go find some silverware to polish."

Peter's lower lip started to quiver as he turned around and quickly exited the locker room. Alcocks followed Soller and O'Malley into the mechanical room, which was adjacent to the men's locker room. O'Malley noticed a metal cart with a long platform that was badly damaged from the fire. The six-foot-long cart was used by the kitchen staff to move large food deliveries into the kitchen. But it was also long enough to move a dead body.

O'Malley went back into the hallway and reentered the room, pretending he was Lenny. "Seconds after Lenny entered the room he was shot behind the ear. Never even saw his killer. The killer put Lenny on this moving cart and moved his body to the black Chevy Tahoe. After the body was loaded into the Tahoe, the killer came back to this room and set the fire to destroy any evidence," O'Malley said.

Alcocks and Soller nodded in complete agreement.

"What's our next move, Chief?" Alcocks asked.

O'Malley stared at the burned out ceiling and said, "Let's go check out Denise's place."

30

A short woman in her early sixties stood behind the podium holding a cordless microphone. The podium was just left of the altar. Her blonde hair was pulled back in a ponytail and she smiled as she sang, "Amazing Grace." Standing seven feet away was a guy strumming his acoustic guitar, but her incredible voice soared over the guitar chords.

Father Carey walked alongside Deacon Terry as they followed the two altar boys toward the altar while over five hundred people stood. Everyone looked ready to celebrate Mass on the grass on a beautiful summer night in Whisper Dunes.

Stan and Lisa stood in front of their golf cart, which was parked in the last row. Lisa was singing along but Stan's lips were nervously pressed together as he eyed Houston, who was standing about twenty yards in front of Stan and Lisa. Stan subtly pulled his phone from his pocket and typed a quick text.

Houston was singing the words very softly while staring at an attractive woman nearby, who was standing next to her husband. Denise was standing tall and singing while staring right at Deacon Terry, who had his head down as he followed closely behind Father Carey. Deacon Terry stood in front of one of two chairs that was positioned just left of the altar while Father Carey stood behind the altar with his head bowed.

Duane glanced at his watch—5:00 p.m. Randy took a deep breath as he stared nervously at Hubert's mansion.

"It's 5 o'clock. Time to Go for Go," Duane said in a measured tone. Randy and Duane both put on sunglasses before exiting the pick-up truck. Randy followed closely behind Duane as they crossed the quiet street.

Randy was overwhelmed with nervous energy. He constantly looked left and right to make sure the coast was clear as they approached Houston's driveway. But Duane wasn't nervous at all. In fact, his confident determination had manifested into sassigassity. A characteristic that was unique to Duane. One day, after another run-in with bullies in middle school, Duane's mom looked him in the eye and told her oldest son that he had something that no one else had...sassigassity. From that day forward, Duane used his sassigassity to overcome many personal and professional road blocks throughout his life.

Duane and Randy hurried up the driveway and within a few seconds were standing outside the back door. Duane checked his watch, which read: 5:02 p.m. He took a deep breath and looked at Randy. "We've got twenty-eight minutes. No excuses, do the job."

Randy nodded then exchanged a fist bump with Duane. They both took deep breaths before Duane opened the back door. Randy entered Hubert's house first, followed closely by Duane.

Randy and Duane, both wearing gloves and booties over their shoes, walked around Hubert's enormous kitchen. Duane glanced at the island countertop in the middle of the kitchen. On the marble countertop were two empty bottles of Merlot, one line of cocaine on a silver plate, and a large glass bowl that had a few homemade kale chips left in it.

Duane casually grabbed the rolled up hundred-dollar bill from the silver plate and put it in his back pocket. "Smells like kale chips and ass in here," Duane said.

Randy looked disgusted as he came across a used condom on the hardwood floor. "What a fucking slob. There's a used condom on the floor," Randy said.

"Considering this prick has probably had a housekeeper picking up after him since he was in diapers, that checks out," Duane said.

Randy watched Duane walk over to the nearest light switch and flick it on and off a few times. "Power's off," Duane said. "Nice job, Frankie boy."

"Looks like Hubert got coked up before he left for Mass," Randy said. "Might explain why he left the back door unlocked."

"You know, before Lenny was murdered, I don't know a single person who locked their back door. I know I never did."

"I have kids and no gun in the house, so I'm very reliant on the bolt lock."

They moved through a long narrow hallway, which led to the massive living room. The living room had a thirty-foot vaulted ceiling with faux wood beams attached. Duane and Randy were both briefly distracted by the large framed photograph hanging over the stone fireplace. The photo was of a beautiful naked woman standing knee deep in a river with a wolf cub lying across her left shoulder.

Randy looked at Duane and said, "You take upstairs, I'll start in the basement."

An intense look appeared on Duane's face as he turned his attention from the photograph to Randy. "I'm going to tear this place apart."

Duane was working up a sweat in the master bathroom, pulling drawers out of the vanity and dumping the contents on the floor. A fifty-inch television was floating in the bathtub. The faucet was still running and the bathtub was on the verge of overflowing. Stuffed into the toilet were four pairs of dress shoes. Duane moved over to the bathroom closet and started grabbing things from the shelves and tossing them onto the marble floor tiles.

Duane walked into Houston's master bedroom and started pulling drawers from the long dresser that was against the wall facing the custom made king-size bed set. Piles of clothes from at least a dozen drawers littered the hardwood floor. The room was a complete mess. The king-size mattress had been cut open. Broken pieces of an expensive vase were all over the floor. A smashed framed photo of the New York Stock Exchange was also on the floor, and the painting over the bed had a dildo pierced through it.

Duane moved to the enormous closet and started opening shoeboxes. But he stopped as soon as he felt his phone vibrate with a text message. Duane pulled out his phone and saw that the text was from Randy. It read: *Get down to the basement!*

Duane sprinted out of the master bedroom, through the long hallway, and down the stairs that led to the foyer. Duane passed through the dining room but stopped abruptly. His eyes locked in on the large china cabinet, and a mischievous grin slowly appeared on his face.

Randy stood over a metal chest in the secret room adjacent to the wine cellar. The chest was open and Randy slowly reached in and pulled out a red leather-bound journal. As he opened the journal he was startled by a loud sound caused by the china cabinet crashing to the floor. He shook his head in disbelief then turned his attention back to the journal. His wide eyes were filled with curiosity as he slowly turned the page.

"Where are you?" Duane shouted.

"I'm in the secret room next to the wine cellar!"

Randy's eyes remained focused on the page as Duane entered the secret room, out of breath.

"What do you got?"

Randy glanced at the chest. "A whole lot of evidence."

Duane looked inside the chest and saw eight different video cameras, four laptop computers, roughly a hundred recordable DVDs, and at least fifty tiny boxes—the kind you would put a ring or a pair of earrings in. On each small box was a label with a name written on it. Duane picked up one of the small boxes. SPACE D—M. SAMMACICCIA was written on the label. Duane opened the box and found a flash drive.

Randy suddenly looked distraught. "Do you think Denise actually slept with all these guys?"

Duane continued to read the names on each of the boxes. "I'm afraid you were one of many, many men, and a few women, who fell into Denise's honey pot. But that doesn't mean she didn't have real feelings for you. Well, she probably didn't, but that in no way cheapens the high quality sex you had with her," Duane said. "That's probably not true either. The point is, you were seduced by a world class beauty. Deep down, I don't think you're guilty of cheating on Vivian. Just like I don't think a guy who avoids paying Uncle Sam every year in order to finance a summer camp for disadvantage kids is guilty of cheating on his taxes."

Randy's eyes remained on Duane. He let out a long sigh before flashing a slight smile. He knew Duane was just trying his best to make him not feel like a total asshole for cheating on Vivian.

Duane started reading off the names on each small box. "K. Barzoni, B. Barzoni, B. Mulcahy, B. Breen, M. Tinio, J. Merrion, M. Wilson, Pastor C. McClintock, M. Knight, B. Knight...I don't recognize most of these names."

Randy continued thumbing through the red leather-bound journal. His eyes widened. "Here we go, Micky Sammaciccia, Space D's head of spaceport development. It's got all his personal information and contact info."

Duane looked for the small box with M. Sammaciccia written on the label. "Here it is," Duane said. "Something tells me Mr. Sammaciccia only became interested in purchasing Houston's 5,000 acres after Denise showed him this video of the two of them playing on top of the feathers."

Randy looked bewildered as he stared at Duane. "I can't believe Denise and Hubert blackmailed Space D into buying the land."

Duane regarded Randy and said, "With this evidence, we can blow up their whole fuckin operation."

A search warrant was taped on the door of Denise's apartment. The door was partially open and inside Chief O'Malley was checking out the bookcase in the living room. He scanned the top shelf, which was stacked with books written by Elmore Leonard. The shelf below was stacked with books written by John Le Carre. O'Malley had read multiple books by both authors, and was well aware that Elmore Leonard was one of the great crime writers, maybe the greatest, and Le Carre was quite possibly the greatest spy writer of all-time.

Alcocks was in the kitchen putting a dirty glass and spoon into a plastic bag used for collecting DNA samples. He slid the blue tab, sealing up the plastic bag. Alcocks then pulled out his phone and took a photo of the bag.

Soller was searching Denise's bedroom. He took his time as he went through her underwear drawer. He finally moved to the night stand. On the nightstand was a lamp and a hardback copy of *The Friend* by Sigrid Nunez. Soller opened up the nightstand drawer. Inside the drawer were two bottles of organic lube, two vibrators, four different paperback novels by Agatha Christie, a hardcover copy of *The Last Thing He Told Me* by Laura Dave, and a hardcover copy of *Gone Girl* by Gillian Flynn.

O'Malley moved over to the desk, which was pushed against the window. On the desk were two spiral notebooks—a blue one and a red one—a vintage Olympia typewriter, and a coffee cup filled with pencils and blue pens. O'Malley picked up the blue notebook and started to look through it. His eyes narrowed as he carefully read. He looked curious as he turned the page and continued reading.

A woman in a yellow summer dress stood at the podium and slowly read the first reading from *The Gospel of Mark*. The crowd was attentive except for those who drank too much on their golf cart ride to Mass on the grass.

Father Carey and Deacon Terry both sat very still in their chairs as they listened to the reading. Terry had no idea that Denise was keeping a close eye on him. Just like Hubert had no idea that Stan was keeping a close eye on him.

Hubert looked very relaxed seated in his custom designed golf cart, but his relaxed posture was quickly disrupted as his stomach started to gurgle. He started to rub his belly in hopes that his sudden upset stomach would quickly pass. But this was wishful thinking. He leaned forward and clutched the steering wheel of his golf cart, as if to brace himself for the fact that he might shit his pants. He took several deep breaths and straightened his posture. Most people seated nearby started to notice Hubert shifting his ass around the seat in great discomfort. He started to sweat profusely as he slowly leaned back in his seat. He focused on taking slow breaths, and to his great relief the aggressive movements in his bowels began to calm down. Hubert slowly exhaled then pulled out his phone and sent a text message.

Denise reacted to the text chime from her purse. She quickly took her phone out and read the text: What the fuck did you put in the kale chips? My stomach is REALLY messed up! Denise looked annoyed as she put the phone back into her purse without responding to the text.

Hubert sat very still on his golf cart, hoping that his bowel movement issues were over. He looked in control for a moment, but suddenly his stomach went topsy-turvy again. Hubert desperately needed access to a toilet, but there was no bathroom in sight. He started to clench his ass cheeks in a last ditch effort to combat the aggressive movements in his stomach. Overcome with a particular anguish he hadn't experienced in years, Hubert's nostrils flared and his upper lip curled back while his sweaty palms tightly gripped the steering wheel.

He turned on his golf cart's flashing neon lights to alert everyone nearby to move their carts. Hubert was now sitting in an unusual position. He was slumped forward with his thighs pressed tightly together. He put his golf cart in reverse, which made a loud beeping sound, and backed out of the parking spot. Hubert then put the golf cart in drive and sped off while everyone watched him barely avoid hitting several parked golf carts.

Hubert, his face dripping in sweat, drove off the fairway and turned right onto the street. Most people in the audience, including Deacon Lutterbach, watched Hubert's lit-up golf cart speed down the narrow street.

Stan desperately searched for his phone in both pockets. Lisa gave him a curious look. "Everything okay?"

"Can I borrow your phone?" Stan said. "I seemed to have left mine in the woods."

"I left my phone at home."

Stan's eyes widened with disbelief. He couldn't hide his nervousness as he checked his watch. Twelve minutes until 5:30. Duane and Randy had to exit Houston's house at 5:30, before the power was turned back on, which is why Stan convinced himself they'd be out of there by the time Houston got home.

"We'll leave after Communion and look for your phone. It won't be hard to find. I remember the tree I was leaning against. It's gotta be right around there."

Stan nodded then kissed Lisa on the cheek. He looked nervous as he kept his eyes on Fr. Carey, who was struggling to wrap up his homily.

Duane held open a purple duffle bag while Randy removed the contents from the metal chest and put them inside the duffle bag.

"I know we should turn all this stuff over to O'Malley, but hear me out," Duane said.

Randy bit his bottom lip, bracing himself for the bad idea that was about to fly out of Duane's mouth.

Hubert, in agonizing discomfort, was trying to hold it in as he drove his golf cart down a quiet residential street. He had been relying on self-talk for the past few minutes, which seemed to make him sweat even more profusely. Sick of hearing his inner voice, Hubert started talking out loud to himself. "Come on, Hubert! You're almost home, my man. You can handle this situation, dammit! A hedge fund manager can handle anything! Control the situation!"

His stomach rumbled louder and he realized that he probably wasn't going to make it home in time. "Son of a bitch!" Desperate, he reverted to a softer tone. "Don't shit your pants, don't shit your pants. Control yourself. You're Hubert fuckin Houston. Win this moment, Hubert! Win it!"

Hubert's eyes started to tear up. His voice cracked into a high-pitched tone as he said, "You're a winner, God dammit! And winners don't shit their pants! Ever!"

His face was bright red as it went through a contorted spasm of embarrassment. The mental anguish was now greater than the physical discomfort. His stomach was still calling the shots and he knew it. "You're almost home. Come on, Hubert! Winning is ninety percent mental! You can out think and outmaneuver anyone. Successful hedge fund managers don't shit their pants! Win this battle! Come on, Hubert!"

Hubert closed his eyes and suddenly broke into transcendental meditation. He breathed slowly in through his nose as he chanted, "Winners don't shit their pants...winners don't shit their pants...winners don't shit their pants...winners don't shit their pants."

Hubert, his eyes still closed, didn't see that he was about to hit a mailbox. He continued to chant with his eyes closed until his golf cart knocked over the mailbox. Hubert opened his eyes and continued to drive as fast as he could while muttering the chant. He leaned forward, resting his chest on the steering wheel. Tears started to stream down his face at the sight of his mansion, just fifty short yards away. Hubert suddenly felt like a man cruising a deserted country road, just minutes after robbing a bank. The cocky glint in his eye had started to return. In his heart of hearts, Hubert believed that he had outmaneuvered his aggressive bowel movements. So much so, he let out a relaxed sigh.

The golf cart sped up the driveway until it reached the top then Hubert hit the breaks. He believed he was going to make it safely to the toilet after all, but just as he stood up he immediately lost control of his bowels. He took two quick steps toward the back door but froze in agony. Hubert's wide eyes looked up at the star lit sky as he shit his pants. A single tear escaped from his right eye. He stood as still as a statue while his bowels continued to empty. Despite the look of sheer disbelief on his face, he stood tall with his hands on his hips as he finished shitting in his driveway. The last time this happened, he was nine and his dad had just watched him sink his first birdie putt. *If your going to shit your pants, do it like a man,* Hubert remembered his dad yelling. Even in that embarrassing moment, he was still desperately trying to make his dad proud. He closed his eyes and took a few deep breaths. Hubert then started walking very slowly toward the back door.

Duane, holding the red leather-bound journal, followed Randy up the basement stairs. Randy, clearly perturbed with Duane, was holding the zipped up duffel bag in his right hand. "After we destroy the flash drive with your sex videos on it, we sell all the other flash drives to a high-powered divorce attorney."

Randy couldn't believe what he was hearing. Duane followed close behind as they walked through the living room then down a hallway. "Or, better yet, we make a sizzle reel and start a bidding war. I betcha we could get at least a dozen different lawyers interested."

"What is wrong with you? We're not going to sell blackmail sex videos to a divorce lawyer."

"Yes, it's tasteless, but don't tell me you couldn't use the extra money. If we split the dough evenly, we'll probably each make two hundred thousand. And that's a conservative estimate."

"It's a terrible idea, let it go."

"You're right. I'm sorry. Sometimes my entrepreneurial spirit gets the best of me."

Randy and Duane entered the kitchen just as the back door opened. They froze at the sight of a brown leather Monaco sandal—almost in slow motion—stepping into the mudroom, which led to the kitchen. Duane and Randy looked like they wanted to run but they were transfixed by the terrible smell that instantly engulfed the kitchen.

Hubert shuffled his sandals across the wood floor very slowly, but stopped in shock as he laid eyes on the two intruders in his kitchen. Randy and Duane both looked more angry than frightened as they stared down Hubert. Duane felt that he had no choice but to address the awful smell coming from the home owner. "Holy shit with a swirl on top! Did you poop your pants, Hubert?"

Hubert mustered up the courage to stand tall and look tough despite the accident in his pants. "What the fuck are you two cocksuckers doing in my house?" Hubert screamed.

Duane's eyes narrowed as he tilted his head to the left and said, "Oh, my God. You did, didn't you? I can't wait to tell everyone that the richest man in Whisper Dunes shit his pants."

Hubert's face turned red. The smell was getting worse by the second.

Randy covered his nose and yelled, "Holy shit you stink!"

Hubert's embarrassment was quickly replaced with shock as soon as he recognized the red leather-bound journal in Duane's left hand. "How did you get that?"

Randy started to dry heave. "Oh, my God, that's awful."

Duane flashed Hubert a cocky look. "Guess who else took a shit tonight? We did, on your entire blackmail operation. You're going down Houston, and so is Denise."

Hubert opened up the nearest drawer and pulled out a steak knife. It was clear to both Duane and Randy that the rage was building up inside of him. His face was bright red with the always dangerous emotional swirl of embarrassment and rage.

Hubert held up the steak knife and said, "Drop the duffel bag, and give me the journal."

Duane and Randy exchanged a quick guilty look before looking back at the home owner.

"Fuck you, Hubert," Duane yelled. "You dirty pimp!"

"Give me the journal and the duffel bag now, or your both dead."

Duane and Randy both felt their heart rate dramatically increase. Duane's eyes got very wide as he glanced at Randy. The adrenaline running through Randy's veins gave him a sudden burst of confidence. Looking right at Hubert, he said, "I guess no one told you that you can't be a pimp and a prostitute too."

Proud of Randy, Duane extended his fist toward him for a quick bump while they both kept their eyes on Hubert. Just as Randy bumped Duane's fist, Hubert threw the knife at Randy's head. Randy closed his eyes for one second, and the knife stuck into the wall six inches above his head.

"Jesus Christ!" Randy said with terror in his voice.

Duane yelled, "You missed, mother fucker!"

Hubert reached for two more steak knives, prompting Randy and Duane to sprint out of the kitchen. Hubert set the steak knives on the counter and quickly removed his soiled pants and underwear. He wiped himself with a dish towel before washing his hands in the sink. He then hurried into the pantry and grabbed a chef's apron hanging from the back of the door. Hubert put on the apron then bolted out of the kitchen.

Randy and Duane ran toward the front door. Randy unlocked the handle and pulled but the door was dead bolted. The only way to unlock it was with a key. Randy and Duane suddenly felt overwhelmed with the kind of fear that comes with being trapped. Randy looked at Duane and yelled, "Fuck!"

Hubert stopped in his tracks as soon as he entered the dining room. The antique china cabinet had been pushed over and pieces of broken plates and crystal glassware were all over the floor. "You cocksuckers! That was my great-grandmother's crystal!"

Randy and Duane ran through the foyer and up the grand staircase. They got to the second floor and looked behind them. No sign of Hubert. Duane looked at his watch. "Shit! The security cameras are gonna power back on in less than four minutes."

Hubert ran into his first floor office and opened the closet. There were a dozen automatic weapons hanging on the wall in the closet. He grabbed an AR-180 and ran out of his office, grinning like a dumb fuck who just found out his dad bought his way into an Ivy League school.

Randy and Duane were hiding in the guest bedroom trying to come up with an escape plan. Randy looked panicked but Duane kept his cool as he thought through his plan. He set the red leather-bound journal on the bed and opened one of the two steel casement windows in the bedroom. Duane looked out the opened window, which was easily wide enough for a grown man to fit through.

"I think we can slide down the drain pipe," Duane said.

Randy was clearly frightened. "I hate heights. Plus, I have weak hands. I'll fall half way and break my ankles."

"Well, that's a helluva lot better than getting murdered by Hubert Houston."

They both reacted to the sound of Hubert running down the hallway. Duane looked like he just got a new idea. "Get in the closet."

Duane and Randy hurried into the walk in closet. Randy stood at the back of the closet while Duane stood right behind the closet door, which he left cracked open so he had a view of the open window. They heard the door to the bedroom slowly open. Randy closed his eyes and stopped breathing, but Duane remained wide eyed and focused.

Thinking they got away, Hubert ran to the open window. He leaned out the window with his gun aimed and carefully scanned the front yard for his targets. Duane burst out of the closet on his tippy toes and relied on a heavy dose of adrenaline to push Hubert out the window. Hubert's face slammed against the asphalt shingles and he lost control of his gun. Both Hubert and his gun slid down the roof, but as his body slid off the roof he was able to grab the gutter with his right hand.

Duane yelled, "Let's go!"

Duane and Randy hurried out of the bedroom and sprinted down the hallway toward the stairs, but Duane lost his footing as he hit the first stair and tumbled down the grand staircase while Randy watched with a pained face. Duane did several somersaults down the stairs but amazingly landed on his feet at the bottom of the stairs. Duane acted like nothing happened as he looked back at Randy. "C'mon! Hurry!"

Duane and Randy had to stop running in order to carefully navigate through the glass covered dining room floor. Once out of the dining room they sprinted down the narrow hallway, then hurried through the kitchen and finally escaped out the back door.

With both hands firmly on the gutter now, Hubert pulled himself back onto the roof. His tan face, knees, and arms were cut up badly from the slide down the roof, but he was too angry to notice. Hubert grabbed his automatic weapon from the gutter then climbed through the window and reentered the guest bedroom. He removed the apron and opened the top dresser drawer. He pulled out a yellow bathing suit and a white t-shirt, quickly changed into his new outfit, and ran out of the bedroom.

Randy and Duane sprinted across the street toward the pick-up truck. Duane got in the driver seat just as Randy got in the passenger seat. Duane frantically searched his pockets for the keys. "Oh, fuck! The keys must have fallen out during my nasty little tumble."

Randy was horrified at what he saw through the driver side window. "Oh, no."

Duane looked out his window to find Hubert pointing his automatic weapon right at him. Randy was terrified, but

Duane didn't look intimidated at all, in fact he looked upset. Duane raised his left index finger and pointed it at the gun.

"You better have a permit for that gun, Houston. Otherwise, you're in deep shit."

"Get out of the fucking truck! Right fucking now!"

Frozen in his seat, Randy was sweating bullets. Duane calmly stared at Hubert while he pondered an idea. Duane finally nodded and said, "Okay, Hubert. You got us. We'll give you the duffel bag and we'll be on our merry way."

Duane slowly opened his door, but stopped when he saw the bright lights from the Venetian Night golf cart parade coming down the street. Hubert turned his head slightly to the left to check out the golf carts that were just starting to pass his house. Duane slammed open his door, which smashed into Hubert, causing him to drop his automatic weapon. Hubert grabbed his right arm in pain as he stumbled away from the truck. Duane jumped out of the truck, with the duffel bag in his right hand, and kicked the gun underneath the truck. Hubert swung his left fist at Duane but missed badly. Duane kicked him in the balls then turned to Randy, who was standing in front of the truck. Duane yelled, "Come on!"

Hubert dropped to his knees in horrible pain as he clutched his nut sack.

Duane and Randy hurried toward the Venetian Night golf cart parade. As they were running Duane yelled, "Find a cart to hide in! I'll meet you at the police station!"

"Okay!"

Hubert looked under the truck for his gun but decided not to grab it. Instead, he got up and ran toward his driveway.

Over 500 golf carts, all decorated with bright lights, were driving past Hubert's mansion. Some golf carts were pulling small floats. Duane spotted a golf cart that was pulling a small flatbed trailer with a dozen people on it wearing elaborate animal costumes. Standing at the back of the trailer was a bare-chested man wearing a cowboy hat and cracking a whip. He was supposed to be Joe Exotic. Duane jumped on the trailer. A girl wearing a sexy cheetah costume looked excited and yelled, "Hey, Duane!"

"Hey, Sandy! Got an extra costume for me?"

"Oh, hell yeah!"

Sandy grabbed a tiger costume out of the bag next to the massive cooler. Duane quickly put it on to Sandy's delight. "You look fabulous, babe!"

Hubert hopped into his golf cart at the top of his driveway. He turned on the bright neon lights under the cart before cruising toward the parade.

Randy was still running against the parade of golf carts, looking for the right float to hide in. He saw a float that got him excited. A golf cart was pulling a trailer and everyone on it was wearing big blond wigs and rocking out to eighties music. There was also a smoke machine on the golf cart that was pumping out way too much smoke. Randy took his shirt off and jumped on the trailer. "Can I rock out with you guys?"

A big guy gave Randy a high five. "You betcha, pal!"

A cute girl handed Randy a big blond wig, which he quickly put on. "Thanks!"

Another guys asked, "Want a brew, man?"

"Heck, yeah!"

Hubert sat in his parked golf cart at the bottom of his driveway. A thirty yard gap between golf carts suddenly opened up, giving Hubert the chance to join the parade. He cruised behind a pink golf cart for about twenty seconds before he veered left and got out of the line. His golf cart slowly cruised up the street, checking out each cart as he passed them on their left side. Hubert thought he saw Randy on a trailer up ahead, so he popped open the top of the center counsel and reached for his hand gun. But as he got closer he realized it wasn't Randy. Hubert continued to check out each and every cart that he passed.

Duane, with his tiger mask on, talked loudly into his cell phone. "No, this is not a prank call! Hubert Houston is on his golf cart in the middle of the Venetian Night parade, and he's flashing a gun! I repeat, Houston is loose, and he's armed and dangerous! I should also warn you, he shit his pants. So I highly recommend wearing gloves when you arrest him."

Denise was walking toward her apartment building, but stopped abruptly at the sight of two Whisper Dunes Police vehicles parked outside her building. "Oh, no," she muttered to herself.

Denise took a deep breath and contemplated what to do next. She gazed into the distance then closed her eyes for a few seconds. She was overwhelmed with sadness because she knew her time in Whisper Dunes was now coming to an end.

When she was living aboard in London and Rome, and especially when she was living in New York City and D.C., she often dreamed of moving to a small town and leading a simple life. But for the first time since moving to Whisper Dunes, she felt regret over her decision to make this town her permanent home.

Denise quickly made a wonderful impression on everyone she met after moving to Whisper Dunes. She made lots of friends and was very active in the community, not just sexually. She loved to volunteer and always made a point to strike up a friendship with a lonely soul, who everyone else tended to avoid. Ever since she was a little girl, Denise always rooted for the underdog. What most people would never know is that she had inspired dozens and dozens of lonely souls in Whisper Dunes to live with a daily intention, and to seek out adventure and romance. Each one of those lonely souls probably remembers exactly where they were when Denise looked into their eyes, smiled, and said, "You're not living unless your seeking out at least a little adventure and romance every week."

Occasionally, Denise even found herself hopeful that she might find a man in Whisper Dunes, or somewhere in the U.P., who would make a good husband and want to start a family. But she came to the conclusion a long time ago, marriage isn't for everyone. Denise's chest and shoulders felt stiff and heavy thinking about how close she was to realizing her dream of buying the llama farm just north of Whisper Dunes. The couple who owned and operated the farm for over forty years had been patiently waiting for Denise to come up with enough money for the down payment. She had visited the farm many times and thought she'd spend the rest of her life there, but she would now have to abandon that dream, like so many others.

Denise's mistakes throughout her life were usually related to her deep insecurities. She never really learned to think for herself when she was a young adult. She was a trained people pleaser. But Denise had been listening to her heart more and more, in hopes of shedding her past and one day becoming proud of the life she was living. She still had dreams and desperately wanted a life where she didn't answer to anyone, except maybe her kids. But the visions of that life had vanished in a moments notice.

A few tears rolled down Denise's cheeks as she looked up at the starlit sky. She felt hopeless for a moment, but her resilient mind did not allow her to wallow in self-pity for too long. She continued staring at the stars as she took a long breath through her nose and exhaled through her mouth. Denise, with a determined look on her face, turned around and walked quickly toward her car.

31

O'Malley was still sitting at Denise's desk, deeply focused as he read the notes in the blue notebook. The notes were written in cursive and not every word was legible, but that didn't discourage O'Malley from trying to read every word. O'Malley's concentration was broken when a voice came on his radio. "Hey, Chief, we just got a call about Hubert Houston. The caller said he spotted Houston flashing a gun while driving in the Venetian Night golf cart parade. Officer Soller is in pursuit to check it out. Over."

O'Malley looked dumbfounded as he set down the notebook and grabbed his walkie-talkie. "Ten-four. I'm on my way. Over."

Hubert continued driving his golf cart slowly along the parade route, carefully checking each golf cart he passed in hopes of spotting Duane or Randy. He saw a wild float up ahead that caught his attention. The Traveling Wilburys, "Handle With Care" was blasting from the two large speakers on the float. Duane was dancing with a woman in a white tiger costume. The guy in a lion costume yelled, "You want another shot, Duane?"

Hubert's intense eyes opened wide as soon as he heard Duane's name being shouted. His golf cart sped toward the Joe Exotic float. He leaned forward in his seat, as if that would make his golf cart go faster. Hubert pulled out a gun from the center counsel as his golf cart got closer to the trailer. He squinted his eyes, quickly looking over each of the thirteen people dressed in jungle cat costumes dancing on the trailer. Hubert thought he spotted Duane, but everyone was wearing masks so he wasn't sure. A few seconds past before Hubert saw two men remove their masks so they could chug a shot. An evil grin appeared on Hubert's face as he steered his golf cart until it was about a foot from the left side of the trailer. He pointed his gun at Duane and yelled, "Peek-a-boo you fuck!"

Everyone on the trailer started to scream at the top of their lungs.

"Where's the duffel bag, Duane!"

Duane calmly walked over to the duffel bag, which was next to the cooler, and picked it up. He held the duffel bag tightly in his right hand as he took a few steps toward Hubert. "Put the gun away, then I'll toss it to you!"

"No fucking way! Toss me the duffel bag! Now!"

Everyone, except for Duane, jumped off the trailer and ran in different directions. Duane was alone and defenseless, but as usual, his sassigassity kept him cool despite the uncertainty of the situation.

Hubert was so focused on Duane, he had no idea that a Whisper Dunes Police suv was behind his golf cart. Officer Soller was watching Hubert closely. For the moment, Soller elected to keep the lights off as he slowly got closer to Hubert's golf cart.

Duane kept his gaze on Hubert, but noticed the police suv following Hubert's golf cart. "You can have the duffel bag, just put the gun away!"

"Toss me the bag, or I'll shoot you! Last warning!"

The police lights started to flash. Alarmed, Hubert looked back at the police suv for a few seconds, which prompted Duane to jump off the right side of the trailer and run away with the duffel bag. Hubert glanced back at Duane but he was gone.

"Pull over now, Houston," Soller yelled through the vehicle's megaphone.

Houston turned off the lights to his cart and slowly steered toward the left side of the street. They were now cruising along an elevated street that was once a tree-covered dune. Just a few feet from the pavement was a steep wooded hill that sloped down at about a forty degree angle. Hubert looked left for a second. At the bottom of the hill he saw a two-story home with a large, flat backyard. In front of the home was a winding neighborhood street.

Soller kept his lights flashing as he followed Houston's golf cart, which was cruising at about ten miles an hour on the far left side of the street. Houston's golf cart finally came to a complete stop, but he kept the golf cart in drive as he glanced in the rear view mirror. Just as officer Soller stepped out of his vehicle, Houston's foot slammed down on the pedal. He made a sharp left turn then tapped the brakes as he made the tricky drive down the wooded hill.

"Stop, Houston! You're under arrest!"

Soller stood there with an incredulous look on his face as he watched Houston navigate the hilly, wooded terrain. He reached for his walkie-talkie. "This is Officer Soller! I need backup! I attempted to apprehend Hubert Houston, but he took off on his golf cart down a wooded hill! He's heading south on Jackson Avenue! The suspect is armed and dangerous!"

Soller hustled back into his vehicle and sped off with the lights flashing but the siren off.

Hubert looked surprised that he made it down the tough hill in one piece. But despite pressing the pedal to the floor the golf cart was slowing down. He drove his slow- moving golf cart another forty feet down the dark, deserted, street before he looked back and saw that both rear tires were flat. "Son of a bitch!" He grabbed his gun from the center counsel, hopped off his cart, and ran down the quiet street.

A man in his mid-seventies, Mr. Nicklaus, was sipping a martini on his front porch while listening to his police scanner. He heard the officers radio communication and realized that Hubert Houston was armed and dangerous, and nearby. "Lulu! Get my shotgun!"

Mr. Nicklaus waited all of two minutes for his wife to deliver him the shotgun. He was now standing on the top step of the porch, looking hyper-vigilant. He looked slowly to the left then slowly to the right. The street was eerily quiet. You couldn't even hear a car in the distance. Mr. Nicklaus almost lost his balance as his wide eyes spotted Hubert running up the street in a yellow bathing suit and leather sandals. He pointed his shotgun at Hubert as he got closer to the house.

"Freeze, dirt bag!"

Hubert took cover behind a massive oak tree. He breathed heavily while leaning his back against the tree. He slowly inched his head to the right and looked across the street, just long enough to spot Mr. Nicklaus standing on his porch with a shotgun. Hubert, considering his options, saw that the two houses closest to him were dark and probably empty for the time being. Like most people in town, the residents of these two homes were likely participating in or watching the Venetian Night golf cart parade. Hubert ran as fast as he could between the two nearby houses—a two-story brick Colonial Revival and a narrow, three-story white clapboard house. Mr. Nicklaus squinted his eyes as he watched Hubert run up the driveway and disappear.

"Dammit! He got away!"

Mr. Nicklaus put his shotgun on the porch table as he spotted a Whisper Dunes police suv speeding down the street. The police suv slammed on the brakes in front of his house and the passenger window rolled down. Chief O'Malley yelled, "Did you see Houston?"

"Yeah!" Pointing across the street, Mr. Nicklaus said, "He just ran between those two houses!"

"Thanks!"

"Careful! He's armed!"

Alcocks sped about forty yards up the street before stopping in front of the driveway that led to the brick Colonial Revival house. O'Malley and Alcocks cautiously exited the vehicle with their guns drawn.

Hubert was inside the house next door to the brick Colonial Revival house. He was scarfing down a banana in the kitchen when he noticed a small bowl on the counter with two sets of keys in it. Hubert grabbed the set with the Chevrolet Traverse smart key. He was about to walk out the back door, but froze when he saw two flashlight beams in the backyard. Hubert, looking like he might have a panic attack, ducked down and lowered his head as if he was praying. He slowly raised his head up to look out the kitchen window and spotted O'Malley and Alcocks walking through the backyard, which led to a hilly wooded terrain. Hubert lowered his head just before Alcocks walked by the kitchen window. The window was elevated just high enough off the driveway so Alcocks couldn't see in. He stopped and shined his flashlight through the kitchen window for a few seconds before walking toward the front yard.

Hubert crawled on his hands and knees toward the front of the house. He got to the small living room and slowly raised up just enough so he could look out the front window. He saw Alcocks pacing in the front yard while talking on his radio. O'Malley hurried down the driveway toward Alcocks. He motioned to Alcocks to follow him. Hubert watched them as they approached their vehicle then huddled close together.

O'Malley turned his back to the house and whispered to Alcocks, "Houston either ran through the forest or broke into one of those two houses. There's no sign of footprints on the trailhead so I think he's in one of those houses. Looks like everyone on this block is at the parade so hopefully no hostage opportunities for him."

"What do you want to do?" Alcocks whispered.

"We're gonna drive away. Then wait for him to escape from his hiding spot."

Alcocks nodded and walked toward the passenger door of the patrol vehicle. O'Malley got in the driver side and waited for Alcocks to shut the door before speeding off. They both checked the rear view mirror as they drove away. "If he's watching us right now, I bet he'll go south then west," O'Malley said.

Alcocks nodded, understanding exactly what O'Malley was thinking. "He wants to get to the airport. Probably already called ahead to make sure his private jet's ready for take off. All he has to do is find a way to get there," Alcocks said.

O'Malley glanced at Alcocks and said, "If he gets on his plane, we'll never see Hubert Houston again."

Hubert remained in his crouching position while he closely watched the patrol vehicle make a right at the end of the street. The taillights were no longer visible so Hubert slowly stood up. He looked out the window for a minute, making sure that O'Malley didn't circle back. He was confident the coast was clear and dashed toward the backdoor.

Hubert got into the black Chevy Traverse and sped out of the driveway. He turned right out of the driveway and cruised down the empty street. Hubert stopped at the stop sign for a minute and debated with himself as to whether to go straight, left or right. He finally turned right onto Bluff Street.

O'Malley and Alcocks sat quietly in their vehicle, which was parked on 6th Street. The quietness was starting to get to Alcocks. He tapped his right fingers repeatedly on his right knee. O'Malley turned to Alcocks and said, "Houston's operating in desperation mode now. He won't hesitate to shoot. If you get him in the cross hairs don't second guess yourself. Understand?"

Alcocks stopped tapping his fingers against his knee. He looked O'Malley in the eyes and nodded.

"If you see that asshole raise his weapon, even an inch, take him out."

The Venetian Night golf cart parade was cruising east down Baraga Avenue and getting closer to downtown. Two Whisper Dunes police officers on police motorcycles were now leading the parade. A Whisper Dunes police suv was parked next to three barricades at the corner of Baraga Avenue and Front Street. The two Whisper Dunes police officers turned their motorcycles left onto Front Street with the lead golf cart of the parade following thirty yards behind.

One by one, the golf carts made a left turn and headed north on Front Street. The historic street in downtown Whisper Dunes was packed on both sides with people, most of whom were cheering as the parade crept up Front Street.

Like a professional race car driver, Hubert Houston looked focused and completely sure of himself. He made a left turn down another quiet street and found himself deep in self talk. *This is why I moved forty million dollars of my clients money from my alpha medallion fund into my secret bank account in the Cayman Islands. I knew this day might come. Now, all I have to do is drive eight miles to the Marquette-Sawyer airport and I'll get to spend the rest of my life island hopping in the Caribbean. I'll have a beautiful girlfriend waiting for me to visit on each island. Maybe even after a few years I can start managing money again under my new fake name, Ashland Pritchard.*

Hubert slammed his hand on the dashboard and yelled, "Fuck!"

His dream scenario was upended by the realization that the cops might be looking for him at the Marquette-Sawyer airport. In fact, it was highly likely, he calculated. And considering he was the only person who lived in Whisper Dunes, or any nearby town, who owned a private jet, it would be very easy for the cops to find him before he took off. But his mind was racing and he quickly developed a new plan. *I got it! I'll drive to Green Bay and get on a direct flight to Orlando. Treat myself to a day at Epcot tomorrow, then fly out tomorrow night to Grand Cayman.* Clearly pleased with his new plan, he grinned and said, "It's all locking in now, baby!"

Hubert had entered into a hyper-focused state of delusional thinking, which created a big blind spot. His hands were in the 10-2 position on the steering wheel while he slumped comfortably forward in the driver seat. Hubert started to fantasize about his future life in the Cayman Islands, where financial criminals move freely and live out in the open without a hint of remorse for destroying the lives of many people. They socialize daily at their favorite country clubs, where they casually conspire to corrupt politicians, steal elections, keep interest rates at or near zero, and defraud the American taxpayers, and the United States government.

Hubert's vision of his future utopia was suddenly interrupted by red and blue flashing lights in his rear view mirror. He leaned back hard into his seat as he shouted, "Son of a bitch!"

Hubert looked straight ahead and closed his eyes tightly before they opened wide. He didn't blink while he allowed himself to pretend for about thirty seconds that a Whisper Dunes police suv wasn't following him. But that delusional thought escaped his mind as he heard Chief O'Malley's voice coming through the megaphone. "Hubert Houston! This is Chief O'Malley! Pull over now!"

Hubert closed his eyes again and sighed. He opened his eyes and convinced himself that he could still make it to the Cayman Islands. Hubert's foot pressed down on the gas pedal. Different thoughts were spinning around his head. He made a hard right turn then slowed down a bit as he ruminated on a clear thought. *If I could do one more thing before I'm arrested and spill my guts to O'Malley, what would it be?*

Hubert looked distracted before a new thought popped into his head. *I guess I picked the right day to snort a few lines of coke off of Denise's perfect tits. God, what a woman.* As Hubert thought deeper about his relationship with Denise his eyes got watery. His conversation with himself continued, *Other than my Mom, Denise may be the only real friend I've ever had.*

On Hubert's left was the first hole of the Potawatomi Country Club. He wiped away the tears as he stared at the golf course. He then looked in his rear view mirror—two Whisper Dunes police vehicles were now following him. Hubert turned on the radio and switched stations until he got to the classical music station. Bach's, "Suite No. 3 in D Major" was playing. Hubert took a deep breath before turning up the volume. He started thinking about a new plan.

O'Malley and Alcocks both looked calm. O'Malley had been in many high speed chases before, but this was only Alcocks' fourth chase. Both the driver and passenger windows were rolled down a few inches, and as they got closer to the

Chevy Traverse they could hear Bach blasting from the sound system. O'Malley shook his head in disbelief as he watched Hubert make a sharp left turn off the street and onto the well manicured grass of the first hole. The Traverse tore up the grass as it sped across the flat fairway.

"Only Hubert Houston would be blasting classical music while leading us on a high speed chase through the golf course. What an asshole," Alcocks said.

"I had a feeling he was going to do that."

"Rock out to classical music, or drive through the golf course?"

O'Malley glanced at Alcocks and said, "Both."

O'Malley made a hard left, followed by the other patrol vehicle. Both vehicles tore across the fairway. Hubert turned off the headlights and the Traverse suddenly disappeared into the dark woods behind the first hole green.

"Ah, shit," Alcocks said. "I don't see him."

O'Malley decided not to drive through the woods. He turned right and sped up a steep hill that led to the fairway on the ninth hole. The two police vehicles sped down the fairway, not sure where they were going. There was silence inside the patrol vehicle for about thirty seconds until Alcocks shouted, "There he is!"

O'Malley and Alcocks saw the Traverse about a hundred yards away, driving up a steep golf cart path. O'Malley kept his eyes on the bumpy fairway as he sped toward the Traverse. "I've never played this course before. You?"

"I don't golf, Chief, you know that."

O'Malley picked up the radio. "Hey, Mulcahy, you ever play this course?"

Mulcahy's voice came over the radio, "Yeah, when I was a youngster I used to sneak on here all the time and play. Be careful. Lot of sand traps, and the back nine has some really steep elevation changes."

"Ten-Four."

The two Whisper Dunes police vehicles sped down the middle of the fairway, tearing up chunks of grass in there pursuit of Hubert Houston. O'Malley saw a bunker up ahead and swerved to the right just as officer Mulcahy's voice came over the radio. "Chief, you follow Houston. I'll try to cut him off before he gets to the thirteenth hole. That's the only hole on the back nine where he can escape to a street. Over."

"Ten-four," O'Malley said. A few seconds later he slammed on the brakes and turned the steering wheel to the right. O'Malley's vehicle drove up the steep, narrow golf cart path while Officer Mulcahy's vehicle veered right, tearing up the fairway before his tires hit a gravel golf cart path. Officer Mulcahy's vehicle created a cloud of dust and gravel as it sped down the pitch-black golf cart path.

O'Malley's vehicle reached the top of the hill and stopped. The tenth tee box was the highest elevation point on the golf course. It was a short par three hole, but the only way to get to the eleventh hole was to travel down a very steep golf cart path. Something O'Malley and Alcocks did not know. It was pitch-black and the only thing visible were dozens of oak trees. Alcocks blurted out, "Where the fuck do we go now?"

O'Malley turned on the spotlight on his side of the vehicle. "I think that's the cart path over there," O'Malley said. He hit the gas and unknowingly drove toward the very steep decline just off the green of the tenth hole. O'Malley's vehicle sped past the green, and as soon as the front wheels dropped off the edge of the cart path, O'Malley lost control of the vehicle. He jerked the steering wheel to the left and the suv rolled over several times down the steep hill. Alcocks swore all the way down the hill until the vehicle stopped rolling. Amazingly, the suv landed back on its tires.

O'Malley and Alcocks both rubbed their necks in pain. "You okay?" O'Malley asked.

"Yeah, I think so."

O'Malley slammed his foot on the gas pedal. A few seconds later the suv crashed into a deep bunker. The air bags deployed, preventing any injury, other than whiplash to O'Malley and Alcocks. But the vehicle's front end was smashed in pretty good. O'Malley was the first to exit the vehicle. He walked with a limp as he made his way to the passenger door. He opened the door and helped Alcocks out.

They both took deep breaths as they attempted to walk off the pain. Alcocks regarded O'Malley. "What do you say we go find Houston and fuck him up real good?"

Before O'Malley could respond, officer Mulcahy's voice came over the radio. "Chief! I'm pursuing Houston on foot! Suspect crashed into a tree and exited the vehicle! I don't know where he is! Need back up! I'm running north on Floral Trail! Over!"

Hubert ran as fast as he could through a backyard but the leather sandals weren't doing him any favors. He slipped again on the wet glass, this time landing hard on his right arm. He got back to his feet and continued toward the street. Once his sandals hit the pavement he started running east on Rock Street toward downtown. The twin bell towers atop St. Peter Cathedral rang out in the distance. Hubert came to a painful stop in the middle of the street and checked his watch—nine p.m. He stared in wonderment at the twin bell towers, which were located only one block northeast of where he was standing. Hubert stood still in a trance as the bells continued to ring out over the neighborhood. To this very day, Hubert is unable to explain to anyone why he stopped to admire the bell towers. But one thing was clear to him as he stared at the bell towers, he no longer had the desire to continue down the path he was on. A path he'd been traveling down since he was a young man.

Hubert felt comforted by the soothing sound of the bells ringing. A feeling he hadn't experienced since he was a kid. With each ring, the memories of his past life became clearer. In the early 1960s the church bells stopped working, and they didn't ring again until Hubert's grandfather—his mom's dad—paid to have them fixed. The bells rang again for the first time in nearly twenty years on his parents wedding day. Hubert served as an altar boy at St. Peter Cathedral for eight years, and even considered becoming a priest. But his dad worshiped money and taught his son to do the same. Hubert wanted to make his dad proud so he took everything he said to heart, until one day when a young Hubert came home from horseback riding lessons on a hot summer afternoon and found his dad in the shallow end of the pool having sex with Giselle. At first glance, Hubert thought Giselle was just hugging his dad tightly with both her arms and legs, but then he heard the moaning as her butt splashed repeatedly against the water. Giselle—Hubert's favorite nanny—was from Panama, and without question the most beautiful woman Hubert had ever seen, until he met Denise.

Everything for young Hubert changed that day. A month after the incident, Hubert confronted his dad in his study. Hubert Sr. stared at his only son for a long while before slapping him hard across the cheek. The asshole then looked at Hubert Jr. as he rubbed his red cheek and said, "You only get one life, Junior. Seek out pleasure every day, take what you want, and don't apologize for anything."

Hubert's hatred for his dad did not stop him from becoming just like his dad. A man who took everything he wanted and apologized for nothing. No need to waste your time apologizing when there's no feeling of remorse. But as Hubert continued to stand still on the dark tree-lined street—completely mesmerized by the sound of the church bells—he was overwhelmed with remorse. So much so, his knees were getting weak. As the bells continued to toll, Hubert was reminded of the person he used to be before he turned into his dad. His wide eyes finally blinked, and tears streamed down his face.

Marge's Ice Cream Parlor would normally have a long line out the door on a Saturday night in the summer, but Front Street was still packed with people watching the end of the Venetian Night golf cart parade. The only customers inside the beloved ice cream shop were a cute couple in their early eighties. The lovebirds were sharing an ice cream sundae at a small table by the window and giggling at each other like they were still in high school. Charlie, the sixteen-year-old behind the counter, was the only worker on duty. He was wiping down the counter but stopped when he heard the small bell above the door ring as the glass door swung open. Charlie's sweet-natured smile vanished as he locked eyes with the injured man limping toward the counter.

Charlie stood still while Hubert Houston sat down at the counter. Hubert regarded Charlie with a kind smile and said in a gentle voice, "Hello, Charlie."

"Hello, Mr. Houston," Charlie said timidly. "Your usual?"

"Yes...please."

Hearing the word please from Hubert Houston, coupled with the fact that Hubert was still looking at him with a kind smile, sent Charlie into a brief state of bewilderment.

Hubert watched Charlie grab one of the five ice cream scoopers from a glass container filled with warm water. Charlie then grabbed a waffle cone before making his way to the far end of the ice cream freezer. He carefully placed two large scoops of chocolate chip cookie dough ice cream in the waffle cone.

Charlie was unaware the police were actively looking for Hubert, and he was especially unaware that Hubert Houston had just experienced a coming-to-Jesus moment. An awakening so powerful, it broke him out of the mold he had spent his entire adult life stuck in.

Charlie handed Hubert his ice cream cone. "Thank you very much, Charlie," Hubert said as he put a hundred-dollar bill on the counter. "Keep the change."

"Thank you, Mr. Houston."

"Please, call me Hugh."

Hubert looked around the iconic shop as Charlie opened up the register. He put in the hundred-dollar bill and grabbed four twenty-dollar bills, a ten-dollar bill and three singles. He quickly stuffed the bills in his front pocket before shutting the cash register.

"Did you know that the average American eats forty-eight pints of ice cream every year?"

"No, I didn't," Charlie said just before flashing a relaxed smile. "That seems like a lot."

"I used to work here when I was your age. I would bug the heck out of Marge with all my questions."

Charlie looked a tad uneasy as he watched Hubert take a lick from his cone. He was obviously in a talkative mood, but Charlie didn't have anything to say. What does a sixteen-year-old boy say to a middle-aged man who had been nothing but an asshole to him?

Hubert licked his cone a few more times before regarding Charlie. "You know something, Charlie, I owe you an apology."

Charlie looked very uncomfortable now. He bit the bottom of his lip and lowered his eyes for a few seconds before finding the courage to look Hubert in the eyes. "I was like you when I was your age, Charlie. Hardworking, kind, and courteous. I felt joy in seeing other people happy."

Charlie didn't bother to try and hide his surprised look. Getting the sense that Hubert had more to share, Charlie reached for the stool by the cash register and sat directly across from Hubert.

"You know, I used to be a lot like my mother. A good person with a kind heart."

Charlie looked more relaxed now. "What did you want to be when you were my age?"

The question caught Hubert off guard, but he still smiled at Charlie. He didn't have to think long before he leaned forward a bit and rested his scraped elbows on the counter. "I loved math at an early age. Never cared about money until I was older, but always cared about math. I was living my dream as a math professor in upstate New York. I loved everyone in the math department. I had an amazing girlfriend, I liked the area a lot, and I liked that I pissed off my dad by not going to work for him. He was a wealthy entrepreneur, who expected me to run some of his companies when I got out of school. But I didn't respect my dad, and had no intention of working for him."

Charlie looked interested and kept his eyes focused on Hubert.

"My only real ambition was to chair the math department, but out of the blue, a guy I'd never met showed up in my office late one evening and offered me five-hundred-thousand dollars a year, plus bonuses, if I would join his new hedge fund. I never imaged living in New York City and making that much money. So I took the job, with the belief I'd do it for a year, two tops, then go back to teaching. But that never happened. The allure of wealth turned into a constant craving. Pretty soon, all I cared about was finding new ways to make more money."

Hubert sat up straight in his seat as he let out a long sigh. He was starting to become emotional, and for the first time in a long time, he was comfortable conveying his true feelings.

"Let me ask you something, Charlie. Would you rather be the world's greatest lover, but have everyone think you're the world's worst lover? Or would you rather be the world's worst lover, but have everyone think you're the world's greatest lover?"

Charlie was clearly surprised by the question. After a few seconds he looked at Hubert and said with confidence, "I'd rather be the world's greatest lover, but have everyone think that I was the world's worst."

Clearly proud of Charlie, Hubert was beaming with joy. "You have an inner scorecard, Charlie. That's a very important thing to have. Means you're the only one who can define your success. Never compromise your standards or beliefs. That way you'll live a very satisfying life and have the chance to help others along the way. Don't ever sell out, Charlie. Not for money. Not for admiration."

Charlie was clearly moved by Hubert's advice. He nodded and smiled at Hubert, who was becoming more emotional.

"Once I threw my inner scorecard away, I no longer lived the life I wanted to live. There's nothing worse than being addicted to money," Hubert said. He looked around the ice cream shop for a moment before his eyes landed back on Charlie. "I would've been a very happy man had I stayed a teacher."

Charlie nodded slowly, trying his best to convey some sympathy.

"I made terrible mistakes, and now I'm going to spend the rest of my life trying to pay off my debts to society. But you, Charlie, are going to be a great success. Based on your own scorecard, and nobody else's."

Charlie's kind eyes continued to regard Hubert. The words had sunk in, and Charlie felt good about his bright future. Most people only get to have a few life-changing conversations during their lifetime...Charlie knew he had just experienced one of them.

32

"You lost your phone in the woods?" Duane asked, clearly dumbfounded. "You really expect us to believe that bullshit?"

Randy was staring down Stan. "You son of a bitch! Houston threw a steak knife at my head!"

"Guys, I'm sorry, but Lisa insisted on having a quickie before Mass on the grass. So we stopped off in the woods for a bit. When I saw Hubert abruptly drive off, I reached for my phone and that's when I realized I lost it in the woods."

Randy clearly did not believe him. "You had a quickie before Mass on the grass?"

"Yeah."

"Why didn't you use Lisa's phone?" Duane asked.

"She left it at home."

Duane and Randy exchanged a frustrated look. Duane then walked over to the small beer fridge in Stan's messy home office.

"Hey, mission accomplished. You guys fucking did it! Time to put your swords away, cause we got some celebrating to do," Stan said.

Duane shut the small beer fridge and handed Randy a beer before sitting back down on the leather sofa. Randy was sitting at the other end of the sofa, and in between them was the duffel bag. "You know what really burns my ass?" Duane asked as he cracked open his beer.

"What's that?" Randy asked.

"The WDPD will get all the credit for bringing down Hubert and Denise's blackmail operation. But no one will ever know that they don't make that collar without our gutsy effort," Duane said. "It took a lot of balls to do what we did...a lot of balls."

"Yeah, it did," Randy said, nodding.

"What are you going to do?" Stan asked. "Hold a press conference and tell everyone that you convinced your ex-fiancé to cut the power in Houston's house so you guys could break in and find the evidence that proves Hubert and Denise were blackmailing Randy, and many other people?"

Duane glanced sheepishly at Stan. "It would be nice to get some recognition for our heroic work, that's all. Maybe you've already forgotten, but Houston pointed his machine gun at me. Not you, me. I'm the one who disarmed that mother fucker and I'm the one who led us to safety."

Randy just thought of something. "Duane, where's the red journal?"

"I left it on the bed in the guest room. Don't worry, I ripped out the page that mentioned you. It's in the duffel bag."

Randy zipped opened the duffel bag and looked relieved as he pulled out a crumpled up piece of paper from the journal. Stan rubbed his forehead anxiously before shooting a concerned look at Duane. "I feel like you should be more worried about getting arrested for breaking into Houston's house. The guy caught you two in his house after you destroyed it."

Duane shook his head and rolled his eyes before looking at Stan. "The cameras were still off and we were wearing gloves so no fingerprints. It's that dirtbag's word against ours," Duane said. "Right, counselor?"

"That's right."

"What's your alibi?"

"We were both in the Venetian Night golf cart parade," Duane said.

"Multiple witnesses can confirm that," Randy said.

Stan's eyes narrowed as he looked at Duane then Randy. "How do you plan on getting the bag of flash drives to O'Malley without raising any suspicion?"

Duane patted the bag while looking at Randy. "Well, now that we've removed the flash drive containing videos of Denise having her way with Randy, I'm going to place this bag into a shipping box and head down to the post office first thing tomorrow morning. O'Malley will receive the package, with no return address of course, and have all the evidence necessary to put away Houston and Denise for a good long while."

Duane and Randy exchanged nods of approval as Stan couldn't help but look impressed. "You boys did good," Stan said. "Real good."

"Oh, here's a fun rumor I just heard. Before Houston stuck his gun in my face for the second time in one night, I was dancing with Sandy on the float. She said that Sir Branch Bradford was spotted having a drink at the bar in the Landmark Inn last night," Duane said.

Randy looked at Duane in disbelief. "The knighted billionaire environmentalist, who happens to own a space company, was drinking at the Landmark Inn last night?"

"That's right."

"Did Sandy actually see Sir Branch having a drink at the Landmark?"

Duane hesitated before he said, "No, but she's been enjoying a summer romance with the Landmark's head bartender, Billy Gunther. Sandy said that Billy talked to Branch for like an hour. Apparently, he's a helluva nice guy."

Stan looked very interested in this wild rumor. "Maybe he read my email," Stan said.

"What email?" Randy asked.

"I emailed Branch Bradford and pitched him my idea for conserving the 5,000 acres. I urged him to develop part of the property into a summer camp for kids struggling with serious health issues and physical disadvantages. It would be just like the Hole in the Wall Gang Camp Paul Newman started." Stan said.

Randy and Duane both looked excited. Thinking it was somewhat plausible that Sir Branch Bradford received and personally read Stan's email.

"I actually wrote him a letter as well. I sent the letter first, then followed it up with a heartfelt email. I mean, who gets letters in the mail these days?" Stan asked. "Who knows? Maybe he was excited to get a letter in the mail and actually read my pitch."

Duane nodded as he regarded Stan. "Hey, stranger things have happened. Like you getting a handjob from a world renowned climate scientist."

Stan looked defensive. "Attempted hand job."

Lisa, wearing a white silk robe, was lying on the king-size bed in the master bedroom staring aimlessly at the television hanging on the wall over the fireplace. She had a glass of red wine in her left hand and the remote control in her right hand. Lisa sighed in frustration as she scanned through all the different Netflix categories: *Totally Awesome 80s, TV Shows, Trending Now,*

Lisa reacted to her phone vibrating on the nightstand. She smiled, thinking it might be Stan, but frowned when she saw Deacon Terry's name show up on the caller ID. She dropped the remote control and pressed the "accept" icon on her phone before hitting the "speaker" icon.

"Hello."

Deacon Terry's slurred voice came over the speaker. "Lisa...Lisa, it's Terry."

"Everything okay, Terry?"

"No, everything is so not okay. I think I took one too many shroom gummies, and now I'm having an emotional breakdown."

"Where did you get shroom gummies?"

A long pause before Terry said, "Fr. Carey."

"Why don't you just try lying down?"

"I tried that, but it felt like I was falling out of a hot air balloon. I'm really messed up, Lisa. I need your help."

"Well, since Fr. Carey supplied you with the illegal drugs, why don't you call him?"

"I tried. He's not picking up. He's probably passed out in his hammock. Please, Lisa, I need your help. There's a lot of weapons in the house and I don't trust myself right now."

Lisa closed her eyes and tilted her head back until it touched the head board. It was moments like this one that made her wish she wasn't raised to be a good Catholic girl. She was always willing to assist others in need, regardless of the situation. Her parents were strict Catholics but didn't embrace charity. They never once volunteered to help out the community or those less fortunate. They liked to talk about what good Catholics they were, they bragged how they were daily Mass goers, but it was their oldest daughter who actually grew up believing that it was important to help others without expecting anything in return.

Fr. Carey was laying in his hammock in the backyard of the church rectory. He had his cell phone pressed to his ear. "Hey, Terry, call me back when you get this. Talked to my brother and he really messed up. Normally, the red shroom gummies he makes are the least potent, and the green and blue gummies are extremely potent. But for some reason with this batch he made the red gummies extremely potent. So if you take a red gummy, make sure you only take half of one. If you take anymore than that, call me and I'll come over with some homemade cherry juice so you can piss that stuff out quicker."

Lisa walked into Terry's kitchen but stopped abruptly. She couldn't believe her eyes. Deacon Terry was lying naked on the wood floor in considerable pain. "Oh, for God's sake, Terry. You're a Deacon!"

"Oh, thank you for coming, Lisa. My little prayer has been answered."

"Terry, why are you lying naked on your kitchen floor with a half-chub?"

"It's the shrooms. They're dangerously potent. I was shaking my martini and I slipped. I must have dropped some ice cubes on the floor."

"But why are you naked?"

"I had know idea I was naked until just now. I'm sorry, but this is the heaviest dose of shrooms I've ever been on."

Lisa looked overwhelmed, having no idea what to do. "Why don't we just call Fr. Carey?"

"No! Please, just help me up. If I can get to the couch in the living room I'll be okay."

Lisa closed her eyes and somehow convinced herself to stay and help. She bent down and grabbed Terry's hand. Lisa kept her eyes firmly on Terry's eyes as she helped him back to his feet. As soon as he proved he could stand on his own, Lisa hurried over to the sink and washed her hands.

"Oh, my God, thank you so much, Lisa. Our Lord sent me an angel tonight...and that angel is you."

Lisa's discomfort was growing, not unlike Deacon Terry's erection.

"Can you please pour me a martini, Lisa?"

"No. I'm leaving."

"Please. The gin helps to neutralize the hallucinogens."

Lisa sighed then blurted out, "Okay, but then I'm leaving. Go into the living and lay down. When I come into the room, you better have a blanket over you."

"Bless you."

Lisa started making the martini in the kitchen while Terry walked into the living room. He sat down on the red velvet couch and stared at the vase on the coffee table. The vase was filled with white roses he bought two days ago. Terry's eyes drifted down until he was staring at his penis, which was no longer erect. But he didn't see his penis, instead he saw an unstable Jenga tower that was about to fall. Deacon Terry was on the verge of great emotion. He started thinking about the last time he had a nice evening with his ex-wife, Vanessa. They were at their neighbors' house for game night. It was a cold January night and they played Jenga until one in the morning. Terry and Vanessa had had an open marriage for two years, but Terry didn't like the fact that she kept changing the rules they created together. Rule number one: no sleeping with anyone who lived within a sixty mile radius of their house. But Vanessa had modified that rule twice—along with nearly every other rule— and when Terry found out that Vanessa was sleeping with his close friend and next door neighbor, Lee Hornsby, he asked for a divorce. Twenty-four hours after the divorce was final, Terry decided to become a deacon. Prior to working with Fr. Carey, he had never tried magic mushrooms before.

Lisa entered the living room with a martini in her right hand and yelled, "I told you to cover up!"

"I'm sorry, but I don't have any good blankets. My ex-wife got them all in the divorce."

Lisa carefully handed the martini glass to Terry, whose emotions had gotten the best of him. Tears were now rolling down his rosy cheeks. "Thank you so much, Lisa." He took a big sip and then muttered, "Oh, good, good, good, good. Oh, that is darn good."

Terry set the martini glass on the coffee table as he regarded Lisa.

"Hope that helps," Lisa said.

"You are so perfect, Lisa. I've been in love with you before I even met you," Terry said as the tears continued down his cheeks.

"Terry, you're tripping so hard right now, your balls might fall off. Finish your martini and go to bed."

"Love is love, Lisa. No matter how altered your state of consciousness is, love is one long trip, and when I come down from this trip I will still be tripping all over you."

"I'm in love with my husband, and I always will be. When your trip is over, I will remind you again that I'm madly in love with my husband. And if you so much as wave at me, I'll tell

Stan, who in addition to having issues with jealously also has issues with rage."

"Lisa, God wants us to be together."

"Jesus Christ! What the fuck is going on here?"

The wind was knocked out of Lisa as she turned around to find Denise standing in the living room with a gun in her right hand.

"Oh my God, Denise, what are you doing here?" Lisa asked.

"What am I doing here? What are you doing here? About to cheat on your husband with a drunk deacon?"

"No! God, no! Terry's going through a bad trip and I'm just making sure he doesn't hurt himself."

Terry stood up, pulled a basket out from under the end table, and grabbed a blanket. Lisa looked upset. "You said you didn't have any blankets."

"No, I said I didn't have any good blankets," Terry said as he draped the blanket over his skinny shoulders. "Denise, I think I know why you're here. Although I'm flattered, I'm not emotionally stable to have a threesome right now. But I'd be happy to take a raincheck."

Denise, full of aggression, walked over to Terry and pointed the gun at his chest.

"Denise, please, as much as I want to, I don't think I'm capable."

"What did you tell Alcocks?"

A puzzled look crossed Terry's face. "I have absolutely no idea what you're talking about?"

"Denise, he's on a heavy dose of shroom gummies. He doesn't know what he's saying."

"Bullshit! I've tripped on magic mushrooms on more than one occasion. He knows what I'm asking him."

Deacon Terry stared at Denise, who kept the gun pointed at his chest. He took a deep breath and nodded. "You win, Denise. I'll have a threesome with you and Lisa, but you have to promise you won't tell Stan."

Denise shook her head in disbelief.

"See, he's really messed up," Lisa said.

Denise clenched her jaw while looking Terry in the eyes. "I know it was you who called me to say you found my orange Nike shoebox."

Terry, clearly confused, put his hands on his hips and said, "What are you talking about?"

"Don't fuck with me, Deacon Terry! I know it was you."

"You must be trippin' worse than I am, Denise. I don't know anything about an orange Nike shoebox. And for the record, I only wear Avias."

"How do you know it was Terry who called you?"

Denise shot Lisa an intimidating look before quickly moving her intense eyes back to Terry.

"I received a call from an unknown number weeks ago from a guy who told me to meet him in the crime section at the library because he said, quote, 'I know what you did.' So, I showed up to the library to find Terry in that section."

"Wait a second, Fr. Carey was also in that section. Maybe he called you?"

Denise looked sure of herself. "No, the caller had a distinctively deep, slightly hoarse voice, just like you. Then just a few days ago, I received another blocked call from someone saying they found my shoebox."

"Denise, I swear to God, I'm not the one who called you."

Denise lowered her gun as she took a step toward Terry. "I saw you talking with Alcocks at that park down in Gwinn. It looked like you two were having a deep conversation."

Terry looked uneasy as he let out a deep sigh. "I was giving Officer Alcocks spiritual advice. He comes to me once a month for marriage counseling. You see, he's thinking about leaving his wife and I've been trying to convince him not to."

"That is total bullshit, Lutterbach! I've tried to seduce Alcocks on more than one occasion and he's always turned me down cold. He's got a gorgeous wife who knows how to take care of her man. There's no fucking way he's thinking of leaving Maria," Denise said.

Terry closed his eyes as Denise aimed the gun at his face. He started to cry uncontrollably. He finally said, "About six months ago, Chief O'Malley pulled me over for speeding. I was a little tipsy. Long story short, he found mushroom capsules and shroom gummies in a bag in my trunk. Instead of going to jail for possession, I offered to plant a bug in the confessional at church."

Denise and Lisa both looked shocked. Lisa stared at Terry with her mouth wide open and said, "Oh, my God. How could you do that?"

Denise had a faraway look while trying to comprehend all the different confessions recorded over the past six months. Knowing that some of the confessions recorded likely revealed to Fr. Carey, and any cop listening to the bug, that she had been blackmailing certain individuals with her sex tapes.

"It was the only thing I could think of to stay out of jail and avoid seeing my rep destroyed. I'm not only a deacon, I'm also a well-respected businessman."

Denise was full of rage. Her eyes were wide and her nostrils flared as she pressed the barrel of the gun against Terry's head.

"Please, Denise, I'm begging you...don't do it. I'll give you whatever you want."

"I want my fucking shoebox back!"

"I don't have your shoebox! I swear to God!"

Fr. Carey burst into the living room with his gun pointed at Denise. "Drop the gun, Denise!"

Denise looked just as surprised as Terry and Lisa, but she didn't lower the gun.

"I will shoot you, Denise, if you don't drop the gun!"

Terry started to cry again as he clutched the blanket. Lisa glanced at Fr. Carey then stared at Denise. "Please, Denise, drop the gun," Lisa said gently.

Denise lowered her right hand very slowly then tossed the gun on the couch. Fr. Carey moved quickly toward Denise. He put his gun in the holster then slapped handcuffs around Denise's wrist. Everyone in the room looked more surprised by the handcuffs than the gun. Fr. Carey started to read Denise her rights. In a state of bewilderment, Denise said, "What the fuck are you doing, weirdo?"

"Wait a second," Lisa said. "You're a cop?"

Fr. Carey finished the Miranda warning before regarding Lisa.

"I'm a special reserve deputy with the Marquette County Sheriff's Office. For the past four years I've been working with the undercover ops team. Before that I worked closely with the K-9 unit."

"So you're not a priest?"

"I've be an ordained priest for nineteen years, and a special reserve deputy for sixteen years. Who says you can't be great at two things?"

Lisa was overwhelmed with shock. Terry looked serious as he stared at Fr. Carey. "Can deacon's be reserve deputies too?"

Lisa, stuck in a state of bewilderment, had to blink her eyes a few times before she regarded Fr. Carey. "Let me get this straight—you're a priest, a special reserve deputy with the Sheriff's Office, and a magic mushroom dealer?"

Fr. Carey smiled as he shook his head repeatedly. "No, no, no, no...my brother's the dealer. He grows and sells high quality magic mushroom products to the overworked, stressed out parents in the area. I just provide protection. In return, I get a kickback, all of which is donated to the church."

Denise seemed to be just as bewildered as Lisa.

"By the way, Terry, did you listen to your voicemail?" Fr. Carey asked.

"No."

"Just listen to your voicemail then delete it."

Fr. Carey started to lead Denise out of the living room. "Guys, I'd love to rap with you, but Denise has some questions to answer."

33

Denise looked calm sitting in the uncomfortable metal chair. She was sitting up perfectly straight, her elbows at her side, her right hand atop her left hand on the metal table. There was absolutely no fear in her eyes as she stared at Chief O'Malley, who was sitting directly across from her. Alcocks, wearing a neck brace, stood in the corner with his arms folded. On the table in front of O'Malley was a blue pen, a yellow legal pad, and a full cup of coffee.

"What happened to your neck?" Denise asked in a concerned voice. Alcocks kept his lips pressed together while staring at Denise.

"Officer Alcocks and I were in high pursuit of your business partner and fuck buddy, Hubert Houston. I lost control of the vehicle and we rolled down the side of a dune. A few seconds later, I crashed into a bunker. Somehow, I walked away without a scratch, but Officer Alcocks injured his neck pretty badly."

"My partner?"

"We'll get to that in a minute. Can I get you a cup of coffee?"

"I don't drink coffee. I drink tea."

"Would you like a cup of tea then?"

"No, thank you."

Denise watched O'Malley sip his coffee. "Let's start with this question, Denise," Alcocks said.

"No, let's start with this question. Why am I sitting in an interrogation room in the Whisper Dunes police station? I was arrested by a Marquette County Sheriff's Deputy, albeit a reserve deputy who moonlights as a priest."

"That's a good question," O'Malley said.

O'Malley set his clasped hands on the metal table and leaned forward. His instinctive interrogation style, conveying patience by using a gentle voice, was developed during his last few years as a homicide detective in Detroit. O'Malley's natural interrogation style was very combative during most of his years on the police force. But after his wife and their two young children moved out of the house, he considered therapy, but ultimately rejected the idea. Instead, he started driving to Bloomfield Hills twice a week to attend anger management classes in a church basement. Eventually, O'Malley embraced a much softer, gentler communication style, not just with his wife and kids, but with criminals as well.

"I issued a warrant for your arrest about two hours ago."

"Now, why would you do that?"

"Earlier today we got a warrant to search your apartment," O'Malley said in a gentle tone. "The only thing I discovered is that you like to write. In fact, I read through several of your notebooks. You're a fine writer, Denise."

"How sweet of you to say."

O'Malley regarded Denise for a good ten seconds before he said, "Hubert Houston was arrested a few hours ago. We had probable cause to search his house, and during the search we discovered a red leather-bound journal in one of the bedrooms."

Denise suddenly felt queasy. But her face was without expression as she kept her eyes on O'Malley.

With his arms still folded, Alcocks took a step toward Denise and said, "Based on the information in the red journal, you have slept with a lot of men."

Denise flashed her sexy smile that she had been perfecting since her college days. "We're not in a despicable country where women don't have rights. We're in America. And I'm a proud American girl, who can happily fuck whoever I want to, whenever I want to."

O'Malley smiled uncomfortably. "That's true. But you committed a serious crime when you decided to blackmail all the people you were having sex with by forcing them to invest their money into Houston's hedge fund."

Denise pursed her lips together while deciding what to say next.

"When did you begin your partnership with Hubert Houston?" O'Malley asked.

Denise licked the corner of her lip as she glanced at Alcocks. "Make me a cup of green tea, would you, sweetie?"

O'Malley looked at Alcocks before moving his eyes back to Denise. "Two officers must be in the room at all times during an interrogation. Alcocks, text Gary and tell him to make a cup of green tea."

Alcocks whipped out his phone and sent the text.

Denise stared at O'Malley for a moment. "Did you know that Fr. Carey was a reserve deputy with the County Sheriff's Office? Frankly, I still don't believe it."

"No, I did not," O'Malley said. "Apparently, he's been working undercover for a few years. Fr. Carey did tell us that he headed over to Deacon Terry's house to return a book he had borrowed and found you in the living room pointing a gun at Terry."

"Fr. Carey also said that Lisa Zbikowski was in the living room with you and Lutterbach," Alcocks said. "Why was she there?"

Denise shrugged her shoulders. Her eyes darted from O'Malley to Alcocks and back to O'Malley. "Deacon Terry confessed that he put a recording device under the kneeler in the church confessional room. How long have you guys been listening in on people's confessions?"

O'Malley and Alcocks both looked surprised. "What the hell are you talking about? We don't know anything about a recording device in the confessional room," O'Malley said.

"Was Deacon Terry tripping on shrooms when he said this?" Alcocks asked.

Denise nodded. "Yes, he was."

"I pulled that nut-job over about six months ago. He was messed up on shrooms. He also had a gun in the front seat. As I was arresting him he told me he would put a recording device under the kneeler in the confessional if I let him go. Shortly after I arrested Deacon Terry, I told Fr. Carey that he should fire his ass. But he gave me the same load of bullshit he always does, 'Hate the sin, not the sinner.' I'm pretty certain Deacon Terry has something on Fr. Carey. What? I have no idea."

Denise looked more relaxed now. She took a deep breath through her nose and exhaled slowly as she leaned back in her chair. "I will tell you nothing but the truth...even though you won't be able to use it in court."

O'Malley and Alcocks both looked confused.

"My attorney is in the air right now. When he arrives he'll confirm everything I'm about to tell you."

O'Malley took a long sip from his coffee then picked up his pen. With his elbows resting on the metal table, his eyes started to narrow. He could sense that Denise was relaxed and at peace with the idea of telling the truth.

"I met Hubert Houston when we were both living in Manhattan."

"Kansas?" Alcocks asked.

"New York City."

"Ah," Alcocks said with a grin.

"We dated casually and connected over the fact that neither of us believed in a monogamous relationship. We also connected over our love for the Upper Peninsula. Hubert was born and raised in Whisper Dunes, and when I was younger I would visit my grandparents in the summer, who lived just north of Whisper Dunes."

Denise watched O'Malley jot down a few notes.

"About a year after Hubert moved back to Whisper Dunes to start his own hedge fund, I quit my job and moved here."

"What did you do in New York?" O'Malley asked.

Everyone reacted to the knock at the door.

"Come in," O'Malley said.

Officer Soller entered holding a cup of green tea and placed it in front of Denise. "Need some honey, or are you sweet enough?" Soller asked.

Denise kept her gaze on O'Malley. "I'm sweet enough."

Soller quickly exited the room but didn't close the door all way. Alcocks walked over to the door and made sure it was securely shut.

Denise regarded O'Malley with her beautiful blue eyes and said softly, "I worked for the CIA."

Alcocks laughed out loud but stopped when he saw that O'Malley was keeping a straight face.

"I was a special agent tasked with collecting highly sensitive information from powerful men. Information that could be weaponized by the CIA to compromise their power."

O'Malley actually looked concerned as he watched Denise sip her tea.

"Before he moved back to Whisper Dunes, Hubert was an analyst for one of the largest hedge funds in the world. Some powerful people at the S.E.C. were concerned that the hedge fund was another giant Ponzi scheme, so my handlers at the CIA ordered me to find out what I could. I targeted a couple guys at the firm, including Hubert. I only had to sleep with him twice before he started sharing highly sensitive financial information with me. I've fucked a lot of men, and yet I've always been amazed how easy it is to get information from them after they've blown their load all over me. They're more talkative than a woman on the night she gets engaged. They'll answer any of my questions in explicit detail. Well, at least that's been my experience."

O'Malley and Alcocks were both at a loss for words. Alcocks kept his wide eyes fixed on Denise as he sat down in the chair next to O'Malley. Denise remained confidently upright in her chair. She glanced at Alcocks before focusing her eyes back on O'Malley. "Hubert didn't know I was a CIA agent until after he moved back to Whisper Dunes. When I told him who I was, for some reason, he didn't get angry with me. I think he was impressed with himself that he was sleeping with a high-ranking CIA agent. Then when I told him I was having serious financial problems, he urged me to move to Whisper Dunes. It wasn't until after I moved here that he told me he was struggling to raise money to start his hedge fund."

"Why were you having money problems?" O'Malley asked.

Denise looked at her cup of tea before taking a sip. She regarded O'Malley. "I was no longer with the CIA. For the first time since I was twenty, I wasn't taking orders from anyone. I moved to St. Barts and partied for a few months then got really bored. I download a few trading apps and started trading stocks to fill the lonely days. I ended up loosing my life savings. I was broke so I pitched Hubert on a partnership. He agreed, and I started targeting wealthy guys to seduce and blackmail. It didn't take me long before I raised a quarter of a billion dollars for his fund. I thought things were going well until Hubert told me he made a couple bad trades and the fund was in big trouble. Then one night, Hubert showed up to my apartment and told me about a few people who were standing in the way of his land deal with Space D."

Denise took a breath and sipped her tea. She looked eager to keep talking, as if it was therapeutic for her. "Hubert told me he received an offer for the land. One hundred million. He advanced me half a million and I was set to receive nine point five million once the deal closed. Considering his hedge fund was on the brink of collapse, he was desperate to make the deal happen."

"Is that why you guys whacked Lenny, because he was going to fuck up your deal with Space D?" Alcocks asked.

The calmness dissipated from Denise's face. She thought about Lenny for a moment. Thinking he'd still be alive had he not discovered the shoebox. "No. He was in my apartment while I was away. As you already know, Stan sent him over to replace the shower head. I have no idea how he stumbled upon my secret hiding place, but he found something he shouldn't have under the floorboards."

O'Malley tried hard to conceal his surprise. His eyes narrowed as he said, "What did he find?"

"Flash drives of me in action with most of Hubert's hedge-fund clients...and a manuscript. He told me I would have to pay him a hundred grand if I wanted the flash drives and manuscript back. I told Hubert and he agreed to pay the fee, but when I showed up at the drive-in-movie theatre to make the exchange he was a no show."

O'Malley shared a look with Alcocks before his eyes landed back on Denise. "We believe that someone lured Lenny to the Potawatomi clubhouse with a bogus emergency plumbing call. Once Lenny stepped into the mechanical room he was shot in the head from behind," O'Malley said. "That wasn't you who shot him in the back of the head?"

Denise looked a bit tense as she regarded O'Malley. "I had nothing to do with Lenny's murder, and neither did Hubert."

O'Malley stared at Denise with a blank face. "Then who killed Lenny?"

Denise had a faraway look. She didn't have to answer the question, she thought, but decided she would. Alcocks nervously bit his lower lip as he watched Denise casually cross her long legs. She looked at O'Malley and said, "A CIA assassin."

Alcocks looked upset as he leaned back in his chair. "You're fucking with us, aren't you?"

Denise shook her head. O'Malley looked up at the ceiling in a state of disbelief. He waited until his face was stripped of any emotion before he locked eyes with Denise. "Now, why would a CIA assassin want to kill a thrice divorced, unlicensed plumber?"

Denise closed her eyes for a few seconds as she considered how to proceed.

"Please understand, I cannot be prosecuted for any crime in the United States of America for the rest of my natural life," Denise said in a confident tone. "So I'll tell you what you want to know."

O'Malley and Alcocks looked bewildered as they glanced at each other. O'Malley slowly scratched his chin as he stared at Denise.

"Let me go back a little bit. I was a junior at the University of Penn when I was approached by two CIA agents one rainy fall afternoon. I was majoring in French Poetry and had just begun a little fling with my professor, who unbeknownst to me was a Russian spy."

O'Malley's eyes got wide with amazement. He didn't want to believe Denise, but he did.

"The CIA offered me fifty grand if I continued on with my relationship with Boris for the next few semesters. I agreed. After I was able to obtain and deliver to the CIA the sensitive information they needed, they were eager to inculcate the principles of sexpionage on me. To the CIA, I was the perfect recruit. In addition to my inimitable ability to get a man to open up to me in bed, I was intelligent, I came from a broken home, and my Dad was a con-man, which is to say I understood the full scope of human behavior."

O'Malley and Alcocks were both completely mesmerized. They looked like two kids sitting around a campfire listening to a ghost story they didn't want to end.

"Two months after my graduation from Penn I entered the CIA's White Swallow program."

Confused, Alcocks blurted out, "White Swallow program...what the hell's that?"

"A top secret sexpionage training program started during the Nixon era. When a target is too sophisticated to be hacked remotely, the CIA sends in a White Swallow agent. We're not assassins, we're seductresses."

Denise finished her tea before glancing at Alcocks, whose cheeks were red. O'Malley looked to be biting the inside of his cheek to keep his stoic look.

"I focused on physical-access operations, designed for individual targets. For eight years, I was the best honey pot in the CIA. I wielded my pussy like James Bond wielded his Walther P99."

Alcocks looked uneasy as he leaned back in his chair.

"I became so valuable to the CIA that they gave me unlimited access to a Gulfstream G650. I had apartments in New York, D.C., London, Paris, and Zurich. A dozen CIA issued credit cards. I once spent over four-hundred-thousand dollars on a long weekend in Paris."

O'Malley let out a whistle and said, "A real *bon vivant*."

"You bet your ass I was. Obscenely wealthy, powerful men would do anything to spend the night with me. It's not just about looks. They love the idea of going to bed with a self-made woman. Once we finished fucking, all they wanted to do was talk business and gossip about all the privileged information they had access to. Never once did I have to drug a target. That's how good I was."

O'Malley kept his eyes on Denise as he sipped his coffee. Meanwhile, Alcocks was forced to move awkwardly in his chair as he casually adjusted himself.

"So, you were trained by the CIA to collect highly sensitive information on powerful government and business leaders, both foreign and domestic," O'Malley said. "Which means..."

"I have incriminating information on some of the most powerful and wealthiest men in the world. According the CIA's top brass, I created the best dossiers they ever read."

O'Malley looked like he wanted to say something but decided to stay quiet. It was clear to him that Denise had more to reveal.

"World leaders, powerful business leaders, billionaires...they are always looking for ways to expand their portfolio of power. My mission was always the same—find out which power players were trying to expand their power and why. If I learned one thing during my CIA tenure, it's that money always defies morality."

O'Malley and Alcocks remained highly intrigued as they nodded.

"Let me say this in defense of the White Swallow program, and all the CIA agents who put their lives in constant danger. The United States government gives the financial services industry hundreds of billions of dollars each year. The vital information collected by agents like myself gives our government some much needed leverage over the sociopaths who control the financial institutions in America and abroad."

"Can you share any secrets with us?" O'Malley asked, not actually expecting Denise to reveal any top secrets.

"Let's see," Denise said as she glanced up at the ceiling before regarding O'Malley. "A number of global accounting firms have developed a system that allows them to hide massive corporate losses. Oh, and most of the CEOs at every major bank in the US have been blackmailed by a group of private equity firms. Under the direction of the private equity funds, the banks continue to create a massive credit bubble, which will eventually pop and lead to another great recession. The billionaire oligarchs will then start to buy up as many properties as they can. When the economy starts to get better only rich people will be able to afford to buy a home."

O'Malley didn't show any emotion, but Alcocks looked like he wanted to slam his fist on the metal table. He muttered, "I fucking hate billionaires."

"That's really all I can talk about. Everything else I know is highly classified."

O'Malley looked almost sympathetic as he stared at Denise. "Why did you leave the CIA?"

"When you're a spy, they teach you how to lie and cover up your tracks. Eventually, you run the risk of being too good at your job. Once that happens, your bosses stop trusting you. After they investigated and cleared me of being a double agent, they gave me a bullshit desk job for six months while figuring out my next list of targets. I was bored out of my mind so I started writing a roman à clef novel. Eventually, one of my bosses found out about the book and asked me to resign. So I did. They gave me a nice pension and total immunity from being prosecuted of any crime in the United States, which is a nice perk."

O'Malley stared at Denise for what seemed like a minute. He finally said, "You're Weslie Addle."

Denise no longer looked at ease. Her body stiffened and she didn't breathe for at least ten seconds. Her gaze finally met O'Malley's. Not knowing what to say, she nervously licked her lips and took a deep breath.

"I read your manuscript. Incredible story. Especially considering its a roman à clef. I was blushing for most of the book, but I couldn't put it down. They say write what you know, and you clearly took that advice to heart. Wow. Those chapters set in the Caribbean, specifically all the action happening on that Swiss banker's yacht. Holy cow. Did all of that actually happen?"

Denise looked incredibly tense. She lowered her elbows on the table and leaned forward. "How did you get your hands on my manuscript?"

O'Malley glanced at Alcocks, who was clearly staring at Denise's cleavage. O'Malley calmly leaned back in his chair and folded his arms. "An orange Nike shoebox containing your manuscript, *French Poetry Majors Make The Best Spies*, was discovered in Lenny's fishing cabin."

Denise looked furious, wondering how her handlers at the CIA did not know about Lenny's secret cabin. She closed her eyes for a few seconds, and when she opened them she said, "Lenny stole the shoebox containing my manuscript from my apartment. In an effort to be extra secretive, I wrote the manuscript on a typewriter. My lawyer has a copy and I have a copy of the most recent draft."

O'Malley and Alcocks both looked uneasy because they realized that Denise was no longer her cool, confident self.

"Beauty is a very reliable camouflage, one that deceives the beholder without offering much protection to the wearer," Denise said softly. "The CIA had no use for me anymore, and with the information I collected over the years they wouldn't mind at all if someone took me out."

O'Malley could see fear in Denise's eyes as she stared at him.

"That manuscript is what has been keeping me alive since I left the CIA. I have an understanding with my handlers that if something should happen to me, say I died mysteriously in my sleep, or the boat I was on exploded, or I was hit by a car while out for a jog, or I had a sudden heart attack while fucking someone in a sauna, my lawyer will submit the manuscript to all the major publishing houses in New York and London. A bidding war will break out and eventually my roman à clef will be published, but only in the event I meet an untimely death."

O'Malley and Alcocks remained quietly seated. Neither moved an inch as they continued staring at Denise. Alcocks had a blank expression, but O'Malley's eyes conveyed sympathy.

"Lenny realized what he had was valuable. He told me he would not return my manuscript until I convinced the CIA to give him ten million dollars. Trying to blackmail the CIA is always a bad idea."

"So you're telling us that a CIA assassin lured Lenny to the Potawatomi Country Club and murdered him?" Alcocks asked. "Then burned the place down? Then dumped his body in a nature preserve? Just because he stole your manuscript?"

"I'm not an assassin so I can't speak intelligently about the planning or mentality of a CIA assassin. After they took Lenny out, I was visited by a high-ranking CIA agent, who told me if the manuscript is discovered by anyone but me, more people will be taken out."

Alcocks looked at O'Malley, who lowered his head and rubbed the bridge of his nose. "How do we handle this situation?" O'Malley asked.

"Where's the manuscript now?"

"In my office. Considering it's evidence in a murder case, I was going to have it locked up in the evidence room after our interrogation ends, but I'm having second thoughts."

Denise took a deep breath in hopes of slowing down her racing mind. She then grabbed O'Malley's notepad and pen and wrote—*Return the manuscript to Lenny's cabin tonight. Give me the address and I'll pick it up. As far as you and Alcocks know, the manuscript doesn't exist.*

Denise slid the notepad back to O'Malley. He squinted his eyes as he read Denise's small handwriting. He looked at Denise and nodded. "Okay. But then I want you to leave Whisper Dunes. For everyone's sake, including yours."

Denise looked relaxed again. She grinned and said, "But I love living here. It's an absolute paradise for a nature lover like me. It's also a wonderful place to raise kids."

Alcocks looked confused. "You don't have any kids. Do you?"

"No, but I've always wanted to be a mom. Just need to find me a husband who doesn't ask a lot of questions. I don't know if I could pass for a traditional housewife, but I'd have fun pretending to be one."

O'Malley smiled slightly and said, "We are what we pretend to be, so we must be careful about what we pretend to be."

Denise smiled back. "Are you a Kurt Vonnegut fan, or do you just like quoting him?"

"I'm a fan."

"Me too," Denise said as she straightened up in her chair. "Being a good spy is not unlike being a good housewife. It all comes down to how well you can pretend."

O'Malley stared at Denise for a long moment. He finally said, "Why the pen name, Weslie Addle?"

"I grew up in West Seattle," Denise said.

"You've reached the end of the line in Whisper Dunes," O'Malley said. "Why don't you move back to West Seattle and start over?"

Denise's eyes closed for a few seconds before she took a long breath. She glanced at O'Malley before her eyes focused on the door, wondering what her life might be like back in West Seattle.

34

Russ stood on the concrete landing outside Town Hall, surrounded by two-dozen reporters and six men pointing cameras at him. The mayor had been ambushed so many times by reporters during the past three months, he'd developed a certain ease around the nosey reporters. Russ patiently regarded the reporter who had her microphone an inch from his lips.

"As much as the corporate media giants would love to see the people of Whisper Dunes turn against each other and become vindictive, that's not going to happen. The power-brokers back in LA and New York saw an opportunity to treat the town of Whisper Dunes like they treat America's political system and the NFL...like one big show, packed to the brim with drama, drama, and more drama. But the corporate media giants failed at turning Whisper Dunes into one big dramatic circus because they doubted the resolve and the integrity of the people who live here. You see, the folks who live in the Upper Peninsula haven't had their minds weakened and corrupted by social media companies. Up here, we're still a bunch of free-thinking humans who are grateful for our beautiful environment, and grateful for each other, despite our differences. And long before climate scientists became infatuated with the U.P. and long before the media showed up, every single person living up here already knew that Whisper Dunes was America's Best Place to Live."

Carol entered Russ's office holding a magazine in her right hand and a cup of coffee in her left hand. Russ sat behind his desk, looking disgruntled while reading a handwritten letter. A hundred sealed envelopes were on the desk, and on the floor in front of the desk were six cardboard boxes stuffed with envelopes.

"Looks like you're reading that one closely. Is it a nice letter or another death threat?"

Russ read from the letter, "'Only God Almighty can change the climate, you soulless bastard. I pray that a pit bull gnaws at your nutsack until you bleed to death. Have fun burning in hell.'" Russ looked at Carol. "She even signed her name. Bayou Betsy. Although I don't think that's her real name."

Carol set the coffee cup next to the other two cups on Russ's messy desk. She tried to keep a positive expression on her face while fishing through one of the letter boxes. She grabbed an eight-by-ten manilla envelope and handed it to Russ. "Here, I bet this is a nice one."

Russ couldn't hide the discouraged look on his face. "For some reason, any letter that comes out of an eight-by-ten manilla envelope is almost guaranteed to be a death threat."

Russ picked up the silver envelope-opener next to his coffee cup and opened up the manila envelope. He pulled out a handwritten letter and started to read. "'Dear Mayor Tillinghast, the Earth is not on fire, but your house will be soon...you communist fuck.'"

Carol gently patted Russ on the back as he dropped the letter into the trash bin. He leaned back in his chair and looked at Carol, who was dressed in an expensive light blue pants suit and wearing heavy makeup. "Well, as much as I don't agree with what they're saying, I'll vigorously defend their First Amendment right to say it."

Carol smiled as she handed Russ the magazine in her hand. It was the latest issue of *Forbes*. On the cover was Sir Branch Bradford. Russ squinted his eyes as he held the cover close to his face. In the cover photograph, Branch Bradford was standing near the edge of a sandstone cliff on Presque Isle Park. Behind him was Lake Superior, and to his right was a sandstone peninsula covered with pine trees. Near the bottom of the cover it read: *"Don't touch it." - Frederick Law Olmsted/Sir Branch Bradford.*

Russ was beyond amazed as he continued to stare at the cover. Carol looked happy, both for Russ and Whisper Dunes. "I brought you a fresh cup of Joe, now sit back and enjoy reading the article," Carol said.

"When did Sir Branch Bradford visit Whisper Dunes?"

"Not exactly sure. The article confirmed that he spent four days in Whisper Dunes inspecting the 5,000 acres. According to the article he's going to turn the land into a protected nature preserve, and start an international kids camp dedicated to providing an environment of healing and adventure for children with serious illnesses as well as kids growing up in poverty. It's modeled after The Hole in the Wall Gang Camp started by Paul Newman."

Russ's emotions got the best of him and tears began to run down his cheeks. He moved his eyes from the *Forbes* cover to Carol. "Well, that is just the greatest news I've ever heard."

A 2008 Sea Ray 28 Sundancer was anchored in Lake Superior, about a mile from Whisper Dunes' downtown shoreline. Duane, sitting in the captain's chair, looked uneasy as he spoke into his cell phone. "Hal, honey, calm down. You tell your bro he has nothing to worry about. Yes, they found the keys inside the house, but he has a rock solid alibi, so there's no way the police can connect him to the break-in. Work trucks get stolen all the time for robbery jobs. Has O'Malley even brought him in for questioning? Exactly. O'Malley knows that whoever had the balls to orchestrate the break in at Houston's house is the reason that fucker's going to jail. Case closed, nothing to worry about. See you at dinner," Duane said as he ended the call. "God, what a drama queen."

Stan and Randy both shook their heads in disbelief. Duane took a puff from the joint before passing it off to Randy, who tossed it in the lake. Duane and Randy listened closely as Stan read from the *Forbes* article on Branch Bradford. Stan, emphasizing nearly every word, said, "'Thirty-four years after he started work on designing New York City's Central Park, Frederick Law Olmsted visited the Upper Peninsula of Michigan with grand plans for his next park design. But upon walking the land that would soon be known as Presque Isle Park, he famously told the city leaders, 'Don't touch it,' and headed back east the next day.'"

Stan took a sip from his beer before continuing to read out loud. "'One-hundred-thirty-two years later, several space companies submitted plans to build a rocket launch spaceport just north of a small town in the Upper Peninsula of Michigan. But just hours after arriving in Whisper Dunes and exploring the potential site for the rocket launch spaceport, Sir Branch Bradford pulled out his phone and texted his top lieutenants, 'Don't touch it.'"

Stan stopped reading and looked up to see Duane and Randy both on the verge of tears.

"'After Sir Branch purchased the 5,000 wooded acres along the Lake Superior shoreline, he declared that 4,000 acres will be a protective nature preserve that will be open to the public all year round. But the remaining 1,000 acres will be developed into a summer camp for kids from all over the world who are struggling with severe illnesses and disabilities, as well as for kids who are living in extreme poverty. The camp will be dedicated to providing an environment of healing and adventure for these children. The camp is completely free, including room and board, and Sir Branch will pick up all travel expenses required to get the kids to the camp and back home. Despite personally financing the entire cost to run the camp, Sir Branch was quick to deflect praise, making a point to mention that the idea was inspired by The Hole in the Wall Gang Camp started by Paul Newman.'"

Stan stopped reading so he could wipe the tears streaming down his face. Duane and Randy also subtly wiped the tears from their cheeks. The guys all took a minute to gather themselves while they stared out at the sea. Duane put his sunglasses back on then stood up and grabbed three beers from the cooler. He opened the bottles and handed one to Stan then Randy. Duane looked emotional again as he raised his beer. Stan and Randy stood up and raised their beers toward the sky.

"Here's to sticking together through thick and thin. And here's to a man whose heart is bigger than his beautiful brain. Would it have been better for all of us if this article was released by *Forbes*, say a month ago? Yes, but let's not waste time crying about the past. Time to move forward, together."

The guys clinked their bottles and chugged down their beers. "I gotta tell you guys, I am not regretting putting in most of the dough to buy this boat. Look at us! We're floating on Lake Superior, sipping brews and breathing fresh air," Duane said.

"It's pretty incredible," Stan said. "Thank you, Duane, for stepping up and making this happen."

"My pleasure. I've already got a name picked out, and I don't care if you like it or not because I paid sixty percent of the purchase price," Duane said.

"What's the name?" Randy asked.

"Private Dicks."

Duane could tell that Randy and Stan did not care for the name. "Like I said, I don't give a shit if you don't like it. That's the name."

Randy looked at Duane then Stan. "I love you guys. You stepped up and helped me when you didn't have to. You both went to incredible lengths to save me from my horrible mistake. If there ever comes a time down the road when either of you need me, I want you guys to know that I'll be right by your side, every step of the way."

Stan then Duane gave Randy a big hug. After a quick embrace, the guys sat back down and admired their surroundings for a minute. Stan and Duane were looking in opposite directions at the calm, sparkling water while Randy took in the beautiful view of downtown Whisper Dunes. "Do you guys think this town will ever be the same again?" Randy asked.

"Change is coming to Whisper Dunes, but that doesn't mean we have to change," Stan said. "As long as people come up here and respect our way of life, I'm open to welcoming anyone and everyone."

"I'm just happy to see all the news reporters and protestors finally leave. It's such a relief not to have to stand in line for thirty fucking minutes at Babycakes for a coffee and a blueberry scone. Although I'd be lying if I said I'm not going to miss seeing some of those news reporters jogging around town."

"By the way, did your accountant get back to you?" Stan asked.

"Yeah. Bob said it's perfectly legal to write off the boat, as long as we're able to prove we're using it to support our not-for-profit entity's volunteer mission," Duane said.

Stan looked excited as he high-fived Duane then Randy. "Oh, that is good news!"

"Bob also said we can write off food and booze expenses. We just have to make sure we keep good records in case we get audited."

Randy looked at Duane and said, "Did you fill out the paperwork yet for the half-marathon fundraiser?"

"No, not yet," Duane said.

"I'll have my new assistant fill it out," Stan said.

Duane and Randy both conveyed a doubtful look. "That stripper you hired to answer your phone and make copies? She can't even type," Duane said.

"She's not a stripper, she just dresses like one," Stan said. "Hey, I got an idea. What if we dropped the men's club title and invited Lisa and her friends to join?"

"Can Vivian join?"

"Sure, if she wants to."

"A co-ed social club? I like it. Makes it less likely will get audited," Duane said.

"I think we've got some fantastic fundraising ideas, but let's face it, if you want to get shit done you need to get the moms involved," Stan said.

"Great. Paperwork problem solved," Duane said.

Stan, Duane and Randy looked out at Lake Superior, each with a different thought running through their mind.

Denise was still sweating, even though her pilates class ended twenty minutes ago. She walked down the hallway without a care in the world until she stopped at her apartment door. She grabbed the key from around her neck, unlocked the door, and entered her apartment.

Denise took two steps inside her apartment and froze. In the living room, a man in a dark suit and tie was sitting in her Danish mid-century armchair. The man, who looked to be in his late sixties, was short but had a strong upper body. His skin was pale, the result of spending nearly every day of his life for the past forty years inside an office building.

Denise tried hard not to show any emotion, but her unwavering self-confidence dissipated as she considered why this man was in her living room. The man she was staring at nodded, but did not offer a smile. Unlike virtually every man she had ever encountered while in her pilates outfit, this man did not look her up and down. His eyes were sympathetic as he kept them firmly on Denise's face. She breathed slowly and finally took a few steps toward the man, who said, "Hello, Denise."

"Hello, Gus."

Gus remained perfectly still in the chair. His lips barely moved as he said, "So, you're a pilates instructor now?"

"I don't answer to you anymore. Why are you here?"

"Where's your manuscript?"

"It's in a secure location."

"So there's absolutely no chance that someone will find it again and try to blackmail the CIA?"

Denise's eyes narrowed as she shook her head. "No."

"You've put yourself in the middle of quite a mess in this lovely town. I think you should consider moving back East."

"I'm done getting on my knees and lying on my back for the CIA."

Gus closed his eyes for a moment and shook his head in frustration. He took a long breath and finally regarded Denise. "You were an outstanding agent, who brilliantly executed every one of your missions. Your missions saved lives, Denise. Your missions protected our democracy. All those billionaires never thought in a million years that their secret trust deeds would be discovered by the United States government."

Denise did not have any expression on her face as she sat on the couch across from Gus.

"I guess you still don't understand all the good you did for your country. You've been very good to your country, but maybe your country wasn't always good to you."

"I love my country, it's the CIA I hate."

"Come now, you don't mean that," Gus said. He crossed his right leg over his left leg and leaned back into the chair.

Denise's mind was flooded with emotions. She walked over to the kitchen, grabbed a dish towel from the drawer, and wiped the sweat from her face. She then grabbed a bottle of water from the fridge and walked back to the living room. When Denise had first spotted her former CIA handler in her living room she honestly thought he had come all this way to kill her...even though she knew that Gus had never once fired his weapon. Still, her nerves were unsettled, which made her knees weak. Denise tried her best to convey a relaxed look as she sat back down in the middle of the couch, directly across from Gus.

He smiled slightly and said, "You know, I've always been curious about your book."

"The only way you'll ever get to read my book is if I'm declared legally dead. You know that."

Denise and Gus stared at each other for a minute. Long ago, they recognized in each other a vulnerable quality that others had missed—the expectation of being looked at without being seen or understood.

"You are one of a kind, Denise."

Denise was playing with her long hair. "I always considered you one of the good guys, Gus. Just not sure why you haven't retired yet. Still planning to live out your final years in Montana?"

"Wyoming."

"Might as well be the same state."

Gus's face no longer showed any expression. His cold eyes stared at Denise, hoping the uncomfortable silence might force her to say more, but her lips stayed sealed. She almost looked disoriented as her eyes moved freely around the room. Denise closed her eyes for a few seconds and allowed her back to sink into the couch.

"Without question, the most important legislation ever passed by Congress was the Civil Rights Act," Gus said. "Five hundred years from now, the Civil Rights Act will still be considered the most important law Congress ever passed. The bill was actually written in 1957 by three Democrats and two Republicans. But the architect of the Civil Rights bill was a Catholic priest by the name of Fr. Theodore Hesburgh. He was appointed by President Eisenhower to lead the Civil Rights Commission in 1957. Despite all the work the commission put into drafting the legislation, President Eisenhower knew he would never be able to get the bill through Congress so he left the bill for President Kennedy. JFK quickly concluded that there was no way he could find enough votes to pass the bill. But when Lyndon Johnson became president he figured he only had a year in office. So he decided to go all in on trying to find enough votes to pass the most important piece of legislation in American history. Of course, everyone told him it was impossible and that he shouldn't even bother trying."

The stress that had overwhelmed Denise at the sight of Gus in her living room had melted away as she became completely engrossed with the story. She crossed her legs, then didn't move a muscle. Her eyes had narrowed and didn't blink until Gus said, "Do you know how President Lyndon Johnson got the Civil Rights Bill passed into law?"

Denise slowly shook her head. "No," she said softly.

"Before the bill was going to be put up for a vote, President Johnson already knew every senator and congressman who was going to vote against the bill. Everyone on his staff urged him to put the bill in his desk and forget about it because there was absolutely no chance the bill would pass. But what they didn't know is that President Johnson had personal files on every member of Congress, thanks to the CIA. LBJ knew that most of the racist senators and congressmen had more than a few young mistresses. So what he did was, one by one, he would call a senator or congressman in the middle of the night and ask them why they wouldn't vote for the bill. And they'd all say the same thing, 'If I vote for your bill, Mr. President, I'm dead in my state.' And LBJ would tell them that if they didn't vote for the Civil Rights Bill they were soon going to wake up to a front-page story in the *Washington Post* about what they liked to do every Monday night at the Mayflower Hotel. Bang! One by one, he called up each and every one of those racist assholes and explained to them that pretty soon everyone back home would find out about their young mistress. And that's how LBJ got the votes to pass the Civil Rights Bill. In reality, the votes that passed the Civil Rights Bill into law didn't come from those racist senators and congressmen...they came from the women who compromised their power."

Denise was experiencing a moment of enlightenment that made her entire body tingle. She allowed her wide eyes to stare aimlessly at the plant on the coffee table as Gus's story seeped into her mind. Her missions had created so many dossiers for the CIA, but she sometimes wondered whether any of those secret files were ever used to make a difference and create positive change. Stopping evil people from doing more harm was always the goal of each mission. But Denise never had any way of measuring her efforts to see if they had any sort of positive effect on society.

"You always carried out your missions to perfection, Denise. Your efforts, like the women in the program before you, strengthened our democracy. Americans are better off thanks to some of the information you were able to uncover."

Denise moved her eyes from the plant to Gus. "I never wanted this life."

"I understand that," Gus said in a sympathetic tone. "But right now your country needs you...for one more mission. A mission that only you are capable of handling."

Denise's head was spinning with thoughts. Looking a bit nervous, she licked her top lip then took a deep breath. For a moment she fantasized about publishing her roman à clef then moving to Costa Rica and leading a secret life. But the CIA would eventually find her.

"You'll never have to worry about money again, Denise. I promise. There's risk involved, but once you complete your mission, you can live freely anywhere you want. You'll have a 200,000 dollar a month allowance and access to a private jet for the rest of your life."

Her eyes were fixed on Gus, who stood up out of the chair while keeping his eyes firmly on Denise. She concentrated on breathing slowly in hopes that her mind would stop racing. Denise looked out the window and started to think clearly. She realized that a decision had already been made on her behalf and that she didn't have much of a choice. The life she continued to dream of would not be possible, at least not in the near future. But she believed Gus. If she could complete the mission she could find another idyllic town to live in. A town where she could live in peace and fall in love and finally start a family. She was only thirty-five, she thought. There was plenty of time left in her life to pick up and start over again. She still believed she might one day get the chance to live a life that she was proud of.

Denise swallowed to clear the lump in her throat and finally said, "One more run...then I'm done."